D1005493

Sharlene MacLaren's *Courting Emma* takes you through a gamut of emotions. You'll experience life with her very real characters, delve into your own heart on spiritual issues, smile and rejoice when victories are won, and find deep satisfaction in a story well told. This sweet novel will keep you enmeshed till the end as it weaves its spell around your heart.

—Miralee Ferrell
Author, *The Other Daughter*

I highly recommend *Courting Emma* by Sharlene MacLaren. It's a soulful journey back in time to the late 1800s....The author took the time to set the scene with careful detail, which included getting to know each character, from their smiles to minute mannerisms. But it's the heart of Emma and her spirit that propel the reader from chapter to chapter. If you like to read historical fiction, then this is a must-read. If you are unfamiliar with this genre, then this book is a good place to start, but be sure to get the complete series of MacLaren's Little Hickman Creek....

—Robin Shope
Author, *The Chase, The Replacement,* and *The Candidate*

Watch for this author when you want just the right touch of detail and depth mixed with humor and meaningful emotion brought to a satisfying ending.

—Mildred Colvin
Author, Winner of Reader's Choice Award

Sharlene's Little Hickman Creek series just keeps getting better! Flawed characters with painful pasts embark on a spiritual journey where love and reconciliation team up to make for an exciting tale. And as usual, the romantic tension was delectable. I loved it!

—Michelle Sutton
Book Reviewer
Author, *It's Not About Me*

Sharlene MacLaren's characters in *Courting Emma* will incite strong feelings in readers—anger at their selfish behavior, understanding of their humanity, and hope for their future. A love story to remember!

—Vicki McCollum
SavVy ReViews Blogspot and
Infuzemag.com contributing reviewer

What Readers Are Saying about
Sharlene MacLaren & Her Books

Through Every Storm

Wow! I've read many Christian novels and many authors, but after reading this one, I must say, you are at the top of my favorites. Keep up the good work.

—*Bev* from Michigan

Reading *Through Every Storm* reminded me that God is surely our strength in times of trouble.

—*Joyce* from Pennsylvania

I loved this book. I can't wait to read everything else you've written.

—*Mandy* from Johannesburg, South Africa

Oh, what a read! I laughed, cried, and felt my heart stop in places. This is an absolutely great book!

—*Ashley* from Wolverhampton, England

I've just read your book after checking it out at the library. Thank you so much for letting God use your talents in writing such encouraging words.

—*Denise* from Alabama

This is the best, most emotionally moving book I've read in years. In fact, I read it twice. The only other book I've ever read more than once is the Bible! Your writing evokes poignant images that have branded my mind.

—*Cheryl* from California

Loving Liza Jane

From start to finish, I could not put this book down. I can't wait for the next one!

—*Ash* from the United Kingdom

I loved this book and how you weave Scripture into your stories.

—*Staci* from Michigan

Loving Liza Jane

Your writing style reminds me very much of Karen Kingsbury. Excellent!

—*Lori* from Michigan

I'm a bookstore manager, and I loved this book! We are ordering more!

—*Ann* from Indiana

HIGHEST praises for *Loving Liza Jane*. Now I can hardly wait for the next one!

—*Sylvia* from Kansas

Where do I start? I am so happy to have found your books. You are touching lives through your writing.

—*Patti Ann* from Oklahoma

Sarah, My Beloved

I was totally enraptured by this wonderful book. Thanks for providing such delightful reading.

—*JBS* from Florida

Oh, what a book. I must tell you the end of the book was so tender and utterly beautiful that I bawled my eyes out! I am tingling in anticipation of the day *Courting Emma* releases.

—*Maria* from London, England

I could barely put this book down to go to bed. I read it in a day. Every one of your books just keeps getting better.

—*Julie* from Michigan

You are an amazing writer. This was a beautiful story.

—*Jennifer* from Florida

I feel like I know the characters by the time I'm done. I can't wait to read Emma's story next! I bet it will be the best in the series.

—*Rosalyn* from Georgia

LHC

Little Hickman Creek Series

Courting Emma

A Novel

Sharlene MacLaren

WHITAKER
HOUSE

Courting Emma

Third in the Little Hickman Creek Series

ISBN: 978-1-60374-020-3
Printed in the United States of America
© 2008 by Sharlene MacLaren

1030 Hunt Valley Circle
New Kensington, PA 15068
www.whitakerhouse.com

Library of Congress Cataloging-in-Publication Data

MacLaren, Sharlene.
Courting Emma / Sharlene MacLaren.
p.   cm. — (Third in the Little Hickman Creek series)
Summary: "Having buried her painful past, Emma Browning begins to wonder if healing and forgiveness are possible after all when the handsome preacher becomes the new tenant at her boardinghouse"—Provided by publisher.
ISBN 978-1-60374-020-3 (trade pbk. : alk. paper) 1. Landladies—Fiction.
2. Landlord and tenant—Fiction. 3. Kentucky—Fiction. I. Title.
PS3613.A27356C68 2008
813'.6—dc22
2007051393

3 4 5 6 7 8 9 10 11 12 **ய** 15 14 13 12 11 10 09 08

Dedication

To Debbie:
My precious friend,
Provider of giggles,
Sharer of secrets,
Spreader of joy,
Partner in prayer.
Life would be much duller without you.
I love you, girlfriend.

Chapter One

July 4, 1896

*E*mma Browning's boot heels clicked out a rhythm on the wooden sidewalk as she strode purposely toward home. She'd just spotted Ezra, her galoot of a father, staggering in her direction, and if she didn't get out of sight soon, he'd be sure to make a fool of her—again!

She glanced skyward and watched as one tiny cloud rolled across a blanket of blue, obliterating the sun's rays for the briefest of moments. Oppressive humidity and uncommon heat created sweat drops that trickled down her back. Without thought for propriety, Emma loosened the tie on her bonnet and rolled her sleeves up to her elbows, exposing skin baked to a golden tan from working in her vegetable garden.

A red, white, and blue banner bearing the words INDEPENDENCE DAY stretched across Main Street from the upper story window of Flanders' Food Store to Community Bank and Trust, catching the eye of every passing citizen. And passersby were something the town of Little Hickman, Kentucky, had plenty of today. In fact, it would seem the whole of Jessamine County had shown up for the town's festivities, which included field games for the children, horseshoes and target shooting for the men, pie-eating contests, food booths, cakewalks, and a host of other activities to keep a body busy for hours.

The slight breeze stirred up the wonderful aroma of roasted chicken. Emma's stomach growled as she stepped down from the sidewalk and passed Irwin Waggoner and Tom Flanders, both donning long white aprons and standing in the alleyway between Winthrop's Dry Goods and Flanders' Foods, turning several chickens on spits over an open fire pit.

"Afternoon, Miss Emma," called Irwin, smiling from ear to ear, one crooked top tooth jutting past his upper lip. Emma waved a greeting, glad when they didn't stop her to make conversation. Earlier, Fancy Jenkins, Bess Barrington, and Caroline Warner had talked her ears nearly off about everything from the weather to this fall's upcoming United States presidential election, Bryan versus McKinley, and, frankly, she was too done in to listen to more banter.

"Miss Browning, Miss Browning!"

Emma stopped at the high-pitched squeal and discovered Lili Broughton running toward her, her toddling younger sister, Molly, clinging to her skirts. Molly's elfin nose was smudged with dirt and her red-and-white checked pinafore was covered with sticky goo.

"Are ya havin' fun?" Lili asked, coming to a stop in front of her, pushing a strand of golden hair out of her eyes.

Emma smiled in spite of the snag in her plan to escape the hullabaloo taking place on Main Street. Tall for her age and sweet as sugar, Lili's own smile stretched wide across her face, revealing a deep dimple in her left cheek.

"Oh, yes, a grand time," she fibbed, glancing behind her and giving a quick sigh of relief to find that old Ezra Browning had disappeared from sight.

"We're having a grand time, too. There's fireworks tonight. Did you know that? Are you plannin' to watch 'em?"

"Oh, I 'spect I'll see 'em, all right. And where are you young ladies off to now?"

Lili's eyes sparked with eagerness. "Papa says me and Molly, er, Molly and I," she corrected, "can go have a mule ride. 'Cept we have to wait for him and my stepmama to catch up."

"Oh?" Emma's gaze meandered to the middle of Main Street, now closed off to traffic, and spotted Benjamin and Liza Broughton chatting with a group of farmers. Ben looked up, no doubt keeping an eye out for his children. He waved at Emma, and she smiled, returning the greeting.

"Did you know Mr. Livingston has the tallest mules in all of Jessamine County?" Lili prattled, her enthusiasm drawing Emma back into the conversation.

"Does he now?" she said. Sam Livingston owned and operated Little Hickman's only livery. Although Emma, sole proprietor of the town's boardinghouse, had little use for a horse, when the rare need did arise to venture beyond the town limits, she'd rent one of Sam's. "I guess I have heard talk about them. Didn't they win a couple of ribbons at the county fair last summer?"

Lili nodded, slanting her face at Emma, the sun's intense rays making her wrinkle her nose and squint. "Did you know a mule is half horse and half jack—well, Papa says I'm not to say the real word for the other half of a mule, even though it's right there in the Holy Bible. I know it's there, too, 'cause Reverend Atkins said it last Sunday right durin' the Scripture readin'."

She couldn't stop the sudden giggle that escaped. "Is that so? Well, your papa's probably right; a real lady watches her manner of speaking."

Molly tugged at her sister's arm and shrieked her impatience. On cue, Ben and his pretty wife of less than a year started toward them. "Hello, Emma," Liza Broughton called on their approach, lifting her skirts as she and Ben scuttled across the dirt-packed road, Ben's boots leaving dust clouds in their wake. With nary a drop of rain in the past several weeks, and a seemingly endless heat wave, the earth's topsoil had turned to dust, and Emma swore it was all coming to settle on her parlor floor.

Nearly five months pregnant, Liza showed the barest beginnings of a rounded belly. Emma smiled at the pair as they stepped up to the sidewalk. Ben took Liza's hand and gazed at her adoringly, making it clear their newly married status hadn't yet worn off.

"Lili here was just tellin' me she's about to go for a mule ride," Emma said, fighting off the urge to add she'd also been about to tutor her on the mule's mutant beginnings.

Ben grinned, took off his battered Stetson to scrape a hand through his black hair, then plopped it back in place. "It's all she's been talking about. Liza and I decided if there's to be any peace in the family, we'd best get over to Sam's before the line of squalling kids grows any longer. After all, it's not every day one gets to ride an ornery old mule, you know."

"Papa, they ain't ornery. Leastways, I don't think they are. And they're prize-winnin' mules. Even Miss Browning says so."

"*Aren't,* Lili," Liza corrected, stepping forward to give one of Lili's braids a tiny, tender yank. "They *aren't* ornery." It would seem Lili didn't stand a chance with her countrified drawl and misuse of grammar. Liza, Little Hickman's former schoolteacher, would no doubt see to it that her new daughters spoke proper English.

"Gus Humphrey told Andrew Warner that Sam Livingston's mules was the tallest mules in all of Kentucky. It's so, ain't it, Papa?"

Liza angled a weary glance at Ben and shrugged her shoulders. It was all Emma could do to hold in her laughter.

"Would you care to join us for supper?" Liza asked, putting a hand to her belly and turning her attention on Emma. "I packed plenty of food. Ben's already laid out our blanket where we can get a good view of tonight's fireworks, and we've a basketful of goodies all set for our evening meal."

Although Emma appreciated the invitation, she looked forward to enjoying a casual evening of uninterrupted solitude. A good book was more to her liking on a night like this. "I thank you for the invitation, but I 'spect I should head back and tend to my own evenin' meal. No telling how many will show up at my table tonight, but I best be prepared."

Ben's brow arched. "I hear one of your boarders moved to Oklahoma. Doesn't that leave you with an opening?"

She had a notion what he was getting at. Since late spring, Ben's lifelong friend, Jonathan Atkins, Little Hickman's new preacher, had been hounding her about taking a room in her boardinghouse. Short on room, she'd had a good excuse for turning him down. Besides, her boarders consisted mostly of loud-mouthed ruffians, not the sort suited for any preacher's company. Moreover, Jon Atkins had a way of setting her on edge with his jocular manner and handsome looks, not to mention his blatant Christian testimony. As if her boardinghouse wasn't already a mishmash of unfortunate misfits, adding a man of the cloth to the pot might really stir things up.

"Shouldn't take long for another hooligan to come knockin' on my door once news gets out."

Ben tipped back on his boot heels. "Wouldn't hurt to let Jon take a room, you know. You probably heard he's sold his farm. Plans to donate most all his profits to building a new church."

"That's a mighty generous act," Emma said. *Foolhardy, too,* she silently added. What man in his right mind did a thing like that? Sold his property, then wound up giving his profits to the church? These were hard times. It was a fine fix she'd be in if she let the man take a room with her only to discover he hadn't the means for paying his rent. She didn't imagine the congregants of Little Hickman Community Church indulged him in much of a salary.

"All he needs is a place to lay his head," Ben said. "Might be a smart thing to allow his good influence in your establishment. Matter of fact, I should think you'd welcome it."

The last thing she needed, or wanted, was some preacher forcing his beliefs on her, and she didn't imagine the bunch of sad sacks she housed would appreciate it, either. Keeping her opinions to herself, she said instead, "I'll give it some thought."

"Can we go now, Papa?" Lili asked, tugging on Ben's arm with her free hand, her other one clutching tightly to little Molly.

The nearby aroma of fresh baked bread blended with the roasted chickens, reminding her it'd been awhile since her meager lunch, an apple and a bowl of vegetable soup. She smiled at the little family. "You'd best get over to Sam's before them mules start balking at all the free rides they're forced to give."

"I think you're right," Liza said, bending to take Molly into her arms. The child nestled her head into the crook of Liza's neck, rubbing her eyes with her pudgy fists. "If you change your mind about the supper offer, be sure to join us," Liza said over the child's head. "It's to be quite a fireworks display from what we hear. Ben says Clyde Winthrop footed the entire bill, sending for some company out of New York."

Emma had no doubt it would be quite the show, but it didn't interest her. What did interest her was going back to a quiet boardinghouse, making a simple supper, then running a tepid bath. Perspiration dotted her forehead and ran in little droplets down her temples. About all she could think of now was getting out of this heavy dress and into her cotton chemise. Perhaps later, after the sun went down, and folks gathered out behind the livery in the big open field for the fireworks display, she would sit at her open window and watch from afar.

"I'm sure it—" Emma was interrupted by a huge commotion. Everyone's eyes alighted on the staggering, slightly round man coming up the street. Dirty trousers sagged below his belly, one suspender keeping them from sliding to the ground. A bottle of booze swung from his hand as he belted out some indecipherable song.

Emma put a hand to her throat. It was what she'd feared. Disgust and shame roiled in the pit of her stomach. How could Ezra Browning keep doing this to her—mortifying her in plain daylight? *Someone ought to shoot the miserable, tanked-up, tangle-footed jug-head,* she thought, *then heave him facedown into Little Hickman Creek's deepest waters.* If she weren't afraid of the consequences, she'd do it herself.

Hauling in a heavy dose of air, Emma mopped her damp forehead with the back of her hand and sighed, avoiding the gazes of Ben and Liza. "Guess I should get him off the street."

When she stepped forward, Ben reached out a hand to stop her. "He's not your responsibility, Emma. He may be your father, but Sheriff Murdock should be the one tending to him."

She breathed past a knot welling up in her chest. "He has enough on his hands what with all the extra folks in town today. Besides, the people of Hickman shouldn't have to put up with that barrelhouse bum another minute."

"And what do you propose to do with him?"

She knew what she'd like to do. "I'll stick him in that old tin tub out back. He can lay there till he sobers up."

Ben frowned. "I'll go get the sheriff."

"No, don't bother," Emma muttered, raising her chin a notch. "I'll just...."

"Well, my Aunt Gertie's gravy! Would you look at that old coot? Such a disgrace." Iris Winthrop, Little Hickman's own over-the-fence ear duster and owner of Winthrop's Dry Goods, joined the small throng of citizens gathering on the sidewalk, face pinched into a contorted frown. "Doesn't he have an ounce of sense under that filthy cap?" she sputtered. Always dressed to the nines, the high-nosed woman sniffed, her multicolored, feather bonnet bobbling in the breeze. Some nodded their agreement; still others merely watched as the pathetic Ezra Browning tripped and nearly fell flat on his whiskery, red-eyed face, then managed to right himself. Ezra laughed at his blunder, had a coughing spell, then resumed his off-tune song, swaying and teetering as he went.

"Oh, my stars in heaven," Mrs. Winthrop spat.

"One of these days he'll drink himself to death," someone at the back of the crowd mumbled. Emma recognized the voice as that of George Garner, Little Hickman's new postmaster.

And not a day too soon. A fresh dose of bitterness stirred in Emma's heart. Wasn't it enough that Ezra Browning spent every waking minute of his life making her miserable? Did he have to punish the entire town?

More under-the-breath comments came from several onlookers, as mothers herded their children to the opposite side of the street, away from the drunken ignoramus. Emma wanted to crawl into the nearest hole. Instead, she gathered her wits and faced the hodgepodge of curious faces. "Please.

You folks go about your business," she instructed, shoulders pulled back. "I'll tend to old Ezra."

"I'll help," Ben offered, stepping forward.

"No." The single word came out harsher than she intended.

"Emma...." Liza gathered a wide-eyed Lili close to her side with one hand, her other arm still supporting Molly. Her brow furrowed with sympathy.

Emma shook her head. "He's my father. I thank you for your concern, Ben, Liza—and everyone—but I'll take it from here. Please. Go on about your day."

Ben didn't look convinced, but at least he respected her wishes enough to step aside. The other spectators followed suit, moving back when Emma started down the sidewalk in the direction of her drunken father.

*****

Reverend Jonathan Atkins took another swig of fresh-squeezed lemonade and licked his lips in pleasure. "You do make the finest lemonade in town, Mrs. Baxter," he gushed, setting the ice-cold glass to his sweaty temple. The temperature had to be pushing ninety degrees and not a cloud in the sky.

Frances Baxter and her daughter, Rosie, had set up a drink stand in front of Bordens' Bakery to accommodate the number of visitors in town, and by the look of things, they were doing a fine business. The line for refreshment extended to the middle of Main Street.

Frances looked flushed, and Jon couldn't tell if it came from his compliment or the excessive heat. "Why, thank ya," she said, hurrying to prepare another glass for the next eager customer, stuffing the nickel he offered into her deep dress pocket. "It sure is a scorcher t'day."

"I'll grant you that," he replied, mopping his brow with the back of his hand.

"Afternoon, Jon," said a passerby.

Jon craned his neck toward the low-timbred voice, then grinned when he recognized its source. "Well, if it isn't the Callahans. Where are your youngsters?" Jon tipped his hat at Mrs. Baxter, then turned his attention to his good friends, Rocky and Sarah Callahan. Their wedding had come on the heels of Ben and Liza's, a sort of marriage of convenience, Rocky needing a mother for his niece and nephew, whom he'd acquired at the death of his sister. If Jon were to judge, though, he would say the two had scrapped the whole notion of convenience and fallen in love. They were holding hands and smiling as if they hadn't a care in the world.

"Bess Barrington offered to take them over to Sam's to ride them blasted mules," Rocky said. "And we didn't refuse. It's afforded Sarah and me the opportunity to visit without Seth's persistent begging."

Jon laughed. "From what I hear, those mules are quite the attraction. Don't know what anyone sees in those big-eared hay burners, but I suppose if Sam's offering free rides to the kiddies, that'd be the draw."

Rocky nodded, opened his mouth to reply, then shut it again without speaking. His eyes were fixed on something just over Jon's shoulder.

"Come on, Ezra, you ole fool."

Jon turned his head at the sound of Emma Browning's voice. The mite of a woman was doing her best to steer her drunken father in a straight line.

"Emma, you need some help?" Rocky called out, stepping

off the sidewalk to saunter across the street. Jon and Sarah followed.

She paused to acknowledge the threesome with a tiny smile. "Thank you, but I believe I can manage," she replied with curtness, resuming her step. Her arm was looped through Ezra's, her willowy frame doing its best to support his swaying body. Emma was nothing if she wasn't stubborn—and a paradox of a woman if there ever was one. A delicate beauty, she was also hard to the bone, Jon pondered.

Younger than Jon by a couple of years, Emma had grown up with Benjamin, Rocky, and him and had attended the same one-room schoolhouse. Jon distinctly remembered chasing her around the playground on their recess breaks, pulling at her blond braids, and teasing the occasional smile from her plump lips. She'd been shy in those days but had an edge to her even then. Maybe it was her need to survive that had made her that way. Her bleary-eyed father had been buzzed as far back as Jon could remember. And half the time, if recollection served him right, she'd come to school with bruises on her face and arms, a result, everyone had presumed, of having pushed one of Ezra's wrong buttons.

Now, all grown up, Jon saw Emma for what she was, a child in adult skin, tough as a hickory nut on the outside, but underneath, uptight and scared. He had to give her credit for her willful spirit, but there always had been a part of him that longed to see into her depths. What really went on inside Emma Browning's head? Then just as quickly as the question surfaced, he'd remind himself that he was Little Hickman's one and only parson, and he had no business courting one so obstinate, never mind that she seemed to have no use for the church.

"He's drunk as a skunk," Rocky muttered under his breath.

"What do you suppose she plans to do with him?" Jon whispered back, as the unlikely pair drew nearer.

"Can't tell," Rocky answered. "Best leave her be, though. Emma's a proud one."

"With a head set in concrete," Jon added.

Sarah spoke for the first time. "She's really something, isn't she? That man doesn't deserve to shine her shoes, and yet there she is doing her best to help him."

"Get him out of sight is more like it," Rocky said. "He's a downright embarrassment, not only to Emma, but to all of Little Hickman."

"Way down upon the Schwanee Riv-eeer," Ezra bellowed, his body leaning heavily into Emma's, his bloodshot eyes heavy-lidded and glazed over. The old codger was so crocked he didn't even know where he was, or that his daughter was hauling him up the street.

On instinct, Jon stepped forward and grabbed hold of Ezra's other arm. He was the preacher, after all. It was his job to serve. Ezra gave Jon a distant look, as if trying to place just where it was their paths had crossed. Soon, though, he shook his head and continued his off-key song. "You taking him to your place?" Jon asked above the ruckus.

Emma looked abashed. "Unhand him, if you please, Reverend. I already said I can manage him just fine."

"And I happen to disagree. Are we headed to the boardinghouse?" When it came to tenacity, he could play with the best of them.

She stood stock-still for a split second and eyeballed him around her father's head, thin strands of white-blond hair falling out from her loose sunbonnet. Perspiration had soaked through her blouse, plastering it to her skin. Jon swiped his arm across his forehead. He frowned. "You have a problem with my helping you?"

A look of contempt crossed her face. Someday he would like to ask her what it was about him she detested. Jon clenched his jaw. "Fine," she said. "I'm taking him to the boardinghouse. I've a big tin tub out back he can sober up in."

Jon gave a half-grin and nodded. "Sounds like a fine place for him. Maybe he'll sleep a few days if we toss in a pillow."

Emma blinked, refusing to see the humor in his remark. When she started walking again, Jon took a firmer hold of Ezra's arm. Then, throwing a backward glance at Rocky and Sarah, he silently mouthed, "She hates me."

Chapter Two

*I*t was plain humiliating, no other word for it. Once she and Jonathan had plunked her father into the rusty horse trough out behind the boardinghouse, the man had wet himself and promptly fallen asleep. He certainly wouldn't wake up fresh as a daisy in the morning.

If he was still here, that is.

With a little luck, he'd awaken and saunter back to Madam Guttersnipe's den of iniquity—which was exactly where he belonged. Matter of fact, Emma should have taken him there right off, and might have, had it not been for the Reverend Jonathan Atkins' interference. A man of the cloth would surely have argued with the notion of dumping old Ezra at the beer house.

She harrumphed and strode from the kitchen into the dining room to give the table one last swipe with a damp cloth. Why had the preacher stepped forward anyway? Did he not worry about his reputation? Surely, tongues would wag about the minister walking through the middle of town arm in arm with the town drunk, and in plain daylight, no less. Why, she could almost picture Iris Winthrop now, gums batting at full speed as she made it her duty to inform her merchants of the minister's objectionable behavior. Never mind that he was simply doing a good deed by getting the old bum off the street.

And that was another thing. Wouldn't his good deed now put Emma in his debt? She surely didn't want to be beholden to Jonathan Atkins. She had no use for him, his Bible, or his God. Before she knew it, the handsome parson would be wheedling his way past her front door, eating at her table, conversing with her tenants, and doing his best to convert everybody within hearing distance.

Raucous laughter outside her boardinghouse collided with her nagging thoughts, drawing her to the window for a look. On the way, she checked the old grandfather clock, which stood like a majestic monarch against a far wall in the front parlor, its ever present tick-tock soothing her taut nerves.

Dusk was falling fast. In another hour or so, explosions of light would rocket through the sky, astounding young and old alike. She hoped they would be loud enough to rouse old Ezra and send him on his way.

Pulling back a lace curtain for a better look, she noted that Harland Collins and Wes Clayton, two of her boarders, the only ones who had shown up for her supper of beef stew and biscuits, were lounging on the porch, taking slow drags off their cigarettes. She had a strict rule about no smoking in the house, so when one of them had the need to light up, he took his habit outside. She scowled. Even from here, she could smell the nicotine smoke as it drifted past the open window.

She swabbed her damp brow with the corner of her apron and looked out over the street, still abuzz with activity. Come morning, the streets would be blessedly peaceful again, save the usual traffic. There would be the clip-clop of horses' hooves, the occasional shouted greeting, and the scurrying feet of children racing up the sidewalk, but not the clack and clamor of hundreds of extra folks swirling dust into the hot, dry air, dropping debris along the way, and talking in fast, excited voices about the upcoming fireworks display.

"Heard Hickman's boozehound is out back sleepin' it off," muttered Mr. Clayton, obviously unaware that Emma stood in the window behind him. The rocking chair he sat in sang a slow, mournful tune as he set it in motion. "Miss Emma and the reverend dropped him in that old horse trough. Guess they made quite the trio traipsin' up Main Street, Ezra trippin' over his own feet whilst Emma and that preacher fella dragged him along."

Harland Collins let out a mighty chuckle, rubbed his whiskered jowls, then took a deep draw on his cigarette before blowing out a perfect smoke ring. Emma hung back in the shadows, glad she'd chosen not to light the parlor lamps. Up the street, the tinny sounds of Madam Guttersnipe's piano filled the dusky night.

"Yep, had to be quite a sight," Harland was saying, looking out over the street. He lifted a hand to wave at a passerby. "Don't imagine Ezra will remember a thing come mornin', but the ones spectatin' shore will. It's a dirty shame what that little lady has to put up with."

"Pfff. Tain't nothin' new for her," Wes argued. "Miss Emma's been puttin' up with that beerified ragbag since she was a little missy. Cain't have been easy on her, though, 'specially with no mama to fend fer 'er. No wonder she's so full o' vinegar. Had to learn life the hard way."

Emma hated that she was the focus of their discussion; even more that she'd garnered their sympathy. She needed no one's pity, leastways not from these two old coots. She had a mind to march out the back door and toss a bucket of slops over that worthless, sleeping fool. It was, after all, entirely his fault that folks were talking about her.

Not for the first time Emma brooded over the mother she'd never had and wondered how different life might have been. Would she be living in Little Hickman today, or might her mother have whisked her away at a young age, perhaps straight from her cradle, and into some distant, remote place, far from Ezra Browning's reach? Like so many times before, she imagined the scene— Emma, a mere babe, snatched from her bed in the wee hours of morning into a waiting carriage driven by some noble defender, wrapped safely in her mother's warm embrace. Of course, they would have traveled miles, maybe even crossing over the Tennessee border, before Ezra finally awoke from his drunken stupor and discovered their absence. Naturally, it would've been futile to go in search of them, for they would have covered their tracks so skillfully. And, besides, Ezra would have lacked the town's help and support, for everyone would have silently applauded the young mother for her indomitable strength and courage.

Emma shook her head as if to ward off her foolish meanderings. Who was she kidding? Lydia Baxter Browning had died giving birth to her, and the only proof Emma had that she'd even existed was a tattered photograph she kept between the pages of a book. Matter of fact, Emma didn't even have grandparents as far as she knew.

Maybe Mr. Clayton was right; she'd learned life the hard way, and it had made her the person she was today, strong and self-sufficient. If people mistook that for bitter and steely-edged, well, so be it. She wasn't here to impress anybody, least of all the men living under her roof.

"Vinegar, you say?" Harland joked. "Ha! Miss Emma's as scrappy as a hog-tied Indian squaw. I daresay she could swallow down a teaspoon o' vinegar with nary a wince." To that, both men cackled loud enough to wake the mongrel dog lounging under Emma's porch. The mangy mutt sauntered out and shook the dust off himself, then voiced his annoyance with a low growl.

Emma frowned and turned away from the window.

It was high time she drew herself a bath and tried to wash away the memory of this day.

*****

"Mr. Atkins, come and sit by us," came the shrill invitation from Lili Broughton.

"*Reverend*, Lili, not *Mister*," Ben corrected. The entire family scooted over on their blanket, making room for Jon's approach. He grinned and filled up the distance between them with a few long strides.

"Mister will do just fine, Lili," he said, dropping down on the blanket in the precise corner that Lili patted with her hand. Her entire freckled face was awash with excitement. By contrast, her little sister Molly lay sprawled across her stepmother's lap, dead to the world, her plump, round face smudged with grime, her dark hair mussed and coming loose from its short pony-tail.

Jon couldn't hold back a chuckle. "You're not excited about these fireworks, are you, Lil?"

"My insides is 'bout to explode!" she exclaimed. "Papa says it'll be at least another half hour. The sky needs to get a lot more stars in it."

Jon couldn't blame her for her excitement. If he were honest with himself, he'd have to admit to having a few butterflies himself. It'd been a good long while since Little Hickman had sponsored a fireworks display. Jon reached in his pocket and pulled out a piece of wrapped taffy. "Maybe this will tide you over?" he asked, handing it to the eager child.

"Mm, thank you, Mister—uh, Reverend." All fingers, Lili hastened to unwrap the concoction, momentarily losing her-self in the effort. Jon chortled to himself. In the unlikely event he ever had children, he would want them to be just like Lili and Molly.

"Did you get that tanked up Ezra Browning situated over at Emma's place?" Ben asked. Sitting close to Liza, he had propped an arm over his bent knee and was chewing on a long blade of grass, his hat tilted so that it nearly covered one dark eyebrow.

"How'd you hear about that?" Jon asked, dragging his eyes away from Lili.

Ben harrumphed. "Who in Hickman hasn't heard about it? 'Fraid you were an interesting topic this afternoon, my friend." Eyes twinkling, Ben went on. "Topics ran the gamut, too. Everything from 'What would possess the preacher to be seen with that pickled fool?' to 'Did you notice Reverend Atkins' new boots?'"

Jon shot Ben a curious look then glanced at his boots, not new, but shined that morning by a young lad anxious to make a dime. "You're joshing, right?"

Ben shook his head and laughed. "I'm serious as a double-barreled shotgun. Course, in this town, it doesn't take much to get tongues wagging. I have a feeling Iris Winthrop was a mite put out with you for walking down the same side of the street as Ezra Browning, much less helping him along."

"It was no less than Jesus would have done," Jon countered. "Does she not know that our Lord took meals with the scum of the earth? In fact, He associated with them every day."

"You don't need to convince me of that, but do you think that matters one bit to Mrs. Winthrop? Everyone knows that woman is all about upholding her fine character. Nothing is more important to her than status and maintaining Little Hickman's spotless reputation." Ben cut loose with another low-throated chuckle. "Mightn't have been so bad if we hadn't had so many visitors today."

Jon's eyes scanned the field where literally hundreds, maybe even a thousand or more, folks had heard about Little Hickman's fireworks and come out to watch. Buggy after buggy lined the outskirts of town, where folks had left them and their horses tied to makeshift hitching posts and various shade trees. Here and there, lanterns dotted the landscape like dozens of fireflies. In the distance, a child's excited whoop filled the air, followed by whinnying horses and impatient, barking dogs. Yes, it was unfortunate that so many had had to witness Ezra Browning's drunken display, Jon mused, but it was nothing new to most of Hickman's townsfolk. It irked him how people placed so much importance on outward appearance and less on the decaying souls of men.

"Well, I imagine Mrs. Winthrop won't be too pleased tomorrow mornin' when she learns I've taken old Ezra to the bathhouse and cleaned him up," Jon said, taking a gumdrop from his shirt pocket, tossing it straight up, and catching it in his open mouth.

Ben whistled through his teeth. "You serious? I'd venture to say Emma won't be so happy herself. She prides herself on handling her own affairs, you know."

Jon made a scoffing sound. "It's high time Emma Browning swallowed some of that pride."

*****

A rooster crowed at precisely five-thirty the next morning. Precisely, because, no sooner had he screeched out his morning call than the grandfather clock took up its chiming. Emma groaned, buried her face in the folds of her cotton blanket, and squeezed her eyes shut against the early stages of dawn. Had she slept a wink? Last night's fireworks, although an impressive display of glitter and dazzle from her second-story perch, still echoed through her brain, the crack and boom of each explosion singeing her nerves. To make matters worse, after she had settled in for the night, each of her boarders had plodded up the stairs at varying times, some moaning and mumbling to themselves, others tripping along the way, the result of over-imbibing. The only two who had come in at a decent hour and, thankfully, sober, were Elliott Newman and his son, Luke.

She heard the twitter of waking birds out her open window, felt a warm, tickling breeze creep past her bare arms, and noted that the temperature in her room had barely dropped a degree in the night.

With a sigh, she yanked back the cotton sheet and hauled herself up.

It was going to be another sweltering day.

*****

Breakfast had been a quiet affair. Of Emma's six boarders, four had missed the meal, either sleeping past the deadline for receiving a hot breakfast and settling for a cup of coffee and a piece of buttered bread on the run, or choosing not to eat at all for lack of appetite, hoping to slip out the door unnoticed. While she'd been scrubbing a fry pan, Gideon Barnard, who worked at Grady Swanson's Sawmill, had sauntered past the kitchen door looking fuzzy-eyed. He'd shot her a wary look, as if to say, "I know, I know. Don't lecture me." Not that she'd intended to do so. She'd lived long enough to know lectures didn't solve a thing; they certainly didn't deter a man's drinking habit. Proof of that lay out in the old tin tub in the backyard.

"D-did you like the f-fireworks, Miss Emma?"

Emma looked up from her bread making. It was just past nine-thirty. Luke stood in the doorway, thumbs hooked in his suspenders, dark brown hair haphazardly brushed to one side, close-set eyes darting about, avoiding direct contact with hers. Pug-nosed and rosy-cheeked, it was his ever-present grin that most endeared him to her. A grown man with the innocence and intelligence of a youngster, he was Little Hickman's lamplighter, faithfully lighting the lamps along Main Street at dusk. During the day, he made himself available for jobs that didn't require mind power. Most of the time, she had no trouble keeping him busy, but on those days she couldn't, she'd send him off to his father's wheelwright shop, Flanders' Foods, Eldred Johansson's Mercantile, or Sam's Livery. Thankfully, they always had a job waiting for him.

"They were a sight to behold, weren't they?" she replied, pausing for a second to recall the event, then quickly going back to kneading the large lump of dough beneath her hands. When she finished, she molded the clump into a ball and laid a towel over it. Then she wiped her floured hands on her apron. Luke kept watch from his place in the doorway.

"M-me and Pa, we liked them big ones," he remarked in his flat, monotone voice, his words always coming out slow and labored, with intermittent stuttering. "They made me sh-shake right here." He put a stubby hand to his chest.

Emma laughed. "I know what you mean."

Luke took a step forward, eyes eager. "Want me to sweep the f-floor?"

She glanced around the tidy kitchen. "It's been done, but you could take the broom to the front porch. That could use a goin' over. After that—"

Just then, a squawking male voice made her pause mid-sentence. She walked to the kitchen window overlooking the backyard. A sudden gasp escaped her throat.

Luke came up beside her. "Ain't that the p-preacher?"

Her shoulders slumped as she heaved a sigh. Jon Atkins was helping old Ezra out of the tin tub, and from the sound of things, her father wasn't too happy for the help.

Why couldn't the reverend mind his own business?

Chapter Three

"Lemme go," Ezra screeched, both hands flailing. "I don't need no help."

"I beg to differ, old man," Jon argued. "You can't even stand up on your own. Look at you."

Jon caught sight of Emma Browning bounding off the boardinghouse back stoop, skirts flaring, wisps of blond hair coming loose from their tight little bun. Her blue eyes sparked with a mixture of anger and confusion as she marched with purpose in their direction, Luke Newman on her heels.

"What do you think you're doing, Jon Atkins?" she asked.

"I'm about to take this odorous fellow to the bathhouse."

Emma fixed him with a perplexing stare, squinting against the sun. "Why would you do that?"

"He could use a bath, don't you think?" The man's stench was enough to knock a skunk to its knees.

"Don't need no bath," Ezra grumbled. "Had one already."

"When? Last spring?" Jon asked, trying to make light of the situation. It had been at least a week since the guy had even shaved, let alone bathed himself.

Ezra coughed and spat, just missing Jon's boot. It was all Jon could do not to set the oaf back down in the tub and let him sleep awhile longer. But he'd determined to get involved in the fellow's life—actually, God had prompted him to get involved—and so here he was defending himself to the drunken fool's daughter.

"It won't do you any good," Emma said. "Matter of fact, you'd be wastin' your time." Her eyes skittered over Ezra's slouched frame. She crossed her arms and stuck out her obstinate little chin. "He's nothin' but a drunk."

Jon took a moment to study Emma's stance, spine straight as a pin, jaw tense, eyes hard and proud. She'd learned that stance from years of struggling to survive. "When was the last time you saw him sober?" he asked.

Emma laughed, but there was no warmth in the sound. "Well now, that'd take some recollectin', preacher."

Preacher? Jon? Reverend Atkins? Which was it? Jon mused. She'd known him all her life, but since his return to Hickman a little less than a year ago, she didn't seem to know quite how to address him. Furthermore, she was determined to dislike him.

Ezra swayed, and Jon got a firmer grip on his arm. The bum was still so liquored up he didn't even know he was the topic of conversation.

"Come on, old man," he said, turning Ezra around and pointing him in the right direction, slanting his face away from the worst of Ezra's overpowering odor.

"You w-want some h-help?" asked Luke. Up until now, he'd been the silent observer. Matter of fact, Luke spent most of his time on the sidelines watching life go by. Jon wondered if the boy didn't know a whole lot more about living than most folks gave him credit for knowing.

"That'd be real nice, Luke. You take the other arm."

Luke stepped forward and Emma's frown grew. "There's no hope for Ezra, Jon. You might as well accept it."

Ah, so now he was Jon again.

He paused and smiled at her. "Oh, there's hope, Emma. As long as there's a God in heaven, there is hope."

She made a scoffing noise. "You'd best save your sermonizin' for your congregation."

His grin widened as he tilted his face at her. "I will if you promise to come hear me sometime."

He detected the slightest hitch at the corner of her mouth. "Now, why would I bother comin' to hear one of your sermons?"

"To please me maybe?" She gave him an odd look, and how could he blame her? She'd be blown away by the knowledge that he was attracted to her, had been since he was a snotty-nosed kid. Of course, his attraction made zero sense. He needed a wife, yes, but a good *Christian* wife, someone to support his ministry, not someone like Emma Browning who openly admitted she had no use for God.

He gave himself a mental scolding.

Ask her about the room, Jon.

The nudge was as strong as if Jupiter, his horse, had plowed straight into his side. *I've asked her plenty, Lord. She's made it clear she doesn't want me under her roof.*

Ask, Jon.

"You rent that extra room out yet?" he asked.

She gave him a stunned look, probably still mulling over his invitation to come to church. "What? No." Her arms remained crossed, except now she hugged herself more tightly and added a scowl to her pursed lips.

"I'm still in need of a place."

Ezra belched loud enough to scare the birds from their perches. Not only that, it carried a vile stench. Emma lifted a hand and batted the acrid air to ward off the worst of the smell.

"Oh, for crying in a bucket! If you get him out of here, you can rent a blasted room."

Jon grinned. It was a victory grin, he knew, so he tried not to let it grow to extremes. *Thank You, Lord.* "That's a load off my shoulders, Emma. Tom Averly, who bought my place, will be pleased to know I'm finally moving out."

He and Luke started hauling Ezra out of the yard.

"Rent's twelve dollars a week, but my long-termers pay by the month," she called to his back. "I'll expect you to pay the first month's rent on the day you move in. Thereafter, rent's due the first of every month. And if you get behind, there'll be no mercy."

Jon waved, hiding his victory grin. "I always pay my bills on time."

"And I won't stand for any of your preaching, either, you hear?"

"Will you sit for it?"

She didn't respond to that, just made a grumbling noise.

He was still grinning when they passed Winthrop's Dry Goods and he caught a glimpse of Iris Winthrop through the glass, her wide-eyed, gaped-mouth reaction when she saw Luke and him escorting Ezra through the center of town only adding to his satisfaction.

The bath was no easy affair, but when it was finished, Ezra Browning did smell as nice as a field of daisies. Of course, he'd sauntered in the direction of the Madam's saloon shortly thereafter, much to Jon's dismay, not in the least bit grateful for their help.

"Let me take you back to your house, Ezra," Jon had offered. "Luke and I will help you clean up the place and fix you a decent meal." But Ezra had shaken his head and mumbled something about needing a drink instead.

"I guess h-he don't like ar cookin'," Luke had said while they stood there next to the bathhouse watching Ezra amble off, Jon's arm looped over Luke's hunched shoulders.

Jon slanted his head at Luke. "He doesn't know what he's missing. I cook a mean bean soup."

Luke shot him a twisted grin. "Me and Pa like bean soup,

but Miss Emma don't n-never make it. She says she don't dare m-make b-bean soup for a houseful of r-rude men."

At Luke's remark, Jon clutched his stomach and bent over laughing.

*****

Emma dusted with a vengeance. Now, why had she gone and offered her vacant room to Jonathan Atkins? Hadn't she just been telling herself she neither wanted nor needed the company of a preacher in her establishment? So why was it that when he'd looked at her with those powder blue eyes of his, she'd crumbled like a month-old cookie? Was it because he'd taken old Ezra off her hands? It seemed a likely excuse. After all, one good deed deserved another, and Lord knows she wasn't about to take her father to the bathhouse herself, much as the old codger did need a bath. But then she had to confess there was more to it than that.

Emma dusted even faster. Truth was, she wasn't willing to delve much deeper into her reasons for relenting. All she knew was that the town's young preacher was about to make his home in this very room, and she'd best get it ready for him. She lifted a lace doily from the chest of drawers, gave it a little shake and replaced it, smoothing down the corners with care. Then she glanced up at the ancient picture hanging crooked above the chest and righted it.

Standing back, she made a sweeping assessment of the room: clean sheets on the old four-poster bed, braided rug freshly beaten, gingham curtains laundered and pressed, and the cracked leather seat of the old wooden rocker wiped clean. She had no idea when Jon Atkins planned to move into Mr. Dreyfus's old room, but at least it would be ready for him when he did.

She dropped her hands to her sides and felt a bulge in her apron pocket. Stuffing her hand into her pocket she withdrew the lone wool sock she'd found under Mr. Dreyfus's bed, the one she'd darned for him on numerous occasions. More than likely, he hadn't missed it yet, but come winter he'd be wondering what had become of it.

Fingering the woolen fabric, an unwelcome memory poked to the surface.

Blustery winds sneaked through the cracks of the poorly heated cabin, the pile of firewood next to the stone fireplace dwindling down to almost nothing. Papa staggered through the door, eyes watery red, snowy boots leaving a trail of white on the just swept rug as he stomped his feet. An icy look on his round, whiskered face matched the frigid temperatures. Emma shivered in the straight-back chair and drew the wool blanket up closer around her neck, tucking the book she'd been reading beneath its folds.

"What you doin', girl?" he growled, slamming the door shut behind him, eyes narrow and suspicious. "How come I don't smell no supper cookin'?"

"We're outta most all the food, Papa. All that's left is some flour and oil and a few cans of beans." She drew her knees up close to her chest, hoping he wouldn't find her book. He'd accuse her of laziness for sure. No matter that she'd spent the afternoon sweeping, dusting, and shoveling a narrow path to the rickety old outhouse. Her ten-year-old muscles felt sore and fatigued.

"Then cook the lousy beans, missy."

"We've had beans three times this week, Papa."

As soon as the words left her mouth, she wanted to reclaim them. Papa didn't take nicely to backtalk. He reached her in two long strides and gave her the back of his hand. The force of the blow was enough to knock her off the chair, sending her precious book of Bible stories in another direction.

With his beefy hand he retrieved the book and held it at arm's length. Papa squinted his bloodshot eyes at the cover and tried to make out the title. "What's this nonsense?" he asked.

"Miss Abbott gave it to me," she confessed, her cheek still burning like hot coals where his hand had struck it. She wouldn't mention the book's contents.

"That lady what runs the boardinghouse? How many times I gotta tell you to stay away from that religious crazy?"

Emma pulled herself upright. "Can I have my book back, Papa?" she squeaked out, ignoring his remark. Miss Abbott was as close as Emma would ever come to having a mother, or a grandmother, for that matter. Nearly every day after school she took an extra minute to swing by the older woman's boardinghouse to receive a warm hug and, if she was lucky, cookies and a tall glass of milk.

Papa took one look at the fireplace. The fire was now only a few red embers. Without a second's hesitation, he tossed the treasured volume into the fire, ignoring her sudden gasp. Puffs of black smoke climbed the chimney until the hard cover of the book took hold, reigniting the flames to a rich orange-red.

A trudging sound coming up the stairs dragged Emma's sullen thoughts back to the present. She took a gander at her watch and found it near suppertime. Gideon Barnard glanced inside the open door on his way past then halted and backtracked. "You lookin' for somethin', Miss Emma?"

She jammed the wool sock back in her apron pocket. "Just cleanin' out Mr. Dreyfus's old room, makin' way for the next boarder."

Gray eyes slanted under a crinkled brow, reinforcing the older gentleman's perpetual frown. "Yeah? Who's movin' in?"

"The Reverend Atkins." She purposely kept her answer short, not wanting to elaborate. Bending, she picked up the bucket of water she'd used to mop the wood floor, gathered up the dusting cloth and a few other items, and headed for the door, hoping to slip past Mr. Barnard without further incident. But it wasn't to be.

"That so? The preacher?" He moved aside to let her pass, then, rather than go to his room as he'd earlier intended, he followed a few paces behind her. "That mean we have to clean up our talk around here?"

"I've been askin' you hooligans to do that for some time now. I don't imagine a preacher will have any more success at it than me." On the way down the hall, she stopped, set the bucket down, and, with her free hand, righted another picture, then ran her fingers along the top of the frame, pleased to find it dust-free.

"I ain't cleanin' up my mouth—or my actions, for that matter."

She sniffed. "Fine. Now, if you'll excuse me I need to be checkin' on my supper." She picked up the bucket and resumed her steps.

When she turned to take the stairs, Gideon Barnard was muttering something under his breath.

Chapter Four

After cleaning up the supper dishes, Emma plopped a wide-brimmed hat on her head and went out to her garden to do some weeding and to cut a few stems of blue Larkspur for a bouquet. Harland and Wes retreated to the front porch to have their smokes, and Charley Connors and Gid Barnard headed for the parlor with their playing cards. The last she saw of Elliott and Luke Newman, they were retiring to their room.

It was a quiet summer evening, the kind that made one linger awhile just to catch the sights and smells. What a contrast from yesterday's hubbub, Emma thought, while stooping to pull a few weeds on her walk to the garden, then snipping off some wild clematis that grew near the path, their purple hue a nice complement to the larkspur. Even the humidity had leveled off, making the hot-as-an-oven temperatures somehow more livable.

The voices of children at play carried over the motionless air while, overhead, a couple of squirrels quarreled over their rightful places on an oak branch. Through the narrow alleyway, between her place and Flanders' Food Store, she spotted Mr. and Mrs. Crunkle crossing Main Street, a little brown dog on their heels. Out for their usual stroll, she mused with a smile, bending to snip a few larkspur stems, their fragrance wafting through the air. The orange tabby who'd wandered into the yard last spring and never wandered back out, probably because Luke had started feeding it suppertime scraps, moseyed over to rub against her leg. "Well, if it isn't Miss Tabitha," she said, bending to give the cat a gentle scratch behind its ear. She scanned the yard for Luke's scruffy dog, another one of his projects, but didn't spot it. No doubt, the no-name mutt had found a cool spot in which to lounge after downing a plateful of leftovers.

Her garden, a mix of varied vegetables and an array of flowers, grew healthy weeds as well. With a sigh, she hunkered down and started yanking them out one by one.

"Lovely evening, isn't it?"

A rustle of approaching footsteps coming from the side of the house and the mellow-sounding voice accompanying them so startled her that she lost her balance and fell backwards on her rump, legs sprawling. Jonathan Atkins, all six-foot-plus of his lean frame, sped ahead to offer his hand. "I didn't mean to frighten you. Here, let me help you up." When he bent forward, his sand-colored hair fell across his forehead.

Batting at his long-fingered hand, she righted herself in record time, scrambling to her feet, not missing the flash of humor that washed over him when he straightened. Jumpin' Jehoshaphat, what must he think? One part of her cared more than she wanted to admit, but another part rose up with defiance. How dare he sneak up on her like that, then give her that innocent look, oozing with charm no less.

Well, he could use his charms on her all he liked. She wouldn't be falling for them.

*****

"I thought I'd let you know I intend to start moving some of my things in tomorrow—if that's all right with you."

She wiped her dirt-smudged hands on her skirt. By the look of it, she'd been wiping it with more than just dirt. Jon thought he detected a hint of tomato sauce, and what else—grape juice?

"So soon?"

"Is there a problem?"

"No—not—a problem." She swiped at her brow and left a black streak there, lending to the bedraggled look. It was downright endearing.

Bending, she retrieved a bouquet of fresh-cut flowers, whisked up her hat, then slanted a wary look at Jon. "I'll show you where your room is so you'll know where to put your things."

"Great."

He followed her up the back stoop, shocked by the discovery that he couldn't take his eyes off her. The screen door squeaked in protest when she opened it.

Inside, he gave the kitchen a quick assessment. He'd been in the house before, but on those occasions, he'd only gotten as far as the front parlor and living room. The kitchen was quite large, with an attached washroom to his left. In the center stood a massive butcher-block table over which a myriad of copper pots and kettles hung on hooks from the ceiling. On the opposite wall was a big cast-iron oven with a stovepipe vent, and next to that a shiny, white, floor-to-ceiling cabinet with glass doors that revealed stacks of dishes. Beside the cabinet was a wide door leading into the dining room. Through the opening, he spotted a long oak table with about a dozen chairs surrounding it.

"We had roast beef for supper," she informed him in a matter-of-fact tone.

His mouth watered at the mere thought of a home-cooked meal every night. He'd grown accustomed to settling for meager meals during the week, the kind that required little preparation. Occasionally, one of his parishioners would take pity on him and drop off a basket of fried chicken or a big container of vegetable soup, and most Fridays, he went out to Clarence and Mary Sterling's place for supper. The rest of the time, he fended for himself.

Emma hung her hat on a hook behind the door, then laid the flowers on the counter. Walking across the room, she stretched to reach a white antique vase on a high shelf. "I'll just be a minute," she said, turning slightly. "I want to put these in water."

"Take your time," he said. Harland Collins ambled down the hallway. When he spotted Jon, he gave a slow smile. "Well, if it ain't the preacher," he hailed, stopping in the doorway. "Hear tell you're goin' to be stayin' here. Hope the bunch o' sinners what lives here won't infect yer soul, you bein' a preacher an' all."

A hearty laugh pushed past Jon's chest. "I wouldn't worry about that, Mr. Collins. My father was the biggest sinner I know. Matter of fact, I'm one myself but for God's grace." From the corner of his eye, he watched Emma bristle. Was it the reference to his worthless father or the fact he'd mentioned God?

Harland sniffed. "That so? Well, that bein' the case, you wouldn't want to join me and Wes in a round o' poker later, would ya?" His beady eyes twinkled with mischief.

"'Fraid I'll have to draw the line on that one," Jon said with a grin. "I doubt that would sit well with my parishioners. Besides, I'm just here to find out where to put my things. It's going to take me a few days to settle in."

At that, Emma set the vase full of fresh flowers on the kitchen worktable and turned. "I'll show you to your room now," she announced. "We'll take the back stairs." She led him across the hall and past a tiny water closet. Halfway up the stairs she paused. "It's a bunch of brutes livin' under my roof. Don't expect any mollycoddling from them."

He felt the corners of his mouth twitch upward. Because she was two steps above him, their eyes were nearly level. "What about their pretty landlady?" he inquired.

She appeared to be counting to ten before replying. "I coddle no one." An abrupt twist of her body had her skirts flaring and Jon chuckling under his breath.

They made a right turn at the top of the stairs. "Those are my quarters," she said, gesturing toward the back of the house. So, she lived just above the kitchen, he mused. He would like to be a little mouse and slip under the door. A glimpse into Emma Browning's private domain might reveal a great deal about the person.

They passed rooms on either side, and he silently tried to imagine which boarder went with which room. To his left was another water closet. A hasty glance inside revealed a wash sink and raised claw-foot tub. Through the room's lone window, a patch of late afternoon sunlight cast its reflective glow across the light blue, plaster wall.

It was a rambling old house, built back in the sixties. Nothing spectacular or extravagant about the structure itself, except that it was solid. Simple crown molding, aged oak floors that creaked and groaned, and rose-colored, floral wallpaper, peeling at the edges, all added warmth and charm to the place. Strangely, having entered the second floor for the first time, it already felt like home to him. Was this the Lord's way of affirming his decision to sell the family farm? He'd had no regrets about it—doubts perhaps—but the feelings washing over him now quickly melted even those away.

Emma came to a stop at the end of the hallway and flung open the door to the last room on their left. Remaining daylight filtered through the open window, which overlooked the covered porch and Little Hickman's Main Street. A warm, gentle breeze played with the curtains. Emma stepped aside to allow Jon's entry.

"I serve two meals a day. Breakfast is served from seven to eight and supper's at six o'clock on the dot," she spouted from the door, hands stuffed into her apron pockets. "Fridays and Mondays are washdays, but don't think that means I'll be washing your personal items. You'll have to go down to Rita's Laundry Service for that. I do wash the linens, though—if you tear them off your bed ahead of time. If you don't, I'll assume you want to go another week. Pile them outside your door on Friday morning. I'll remake your bed after I've cleaned and pressed the sheets, but that's the only day I'll make your bed.

"We passed the bathroom." She nodded her head in the direction from which they'd come. "Everyone's allowed one bath per week." He raised his eyebrows at that pronouncement, but kept his mouth buttoned. "There's a schedule posted inside the bathroom. Some don't take advantage of their weekly bath, so you can take someone else's turn if you make sure it's okay. I got one of them new fangled water heaters, a pipe that coils down the chimney, starting up in the attic. The water heats as it passes through the coil."

"I've heard of them. It'll be a nice change for me not to have to haul my water from the stove."

She ignored his remark and forged ahead. "You are to wipe your feet at the door and clean up after yourself. You will know my wrath if you leave the remnants of an apple on a table or drop peanut shells on my parlor rug."

"I can only imagine your wrath at its worst, Emma," Jon said, feigning a chill, trying to wheedle a smile out of her.

Not even a hint of one cracked her porcelain face. She lifted a hand to sweep at a stray hair, a self-conscious move.

"Do we have a curfew?" he asked more or less in jest.

She breathed a loud sigh, as if she'd had about enough of him. "Not as such. I lock the doors at 11, but everyone but Luke, Mr. Newman, and Mr. Clayton enjoy their carousing. They've all gotten very good at picking the lock." At last, the first trace of a smile pushed past the hard lines of her mouth, and for one tenuous moment he thought it might materialize. No such luck.

A whinnying horse galloped down Main Street, the wagon it was pulling loaded with supplies. Jon pulled the curtain back to watch the action from his second-story station. "Nice view," he stated, not really expecting a response. Turning, he gave the room a cursory once-over. It was about the size of a peanut, he mused, and would definitely take some getting used to. But it would suffice. "Anything else?" he asked. "In terms of rules, that is?"

She lifted her head and pursed her pretty lips in thought. "There's no smoking or drinkin' of alcoholic beverages in the house—but then I guess I needn't tell you that."

"No."

"And no entertainin' women in your room, either, but I suppose...."

"I'll keep that in mind," he furnished.

"Well then," she wrung her hands, "I guess that about sums it up, Reverend Atkins. You can start haulin' your stuff up the front stairs whenever you have a mind to."

"You can dispense with the formalities, Emma. After all, we've known each other since we were this high." He indicated with flattened palm a distance of about three feet from the floor.

She cleared her throat. "We'll see. I keep a professional distance from my boarders—except in Luke's case, of course. You understand."

He nodded. No, he didn't understand, but he didn't think now was the time for voicing it. In time, he hoped to learn what it was that made her tick, what she disliked about him, and just what had turned her off to God and all matters of the gospel.

"Well then...." She turned, as if preparing to leave, then paused and cleared her throat, angling him with a sheepish look. "One more thing. I wanted to uh—thank you for tendin' to Ezra. It was totally unnecessary."

"You can't be expected to look after him, not when you have a business to run. I had some extra time on my hands, and besides, I wanted to help."

She looked taken aback. "Well, just the same. He's an ungrateful old coot who don't deserve anyone's time or attention. Lord knows he probably can't remember a thing about last night—or even this mornin', for that matter. His memory's not what it used to be. All that firewater has purely fried his noggin."

"I didn't do it for the recognition, and I don't need his thanks, Emma—or yours. Simply put, I'm in the business of helping my fellow human beings."

"Pfff. He hardly qualifies," she answered, her blue eyes sparking with bitterness. He'd like to know what hideous things Ezra Browning had done to his daughter to provoke such open disgust. Then again, maybe he wouldn't. He knew she'd suffered some form of physical abuse. He remembered the bruises she'd shown up to school with. But she was a grown woman now. How long before she realized her anger would one day fester to the point of never healing?

It wasn't that he meant to excuse Ezra Browning's atrocious behavior. Far from it. He understood the effects abuse and neglect played in a person's life, and he wasn't about to diminish them. He should know; he'd suffered under his own father's iron fist, as had his mother. In fact, he'd watched his father's abuse send his mother straight to the grave. One day after arriving home from school, he'd gone out to the barn and discovered her hanging by her neck from a rope, a note stuffed in her dress pocket saying she couldn't take it anymore.

But his resultant hatred for Luther Atkins had done little to assuage the pain of losing his mother. And it had done even less to bring about any sense of closure or peace. In the end, he'd found his only hope for healing lay in quiet surrender to his Lord and Savior, Jesus Christ. Only then had he found the strength to go on, somehow finding it possible to lay aside his hostility toward his father and make a life for himself.

He wondered what it would take to convince Emma Browning of her great need for a loving God.

"Do you believe in second chances, Emma?"

She frowned. "In most cases, yes. In Ezra Browning's case?" She shook her head and scoffed. "He blew all his chances long ago."

Jon tucked his hands into his trouser pockets and advanced one step closer to Emma. "How bad was it, Emma?" he dared ask.

She sucked in a loud breath. "I don't have a mind to talk about the past, leastways with you. You'll just start exhortin' Scripture at me as if I was one of your flock." She spun on her heel and headed for the front stairs.

"No, I won't," he argued, sticking his head out the door to watch her fast retreat. "It was a simple question."

"Nothin' simple about it," she called over her shoulder, her slender frame vanishing around the corner. From the doorway, he heard the click of her hard-soled shoes hit the wooden steps.

Chapter Five

The old Browning farm wasn't much more than a tumble-down shack, a barn and a couple of sheds in even worse repair, and acres and acres of fallow soil. Where once straight rows of cornstalks bent and shifted in July's hot breezes, a mishmash of tall brown weeds now swayed in random fashion. A kind of forlornness swallowed Jon up at the sight. It wasn't that he'd never ridden past the place before, but today he seemed to look at it through different eyes, and it moved him in ways he hadn't expected.

Situated just a mile out of town on the other side of Little Hickman Creek, Ezra's house stood crooked on a slender slope of land. Curtains blew out the open windows, and he wondered if the panes were broken out or just open to the elements.

Jon clicked his tongue at Jupiter and guided him toward the tottering farmhouse. Glancing heavenward, he noted fast-moving clouds, heavy with certain rain. *I probably could have picked a better day for paying a call on Ezra Browning,* he mused. He could only imagine lightning moving in and forcing him to stick out the storm with the bullheaded old man.

"God, am I reading You right? Do You really want me befriending this alehouse lush, and if so, why now? I'm in the midst of packing up my belongings, trying to drum up volunteers for building the new church, getting my pastorate underway, and making an effort to call on potential churchgoers. Surely, I'm wasting my time with Ezra."

Inasmuch as you have done it unto the least of these, my brethren, you have done it unto me. The passage he'd read just that morning repeated itself in his head.

48

"I get the message, Lord, but I'm not sure I have the wherewithal to reach someone like Ezra Browning—or even the patience. He's too much like my own father was, and when I think of how he mistreated Emma…."

His thoughts trailed off as he drew nearer the place and watched a lone goat rummaging through thin grasses and a few chickens picking at the earth. In a weedy field were a couple of grazing horses. He reigned in Jupiter next to a broken-down shed, dismounted, and tied him to a rickety hitching post. The horse whinnied, as if to voice his dubious opinion of the shaky post.

"Stop right there," came a distant, gruff command.

Surprised, Jon whirled at the voice and saw Ezra standing on his porch, rifle aimed straight at him. In one spontaneous move, he raised his arms. "Hey, don't shoot me, Ezra. I'm not here to cause any trouble."

"What you want then?" he asked, squinting and taking care not to lower his aim. He coughed then dropped a wad of spittle at his feet. It looked to be mixed with some blood. "You that preacher kid?"

Despite himself, he chuckled. "I am. Came out to check on you."

"Huh?"

Lord, what am I doing? This man doesn't want my help. The rifle went down a smidgeon, but not low enough to warrant Jon's arms going down. "How about you put down the rifle, Ezra? I don't even carry a weapon, so it'd be pretty foolish on your part to kill me."

"Yer trespassin'. I got a right to protect my property."

Jon would like to ask him what it was he was trying to protect. As far as he could tell, there didn't appear to be much of anything worth looking after. He dared say every cent the old fool earned as barkeep at Madam Guttersnipe's Saloon—the worst place a man with his predisposition to alcohol could work—went right back into feeding his habit.

"I'm not here to cause trouble. Put the gun down—please."

Slowly, the rifle went down, as did Jon's arms. When Ezra propped the gun against the porch railing, Jon set out on a slow walk to the house, Ezra glowering the closer he came.

"Don't never get any visitors out here," Ezra mumbled, throwing another wad of spit.

"You should be happy to see me then," Jon responded.

"Pfff. Ain't got no need for a preacher. It ain't like I'm on my last legs—yet."

Jon smiled. "I can see that." A far-off clap of thunder sounded about the same time a cooling breeze ruffled his shirtsleeves. His gaze shot upward at gathering gray clouds.

"You best hightail it back ta town 'fore you get caught in a rainstorm," Ezra warned. "Sky don't look promisin'."

Jon perused the house's exterior, noting the windows on either side of the porch *were* missing their panes. On the ground lay shards of broken glass. "It appears you're the one who should be worrying about rain. How do you expect to stay dry with those busted-out windows?" He put a foot to the first porch step to test its strength. When it started to give, he determined to stay on ground level for the time being.

Ezra shrugged his hunched shoulders. "It leaks a tad, but I hang sheets up to catch the worst of it. 'Spect I should be gettin' to it." And just like that, he turned and headed inside. Jon stood there with his mouth agape. Had Ezra just dismissed him?

Deciding to chance it, he took the porch steps and invited

himself inside the tumbledown house, the door already open and hanging warped on its hinges. With care, he stepped over the threshold and held his breath at the stench, a combination of perspiration, stale alcohol, filthy clothes, and rancid food. A quick perusal of the one-room shack revealed a sink overflowing with dirty dishes, an upturned chair, strewn-about clothes, and a layer of dust on every stick of furniture. The urge to wretch was strong, but he fought down the impulse with sheer determination.

"I ain't cleaned in awhile," Ezra muttered, picking up a stained sheet from a rickety kitchen chair. When he reached to hang it over a window by two protruding nails, Jon stepped forward to lend a hand.

"Let me," he offered, taking the sheet and hooking it in place. "How'd the windows break?" he asked.

Ezra harrumphed and ran a hand over his thinning hair. "Who knows? Some scallywags rode out a month ago an' throwed rocks at 'em." He scratched himself. "They's jus' havin' fun I guess, but, boy, did they skee-daddle when they heard my gun go off."

Jon's gut twisted with an unexpected knot. Everyone around town knew Ezra for his loutish manners, but that didn't give anyone license to vandalize his property. He'd like to knock a few heads together.

"Did you let the sheriff know?"

Ezra snorted. "You kiddin'? Will Murdock don't have a good word for me."

"Will's a good man—fair, too," Jon said in his defense.

"Ain't no matter. It's over an' done. 'Sides, what do you care? I ain't a churchgoer."

Jon chuckled. "You don't have to attend my church to be my friend."

Ezra threw him a disbelieving look. Did no one care about him?

A crack of thunder sounded in the heavens, louder and closer. Jon watched the fellow fuss with another sheet. His wheezing lungs rattled. *What a pathetic character,* Jon thought.

Inasmuch as you have done it unto the least of these….

"You ever been to church, Ezra?" Jon asked, pulling up a wooden chair and dusting off a month's worth of breadcrumbs before sitting.

Ezra grimaced. "Ain't got no cause for goin'."

"Anyone ever invite you?"

"I can't recall as much." He sniffed, and a tiny smirk cracked his thin lips. "Guess I ain't the only one knowin' I'm a lost cause."

"You're not a lost cause, Ezra. There's plenty of folks that have done far worse than you and yet somehow have discovered God's love and forgiveness."

Ezra snatched a bottle of ale off the filthy counter and pointed it at Jon, eyebrows raised. "You want one?" he asked. There was a definite sneer in his tone.

Jon couldn't help the grin. Most would consider the blatant offer nothing short of blasphemy. "I'll pass."

Ezra wrangled the cap off the bottle and took a long swig. "Good. I ain't into sharin' anyways." He held the bottle up as if it were some prized possession. "This stuff ain't cheap ya know." His rancid breath carried across the room. Jon had all he could do to sit still.

Resting a booted foot across his knee, he watched Ezra take another swig. "God's in the business of healing wounded souls."

Ezra's eyes bulged. "Tarnation! My soul ain't wounded; it's dead!"

Rather than react to the remark, Jon sucked in a calming breath. "How would you like a little help with this place?" he asked, deciding he'd pushed enough for one day.

"Huh?"

"I was thinking about asking some of my parishioners to lend a hand out here. We could have your yard cleaned up in no time. A couple of the ladies could make fast work of your kitchen.

"I notice your porch is sagging. Wouldn't take much more than a few boards and nails to bring it to rights. We could special order the windowpanes if Eldred doesn't already have them in stock. A good coat of white paint would spruce up the outside."

Dead silence filled the space between them, save Ezra's persistent wheeze—until a loud clap of thunder rumbled past the little house's thin walls and a streak of lightning scorched the sky, giving instant light to the dimly lit room. On its tail came the first drops of rain, their pinging sounds bouncing off the old tin roof.

"I ain't needin' no charity," he grumbled.

"It wouldn't be charity. I'd expect you to work alongside us, and you'd be paying for your own windows and paint."

Ezra scratched his head, and for the first time, Jon noticed a slight tremor. Nerves? Or a result of years of imbibing? He glared at Jon through bloodshot eyes, then lifted the bottle to his mouth and drained it in a matter of seconds.

"You'd need to sober up though—at least till after we finished all the work," Jon said with practiced calm, leaning forward in the chair, clasping his hands together between his spread knees. "Think you could do that?"

"Pfff. I'm sober now, ain't I?" Ezra slammed the bottle down on the counter and moseyed across the room, his less than sure-footed gait an indication he was anything but.

53

"I'd expect you to lay off the sauce completely. We wouldn't want folks thinkin' you were incapable of a little self-control, would we?"

Ezra shot him a sideways glare. "Don't rightly care what folks think. 'Sides, ain't no one I know who'd be willin' to lift a finger on my account."

He was probably right. "We'll see about that. There are a lot of good people in Little Hickman."

Ezra didn't look convinced. Jon rose just as the sky pulled back the last of its draperies and cut loose a torrential downpour. A powerful wind steamrolled past the open windows, dousing the sheets Ezra had used as makeshift barriers, the rain coursing in like a waterfall. Miniature rivers spawned on the ancient wood floor, finding a slanted pathway to the center of the room.

"Got some extra sheets?" Jon called above the sudden flood of commotion, feeling helpless.

Ezra shook his head. "Naw. 'Taint no use anyway."

"Somehow we need to block these windows."

The man stood there as if missing a good share of his brain, which he probably was. Jon couldn't let the rain do more damage than it'd already done. Out the back window, he spotted something draped from a clothesline, lying flat to the wind. "What's that?"

Ezra shuffled to the window as if he hadn't a clue his house was the hub of a true gully washer. "An old piece of canvas I used to throw over my chicken yard. Fool chickens won't stay under it though."

"Got a hammer and some more nails?"

Ezra scratched his head again and pulled his brow into a deep frown. "Yeah, right in that there box."

While he sauntered across the room, Jon pulled up his collar and dashed out the back door.

It took a full hour for the rain to slow its course, but by the time it had, Jon had nailed a piece of canvas to each broken window, helped Ezra mop the floor, did what he could to tidy up the kitchen, then made them a pot of coffee.

"I best get back while the storm's at a lull," Jon said, setting his empty mug on the marred tabletop.

Ezra angled him a wary look. "Why'd you come out here, preacher kid?"

Jon stood. "I told you. I wanted to check on you."

Ezra's graying eyebrows furrowed with uncertainty. "That don't make no sense."

Jon chuckled. "Maybe not now, but it will."

"Huh?"

Thunder rolled in the distance, indicating the worst of the storm had passed. "I'll be back. You work on sobering up now. You'll need your wits about you—and your strength." He stretched. "We'll have this place looking spiffy."

Ezra's eyes narrowed into beady little circles, putting Jon in mind of a cornered banty rooster. "Word has it you sold your place to Tom Averly and you're movin' into my girl's boardin'house."

Jon was surprised the news had reached Ezra Browning—and that he'd remembered it. He was almost certain the fellow remembered nothing about his drunken episode on Independence Day or the bath the morning after. "You heard right. Still have a few more trips to make before my move is complete. Tom bought most everything 'cept for the clothes on my back."

Ezra grumbled low in his chest. "Fool thing you did, gettin' rid of that place and donatin' the funds to a new church buildin'."

Ezra wasn't the first one who'd voiced his opinion on the matter. Perhaps it had been extreme on Jon's part, but sometimes obeying God called for extreme measures. He had no doubt God would meet his needs. "I'd be a bigger fool to disregard God's direction for my life."

Ezra shook his head as if to wrestle it free of a swarm of pesky flies. "That's a bunch of hooey."

"To you it probably is, Ezra," Jon said. "I best be on my way. I have a sermon to prepare for. Don't imagine you'd want to come to Sunday services and critique my delivery?"

For the first time, a smile, or more like a smirk, popped out on Ezra's face, revealing yellowed teeth, one missing on top, probably due to decay and neglect. "I ain't never set foot in a church—'ceptin' when I married Lydia Baxter. Don't 'spect I ever will."

It'd been a long while since he'd heard mention of Ezra Browning's wife—Emma's mother. There'd been talk how she'd died after giving birth to Emma, but beyond that, he knew very little. He suspected her death held the key to much of Ezra and Emma's animosity. "You must have loved her very much."

Ezra scoffed, cursed, then moved to the sink, putting his back to Jon. "Long time ago," he mumbled, picking up one of the dishes Jon had just washed to study its sheen.

Jon walked to the door and put his hand on the knob. He turned back. "I'll be on my way then. Remember what I said about sobering up. And, Ezra, you might want to have Doc check that wheezing cough you got."

The only response he received from that was another flat-out curse.

*****

Emma's steps were purposeful. She had a number of things to tend to, and she didn't welcome the thought of getting wet in the next wave of rain. A deluge had already fallen earlier in the day, for which much of Little Hickman was grateful. At least the dust would finally settle. But enough was enough.

A child's shout of glee had her pausing mid-step to glance down Main Street where she glimpsed a mother and her child. The toddler, having slipped from his mama's hands, had discovered a puddle the size of a small lake and was hopping around in it like a frog, squealing with delight when the water splashed past his knees, soaking his trousers. Emma smiled at the scene, recalling a time when she too had relished the feel of mud between her toes.

"What you doin' in that mud hole, girl? Ain't you got no sense atall? Git back to the house 'fore I tan yer li'l hide. There's work to be done."

It was a scorching day, the kind that made the sweat stick to one's armpits.

"But it feels so good, Papa," she squealed, her six-year-old enthusiasm difficult to curb. "You should try it." She waded further into Little Hickman Creek, soaking the hem of her cotton dress despite lifting it above her knees. "Ain't ya hot, Papa?"

"Not as hot as your backside's gonna be if you don't haul yourself outta that water hole 'fore I count ta ten," he roared. His face was red as a tomato, whether from heat or rage Emma couldn't say. "You ain't finished washin' the breakfast dishes yet. And after that, you got ta tote in those pails of milk from the barn."

She'd grown accustomed to Ezra Browning's fits, learned how far she could push before he laid a hand to her. This seemed to be one of those times, so with a sigh she meandered back to shore, choosing her favorite flat rocks as stepping-stones, knowing them by heart from previous trips to the creek. That's why it so surprised her when she found herself sprawled on her backside, having slipped on a slimy pebble, soaked from head to toe.

"Now look what you done!" Ezra bellowed, wading a foot or so in to drag her up by the arm. Pain surged through her side where she'd collided with a sharp, protruding twig, but she was too proud to confess it. And what good would it have done her? There'd be no sympathy, not when the entire incident was her own doing.

Even the silent tears she shed as they trudged up the hill toward their one-room cabin seemed not to affect him. She struggled along-side him, barely managing to keep up with Ezra's long strides.

And just like that, the joy of cool mud between her toes shriveled like a rose in winter.

Emma blotted out the pesky memory with a tiny shake of the head. She dragged her gaze away from the youngster and his mother and resumed her step, passing Flanders' Food Store. Stepping down from the sidewalk, she crossed the alley, bypassing a puddle. Rivers of rainwater still drained off one corner of the roof of Winthrop's Dry Goods, creating a stream that followed a downward path toward Zeke's Barber Shop, a square little building situated down the alley and just behind the dry goods store.

A jangling bell welcomed her when she walked into Winthrop's. Fancy Jenkins was just picking up a box of purchased goods from the counter. Iris Winthrop turned at the sound. "Why, good afternoon, Miss Browning," the proprietor greeted from behind the counter, her usual pasted-on smile lacking genuine friendliness. Everyone knew the woman was more about appearances than actual benevolence. Emma was certain her father's presence in the town had always been a thorn in Mrs. Winthrop's side, and the fact that Emma carried the Browning name made her an automatic detriment to Little Hickman.

Fancy Jenkins, on the other hand, wore a smile of the warmest kind despite her missing upper tooth. "Hello there, Miss Emma." She hefted the box of supplies higher. "Ain't it a drippy day today? I 'spect it'll stay like this fer awhile." She was a small-boned woman, perhaps frail-looking at first glance, but in her clear blue eyes, there was a depth that spoke of courage and spunk. Life had not been easy for her, she having lost her husband to heart problems a year or so back when her only daughter, Sarah, was about thirteen. Somehow, she eked out a living by managing a small piece of farmland and selling eggs. Emma admired her grit.

"It's a wet one, but the lower temperatures are a welcome relief. I'll say that," Emma replied, offering up a smile for both women before hauling out her list of needs from her front apron pocket and giving it a quick perusal. Yellow thread to match the fabric she'd bought earlier for making new kitchen curtains, needles, a fresh supply of straight pins, three yards of cloth for a new dress—purple, perhaps?—and a supply of serviceable fabric with which to stitch some new kitchen towels.

"Yes, it was hotter than a stovepipe on the Fourth," Fancy concurred, blowing a graying strand of hair off her cheek. "My, but there was a throng of folks come out for them fireworks. Wasn't that a fine display?" She seemed to want to talk, and she placed her box of miscellaneous items back on the counter, shoving aside some sewing notions Mrs. Winthrop had intended for display. Emma didn't miss the loud sigh the shopkeeper blew out.

"I watched them from my upstairs window," Emma said, trying her best to be polite. Out of the corner of her eye, she watched Iris's mouth pull into a straight line. Clearly, she wasn't in the mood for idle chatter. She fussed with some papers by her cash register. The notion that she didn't approve of either one of them gracing her establishment amused rather than peeved Emma, and almost made her want to prolong the conversation.

"Me and my Sarah sat on a blanket next to the Broughtons and that nice Reverend Atkins. My, but he's a handsome man, the reverend. Hear tell he's movin' into your place."

He'd been moving his belongings in for the past three days now, and so far, she'd managed to avoid his comings and goings. Ever since agreeing to let him take the room Mr. Dreyfus had vacated, she'd been berating herself. Doubtless, there'd be nothing but sermons from morning till night now. Evidence of that came when Luke appeared at the breakfast table just yesterday toting a little black Bible. She'd been standing at the table slicing a fresh loaf of bread.

"R-repent y-ye, and believe the g-gospel!" he'd spouted to a table full of gaping men.

"Huh?" Charlie Conners had asked, his eggs falling off his fork.

"That's what it says r-right here," Luke had claimed, laying a stubby finger on a page about midway through the book.

"You can't read," his father had chided, brow pinched. "Here, give me that." Quickly, he'd pushed back his chair and snatched the book out from under Luke's nose. "Where's it say that?"

Luke had leaned close, his eyes doing a careful search, a look of sheer determination written across his pudgy, round face. Finally, he'd put a chubby finger to the page. "R-right there," he'd announced. "The p-preacher says so."

"The preacher, huh?" His father had scowled then squinted at the printed page. "This here says, **'It is better to dwell in a corner of the housetop, than with a brawling woman in a wide house.'"**

When loud laughter erupted, Emma had turned on her heel and left the dining room.

"He all moved in? That's quite an adjustment for the preacher—from a big farm to one little room. Can't imagine givin' up all that space," Fancy was saying, pulling Emma back to the present.

Talk about adjustments! She could only imagine the grumblings that were sure to come if Jon Atkins used her renters as sounding boards for his sermons. Why, they'd mock him up one side and down the other.

"He's been bringing his stuff in little by little far as I know. I haven't paid him much mind," Emma replied, stuffing her list back into her apron pocket and setting off on a stroll through the little store, fingering various fabrics along the way, scanning the place for just the right color and pattern for stitching herself a new dress.

"Sure is nice of the Winthrops to open their house up for Sunday services," Fancy commented.

Emma glanced up to acknowledge the remark. Mrs. Winthrop sniffed and raised her chin a notch. Since the school burned down, folks met in the Winthrop's massive living room. They did, after all, own the biggest house in Little Hickman. Its central location, one block off Main Street, was convenient for all. Although it seemed an uncommonly generous act from Emma's perspective, she suspected the woman enjoyed the accolades that came as a result.

"I been goin' just so's I can watch the reverend," Fancy added, covering her toothy grin with the palm of her hand and letting go a high-pitched giggle. Emma pinched her lips together to hide a smile and took up a piece of woven cotton to finger its softness. Purple and with a delicate, floral pattern running through it. Wasn't it just what she'd been looking for? "Ain't a more comely lookin' man in all of Hickman if you ask me," Fancy chortled.

"My lands!" Mrs. Winthrop clacked, drawing her shoulders up tight and pushing out her plenteous chest. Emma watched in quiet amusement. "It's improper to think of a man of the cloth in that light."

Fancy shrugged. "Nothin' improper about it in my book. I'm just statin' a plain fact. Course, he's a fine speaker, too. I ain't denyin' that. Since he got that preacher schoolin' out East, he sure talks a fine piece, usin' all them nice words. Holds the ear of most folk much better'n Reverend Miller ever did. Frankly, I'm glad that man got too old for circuit ridin'. His sermons were startin' to wear."

Mrs. Winthrop sucked in a raspy breath, visibly addled. "Well." She pursed her thin lips and raised two pointy eyebrows, taking care to look straight at Emma, her eyeglasses resting low on her oversized nose. Emma looked away. "At least Reverend Miller guarded his reputation. This one doesn't seem to care who he's seen with or where he resides."

The comment did as intended, set Emma back for an instant. The bolt of cloth she'd been stroking slipped from her fingertips. Of course, Mrs. Winthrop was referring to the preacher's dealings with Ezra Browning and the fact that he'd chosen to take up residence in her boardinghouse, joining her flock of ne'er-do-wells. She wasn't thrilled about the preacher's presence in her house, either, but she resented the pompous woman's implication that she ran a less-than-respectable business.

"My boarders are not the most befitting characters, I'll grant you that," she said, matching the proprietor's pointed gaze. "But I'll have you know I operate a dignified business, certainly a step up from Madam Guttersnipe's establishment."

"A giant step," Fancy put in, bobbing her bony head up and down so that her sunbonnet tipped to one side, revealing her patchy gray hair.

Mrs. Winthrop made a clicking sound with her tongue and put a hand to her throat to adjust her close-fitting collar. "Well, of course that goes without saying. I'm merely suggesting the minister should have thought twice before deciding to live among such—such ill-mannered men. Why, it could prove scandalous."

Since Emma wasn't in the mood for arguing, she swallowed down a retort and dropped her gaze to the purple fabric, fingering it one last time. She knew Eldred Johansson carried a limited supply of fabrics in the mercantile. And what he didn't have she could always special order. Suddenly it seemed important to take her business elsewhere. Her decision made, she turned and walked to the door.

"Surely you're not leaving already," Mrs. Winthrop asserted, her jaw dropping to her waist. "Didn't you come in with a list?"

Emma opened the door then paused to turn, applying a forced smile. "Why, yes, I did." She squeezed the rumpled piece of paper at the bottom of her deep pocket. "But the air is just too stuffy for shopping."

Iris Winthrop's eyebrows shot up in dismay as she nervously moistened her lips and patted her forehead with a silk hankie. "Well, I never...."

Fancy Jenkins' mouth curved into a knowing smile as she hoisted her box of goods into her arms. "Well, I declare if you ain't right, Miss Emma. It is a mite stuffy in here."

Chapter Six

The air was dank and clammy, scented with the smells of perspiration, dusty clothes, horse manure, and Lily of the Valley. It was all Jon could do to sing the morning hymn, "Rescue the Perishing," led by Carl Hardy and accompanied by Bess Barrington on the Winthrop's upright piano. About the crammed living room and parlor, paper fans fluttered before flushed faces, children cried and wiggled with boredom, and pesky flies zoomed about, eluding the swipe of death.

Jon mopped his damp brow with his handkerchief and examined his audience of faithful Sunday morning worshippers—all packed in close like a bunch of wayward lambs awaiting their shepherd's direction. There was Anna Johnson and her twin boys squeezed in the front row, one toddler on the floor at her feet, the other squirming in her lap. Robert, her husband, leaned against a far wall by the front door, yawning so big Jon thought he'd catch a fly for sure. Ben Broughton stood nearby, shifting from one foot to the other, his lips moving to the hymn's final chorus.

On either side of Anna sat Fancy Jenkins and her daughter, Sarah. Sarah seemed intent on helping Anna watch her children, while Fancy contented herself with watching *him*. Jon nodded politely at the widow. Liza Broughton and her stepchildren, the elderly Mr. and Mrs. Crunkle, Mrs. Martin, widows Ila Jacobsen and Rose Marley, and finally Lucy Fontaine and her brood of youngsters took up the first two rows of chairs. The rest of the worshippers either sat on the floor or stood along the walls, with a sparse number of occupied chairs in between. The crowded situation only stressed Hickman's necessity for a new church building—the sooner the better— but first he intended to mention Ezra Browning's need for benevolence—and pray for hearts of compassion.

"Rescue the perishing, care for the dying," folks sang wholeheartedly despite the punishing heat. "Jesus is merciful, Jesus will save." A thunderous "Amen!" echoed across the room with the hymn's final chord. Jon rose and approached the makeshift pulpit, a wooden box stationed on a sturdy table. Bess rose, too, and wove her way through the masses to reach her family, all situated in the front parlor to the left of the entrance, just out of view.

Jon cleared his throat. "This morning's passage comes from 1 John 3:17–18." He hauled his big Bible up to the box and opened it to the place he'd bookmarked. Giving his congregants an encouraging smile, he began to read. **"But whoso hath this world's good—"**

A baby's loud cry stopped him mid-sentence and redirected the eyes and attention of several parishioners. He gave the mother a moment to hush her child with a bottle, then continued. **"And seeth his brother have need, and shutteth off his compassion for him, how dwelleth the love of God in him? My little children, let us not love in word, neither in tongue; but in deed and in truth."**

Jon surveyed the gathering of folks. They were good people, honest and hardworking, and, for the most part, compassionate toward others. He recalled numerous times when they'd demonstrated selfless giving—like the barn raising out at Rocky and Sarah Callahan's farm this spring, the Christmas bazaar a couple of years ago when they'd donated all proceeds to disadvantaged families, and the work day last fall when they'd served the widows of the community. Then there was the time the bridge over Little Hickman Creek collapsed and the men united as one to rebuild an even sturdier one, completing the job in just three days. Yes, these were good people, made of strong moral fiber, courageous and full of spirit. He had confidence in them. Just the same, he approached the topic with caution.

"I want to talk to you today about our Christian responsibility to help and encourage those less fortunate than we. Now some of you might say, 'I don't have a spare dime to give. How can I help the needy when I'm in need myself?' I'm not talking about emptying your pockets; I'm talking about emptying your hearts."

Just then, Anna Johnson hefted a squirming twin into her arms, motioned for Sarah Jenkins to look after the other one, then wove her way to the front of the house, creating a momentary disturbance. Jon watched while folks made room for her passing. Against the west wall, Harvey Coleson, the town's only barber, mopped his sweaty brow and shifted his two-hundred-pound frame, angling old Mrs. Jarvis with a perturbed look when she succumbed to a coughing fit. Jon sighed. If he had to guess, he'd say he'd lost his audience at the words *Christian responsibility*. Still, he forged ahead.

"The early church carried each other's burdens, looked for opportunities to help. Jesus said in Matthew 25:35, **'For I was hungry, and ye gave me meat: I was thirsty, and ye gave me drink: I was a stranger, and ye took me in.'**"

Jon proceeded to speak about the duty of all Christians to uplift the downhearted, provide hospitality, and work as onto the Father—without grumbling or complaining. He cited relevant Scriptures and gave examples of the generosity of the first Christian church. As he sought to end his message, he scanned the people's faces. "God calls each of us to live holy and righteous lives, following after Paul's example to come together as laborers with God," he charged. "Why, right in this fine community there are those without hope who could benefit from the fruit of our labors."

Outside, a brisk breeze blew through the open windows, parting Mrs. Winthrop's long, velvet curtains and providing momentary relief from the sweltering air. Jon removed a handkerchief from his hip pocket and made a sweep across his face. Again, he studied the roomful of faithful worshippers, comforted by Ben Broughton's encouraging look.

"Our number one responsibility is to reach lost souls for Christ," he continued, "but often that is accomplished by first healing the sick, feeding the hungry, and befriending the lonely. I would hope that folks would see Little Hickman Community Church as a place that cares."

"Amen to that, Reverend," offered the elderly Esther Martin from the second row, her floral hat so big that those sitting behind her had given up trying to see around it.

Jon smiled. "I think it's clear we need to erect a new church building."

A resounding "Amen!" came from several different directions along with nods of agreement.

"And I'm ready to proceed as soon as you are, but first there is a pressing situation in our community we need to address, an individual that sorely needs our help. His house is in sad shape, I'm afraid, missing windows, peeling paint, broken porch steps. And the inside is just as bad. With the aid of several able bodies, men and women alike, I believe we can help get this poor soul back on his feet. Can I count on you to lend a hand?"

Heads turned toward each other and waggled up and down. Faces rife with eagerness sought Jon's challenge, awaited his direction.

"Who is it, preacher?" someone asked.

Jon swallowed down a lump the size of his breakfast of grapefruit and sucked in a cavernous breath. "It's Ezra Browning. I paid a visit on him three days ago."

Gasps and whispers rose up all around, the mumbling and buzzing akin to a roomful of bumblebees. At the front of the house, Mrs. Winthrop suddenly came to life, pressing a hand to her ample chest. If Jon didn't know better, he'd say she was about to have a coronary right in her own living room. He gripped the corners of the box that held his big King James Bible and uttered a silent prayer for guidance.

"What's this about, Reverend?" asked Elmer Barrington, his voice carrying over the simmering crowd. Elmer, who'd been sitting around the corner in the front parlor with his family, came out in plain view to ask the question. "Why would you bother visitin' him? He ain't nothin' but a foul-mouthed, drunken dolt. His own daughter don't have nothin' to do with 'im."

"I'll say," came the voice of Martha Atwater. "He's rude and obnoxious. I don't even want to walk down Main Street when he's out and about. Smells to high heaven, if I do say so. Cain't even walk a straight line in broad daylight."

"I've made him promise he'll sober up," Jon offered. Well, saying he'd squeezed a promise out of the fellow was a bit of a stretch, rather like saying he'd wrestled a bull into submission, but Jon refused to retract his words for fear of losing more ground.

"What makes you think anything will change if we do fix up his place?" This from Clarence Sterling, an aging farmer who'd lived in Hickman most of his life. He stood next to an open window, his petite wife, Mary, sitting in front of him in an English club chair fanning herself, her white hair wrapped in a tight little bun.

"I don't know that anything will change, Clarence," Jon replied. "For all I know, Ezra Browning will curse the ground we walk on, might even kick us off his property. The man's rarely been shown any kindness, so he won't know how to handle it. On the other hand, our good intentions just might provide a channel for some positive changes. Sadly, there are no guarantees when a Christian steps out on a limb to help a wayward soul. One thing I do know. If we don't start showing him some brotherly love, he'll never see God's grace in action.

"Think of it, Little Hickman Community Church just could be his only hope for salvation."

"I'm all for it," said Ben Broughton.

Several others offered nods of agreement, but then Iris Winthrop's emphatic throat clearing drained his hopes. "Well." She pushed herself to a standing position and the room went quiet as a cemetery. It was a known fact she carried weight in the town, and even more in the church since she opened her home every Sunday for morning services, a generous act to be sure. Because of that, folks paid her heed whenever she called for it. Jon braced himself for the coming lecture, her expression enough to scare off a bat.

"I, for one, think the idea quite preposterous. What has this insufferable man ever done for Little Hickman except embarrass us? His actions at the Independence Day festivities were quite inexcusable, if you ask me, not to mention humiliating."

Humiliating for whom? Jon wanted to ask.

"Mrs. Winthrop, I—"

"Furthermore, the people of this town would do well to concentrate their efforts on finishing the schoolhouse and church before wasting precious time on the likes of Ezra Browning. Most lead busy lives, and expecting folks to donate their time and energy at this abhorrent man's house is not only foolhardy, it's—it's insolent."

"Insolent?"

"And disrespectful," she added, as if he needed another insult.

Upon finishing her speech, she clicked her tongue in disgust, the flowers on her wide-brimmed hat fairly trembling. Slowly, she sat herself back down, taking care to fix her bountiful skirts on the way to her wingback chair.

"I'm not asking for the town's help, ma'am," Jon said while begging the Lord for patience. "I'm asking the church to step in. God has called us to be His servants, to rescue the perishing, care for the dying. Did we not just sing those very words in the morning hymn?"

"I don't care what we sang," she said with a cool stare. "Wasting our time on this man is—"

"Oh, Iris, for the love of all that's good, be quiet." Jon was certain God Himself had intervened until he recognized the voice of Clyde Winthrop.

"Amen!" mumbled Esther Martin quite loud enough for everyone to hear. A few snickers filtered through the air.

Normally sedate by nature, if not downright compliant, Clyde possessed the innate ability to rein in his blustering wife at the most opportune times. Jon believed he also had the patience of Job to have lived with Iris for nearly half a century. With surprising servility, she lowered her chin, expelling a loud sniff.

Clyde moved to stand behind his wife. "Now then," he said. "It seems to me we ought to hear the reverend out. He's spotted a need within our community and apparently has a plan for meeting it. I, for one, am curious to hear what that plan might be."

Heads bobbed and faces once full of doubt now sparked with interest. It was a start, Jon mused, nodding his appreciation to Clyde for defusing an otherwise tense situation, then sweeping his gaze out over the small congregation before presenting his proposal.

*****

"Supper's on!" Emma called from the dining room just as the clock in the hallway chimed six times. "And ya best not dawdle."

All around the house, a clatter arose as feet hit the floor. Then came the pounding traffic on the front and back stairs and the slamming of the front screen door, its squeaky hinges making it quite impossible for anyone to enter the house unnoticed.

Tonight there was an extra place setting at the table—in the spot where Mr. Dreyfus used to sit. It was the reverend's first official meal with the other boarders. For that matter, tonight, Sunday, would mark his first night's stay. She wondered how long it would take him to regret his decision. Surely, Gideon Barnard's foul mouth would do the trick—or the loud Saturday night carousing. And if those didn't do it, then their poker games would—or their blatant mockery of his beliefs. Whatever, he'd be gone before any of them could spell *pig snout*. She'd bet money on it.

As usual, Luke arrived first, his hair neatly combed to the side, with the exception of a few unruly strands at the back of his head that stood straight and tall as a cornstalk.

"The p-p-preacher's comin'," he announced to the floor. "He'll sit here." Luke pulled out a chair and stood behind it like a soldier awaiting his commanding officer, no doubt anticipating Jonathan Atkins' grand entrance. A tiny smile tickled the corners of Emma's mouth as she took her place at the head of the table and closest to the kitchen.

Harland Collins sauntered in next. A widower in his sixties, he was one of Little Hickman's blacksmiths, keeping shop in a room off the livery. No matter how hard he scrubbed, his hands never seemed to come clean, much to Emma's chagrin. He nodded at both of them and took his usual seat, opposite Luke's chair. On his tail came Wes Clayton and Elliott Newman. Wes took the chair at the far end, same side as Luke, while Elliott sat on Luke's right and next to Emma. "Why ain't you sittin', boy?" Elliott asked, deep lines etched into his long, haggard face, making him look as if he'd already reached the century mark, even though Emma knew him to be no older than Harland Collins. Of all her boarders, Emma felt sorriest for him. He had watched a malignant tumor eat away at his beloved wife, Matilda, before she finally passed on, leaving him with a teenage boy and a mountain of doctor and hospital bills. One year later to the day, his house burned to the ground. Because he'd let his insurance expire, there'd been nothing with which to rebuild. And that's when he'd come knocking on her door.

"I'm w-waitin' on the preacher," Luke explained in his slow voice.

His father took up his napkin and laid it out on his lap, the only one of her boarders who used the cloth for its intended purpose. On more than one occasion, Harland Collins had used it as a handkerchief, while Gideon Barnard thought it most useful for shining his belt buckle.

"You might be standin' awhile then," Elliott said. "Last I seen the preacher, he was sprawled out on his bed, plain tuckered, I believe. You best sit, son." With sunken spirits, Luke plopped into his chair.

Charley Connors and Gideon entered then and walked directly to their usual spots. "Yep, that preacher's still sleepin', far as I can tell," Charley said. "Guess all that movin' and what-not did 'im in."

"Or maybe ar company ain't to his likin'," said Gideon, pulling back his chair. "Figure them innocent ears o' his ain't used to ar kind o' talk." The man wore a perpetual scowl, but now the briefest of smiles flickered like a flash of light from a lone candle. He ran a hand over his bumpy, sallow skin and sat.

A cackling Mr. Clayton nodded his head and pulled at the gray beard that matched his thinning hair. "We'll break 'im in."

"Heard he had a cantankerous father," said Mr. Newman, wiping at the corner of his mouth with his napkin, even though he hadn't yet touched his food. "And a mama who hung herself when he was just a lad. Somethin' tells me he ain't as innocent as one might expect."

That seemed to shut up the lot of them for the time being, particularly when Harland made a harrumphing sound and took up the bowl of mashed potatoes in the center of the table. Others followed suit, reaching for the platter of chicken, the bowl of green beans, and the tureen of gravy. Soon the clang of forks and knives on plates and the loud chomping of food made up the only sounds in the room.

Emma cleared her throat and put her napkin beside her plate. "I'll go check on the preacher," she announced, pushing back her chair, its legs scraping shrilly on the fresh scrubbed floor.

Several pairs of inquiring eyes gawked at her. "You ain't never checked on me when I missed a meal," Harland Collins remarked.

Luke jumped to his feet. "I'll go with ya."

"Sit down, Luke," his father ordered. "The preacher ain't none of your business." Luke sat begrudgingly.

"Yeah, why's he get the special treatment?" Charley asked, shoveling a forkful of food into his mouth, his eyes trained on her while he noisily chewed.

Why indeed? It irked her plenty, this need to explain when she wasn't sure herself why it should matter one jot. Shoulders stiff, she drew in a breath, then glanced from one to the other. "If one o' you was ailin', I'd fetch the doctor. I'm merely going to see if he has need of one." She turned. "And I'd appreciate it if you tried eating with your mouths closed from now on." That said, she marched out of the room.

"Well, if that don't beat all," Charlie said with a sniff and a hoot.

*****

"Get off my property, you no-good, snoopin' tadpole! I'll shoot ya right on the spot! I ain't afeard to pull this trigger." Shotgun raised and pointed straight at his head, Jon scrambled for breath, his heart nearly leaping out of his chest. Sweat trickled down his face, dripping off his chin to pool at his feet.

"God loves you, Ezra," he managed. "He loves you. All you have to do is surrender to Him, accept that you need a Savior, ask Him...."

A blast of curse words erupted from the drunkard's mouth. "Shut up!" he barked. "Ain't no God big enough for the likes o' me."

"You're dead wrong." He cringed at his poor choice of words. Ezra stepped closer, cocked the gun, and poked its long, steely barrel into his temple.

"Pull the trigger, you insufferable, cussed fool." Confusion mingled with awareness. He angled just his eyes in the direction of the

voice. There stood Iris Winthrop in a pair of men's coveralls, booted feet spread, hands stationed on her extensive hips, the harsh lines of her face yielding their standard scowl. On her head was a flaming-red, wide-brimmed hat with at least a dozen or more multicolored roses shooting upward. "It's time the elders sought out a different preacher. This one has too many outlandish notions."

"No, d-d-don't shoot," *wailed a boyish-sounding voice. Luke.* "He's sick."

Sick? I'm not sick, *he tried to eke out.* I'm just tired.

"You sick?" *Mrs. Winthrop asked, arms dropping to her sides.*

The gun went down. "You sick?" *Ezra asked.*

"You sick?" *asked an altogether different voice, this one faceless and from some distant place, its timbre soft and almost melodic. He fumbled his way through a sudden fog, trying to identify its owner.* This is a dream, *he assured himself.* Wake up.

He put a hand to his forehead and let it linger there. Eyes heavy, he fought to open them, but they felt like lead blankets.

"You sick?" she repeated. "You're sweatin' bad as a fireman walkin' on ashes."

His meandering mind finally made it back to the present, and when it did, his eyes shot open in a flash. Emma Browning jumped back as if she'd just witnessed a ghost coming out of its skin. Jon bolted upright, swabbed his damp brow, and stared at the jumpy woman who'd squelched his nightmare.

Chapter Seven

I asked if you're sick." The skittish expression gone, Emma now wore a look of impatient smugness.

"Why does everybody keep asking me that?" Jon hauled his legs over the side of the bed and shook his head, trying to rid it of the few remaining cobwebs.

"What?"

"Never mind. What time is it?"

"A quarter past six. The others are eating their supper. I called, but you didn't come down. The food don't last a long time around here, so if you don't come on the first call, you could be out of luck. And after today I won't be checkin' on ya."

He swiped a hand over his face then wove it through his unruly head of hair before peering down at his bare feet. He was a disheveled mess, and he could only imagine what he looked like from Emma Browning's perspective. He noticed that she kept her eyes trained on something just over the top of his head. Was there something else amiss about his appearance, or had she never seen a barefooted man before?

"Thanks for the warning," he muttered, giving his head another shake. "I guess I was more tired than I wanted to believe. I never expected to sleep through supper."

"I suppose you have been busy moving." She made a sweep of the room with her silvery blue eyes. "You're all settled in then?" she asked, still refusing to meet his gaze. She clasped her hands at her waist, and he noted a torn sleeve and several smudge marks on the front of her dress, no doubt from tending to her myriad house chores. Did the woman ever stop to rest? A passel of guilt for having taken time out for a midday nap pestered his conscience.

"I haven't unpacked those boxes full of books yet, but everything I'll ever need is right here in this very room. Left all my furniture behind except for that desk and chair." He pointed to the country walnut desk and matching swivel office chair he'd stuffed in the corner of the room and to the left of the window. "Ben Broughton helped me carry them up the steps. I don't think you were home that day."

She nodded and strolled across the room to run a hand over the desktop. Looking for dust, was she? He never had been much for tidying up. That was another reason he was glad to be rid of the house. Smaller living space meant smaller mess. She gave the wooden chair a couple of twirls with her index finger.

"I inherited both from a kindly seminary professor after he retired."

She turned her slip of a frame around to face him. "Teacher's pet?" she asked with a glimmer of mischief.

"In a manner of speaking, I guess. He took me under his wing that first year and every year thereafter. Students called me hard-luck-Kentuck. I didn't have one dime to rub against another, and I guess it showed. It must've been that single pair of gray trousers, white shirt, black bow-tie, and frock coat I wore every day of the week." She gave a gentle laugh, and the sound washed over him like fresh spring water. "It wasn't long, though, before the professor's wife got wind of me and started collecting used clothes from every source imaginable." He shook his head. "You should have seen the assortment. Out of respect I wore some of it, but most of it went right back into the school's charity bin."

She laughed again but quickly stifled the sound with her fingertips. "You're not sick then?" she asked, moving toward the door, clearly finished with the conversation. At the doorway, she paused and turned, awaiting his reply.

He rose and stretched, hands reaching high above his head. "I'm as chipper as a bird in May."

She gave a curt nod. Several strands of hair fell loosely about her tanned cheeks. "Well then, if you want any supper you best get downstairs. You'll soon discover these men wait for no one."

"Thanks for the tip."

He reached for a boot, and in the second it took to snag hold of it, she was gone.

*****

"What say we play some poker?" Charley Connors asked, coming in off the porch, the front screen door closing with a whack. The smells of nicotine and rum carried through the air when Charley sauntered into the parlor. Across the street and up the block, sounds of riotous music coming from the saloon penetrated the walls of Emma's Boardinghouse.

Dusk settled in, lulling some in this dusty town into restful slumber but unleashing roving, dark spirits in others. Jon hadn't felt prepared for the sense of foreboding nighttime brought, having lived his entire life in the country where the only sounds he heard came from creaking tree branches, a reclusive coyote's howl, or croaking frogs on the shores of Little Hickman Creek.

"I'm in," said Harland, rising from the ancient brocade divan. He tossed a well-worn novel on a nearby sofa table.

Without glancing up from the newspaper he'd been poring

 78

over for the last half hour, Elliott Newman gave a crisp, "I'm out."

"What about you, Wes?" Charley asked, eyeing the fellow who'd been dozing in a leather chair in the adjoining library, also designated the music room if one considered the upright piano along the east wall.

Wes looked up through the double French doors. "What? No, I'm tuckered. Grady don't take to me comin' in late on Monday mornin'. Think I'll surprise him for a change and be on time." The fellow's knees groaned when he rose. He gave a slight nod all around and ambled toward his room, which was on the main floor and across from the kitchen. It was hard to miss the slump to his shoulders and the subtle limp.

"Did I hear poker?" Gid Barnard descended the creaking stairs and sauntered into the room. "I was about to have a smoke, but I can be persuaded to play a round, providin' you don't cheat." He stuffed his unlit cigar into his shirt pocket.

Charley grinned then withdrew a deck of cards from the top bureau drawer. "How about you, preacher?" His quizzical gaze held a challenge. "You oughta have some bettin' money left over from the sale o' that farm."

Jon smiled. "It's not mine to bet with, my friend. In case you haven't heard, we're building a new church with most of the proceeds."

Charley's eyebrows slanted in a frown. A mild curse slipped out. "Awful waste if ya ask me, but pretty noble of ya."

Jon might have told him that gambling away hard-earned money was the true waste but passed over the opportunity. These men weren't about listening to his sermons. What they needed were sermons of example, not words. "Nothing noble about it. I'm plain weary of meeting in the Winthrop's living room week after week. Donating my funds seemed like a good solution to the problem. But I surely didn't do it for the recognition."

Charley looked halfway thoughtful then took to some fancy card shuffling, the likes of which Jon had never before witnessed. "Miss Emma? Join us?" he asked, bedevilment in his tone, his eyes trained on the cards that shot back and forth between his hands in a magical formation. Looking just past forty, the amiable Charley Connors tossed his head of reddish-brown hair and grinned widely, this time causing the dimple in the center of his chin to sprout. "You could be our weak-passive player who doesn't raise or fold much, just the kind of player we like to have in the game." He winked at Jon, as if letting him in on one of his best-kept secrets.

Without so much as a glance up from the puzzle she and Luke were working on in the middle of the floor, she made a clicking sound with her tongue. "I haven't the slightest idea what you just meant by that, and anyway, don't be ridiculous. I won't be throwing away my money on that fool game."

Well, at least they had that in common, Jon mused. He had situated himself in a chair in the corner, quite content to watch her and Luke over the top of a history book he'd drawn from the library shelf. He should have been studying for next Sunday's sermon, he told himself, or writing a letter to Professor and Matilda Whiting, or at the very least, compiling a to-do list for the upcoming week. But, alas, here he sat, soaking up the sights and sounds of his new environment, testing the waters, wondering how and where he fit into this strange assortment of folk who made up Emma's Boardinghouse.

He felt like one of the many puzzle pieces Luke picked up to study. "This d-d-don't fit nowhere," he announced, sticking a piece under Emma's nose, clearly frustrated at his lack of success.

"Be patient, Luke. These things take time."

Well, there was a sermon in itself.

*****

By midweek, the temperatures had climbed to the mid-nineties. That is, if one went by the thermometer George Garner had hung from a nail on a tree outside the post office. Emma went to stand in the shade of the old oak to study the instrument, its red needle clearly pointing square between the 90 and 100 marks. Just knowing the temperature seemed to make the perspiration flow more readily.

She mopped her brow then absently looked at the letter she held in her hand, its postmark stamped Chicago. In the upper left-hand corner was the name Grace Giles, but since no address followed, the source remained a mystery. A ridiculous shiver of apprehension made an erratic path up and down her spine despite the midday heat.

Why would a complete stranger be writing her?

It reminded her of two other missives she'd received just last month, also from Chicago. Across the page on the first one had been the carefully written words: ***"For if ye forgive men their trespasses, your heavenly Father will also forgive you."*** The signature had consisted of mere initials—G.G. The second letter, arriving two weeks later, seemed to have been a continuation of the first, for it stated simply: ***"But if ye forgive not men their trespasses, neither will your Father forgive your trespasses."*** Under the verse, which she could only assume came from the Bible, were the words, *If you desire the truth, dear Emma, it will be given you.* That too was signed *G. G.*

Mystified, she'd stuffed the notes away in her top drawer and tried to forget them. And for the most part, she had, casting the foolish notes off as someone's silly ploy to addle her senses. Now she wondered what game this Grace Giles from Chicago was trying to play, for she could only assume that Grace Giles and G. G. were one in the same.

"It's hotter 'n my mama's chili," claimed Will Murdock, tipping his hat at Emma in a friendly manner before sidling up next to her to read the thermometer for himself.

She quickly crammed the envelope deep into her dress pocket. "Well, hello there, sheriff. Your mama's chili, huh?"

"Yep. And she used to use her ripest chili peppers straight from the garden. Like to've ripped my stomach linin' right out. My, that was good stuff. I got the recipe if you want to borrow it."

She giggled, thankful for the diversion Will Murdock provided. "I believe I would, Will. Sounds like something I could use against that motley bunch of men I'm housin'."

"Oh, it'll curl their toes, Miss Emma. Might even burn their tongues enough to shut 'em up for a few days."

Now they both laughed. Hickman's middle-aged sheriff rocked back on his heels, took off his hat to run a hand through his scraggly, damp hair, replaced it, then looped a thumb in his shiny belt buckle. His eyes crinkled at the corners. "I don't know how you do it, Miss Emma, keep your wits about you when you've all those mouths to feed. Keepin' the peace must be a twenty-four-hour job, and I thought I had it bad. You got yer work cut out."

"Pfff. There's no keepin' peace. If they can't get along, that's their problem. I'm not their mother, and I've told 'em so. It's not so bad most days. Long as they take care of their own stuff, mind their business, and don't break the law, I'll keep washin' their sheets and feeding 'em."

"I like your thinkin'. Makes my job easier, you holdin' that law business over their heads. From what I hear, you're quite a remarkable cook, Miss Emma. And a wonder, to boot."

"Oh, fiddle. Who told you that?" They raised their heads to watch a flock of birds navigate across a brilliant, azure sky.

"Jon Atkins. And you know preachers—they're prone to tellin' the truth."

A tiny seed of satisfaction sprouted, causing a smile to emerge. She'd been pleasantly surprised to discover the reverend had been keeping to himself, not spouting off about his religious beliefs, and most evenings climbing the stairs to his room, where she presumed he spent time studying all those religious books he had stacked against the wall on a shelf. Of course, his silent prayers before mealtimes were a bit noticeable, but who wouldn't expect a man of the cloth to thank the Lord for his daily bread? As long as he didn't force the rest of them to comply—other than Luke, who'd already taken to bowing his head along with the preacher—she had no reason to complain about his presence.

"My meals are quite plain," she stated. An unexpected breeze lifted her skirts nearly to her knees, and she hastily pushed them down. Overhead, a squirrel scampered out on a limb.

Will grinned, revealing his signature, silver eyetooth. "Don't go sellin' yourself short, Miss Emma. I've never heard your cookin' referred to as plain. Harland Collins is always braggin' on it, makes me plain jealous I'm not reapin' the benefits of livin' there. A bachelor grows plenty tired of his own vittles."

Emma laughed. "And what about Mrs. Harwood? Last I heard she was leaving platters of cookies on your office doorstep, her way of sayin' thanks for arresting that no-good, moonshinin' neighbor of hers and closin' down his outfit."

"Well, you got a point there, and don't get me wrong, her cakes and cookies are pure pleasure. But they don't stick to the ribs like a juicy piece of chicken and a pile of spuds and gravy."

"Will Murdock, if I didn't know better, I'd say you were fishin' for a supper invite."

He tossed back his head and gave a hearty laugh. "Well now, 'sides havin' culinary skills, seems you're also quite the mind reader, Emma Browning."

"And you're quite handy with the flattery," she jested.

A rig carrying a load of hay rattled at a faster-than-usual clip through town, its driver, Herb Jacobs, lifting a hand to wave at both of them on his way past. A mongrel dog ran to keep up, barking at the back wheel.

"I wouldn't be worth my weight if I missed the opportunity to pay a fine lady such as yourself a well-deserved compliment, now would I?" he said over the noise and clatter, batting a hand at the sudden cloud of dust.

"Well, I thank ya for—" An ear-splitting scream had them turning their heads.

Up the street and in front of Bordon's Bakery, a crowd gathered. Herb Jacobs brought his wagon to a stop and leaped to the ground, running to the excited group. Emma shielded her eyes from the sun and squinted at the scene but couldn't make any sense of it.

"What do you think's going on?" she asked.

"I don't know, but I think I'm about to find out," Will answered, tipping his hat at her before sprinting off.

*****

"Fetch the doc!" someone screamed.

"Is she breathing?" asked another.

"Lord help us. How did this happen?" asked Truman Atwater. In his hand, he carried a fresh loaf of bread wrapped in brown paper. His wife, Martha, clung to his arm, her eyes pools of concern.

"Think she ran right out in front of Herb's rig," offered Orville Bordon, owner of the bakery.

Herb's face was pasty white as he shook his head in disbelief. "I didn't see her till it was too late," he said, his voice hardly more than a whisper. "Went right under my front wheel."

Flora Swain lay sprawled across her child's lifeless body, three of her other children all standing around her, clinging to her skirts and screaming to high heaven.

Jon made his way to the front of the group. "Step aside, folks, and give us some air. Doc Randolph's on his way up the street now." He tried to hold his voice steady as he crouched down beside Flora and rested a hand on her trembling shoulder. So far, he couldn't tell if the child was even alive, so still was her tiny body. Her face, badly scraped, was a mass of torn, bleeding skin, and out of the one visible ear oozed a thin stream of blood. Her arm, clearly broken, lay grotesquely crooked at her side, a bone protruding. One leg had oddly folded itself beneath her frame so that she lay at an awkward tilt. Jon's heart slid clear to his toes. *Dear Lord, please breathe new life into this child, give her the strength to survive.*

"Wake up, Ermaline!" her mother wailed, cupping the girl's cheeks in both hands. "Open your eyes right now. Oh, my baby!" The panic in her voice rose to deafening heights. And the louder she screamed, the more her three clinging youngsters carried on. In a hurried backward glance, Jon discovered Emma standing directly behind him. When their eyes met, she seemed to read his thoughts and hastily removed all

85

three children from the scene, swooping one up into her arms and coaxing the other two away with promises of sugar.

A path carved itself into the growing mass of curious bystanders, making way for Doc Randolph's entry, Will Murdock coming in behind him. Quiet mutterings and speculations flittered aimlessly as Doc opened his black doctor bag and began to bring out an assortment of instruments.

"Flora, it's me, Doc," he whispered. She seemed not to have heard, so Doc proceeded with his duties as if she weren't there, lifting the girl's eyelids, checking her pulse, then positioning his stethoscope directly to the child's chest, his somber expression denoting his full concentration. A hush fell over the gathering crowd.

"There's a good, steady heartbeat," he announced.

Great sighs of relief passed from one to the other as folks shifted their weight and looked to the heavens. From there, Doc began examining the child from head to toe. "I don't want to move her just yet," he explained. "Flora, do you think you could give me a bit of room? I swear I won't hurt her." Compassion welled in the aging doctor's eyes, his years of experience in caring for the sick and dying showing itself in his kindly expression.

As if waking from a bad dream, she stared at him with unseeing eyes, yet somehow had the sense to sit back. Jon took the opportunity to give her shoulder a gentle, supportive squeeze. The woman fairly fell into his side, as if soaking up what bit of strength he could offer. Tears rushed down her cheeks like torrents of rain.

Doc continued his careful exploration, moving skillful hands from top to bottom, pushing, prodding, and gently poking the lifeless child. It seemed that most had forgotten to breathe, so hushed was the group of folks who'd gathered around the scene. Finally, Doc took a deep breath and leaned back on his haunches, keeping his eyes trained on the girl. "Might be some internal bleeding. I'll have to set her leg and arm, but aside from that, I don't see any other visible injuries, other than some head trauma, which, from what I can see, isn't too severe. Surface wounds mostly. She should start waking up soon, which is why I'd like to get her moved to my office now."

"We'll fetch the stretcher, Doc. It still behind your door?" asked Will.

Doc nodded, his eyes still on his patient.

"Herb, why don't you come with me?" Will suggested. "I'll need to question you about the accident."

"Weren't his fault, Will," offered Harvey. "I was sittin' right there on that bench in front of Bordon's when it happened. Sure, Herb was movin' kind of fast, but I witnessed the whole thing. That little 'n' had a mind to run right across the street without lookin'. Think she must've seen that there black dog."

"I thank you for that, Harv. I'll be talkin' to you later. Right now, we gotta get that stretcher for Doc. Come on, Herb."

Herb Jacobs, still in a seeming trance, gave his head a shake and followed the sheriff down the street.

"She gonna be okay, Doc?" inquired Elliott Newman, who must have heard the commotion and left his wheelwright shop to have a look. Luke, looking sullen and insecure, clung tightly to his father's arm.

A guarded expression splashed across Doc Randolph's face as his gaze went from the unmoving child to her mother. "We'll know soon enough," were his carefully chosen words.

Chapter Eight

The first rays of sun shot over a bumpy horizon like hot honey on a biscuit. Wispy clouds, thin and hairlike, stretched across an already brilliant sky of orange and blue, grazing the tops of Kentucky's low mountain range. Jon tipped his hat back for an unobstructed view of nature's display, rested one hand on the saddle horn and the other on his knee, and breathed in the clean scents of morning.

"Don't get much better than this, right, preacher?"

Jon grinned, never taking his eyes off the resplendent display, to his right a field of black-eyed Susans and to the left a copse of tall pines reaching skyward.

"Nope, Elmer, not much better. Matter of fact, this is church, in my opinion."

Jupiter whinnied in agreement, then continued picking his way down the hillside leading to Ezra Browning's one-room shack. A little caravan of volunteers followed Jon's lead: Elmer and Bess Barrington, Rocky and Sarah Callahan, Ben and Liza Broughton, Tom Averly, Irwin Waggoner, and Gerald Crunkle. The small turnout pleased him. Now he could only hope that Ezra would allow them on his property.

Ben and Rocky clicked their horses into a faster gait and came up alongside Jon.

"Think he'll meet us on his porch with that shotgun?" asked Ben.

"If he does you have my permission to turn tail and run."

Ben chuckled. "And leave you to your own defenses? Nothin' doin'."

 88

Courting Emma

"He brings out that gun," Rocky inserted, "we're all high-tailin' it, you hear? I'll beat you all back to town."

"You always were the chicken-heart," Ben harassed.

"And you were the hothead," Rocky retorted.

Jon couldn't help the grin. "Contain yourselves, men, or I'll have to send you both to the end of the line."

"What—and miss all the fun?" Ben joshed.

A flock of birds flew overhead, settling in a meadow, no doubt in search of breakfast. The men reined in their horses at the top of a knoll, calling a halt to the rest of the group. "Looks pretty quiet down there," remarked Ben. "The guy's probably sleepin' off another night of debauchery. What'll we do if we can't wake him up?"

"We'll work around him," Jon said. "Might be better that way." He glanced behind him at the quiet cavalcade of followers, Elmer, Irwin, Tom, and Gerald riding single file, with the three ladies bringing up the rear in Ben's wagon. The wagon carried a load of building supplies, including glass for the broken windows, donated by none other than Clyde Winthrop.

"Probably should have left the women home this first time," he said, chasing down a smidgeon of worry. If anything happened of a negative nature, there'd be no one to blame but himself.

"Liza wouldn't hear of it. She was ready to head out here last Sunday after dinner."

Jon chuckled under his breath. "She's something. Heart of gold, that woman."

"And a mind of steel," said Ben, shaking his head, his tone a mix of pride and pleasure.

Jon gave Rocky a sideways glance. "And I suppose Sarah refused to stay home once she learned Liza was coming."

89

He grinned and nodded. "Matter of fact, Rachel and Seth would've come too if Ma hadn't insisted we drop them off at their place."

"And what of Lili and Molly?" Jon asked.

"They were still sawing logs when we left. Lili's responsible. She'll hold down the fort till we get back."

They proceeded down the hill until the little cabin came in full view and they found a place to hitch the horses. Chickens scratched at sod, scuttling away the closer they came. Wandering aimlessly was Ezra's lone goat, skinny as a rail. A sort of pity welled up in Jon for the helpless creature.

"It's deadly quiet," Rocky said.

Ben looked back at Liza, who was driving the rig, and motioned for her to stay put. She reined in the horses and stopped several yards back.

"Let me go knock on the door," Jon said, dismounting and loosely tethering the reins to the same crooked post he'd used before.

He walked across rutted terrain, climbed the rickety porch steps, and rapped on the door. When he got no response, he gave the door a slight nudge. It pushed open with ease. "Ezra?" he called.

As expected, the room was a hodgepodge of empty soup cans, heaps of clothing, dirty dishes, and upturned furniture. In the corner, slumped in a chair and out like a dead horse, was Ezra, empty bottles stockpiled at his feet. Jon walked the ten or so steps it took to get to the other side of the room and poked the guy in the shoulder. "Ezra, wake up." A low moan came from his mouth, along with a trail of spittle. "Ezra, you have company."

*****

Emma wrung out the last of this week's laundry, piled the wet garments into a basket, and headed out the back door. Miss Tabitha, stretched out on the windowsill enjoying a patch of sunlight, meowed a greeting.

"Mornin', Emma," called Rita Flowers, Little Hickman's laundress. She was crossing the alley but paused midway when she spotted Emma, putting a hand to her brow to shield her eyes from the blaring sun. "Ain't it a beautiful mornin'?"

Emma put down the basket and cast a smile at the middle-aged woman. "The finest." Although it promised to be another hot day, there was a lovely breeze to offset the worst of it. "You out for a pleasure walk?" Emma noticed she was strolling in the opposite direction of her laundry business.

Rita shook her head. "I'm goin' over to Doc's office to see what I can do about relieving Flora. Lucy Fontaine said Flora's been stayin' with little Ermaline round the clock. Fred's doing his best to keep house and take care of their brood, but it's not an easy time for them. Hear Doc's out to the Thompson farm right now lookin' after their youngest that's got the croup."

"Doc's got his hands full," Emma remarked. "How is little Ermaline?"

"Holdin' 'er own far's I know. Actin' like a regular little sprout, anxious to be out of bed. Course, she can't move what with a broken leg and arm and bruises, to boot. Lucky little thing, if ya ask me."

Emma recalled the accident with a shudder. "It was a terrible thing, but I'm glad that things seem to be workin' themselves out."

"I s'pose we could've been havin' a funeral. Thank the Lord for His great mercy."

It seemed to Emma it would have been altogether more

91

merciful had the Lord prevented the accident, but she refrained from expressing her opinion.

"Sometimes the Lord allows these things so His children will learn what it is to trust Him completely. No matter the outcome, He's the one in control. I suspect the Swains will grow closer t'gether 'cause of this accident. No matter, somethin' good will come of it. Romans 8:28, you know." No, Emma didn't know, but she kept that matter to herself. "Well, I best be gettin' over to Doc's. You have a good day now."

They waved and Emma hoisted up the basketful of wet clothes and walked to the clothesline, the cat joining her to curl around her legs and do her best to make a pest of herself.

"Shoo!" Emma ordered, smiling to herself for no particular reason when the cat failed to obey.

After hanging the last towel, she set to rights a couple of garments hanging in a cockeyed fashion, and that's when she noticed it, the corner of something sticking out of her sopping dress pocket. "What in the world?" she muttered, pulling from the pocket a waterlogged envelope, the writing on it faded and running. It came back to her then, the note she'd received in the mail a few days ago, stowed away for safekeeping when Will Murdock had come along, then completely forgotten about when the accident stole their attention.

A frown pulled at her face. Would she even be able to decipher the contents now that the missive had gone through the wash? Walking to the back stoop, she dropped down to the top step, her skirts falling about her ankles, and commenced to peel back the envelope's gummed flap, taking care not to do more damage to its already fragile state.

As suspected, the message was mostly unreadable, save a few words here and there, *mistakes—past—forgiveness—your father.*

Her frown deepened. The thing made no sense, regardless of the effort she put into decoding the washed-out words. Finally ruling it fruitless, she crumpled the wet letter into a ball, retrieved her laundry basket, and went back inside, tossing the crumpled paper into the waste bin.

Only one thing nettled her senses. The mention of her father.

*****

The evening supper consisted of beef stew and warm biscuits with a side of warm applesauce. Jon ate as if it were his last meal, famished after a day of laboring at Ezra's place, repairing broken fence posts, replacing rotten boards in the front porch, and swapping old shards of glass for new in the broken windows. While he worked at those tasks, Irwin, Elmer, Tom, and Gerald tilled the garden and planted some seed, even though it was late in the season, repaired the roof on a shed out back, and built a lean-to for the wayward chickens. Ben and Rocky fixed broken hinges, repaired sagging cupboard doors, and mended broken furniture, while Liza, Sarah, and Bess scrubbed floors, cabinets, stove and sink, and washed every piece of clothing they could lay their hands on. After that, they baked enough bread to last Ezra into next year, if it didn't mold first.

As everyone toiled, Ezra sat on his haunches, stupefied. No one lectured, no one preached. They just worked as unto the Lord, with no thought of repayment. The verse from Matthew, **Inasmuch as you have done it unto the least of these, my brethren, you have done it unto me**, seemed to permeate the little cabin as the team of volunteers worked side by side. Even now, Jon's heart swelled with gratitude as he lapped up the last of his stew.

For a change, the table wasn't full. Gideon and Wes were working late at the sawmill, and Charley Connors was reportedly butchering a fresh side of beef that had just arrived at Flanders' Foods from Bill Jarvis.

"Delicious supper, Emma," Jon praised, giving his mouth a thorough sweep with his napkin, feeling like he'd downed it so fast that surely he was wearing it all over his face. Luke picked up his napkin and did the same, his eyes mindful of Jon's every move.

"Just a simple stew," she said, giving a dainty nod. She rose and set to picking up plates and spoons.

"That was not simple," he argued, deciding to help. "Simple would be fried hamburger with watered down gravy and a sliced potato added to the mix, my usual mid-week fare."

Half a grin peeked out on her pretty face. His goal was to coax out a full-blown one, one of these days. "You actually ate that?"

"You'd be surprised what I concocted in the name of food. It's a wonder my stomach survived those many years of abuse. I used to toss pickles and sliced apples into a fry pan and eat them like candy."

Her nose wrinkled in disbelief. "That sounds terrible."

Following Jon's example of lending a hand, Luke picked up his soup bowl and carried it to the kitchen. Elliott and Harland remained at the table, scraping out the last of their stew and eating in silence.

In the kitchen, Emma placed a towel on the handle of a steaming kettle and carried it to the sink, setting it on the butcher-block table next to the sink.

"Where would you like these?" Jon asked, holding his bowl, a platter of biscuits, and the crock of applesauce. Luke stood behind him, trying to mimic him.

She put the stopper in the bottom of the sink and turned her head. The long, blond braid that went down the center of her back flopped over her left shoulder. He had the uncanny urge to test it for softness, or worse, disassemble the entire plait and run a hand clear through it.

What was he thinking? He shook his head and squeezed his eyes shut for one brief second, trying to erase the ridiculous image that had bolted across his mind, tinkering with his judgment.

With a nod, she pointed at the table directly under Jon's nose. "Set them there, and thank you very much. In the future, you can remain seated at the table. Long as you pay your room and board, I'll tend to the household chores."

He felt put down, but not beaten. "I'm accustomed to doing my part. I don't mind bringing my dishes to the kitchen."

"My kitchen is my domain, Mr., er, Reverend."

Ah, so she didn't want him encroaching on her territory. "When are you going to start calling me Jon?" he asked, setting the dishes on the marred counter, Luke following suit. She made a point to ignore him, pouring the kettle-full of steaming water into the sink, then turning the faucet to add a sufficient amount of cold. He wondered why the old house had a heated coil in the attic that ran hot water to the upstairs bathroom, but didn't have pipes running to the kitchen.

"Reverend's too formal for old friends, don't you think?"

She sniffed. "Old friends? Hardly. You teased me mercilessly."

"That's what boys do when they have a crush. I chased you over every square inch of that playground just itching to yank at one of your braids. Remember that?"

Her back straightened. He positioned himself against the

table and folded his arms across his chest. She took up a dish and set to washing it.

"That was at least a century ago," she said. "Unfortunately, most of my schoolday memories are rather cloudy."

He could imagine they were, as busy as she had been defending herself against an abusive, alcoholic father. Of course, he'd been doing the same, but at least he'd had Rocky and Ben to run to when things got bad. Who had been her allies? Try as he might, he couldn't remember her having many friends. Was that because Ezra had driven them all away? He thought about the old coot, wondered what he was doing in his spic-and-span kitchen. Was he even now bringing it to ruin, dirtying dishes that would sit for days to come, staggering around in his one-room shack while he spent another night in drunken squalor?

Inasmuch as you have done it unto the least of these.... "You remember our teacher's name? Thornton, Thorpe...?"

"Thurston. Mr. Thurston," Emma answered, pausing to gaze off in thought. "He had a mole on his chin that stuck out like a fly in a sugar bowl. Mean as a bull in a four-foot pen, too. He slapped the tops of our hands with a paddle if we used our fingers to count."

"Ah, yes. I sat on my hands a lot."

This produced the tiniest giggle, and it made him frantic to keep the conversation moving, made him imagine what one of her full-out laughs would sound like.

"Remember Virginia Peabody?" he asked.

She turned just slightly and nodded. "A tall, shy girl with black, curly hair."

He gave a fast nod. "Remember the time we were having a spelling bee and she had need of the necessary? 'Mr. Thurston,' she wailed to high heaven, stompin' from one foot to the other. 'I got to go!' Her face was blood-red. I remember that."

Emma turned full around, sapphire eyes wide as she put a hand to her mouth, applying a dab of soapsuds in the process. "Did he let her leave?"

Jon shook his head. "Nope. He got that stern look on his face where his mouth turned under, his chin dropped, and his eyebrows crinkled into one long bushy line, and in that all-important, deep tone, he said something like, 'My dear, you shall have to wait until the noon break.' Well it wasn't five minutes—I think Howard Fuller was spelling legislature—or maybe it was parliament—when Eddie Hampton pointed at the floor under poor Virginia and shouted, 'Mr. Thurston, Virginia Peabody's a goin'!'"

"Oh!" Emma's hands flattened over her chest, one on top of the other, as the impact of the story dawned in her expression. And that's when it happened. A giggle erupted, not just a tiny, fruitless one, either, but the kind a person can't hold back, bubbling up like a geyser, coming out in lusty bursts, the likes of which he'd never heard. "Oh, dear—little—Virginia," she said between laughing spurts, her eyes beginning to water. She clutched her stomach as if it pained her even to breathe.

As if getting the joke, Luke joined in.

In the doorway, Elliott Newman and Harland Collins stood gape-mouthed and sober as judges—as if they'd never heard anything like it either.

*****

What had gotten into her, laughing like a foolhardy child; worse, knowing *he* was responsible for making it happen.

Emma laid her next-day dress out along with her stockings, petticoat, and underthings. Padding barefoot to the mirror in her cotton nightgown, she gazed at her reflection before yanking free her long, blond braid.

Poor Virginia Peabody, she mused, even now smiling at the silly recollection. My, it'd been a long while since she'd thought about her school days, much less laughed about them, and the notion made her ponder what other events of the past lay buried in her subconscious. She picked up her boar-bristle hairbrush and ran it through her long tresses, gently smoothing out the knots at the ends and working her way up to the top of her head.

"What you doin' up at this hour?"

"I was just brushing my hair, Papa." She lay her mama's hairbrush on the little box beside her bed and tucked her bare feet up under the blankets, a cold chill racing through her spine the closer he came. She was glad she'd stashed her book, Little Women, *under her mattress—and just in time, too. Dear Miss Abbott had given it to her just last week, saying every girl should have the chance to read good literature, and already she was nearly halfway through it.*

He took a gander around the room, his bloodshot eyes bulging like two gigantic boulders, a bottle of ale in one hand. "More'n likely you was daydreamin' again, sittin' there brushin' your hair like you was the Queen of England herself. You put out that light now 'fore I tan your li'l hide."

"Yes, Papa," she said, bending forward to blow out the candle and hastening under the covers.

Next week was her thirteenth birthday.

Was that too young to run away?

Chapter Nine

*J*on had a full day ahead. Late July heat settled on his shoulders as he moved up the sidewalk. Everyone he passed wanted to stop and talk, slowing his progress and keeping him from his duties. Besides calls to make on parishioners, there was Sunday's sermon hanging over his head, the final architectural plans for the new church to look over, clean clothes ready for him at Rita's place, a haircut awaiting him at Zeke's Barbershop, a list of supplies to pick up, and, finally, a letter to post.

"You seen the new school lately, Reverend?" asked Clarence Sterling. The elderly fellow had just dismounted his rig and was crossing Jon's path on his way to the bank, a stack of papers tucked under his arm.

Jon paused. "I was just coming from there, Clarence. Matter of fact, I'm running an errand for Ben Broughton, who's over at the site now." He withdrew a folded piece of paper from his pants pocket and glanced at it, a list of materials he'd volunteered to pick up at the sawmill and mercantile.

"Looks awful near to done, if you ask me. Kind o' nice lookin' up the road apiece and seein' that nice new buildin' takin' shape. Won't be long 'fore we hear them recess bells again. Heard tell they're hirin' Bess Barrington for the teacher job. Ought to be good. Least she won't go runnin' off to get married fore the school year's even up." He chuckled at his own words. "When we startin' that new church, by the way?"

"Rocky says he's ready to break ground this week, but I'm thinking the men will need a breather between projects."

Clarence moved his aged shoulders in a shrug. "Piddle. Won't take long once the frame goes up. Many hands make light work, Reverend. I ain't helped much with the school, but when it comes time to start that church buildin', I'll be there from morning till night, and I ain't the only one, mark my words."

"Well, I thank you for that, Clarence. We'll need all the hands we can get."

"Speakin' of which, how'd it go over at Ezra Browning's place?" he asked, running a liver-spotted hand over his stubbled face.

"We accomplished what we set out to accomplish, but I'm not sure Ezra fully appreciated our visit. He spent the day in his chair watching us and coughing up a storm."

Clarence shook his head. "The old fool."

By three in the afternoon, Jon had a fresh haircut and a pillowcase full of clean clothes hefted over one shoulder. He'd delivered the building supplies to Ben, stopped at the Swain house on his way back through town to visit little Ermaline, who was faring quite well despite her broken arm and leg, and was now on his way to the post office before heading back to the boardinghouse to drop off his laundry. Once done with that, he would head out to Sully and Esther Thompson's farm to see how little Millie, their youngest, was doing after her bout with the croup, pay another visit to old Ezra, and then, if it wasn't too late, stop out at Carl and Frieda Hardy's place for a piece of Frieda's apple pie.

"Afternoon, George," Jon said upon entering the post office. The postmaster looked up from his station behind the counter and grinned, presenting the wide gap between his two front teeth. "You got another letter from that professor friend o' yours." George Garner was notorious for reading the postmark on every piece of mail that came across his desk. It was a wonder he ever finished the job of sorting.

Jon lowered the pillowcase of clothes to the floor. "Thanks, George. And I'd appreciate it if you'd post this one for me." He retrieved the missive he'd written to his professor from his hip pocket and handed it across the counter.

George adjusted the spectacles that rested on the bridge of his nose to peruse the addressed envelope given him then nodded his balding head. "Oh, and since you're livin' at the boardinghouse perhaps you wouldn't mind deliverin' this to Miss Emma?" He reached under the counter and drew out an envelope. Had he been holding it specifically for her rather than inserting it in her postal box?

"I suppose I could do that," Jon said, somewhat hesitant about delivering another's mail, particularly that of Emma Browning. Ever since their amiable exchange of a few nights ago, she'd been treating him as if he were a bad rash.

"It's another one of those notes from Chicago," George remarked with furrowed brow, as if Jon held the key to some unsolved mystery and George expected him to hand it over.

"Oh?" He was admittedly curious, but he would be hanged before he'd stoop to George Garner's level and view the postmark. He stowed it away in his breast pocket.

George's frown doubled in size. "Ain't you even gonna look at it?"

Jon lifted one of his brows and slanted his head at the postmaster with a scolding look, doing his best to mask a grin. "George, George, you'd finish your day a whole lot faster if you'd stop reading everyone's mail."

He looked aghast. "I ain't readin' no one's mail. I just check where it's comin' from. No harm in that."

The bell over the door let off a gentle chime, impelling both men to glance at the entrance. Frank and Mary Callahan, Rocky's parents, walked through the door, their two grandchildren, Rachel and Seth, in tow.

"Well, hello there, Jonathan," Mary greeted, tickled. "Aren't you looking spiffy." She circled him as one might circle a prized horse. Any second now, he expected her to order him to open his mouth so she could inspect his teeth.

He grinned. "And good afternoon to both of you—as well as Seth and Rachel. Look at Seth here, growing like a tomato plant." He ruffled the boy's dark brown hair and noted how Seth stretched to his full height. "And Rachel, if you get any prettier, your uncle Rocky might have to confine you to the house." The girl blushed like a rose.

"You just get a haircut?" Mary asked, persisting with her appraisal. Despite the fact that he was the preacher, and thirty years old, to boot, there were some in town who still viewed him as a kid, and Mary Callahan was one of them. Probably because he'd spent so much of his youth hanging with her son, and had even moved in with them for a time after his pa had died.

Only slightly embarrassed, he combed a hand through his freshly cut hair and nodded. "Is it okay?"

"Why, it's perfect," she answered, looking pleased as pink punch. "Makes you look mature, the way the ends just graze your shirt collar."

"That's good to know then."

She brushed an imaginary piece of lint off his shirtfront and beamed up at him. "And quite handsome, if I do say so." Little Seth, arms at his sides, stared open-mouthed, clearly absorbed, whereas Rachel had wandered over to the wall where all the "wanted" posters hung. "Isn't he handsome, Frank?"

"Mary, for goodness' sake, you'll embarrass the boy."

Boy?

"Oh, piffle. He's used to me."

He was still grinning to himself on his walk back to the boardinghouse. In the alley between the post office and Emma's place, Elmer and Gladys Hayward and Bill and Flora Jarvis were engaged in some political debate about the upcoming presidential election. "I say Bryan's Free Silver Movement is a good idea. Might relieve me and Gladys of some of our debt," Elmer was saying. "We just ain't gettin' enough for our crops these days."

"You get rid of the gold standard, and we'll see inflation straight across the board," Bill argued. "McKinley's got a good head on 'is shoulders; Bryan's a lot of talk."

Not wanting to involve himself in the controversy, Jon tipped his hat at the foursome and kept moving, thankful no one objected to his lack of sociability.

He found Emma in the kitchen kneading a big batch of bread dough. Four greased bread pans were set in a row on the butcher-block table. She did a double take when he entered the room. Was it the haircut? But then she hastily covered her reaction with a cursory nod, seeming to apply herself the harder to the business of punching the dough. The notion that she envisioned herself pummeling his face in place of the dough gave him pause. What had he done to deserve her wrath besides draw out a burst of giggles the other night? To say she left him flummoxed was putting it mildly.

"Brought you something," he announced, extracting the missive from his pocket. It took every ounce of his willpower not to glance at the postmark or the sender's name in the process of handing it over.

She wiped her floured hands on her apron front and took the letter, inspecting it in haste before positioning it under the sugar bowl beside her—and completely out of sight. Was it his imagination, or had a muscle flicked in her jaw when she first saw it? "Thank you," she replied with definite curtness. "Don't know why George expected you to deliver my mail."

"I don't know, either, but he asked me to do the favor, so I obliged. I hope you don't mind. I didn't look at it, if that's what you think."

She lifted a brow and shrugged. "I wasn't worried that you had. Anyway, it's just some silly…."

He waited for her to finish the sentence, but she left it hanging.

"Some silly…" he prodded, leaning toward her.

She tossed her head, and her blond hair, which she'd pulled into a single ponytail then tied with a green ribbon to match her dress, flopped over one shoulder. Truth be told, he thought her quite a fetching sight. "Nothing," she replied, pinching her lips together as she threw herself back into her task. "Nothing at all."

He stared at her for at least a full minute before her hands ceased and she turned to look at him, clearly perturbed. "Was there something else you wanted?"

He couldn't stop the grin, which he knew rattled her. Without taking his eyes off her mouth, he reached in front of her to snatch a shiny apple from a fruit bowl. She took a full step back. "Nothing," he responded, sinking his teeth into the juicy apple and sauntering out of the room. "Nothing at all."

An hour later, he knocked on Ezra's door.

"What you want, preacher kid?" Ezra asked through a two-inch slit in the door, his bloodshot eyes roving over him with obvious suspicion.

Jon nudged the door open a couple of inches more with the toe of his boot. "Just checking on you."

"Humph. Don't need no checkin' on." He choked on his own spittle and wheezed as if it were his last breath. A trace of blood mixed with the dirt that covered his shirtfront. Jon pushed the rest of the way through the door. As he'd feared, the place was a shambles. He mentally counted to ten, then figured praying was the better route. *Lord, give me patience*, was about all he could muster.

"Ezra, you're killing yourself, you know that?"

The man glared through glazed and watery eyes. In those eyes Jon read the deepest kind of sorrow, detected a lostness such as he hadn't seen for some time.

"Ain't none of your concern," Ezra grumbled.

"I've made it my concern."

Jon kicked the door shut with his foot and walked across the room to pick up a chair. On his way, he bent to retrieve a number of other items—a tin bowl; a slice of bread, half gnawed; an empty can; wads of paper with scribble marks across them, and other waste. All the while, Ezra followed him with curious, wary eyes.

"What you want?" he asked for the second time.

Ignoring the question, Jon sat down on the chair, the back of which was missing a couple of spindles. "Have a seat," he invited, pointing at the only other chair in the room. Amazing as it was, Ezra shuffled across the floor and dragged the chair over to the table. Keeping a cagey eye on Jon, he took a seat.

"I ain't got any coffee ta offer ya," he said. "Used up the last of it two days ago."

"I don't need any coffee." Jon scooted closer to the table, clasped his hands together, and rested them in a pile of crumbs on the marred, wood surface. "What brought you to Little Hickman all those years ago, Ezra?" he asked.

A cold, congested expression passed over hard features. Ezra swiped a grimy hand down his face. Jon waited, wondering if he'd get an answer.

"Ain't nobody ever asked me that before."

And was it any wonder? Why should anyone inquire after an unapproachable old geezer who'd spent the better share of his life tanked?

Jon pulled back his shoulders and offered up a silent prayer. "I'm asking."

Ezra leaned forward and sucked in a winded breath before speaking. "Lydia and me wanted a fresh start—away from her parents."

"Lydia. And where was she from?"

"Danbury, Illinois. I was wanderin' around back then. Come upon a huge farm. Her daddy give me a job, never guessin' I'd fall for 'is daughter." A sour chuckle rumbled up. "That was a long time ago."

Desperate to keep him talking, Jon remarked, "I bet she was a pretty thing."

Sunken eyes gleamed with some kind of proud yet faraway sheen. "Pertiest ya ever seen. Golden hair, blue eyes, the smoothest skin."

So Emma's fair looks came from her mother. "And you loved her," he pressed.

Jon's trained eye detected unspoken pain, and as if Ezra sensed it, he quickly yanked his head up to glare at him. "Course I loved 'er. We eloped eight months after we met." He harrumphed. "Her folks was madder than two sick dogs, threatenin' to undo the marriage, so we left Illinois and come to Little Hickman. Didn't even tell 'em where we was for awhile. Land was cheap back then, and we had us some big dreams for the future, figured we could make do on our own. But Lydia was deep hurt. She finally wrote to her folks when she was carryin', thought they'd want ta know, but by then they dint want nothin' to do with either one of us. Said she threw 'er life away when she married me and they was washin' their hands of 'er. Guess they thought I married 'er for 'er money." He scoffed, as if the notion itself were utterly detestable.

"After she died, they found a way to blame me for it. Said I'd never get a red cent from them. Wanted nothin' to do with Emma neither."

"So Lydia died—just after—Emma...."

Ezra screwed up his face in a sour scowl. "Givin' birth was hard on her. She'd been sick the last half of her bein' in the family way, so she was already weak and frail, then ta have ta go through all that pain.... It took its toll. There weren't nothin' I could do for 'er."

His gaze traveled to the shiny new windowpane and beyond. "Buried 'er that very night up in those hills. Doc Randolph was the only one what knew us back then, so he helped dig the hole. Emma slept in a box beside the grave."

Hardly daring to breathe, Jon gave a slow nod, terrified the fellow would stop talking, terrified he'd continue. While he allowed the privileged information to settle in his brain, they sat for several seconds in utter silence, save for the high-pitched blather of two cardinals outside the window. "Waacheer! Waa-cheer!" they chattered between them.

"Must've been hard, raising a little one on your own. What about Emma's grandparents—your folks, I mean? Couldn't they have lent a hand?" To his knowledge, not one relative had ever paid the two of them a visit.

107

He might have known the question would push him over the edge. It was a miracle he'd wrung this much out of him. Like a bank vault, the old guy clamped his mouth up tight and sent a glowering look across the table. Jon stared back, nervous energy precipitating the tapping of his fingers on the table. "I meant no offense," he offered. "I'm just trying to understand, Ezra."

"Understand what?" he growled. "Why I growed up to be an infernal, villainous old numbskull?"

He'd nailed it, all right. "I'd like to help you, Ezra—if you'll let me."

He shook his head hard. "Too late."

Jon shook his just as vehemently. "It's never too late. God has a plan, no matter what you may think. And whether you know it or not, He loves you."

"Don't tell me about God, preacher kid. If He cared one bit He'd have let my Lydia live all them years ago."

"He gave you Emma, and she's still very much alive. That ought to count for something."

A scoffing sound blew through his lips. "She don't want nothin' ta do with me."

Jon opened his mouth to reply but changed his mind. How did one argue with the truth?

On a tree branch very near the window, the cardinals were still going at it.

*****

Emma jammed the foolish letter back into its envelope and laid it in her top dresser drawer with the others, doing her best to forget it. But the more she busied herself around the room, the more it pestered until finally she retrieved it for another read.

I know you don't believe this, Emma, but there is a good reason why your father turned out as he did. Believe me, I know. Please do this one thing—ask God to help you understand. He will lead you one step at a time.

If you desire to know more, I will enlighten you, but you must ask. Until then, I will continue to hound you with special promises from God's Holy Word.

Mark 10:27 says, "With men it is impossible, but not with God: for with God all things are possible."

Very Truly Yours,
Grace Giles

Who in the world was Grace Giles?

Chapter Ten

*Y*ou s-s-sewin' a new dress?"

Emma looked up from her stitching and smiled at Luke standing in the doorway. She didn't normally keep the door to her private quarters standing open, but it was so hot today that the cross ventilation coming from the window at the end of the hall and her own open window provided a gentle, cooling breeze.

"I am, and after that I plan to stitch some new curtains for the kitchen."

The fabric she'd ordered from the mercantile had arrived by freight two days ago, a beautiful purple cotton with tiny, delicate red and yellow roses, and she'd been so excited she'd torn the brown paper off the parcel right there on the spot, in front of Eldred Johansson, Gus Humphrey, and Tim Warner. Of course, they hadn't understood or appreciated her enthusiasm, but when Lucy Fontaine ambled through the door, a babe on her hip and a toddler at her side, she'd sufficiently oohed and ahhed, smiling and running a hand over the cloth, as if it were a priceless treasure. And it was, for it had been more than three years since Emma had indulged herself in a new dress.

"Y-y-you goin' to wear it to a p-party?" he asked.

"Party? Don't know of any upcomin' parties, Luke. I 'spect I'll just wear it around the house since my other dresses are gettin' so worn."

He stuffed his hands into his pockets and stared at her. She smiled to herself and went back to sewing, powering the machine with a slow, rhythmic pumping of the foot treadle, concentrating all her efforts on steering the up and down movement of the needle as it made a path over the pinned hem.

Luke spoke over the machine's gentle hum. "My m-m-mama could sew."

Emma ceased pumping the pedal. "Really? Did she sew dresses?" She started pulling pins from the section she'd just sewn and stabbing them into her tomato-shaped pincushion.

"I think. She m-made me a shirt once. My mama, she was real p-pretty."

"What did she look like?"

Luke leaned into the doorframe, the wheels in his head spinning. "She was this tall." He laid his palm flat about five feet from the floor. "She had yellow hair—like you—and soft hands."

The simple description put a tiny ache in her heart. "She sounds lovely."

"Who sounds lovely?" Jonathan Atkins sneaked up behind Luke and placed both hands on his shoulders. Emma's chest gave a strange lurch at the sight of him.

A wide grin washed over Luke's asymmetrical face. "My m-mama," he replied. "She was as p-p-pretty as Miss Emma."

Jon's burning eyes held her captive as he looked around Luke's head. "Then your mother was a beauty."

Knowing she blushed, she put up her defenses and concentrated her efforts on her sewing. Men didn't discombobulate her as a rule, so the notion that the preacher had managed to do so made her want to stomp her foot in protest.

"I got her picture," Luke said. "Want me to go g-get it?"

Even though she dove into her task, she knew he'd trained his eyes on her blushing cheeks, probably felt tickled to have rattled her. "I'd like nothing more," Jon said. "I'll wait here."

No additional prompting necessary, Luke disappeared down the hall. Emma stared at her handiwork and felt her shoulders drop in frustration. She'd been stitching straight as you please until *he* walked in. Aggravated with herself—and with him—she let go a sigh.

"Something wrong?" he asked from his station.

"Just some crooked stitching is all. I'll need to rip it out."

"Hm. Sorry if I distracted you."

"What? No—you didn't," she lied. She clipped the end with scissors and started pulling out the uneven threads.

He kept watching her, which didn't help her concentration any. "I went to see your father today," he announced.

She paused in her task. "I don't know why you bother with him. I heard you took a group from the church out there the other day, which was mighty nice of y'all but quite pointless. He won't keep it neat, you know."

"I found that out today." He chuckled to himself. "But we managed to do some much-needed repairs around the property, so it was worth it. And it gave everyone a good feeling to be able to lend a hand."

A wave of guilt slammed into her. He was *her* father. She should be responsible for his care, but she rarely even visited him.

"God's in the business of healing broken people, Emma. He often uses the church to accomplish that. I'm praying your pa will open his heart to the Lord."

"Humph." She didn't want to talk about the church—or God, for that matter. Her fingers fumbled with the thread while he stood in the doorway.

"What makes you close up at the mention of God?"

She shook her head. "I'm doin' fine on my own. I didn't see God intervenin' in my life when I was a sprout, so why bother?"

"Because you need a Savior, Emma." He said her name as if it meant something to him. "We all do, no matter how self-sufficient we try to make ourselves." When she didn't respond, just kept her eyes fastened on her work, he asked, "Did you pray much as a kid?"

The offhand question got her to thinking. "A few times, I suppose."

"How did your prayers go?"

She scowled and gave her head an arbitrary toss. "Once after Ezra hit me, I asked God to let him drown in Hickman Creek. Does that count? Another time I asked Him to suffocate the old geezer in his sleep by letting the roof cave in—just on his side of the house, mind you, not mine. As you can see, He answered neither prayer." Now that she thought about it, they were bizarre requests, and recalling them prompted a bit of cynical laughter.

Jon chortled low in his throat. "Emma, Emma, you're too much."

There was a certain warmth to his tone that she chose to ignore. "I had it all planned out, too," she went on. "How I'd go live with Miss Abbott after Papa died." She sobered. "That wasn't very nice of me, was it?"

"You were angry, and rightfully so. Let me just say that God is angered by injustice. In fact, He hates it, especially when it involves children. But that's anger of a righteous kind. As long as we recognize anger for what it is, it can't steal our joy; but if we give it a foothold, it can do great damage, even cheat us of our ability to trust another human being."

She raised her chin in defiance, felt a stinging sensation at the back of her eyes. In short order, she took up her sewing again, flustered that he'd managed to rouse her emotions.

113

"What he did to you was wrong, Emma." All of a sudden, he was standing next to her, having taken the liberty to walk right into her private domain. "I have a feeling he'd call it all back if he could," he was saying. "The old fool has spent the better share of his life drunk. He knows you hate him for it, but he's helpless to do a thing about it."

"That's not my fault," she said, sudden anger rising up. "And I'll thank you to leave my room immediately."

He didn't move. Just stood there staring down at her—as if he had the right—close enough that she heard each measured breath. "God can help you, Em—."

"Here it is!" Just in time, Luke came bounding into the room, sticking a faded photograph under both their noses.

Emma reached out and took the photo from Luke's stubby fingers. Forcing a bright-eyed smile, she gave him her full attention. "You were right, Luke. She is very pretty."

*****

"Furniture and whatnot's comin' in on the next freight wagon!" reported Gerald Crunkle, dismounting his horse at the site of the new schoolhouse and waving the telegram he'd just received. About a dozen men had gathered to work today, and a few of them looked up when Gerald arrived. Most didn't take the time to stop what they were doing, however, just wiped their brows with their shirtsleeves and granted him a cursory glance. "Want me to read what it says here?" he asked.

Jon grinned, feeling his own brand of excitement at the news. The quicker the men finished the work on this schoolhouse, the sooner they could start erecting the church.

"I'll read it anyways," Gerald said when he got no audible response to his question. "Desks, books, supplies arriving on

28 July. Stop. Anticipate four wagonloads. Stop. Full payment expected upon delivery. Stop." Gerald studied the yellow piece of paper as if it were a juicy piece of watermelon. "Ain't that good news?" he said.

"It's great news, Gerald," Ben Broughton professed, hauling another broken board across the yard to add to the growing pile of debris. There would be one big fire in another week or so. "You'll forgive us, though, for not sharing your same level of enthusiasm. Most of us have been here since daybreak, and right now the news of the furniture's arrival sounds a bit like, well, more work." A facetious tone accompanied his droll grin as he tossed the board on the pile with a clatter, stopped to mop his wet face, and then looked up to exchange a waggish look with Jon, who was perched high on a ladder. Jon shook his head and laughed to himself before returning to the job assigned him, painting the cedar trim around the new windows.

A couple of murmurs of agreement came from Sully Thompson and Edgar Blake, who were coming around the corner of the white clapboard schoolhouse, also carrying armloads of debris.

"And by the way, Crunkle," Edgar said, loud enough for everyone to hear. "Some of us have noticed how it seems like lately we been seein' more o' your backside ridin' out o' here than the other way 'round."

Someone sounded a hearty laugh on the other side of the building. Gerald's mouth turned under as he gave a broad-shouldered shrug. "Hey, I brought y'all lunch yesterday. You best show a bit o' gratitude." Pushing seventy, Gerald found a tree stump to drop onto and gave a loud sigh. He was the sort of fellow who took well to teasing, and for that reason, the men were quick to dish it out whenever they got the chance.

"I'll just sit here and supervise 'fore I head back. Preacher, looks like you missed a spot—a little to your left—higher."

"Thanks, Gerald," Jon said, dabbing the area with his paintbrush, grinning to himself.

"The way I see it, if that furniture comes in the end of July we ought ta be able to use the building for our church service first Sunday in August," remarked Rocky Callahan, who was climbing down a ladder at the end opposite Jon, paint can in hand.

Elmer Hayward found another stump close to Gerald's and made himself comfortable. Broad shouldered and well muscled, and older than Gerald by about ten years, Elmer still managed to work circles around most everybody. With his full, white beard and thick head of white hair, he resembled a lumberjack. He removed a handkerchief from his hip pocket and wiped his brow. "Attendance will jump when that happens."

"I hope you're right," Jon said. "I'm afraid it's dropped off since having to meet in the Winthrop's living room."

"Can ya blame us? Folks is sick o' that woman's fretful looks," Bill Jarvis muttered. "I declare them oriental rugs o' hers belong in a museum instead of a livin' room the way she eyes everybody what walks on 'em."

"She and Clyde have been more than generous," Jon said in their quick defense. The last thing he wanted was word getting back to Mrs. Winthrop that folks were complaining about her lack of hospitality. "Who wouldn't be overprotective about such valuable possessions? I'm amazed she offered her house at all."

Robert Johnson came to stand under the shade of a tree and take a swig from his water canteen. "I'd say it was more Clyde who made the offer. Iris went along with it. You wouldn't think it at first glance, but Clyde Winthrop wears the pants in that house. He mostly just lets her think she's in charge. You see the way he shut her up a few weeks ago when she didn't agree with the preacher here about goin' out to Ezra Browning's place? My, my, that was worth every cent of the price of admission. Come to think of it, I put double in the offering plate that day."

Several hooted and even Jon chuckled, although with his back to the bunch of them. Tithes and offerings had been up, he quietly mused.

When the laughter died down, Gerald asked, "How's that old fossil, Ezra Browning, takin' to your visits, Preacher? He startin' ta come around?"

Jon glanced from his high perch to ponder the question. It appeared that most had decided to take a break, by the look of things, hunkering down in any shady spot they could find to take swigs from their water jars. He chose to finish out his job despite the sun's penetrating rays.

"Truth is, I don't know what, if anything, I'm accomplishing by going out there, but there's one thing I do know. God's commanded me to love the man."

"But you ain't even his pastor," said Bill. "He ain't never once set foot in our church."

Jon shook his head, wishing they could catch his passion. "If I'm not his pastor, what good am I? Did Jesus come only to serve the desirable?"

"Was he talkin' about folks what tote rifles?" asked Henry Johnson, one of Hickman's younger farmers.

Jon cackled. "I see what you're saying, Henry. I'll confess looking down the barrel of a rifle is not my favorite thing to do, but I haven't seen it since that first time. Truth is, I think the old guy's startin' to like me."

Rocky Callahan took a swig of water, screwed the lid back on the jar, and cleared his throat. "I think it boils down to this, men. Ezra's not the most lovable character in Little Hickman, but he's still a child of God. Wouldn't hurt for any of us to show the fellow a little compassion."

After that, the topic of Ezra Browning came to an abrupt end.

*****

Emma viewed herself in her full-length mirror before closing her door behind her and exiting down the back stairs. It was the first time she was wearing her new dress, and for that reason, she'd taken special care with her old high-tops, polishing them to a sheen, selected a purple ribbon with which to tie back her golden hair, set a white bonnet on her head, and pinched some color into her already rose-hued cheeks. Not that it mattered one iota if anyone noticed her.

In her reticule, she carried an envelope of cash, payment from her boarders, three-quarters of which would go into her bank account, and the rest for purchasing necessary supplies from Johansson's Mercantile and Flanders' Foods. As much as she hated to admit it, she also had to make a purchase of thread and a mélange of other items from Mrs. Winthrop, the woman's selection far surpassing that of Eldred's meager stock.

Outside, she paused before crossing the street to Little Hickman's Bank and Trust, lifting a hand to wave at the Bergen family riding past in their ramshackle farm cart. Wagon wheels and a warm breeze sent dust swirling into the hot, dry air. Women traversed the sidewalk, some dawdling to stare into store windows, others hurrying along, arms full of either packages or babies. The scent of horse manure and hay filled the air, as did the sounds of shouting male voices, whinnying horses, and the saloon's tinny, off-key piano.

Holding down her bonnet, Emma crossed the street, stepped up to the sidewalk, pulled back the solid oak door, and entered the bank building.

Ila Jacobsen, Frieda Hardy, Sarah Callahan, and Fred Swain stood in line at the bank window. Millie Humphrey, one of the tellers, was waiting on Ila. Back in his glass-enclosed office, Bill Whittaker, Little Hickman's bank president, sat at his big walnut desk brooding over a stack of papers. At the sight of Emma, Sarah turned and acknowledged her with a friendly smile and wave, Fred Swain granting her a courteous nod.

"How is little Ermaline doing, Mr. Swain?" Emma asked by way of a greeting, coming to stand behind him.

The man's polite nod switched to a beaming smile as he swiveled his body to give Emma his full attention. "You'd hardly know that leg and arm is broke what with the way she gets herself around, manipulatin' her little body so's she can do most anythin' she puts her mind to. Doc says we need to try holdin' her down some, but sayin' it and doin' it is two different things. Yep, yep, yep, she's a rascal, that one. Guess if she wasn't, she wouldn't be in this fix, eh? Herb says she runned right out in front of 'im, and we believe 'im. That accident weren't any o' his fault."

"I'm relieved to hear it," Emma said. "I know Mr. Jacobs was just plain sick about the whole thing. I'm sure he's glad to hear she's doin' so well."

"Pfff. Herb's been out to the house nearly every day. He and Ermaline's becomin' quite the friends. Doc says it's good for both of 'em—ya know, facin' the thing head-on rather than tryin' to pretend it didn't happen. Sometimes that's the best

119

way to deal with the past. Face it and move on, that's Flora's and my philosophy. Ain't nothin' else we can do but thank the good Lord things didn't turn out worse. Yep, there's always a silver linin' if you look hard enough."

His words struck a chord in Emma's heart that she hadn't expected. *Face it and move on.* The notion that Fred and Flora Swain held no ill feelings for the accident was refreshing, if not surprising. Most would have found reason for grudge-holding, particularly for something as monumental as running over an innocent child. She gave the idea a moment to settle in.

"You go on ahead of me, Mr. Swain," Sarah was saying. "I'd like the chance to visit with Emma."

"Why, sure," Fred said, gladly switching places, drawing out a leather pouch from the back pocket of his overalls and preparing to do business at the window.

All smiles, Sarah squeezed Emma's arm. "How've you been, Emma?" she asked, her luxuriant, red locks falling around her temples, the shiny, turquoise comb at the back of her head not quite sufficient for holding the bulk of her glossy hair.

Emma silently admired her, the poised and polished Sarah Woodward Callahan, former mail-order bride from Winchester, Massachusetts, a Boston suburb. Arriving on a stagecoach last winter with the intention of marrying Benjamin Broughton, she'd wound up instead on the hand of Rocky Callahan. And just as well. The two fit like a hand and a glove, despite Rocky's provincial upbringing. Fashionable and sophisticated, she embodied everything that Little Hickman wasn't—and yet somehow managed to win over the entire town. Of course, it hadn't hurt that she'd donated the funds for a schoolhouse. It'd been an anonymous gift, of course, but few doubted the donor's identity.

"I'm fine, thank you…yourself?"

"Gracious, I'm fine as can be," Sarah replied, her oval face simply glowing.

Emma wondered how she could possibly have looked at her image in the mirror mere moments ago and admired her hand-sewn dress when before her stood a woman of elegance and fine breeding, wearing a store-bought, shimmering satin gown and carrying a handbag to match.

"Have you seen the schoolhouse?" Sarah was asking, completely oblivious to Emma's covetous thoughts.

"What? No, not just lately."

"Oh, you must drive out and see it. I stopped there just an hour ago. The men were hard at work, painting, hauling debris away from the site, and finishing up on small tasks. It's as pretty as a picture set against those green, lush foothills and lovely trees. I'm so glad the town council voted to move it out a ways. It won't hurt the children having to walk a bit, and it will give the town some room to expand. And I think the name the council's decided on, Oak Hill Schoolhouse, is downright homey, don't you?"

"Yes. Homey's a good word." Actually, she'd stayed away from the council meetings, mostly because she didn't think her vote much counted. She had no children. It didn't matter one way or the other to her where they stationed the new building or what name they chose to give it.

"And the church should stay at the center of town—right where the schoolhouse used to be," Sarah said. "Oh, I know Jonathan must be chomping at the bit to get that project started. Has he said?"

"What?"

"Jon, er, Reverend Atkins." She made a disparaging face. "It's hard for me to think of him as Reverend when he and

Rocky are such close friends. You must feel the same—especially now that he's taken a room in your boardinghouse, which, by the way, I think is quite lovely."

Of all the words she'd have chosen for describing the preacher's living arrangements, *lovely* wasn't one of them. *Distracting* seemed a more likely word.

Chapter Eleven

*W*ell, if it's not Miss Emma herself. Thought I might be givin' your mail to the preacher again," said George Garner. "But I see you've come for it." The postmaster emerged from the back end of the building, rubbed his hands on his soiled trousers, and shuffled to the front counter, combing a hand through his oily gray hair. His matching gray beard still contained the remnants of his breakfast, which seemed to have been toast and strawberry jam. George's eyebrows flicked upward, like an inverted V. "You got a couple more letters from Chicago." He propped an elbow on the marred counter and leaned forward, his stale breath wending through the air. "One of 'em came in four days ago and another just yesterday."

Emma sorted through the pieces of mail she'd just taken from her slot; a postcard from Mr. Dreyfus addressed to the boardinghouse residents, an advertisement for a new cookstove, a flyer about November's presidential election, and two letters from the mysterious Grace Giles. She stuffed it all into her leather reticule and pasted on a smile.

"Thank you, Mr. Garner, but, um, if you don't mind, I'll pick up my own mail after this. No need givin' it to the reverend." She would have liked to have added that he needn't keep checking the return address, either, but knew the futility in that.

He looked only a little contrite. "If you say so."

"You have a good afternoon now." She turned on her heel.

"And you, too, ma'am."

When she walked to the door to pull it open, he called out, "Mighty pretty dress you're wearin' there."

"Why, thank you, Mr. Garner." She slipped out with a smile on her face.

Mrs. Winthrop looked up when Emma entered the dry goods store and forced a pleasant look. "Well, well, Miss Emma, I see you're wearing a new dress."

Obviously not intended for a compliment, Emma pulled back her shoulders. "Yes."

"Is that fabric from my stock? I don't recall the floral pattern."

"Afraid not. I special ordered it from the mercantile."

Iris's pointy chin shot forward, a hand quickly spreading across her ample chest. "I see. You couldn't have ordered from me?"

It was a known fact Iris Winthrop considered Eldred Johansson her competitor, even though his inventory varied quite drastically, his store carrying hardware and general supplies, while the Winthrops specialized more in sewing notions and household and kitchen items.

Emma recalled the day she'd left the dry goods store and marched straight to the mercantile to place an order for fabric. "I happened to spot this fabric in Mr. Johansson's catalog." She plastered on a smile. "I simply couldn't resist it."

"Well!" Iris huffed. "It's lovely, indeed, but I'm sure Mr. Johansson and I have the same catalog. Was it Sears, Roebuck, and Company by chance?"

Emma withdrew a list from her pocket. "I believe it was." She unfolded the paper and handed it over the counter. "Now, then, if you'll be so kind as to fill my order?"

Iris adjusted her spectacles and perused the paper. "Hm. Needles, thimble, candle wax, yellow thread, one bar of lemon soap, a pair of shoestrings," she read aloud. Emma shifted her weight. Without a word, the proprietress began assembling the items in a neat little pile next to the cash register.

Emma watched as the stuffy woman moved about. "It's another swelterin' day," she said, feeling compelled to converse. "Almost makes a body anxious for fall."

Iris sniffed. "Yes, well, the cooler weather will be upon us before you know it, and then we'll be wishing for summer."

"Isn't that the truth!"

The bell above the door sounded and both women turned. "Afternoon, ladies." Emma sucked in a breath. What in the world would bring Jonathan Atkins to the dry goods store? Apparently, Iris wondered the same, for her jaw dropped.

"Why, Reverend, what a lovely surprise," she gushed. "To what do we owe the honor of your presence?"

Emma fought down the urge to roll her eyes. She didn't know anyone quite as two-faced as Iris Winthrop. Just days ago, she'd been bad-mouthing the preacher for keeping company with the likes of Ezra Browning and the hooligans living in her boardinghouse, and now she fairly blossomed in his presence.

Charming character that he was, Jon removed his hat and smiled, revealing perfectly aligned teeth. His blue eyes glinted with warmth as they meandered from Iris to Emma and back to Iris, his sandy-colored hair falling across his forehead in its usual haphazard fashion despite his recent haircut. Emma silently instructed herself to pay no heed to his exceedingly handsome face.

"I thought I'd stop by to tell you we plan to start up services in the new schoolhouse the first Sunday in August. As part of the festivities, we'd like to honor both you and Clyde that morning."

Iris clasped her throat with one hand, her other spreading flat across her thick midsection. Her black, beady eyes went round with pleasure. "Well, my goodness!" she tittered.

Jon glanced at Emma, and in that instant, she felt some sort of tenuous connection with him. "There's no getting around the fact that if you hadn't offered your house as a Sunday meeting place, Little Hickman Community Church would not have had the opportunity for regular worship," he explained. "We'd simply like to show our appreciation. You will promise to come, right?" he pressed, leaning forward.

Iris looked ready to burst. "We wouldn't think of missing."

Jon heaved an exaggerated sigh. "Of course, the ladies are planning a church picnic to follow." Emma earned an extra long glance from him at the announcement. Was he extending her a private invitation? It wouldn't hurt to go this once, she reasoned, even if it would mean sitting through one of his sermons. Besides, talking to Sarah Callahan had sparked her curiosity about the schoolhouse.

He pulled his gaze back to Iris and turned the rim of his hat in his hands, his engaging smile never fading. "I expect we'll have a big turnout, what with it being the first time for opening the doors to the public."

"Well, I'm sure you're right about that, Reverend," said Iris, cheeks aglow. "And the women will put on quite a spread afterward. I'll be sure to bring my pies."

"You're famous for your apple and blueberry," he remarked, eyes twinkling.

The man had no compunctions when it came to doling out praise. Emma pinched her lips together to avoid a smile.

"As I recall, your fried chicken is the envy of every woman across the county. Why, that last potluck had Flossie Martin and Esther Thompson guessing at your mystery ingredient."

The woman blushed crimson. "I'll be sure to contribute all three then," she exclaimed. "The pies and the chicken."

"How, may I ask, does Clyde manage to stay so fit and trim married to such a fine cook?"

A twittering sound like a warbling bird came from Iris's throat. She took up Emma's list and used it as a fan. "Why, Reverend Atkins, you'll have me swooning."

Later, Emma held her giggle at bay as she made her way to Flanders' Foods next door, a box of goods under one arm. She heard the Winthrop's screen door slam shut with a thwop.

"Emma, wait!" Jon called after her.

She gave a half-turn but didn't slow her pace.

In a matter of seconds, he was at her side, huffing to catch up. "That's a pretty dress you're wearing. Isn't that the one you were working on the other day?"

His memory impressed her. "It is. Thank you."

"You look pretty as a picture in it. You're an amazingly talented woman, Emma Browning. Lovely, too, if I do say so."

She halted in the middle of the sidewalk and stared him square in the face. "Reverend Atkins, you are a clever man thinkin' you can wheedle the same reaction out of me as you did Mrs. Winthrop. I do not charm easily, sir."

He tossed back his head and laughed. She managed not to react. "I have known that about you for some time, Emma, but I've always enjoyed a good challenge."

Emma shook her head and resumed her step.

"You have to admit you came close to smiling back there," he said.

Yes, she had, but she wouldn't admit it. At the door to the grocery, she paused to look at him, a tiny grin even now tickling the corners of her mouth.

"For a preacher, you sure can be a scamp."

She heard his low-throated chortle even after the door closed behind her.

*****

The first letter simply said,

Dear Emma,

I am praying for you. If you have a Bible, please read the entire book of John. (I happen to know that Clara Abbott gave you one.) It will only take a week if you commit to reading three chapters a day.

I eagerly await a reply from you as to what you think after you've read it.

Your heavenly Father loves you with a love you cannot begin to fathom.

Yours very sincerely,
Grace Giles

What did this woman know about Clara Abbott? And how would she have learned of the treasured Bible given to her just before the woman's passing? She thought of the leather-bound book tucked safely beneath her lace handkerchiefs in the top drawer of her bureau. It had been lying there for many years—completely untouched.

The second letter read,

Dear Emma,

Have you started reading John's Gospel? Don't you find it quite fascinating reading about Jesus' life on earth? Please don't hesitate to write me with any questions you might have. You have my return address, and every day I hope to receive a letter from you.

Have you settled matters with your father? I pray for you often.

Yours always,
Grace Giles

Outside, a gentle breeze drifted past Emma's bedroom window, flirting with the lace curtains. A full moon added light to the glowing candle at her bedside. She strained her eyes to read again the letters she'd received earlier that day but only now had found time to read. After perusing them a second time, and then a third, she carefully folded them up and tucked them back into their envelopes, running her fingers over the meticulously written return address in the upper left-hand corner of one of them.

With a tiny frown, she rose from her wicker chair and padded across the room to her bureau, her nightdress tickling her ankles, her long tresses falling over her shoulders. Pulling open the top drawer, she laid the letters atop the others she'd received, noting the growing collection.

Grace Giles, who are you?

When she would have closed the drawer, she suddenly found herself digging to the bottom, pushing aside handkerchiefs, pillowslips, and doilies until her fingers finally clasped hold of the small leather Bible.

Clutching it in both hands, she first stared at it as if it were a menacing object. Soon, though, a jumble of emotions grabbed hold of her—curiosity, eagerness, surprise, and panic. Sucking in a tight breath, she flipped open the cover. *This Bible belongs to Clara Abbott* was carefully penned on the front page.

For some reason she'd thought she would find a clue as to Grace Giles' identity by simply opening the book, but it wasn't

129

there. She thumbed through the first few pages, Births—Family Record—Deaths, but found each page void of any entries.

The next page listed every book of the Bible from the Old and New Testaments.

Without forethought, she traced her finger down the length of the feathery page until it landed on the book of John. "Page 1088," she whispered.

She told herself it was simple curiosity and nothing more that prompted her to find the designated book. But it was something altogether different that had her walking across the room, flopping down into her chair, and propping the book open on her lap. Deep, unsettled hunger?

"In the beginning was the Word, and the Word was with God, and the Word was God," she read aloud from the first verse in chapter one.

Outside, the tinny sounds of off-key piano playing drifted up from Madam Guttersnipe's Saloon.

She settled back and continued reading.

Chapter Twelve

*E*mma guided the rented horse down the dusty trail. It had been several months since she'd found the need for a horse, so when she'd walked into Sam's Livery the next day announcing her request for a gentle horse, there had been a few stares from Sam, Sully Thompson, and Edgar Blake. Even Elliott Newman had emerged from his wheelwright shop at the back of the livery wearing a look of surprise.

"Where you headin', Miss Emma?" Elliott asked.

Not wanting to divulge her destination, and somewhat perturbed with the men for their curiosity, Emma merely shrugged. "Can't a body enjoy a horseback ride for no particular reason other than it seems like a good day for one?"

The men gawked, obviously not swallowing her reasoning. "You want I should send Luke with ya?" Elliott asked. "It's not all that proper for a lady to be out ridin' these hills on her own, even if it is just a pleasure trip."

This was hardly a pleasure trip, she might have said. "No, I'll be fine." This was Little Hickman, for goodness' sake. Yes, there'd been a few problems in the past, the schoolhouse fire namely, but Clement Bartel, the boy who'd started the fire, was dead as a result, and since then very little had transpired in this tiny community—with the exception of Ezra Browning's drunken shenanigans.

Directing the horse down the hillside, she held on to the saddle horn to steady herself, not nearly as adept a rider as most women she knew. Having spent most of her life cooped up in the house with Ezra, and then running the boarding-house from age eighteen on, there'd been little reason for riding.

At a flat, grassy patch, she reined in the horse named Lester and surveyed the familiar countryside spread out before her: the dilapidated barn and old sheds, the acres of wasted farmland, the tottering one-room shack. A row of flowers blossomed along the west side of the old house, a contrast of color against the ancient boards.

Whether she would even find her father at home was a matter of debate. She knew he worked at the saloon several afternoons a week and spent a good share of the rest of his time there. Giving the horse a gentle nudge with her boot heels, she guided him the rest of the way down the hillside. Pansy, the ancient old goat, raised her skinny head to check her out, then went back to pulling up what few blades of grass she could find around the yard. Emma reached behind her and yanked a couple of apples and an overripe pear from the saddlebag. "Here you go, girl," she called, tossing the fruit to the ground. The animal meandered over, took a moment to sniff out the offering, then gobbled it down with fervor. "Thought you'd enjoy that," she said, jumping down from Lester and leading him to a newly repaired fence post.

Some chickens waddled over. "Sorry, I've got nothing for you," she murmured. They gathered round her and clucked, angling their relatively long bodies at her, their rose combs on the tops of their heads wobbling back and forth. A Rhode Island Red variety, these chickens were known for their egg-laying properties, and because of that, her father had rarely decapitated one for its meat. And when he had, she'd never partaken, for they were the closest things she'd ever had to pets.

They parted for her as she made her way up the beaten path toward the front porch. She glanced about, impressed by how neat the place looked, all thanks to the team of volunteers Jon had scrounged up. A tiny pang of guilt for not having helped in the efforts struck a spot in the back of her conscience.

She gave the front door a light rap, surprised to hear approaching footsteps almost immediately. When Ezra opened the door, they both stood speechless for what seemed like an entire minute, and it wasn't until he broke the silence with a series of coughing spasms that she finally spoke. "You should have Doc Randolph check that cough."

"You sound like that preacher kid," he sputtered when the cough let up. He stepped aside so she could enter. "You come out here to yell at me?"

Ignoring the question, she walked past him and looked around. Little had changed, she mused with a sigh, a sudden wave of memories flooding her head when she looked at the dishes stacked high in the sink.

"Ain't you got them done yet?" bellowed Papa, stomping mud off his feet at the door. "I went out to the barn a full hour ago."

Emma reeled where she stood and tasted fear. Papa had a bottle of ale in one hand and a stick in the other. Did he plan to hit her with the stick because she'd been dawdling with her chores?

"I'm tryin' to hurry, Papa, but this here pan has built-up grease in it. It ain't comin' out so easy." She wouldn't tell him that her stitching practice had distracted her for a time. Just that afternoon, Miss Abbott had given her some lessons with a needle and thread and sent her home with the prettiest gingham fabric Emma had ever laid eyes on. It was to be a pillow, Miss Abbott said, and once she finished the

sides, they would stuff it with a wonderful soft filling. Emma planned to put it at the head of her cot.

To her relief, Papa tossed the stick into the fireplace. She felt the breath whoosh out of her and went back to her scrubbing.

"You got your schoolwork done?" he asked, moving to his chair. His eyes were extra red tonight. She figured that after collecting the eggs and milking old Wilma, he must have sat on his bench in the barn and consumed a bottle of whiskey. He had so many of them stored in various places out there. Sometime she would like to find each one and break them all into a million pieces. But that would mean a whippin' for sure.

"I finished it before supper," she fibbed.

He nodded, took a long swig, then reclined his head on his dingy old chair.

The next morning, before she headed off to school, he was still sitting there, eyes closed, mouth drooping, an empty bottle at his feet.

Her eyes roved the one-room house. "I ain't had time to pick up today," he mumbled.

When have you ever lifted a finger around this house?

She nodded and walked to the window. Hanging from it was a pair of brand-new curtains. She fingered the dark blue cotton and wondered who had hung them. Had it been a woman from the church or Jon himself? She marveled that anyone could be so generous to one so undeserving.

She felt her father's eyes bore holes through her back. "What'd you want?" he asked from behind. "I know this ain't no social call."

Turning, she gave him a long, cold look. It felt good not to fear him any longer. She'd passed through that stage some years ago and entered into one dictated more by bitterness and disgust. "You look different without a bottle in your hand," she said, deciding to ignore his remark. It was difficult to keep the mocking tone out of her voice.

He shrugged and tossed his head to one side, then swept a dirty hand across his whiskered face. "I been cuttin' back," he said.

Her eyebrows shot up on their own. "You don't say." Now that she took a moment to look at him, it did appear his eyes were somewhat clearer. Still, she held out no hope. That was another stage she'd passed through long ago.

His chest rattled before he released another string of coughs. She turned her face away so as not to watch the struggle that ensued. It appeared his years of heavy smoking along with imbibing had done a number on his aging body. Even though he was only in his late fifties, he appeared to be at least twenty years older.

"You should sit," she heard herself instruct, pointing at a chair. To her surprise, he took her suggestion. Once he sat himself down, she walked to the sink to study the dishes. Should she or shouldn't she? The rotten smells of caked-on food had her wrinkling up her nose, but something from within made her turn the water valve and dig for the pail he kept stored beneath the sink. She filled it without a word, then lit a flame at the old stove and lifted the full bucket of water to the single burner.

He was sitting in his chair watching her when she faced him.

"Who is Grace Giles?" she asked straight out.

He gave her a blank stare, then his mouth twisted downward. "Who?"

"Grace Giles. Who is she?"

"I got no idea." His tone rang of impatience. "Am I s'posed ta know 'er?"

"You might. She lives in Chicago."

One shoulder lifted in a slight shrug. "Chicago," he murmured. The tiniest glimmer lit in his eyes then quickly died away. "Don't know her. How'd you come to meet her anyway?"

She let go a frustrated sigh. "I haven't met her. She's a perfect stranger to me, but she's been sendin' me letters."

Another flicker of something crept across his face. "Letters about what?"

Rather than go into detail, she gave her head a little shake. "Nothin' really important. Just—oh, never mind."

Rather than prod, he grew silent, which was just as well. He didn't appear to know Grace Giles, so what was the point of pressing the issue? She turned toward the sink and lifted a dirty dish. Something red stuck to the edges of the plate. Tomatoes? Beets? When she looked at him again to ask what he'd eaten, his eyes had closed, and his breathing was coming in labored spurts.

The old fool had drifted off to sleep, and here she was stuck with a pile of dishes.

*****

Right on schedule, the schoolhouse furniture and a number of other building and school supplies arrived on the twenty-eighth of July. A whole slew of men and boys and a sprinkling of women showed up for the unloading, including Jon, who felt like a kid himself when he first laid eyes on the brand-spanking-new school desks.

Irwin Waggoner and Ben stood on one wagon, handing down things, while Tom Averly, Carl Hardy, Rocky, and Fred Swain handed down items from the other two horse-drawn rigs. They'd set up a sort of assembly line, the men handling the bigger items, the women taking the lighter things that had been placed on the ground.

With the big oak schoolhouse doors standing open, there was a constant stream of folks moving up and down the steps and into the fresh new building, a hubbub of excitement stirring the air with shouts of "Where should this go?" and "What's in this carton?" and even "Why, ain't this a lovely picture of George Washington?" It seemed that Sarah Callahan, who'd undertaken the majority of the ordering—with the help of a committee of other folks, including the former schoolteacher, Liza Broughton—had thought of everything, right down to the brand new textbooks, clock, bookcases and wall shelves, flags, maps, and beautifully framed pictures of former U.S. presidents.

A host of school-age children raced up and down the stairs, a few with items in hand, but most just filled with boundless energy.

"Ain't ya glad the school burned down?" Andrew Warner was heard to have said while he skipped through the yard, Todd Thompson chasing on his heels.

"Andrew James Warner!" his mother scolded. Beyond that, she said no more. Jon couldn't help the chuckle that emerged when he heard the innocent remark. He suspected the ten- or eleven-year-old boy had merely voiced what others thought but feared saying. Shoot, he felt it himself. Not that he ever wanted to relive the nightmare of that awful fire in which they'd nearly lost Liza Jane and Rufus Baxter—and *had* lost Clement Bartel. Still, there was nothing quite like the sights and smells of new wood and shiny, unmarred furniture, or the feel of fresh, unused textbooks yet to be read and explored with eager eyes. He handed a crate of books to the next person in line, Clyde Winthrop, with a grin.

"Heard you stopped by the store a few days ago," Clyde said, starting up a conversation before handing off the carton to the fellow behind him, Elmer Hayward.

"As a matter of fact, I did," Jon answered. "Did your wife mention we plan to honor you two at this Sunday's services?"

"She did, and I want you to know it's completely unnecessary, Reverend. We don't need the thanks."

"I happen to disagree," Jon said. "You've made quite a sacrifice Sunday after Sunday."

Clyde shook his head. "Loaning out our living room has been a privilege—for both of us. I know most felt like they were imposing." He leaned in close to Jon and lowered his voice. "Believe me; I know how outspoken that woman of mine can be."

Jon nodded and handed off another box. "Well, don't worry about it." He figured Clyde was mostly referring to the Sunday she'd put up a fuss about his plan to come to Ezra Browning's aid.

"You might not believe this," Clyde whispered, "but most Sunday afternoons when Iris is busy cleaning up the place, she'll comment on how much she likes the Sunday gatherings. I think they do her good—make her feel needed." He gave his head a gentle shake then paused with the box in his hand, dropping his voice to a low murmur. "She doesn't always come off as being the friendliest, but if you want the truth, I think it's mostly a cover-up for her lack of children. Strange, I know, but she still carries around the hurt of her barrenness. You'd think at her age she'd have gotten past it, but I guess that sort of thing sticks with a woman."

Jon moved his head up and down in a show of quiet acknowledgment. "Knowing a person's background usually explains a lot about why they behave the way they do." The two continued passing off boxes as they talked. "You take someone like Ezra Browning, for example. He didn't become an alcoholic overnight. Something drove him to it."

Clyde nodded. "That's the truth." He turned and put another box into Elmer's arms, then scratched his head and looked to the sky, pausing for a breather. "And that daughter of his has suffered plenty. Long as I've known her she's made it her goal to avoid most men because of that old feller that raised her."

"And yet she has a boardinghouse full of men," Jon remarked.

Clyde winked and laughed. "Well, o' course! None of them pose a threat to her." He tilted his face at Jon and grinned, his eyes flickering with bedevilment. "But now that you've moved in, well, that could be another story."

The sentence remained open-ended, causing Jon to cease what he was doing. "What—you think I pose a threat?"

Now Clyde threw back his head for a great peal of laughter. When he finally composed himself, he opened his mouth to respond, but someone at the schoolhouse steps called out. "Hey, what's the holdup down there?"

Clyde took the box Jon held in his arms and chuckled as they resumed passing supplies from hand to hand. "She's a pretty tough little woman, that Emma Browning," he muttered under his breath. "But I got to believe there's someone out there who can tenderize her spirit." He leaned in closer. "Who better than the preacher?" Another one of his hearty chuckles followed.

Speechless, all Jon could do was stare straight ahead and ruminate on his words.

By late afternoon, the place looked ready for the first day of school. Some had left for the day, while others lingered inside to admire the freshly painted walls, the floor's shiny wood planks, and even the big oak desk the new teacher would occupy. Liza Broughton stepped onto the platform at the front of the room, perusing the entire room with bright-eyed wonder. "Oh, it'd be such a pleasure to resume my job as Hickman's teacher." She rubbed her pregnant belly and wrinkled her nose. "But I don't think I'm the one for the job."

"No, ma'am, you're not," Ben said, stepping up beside her to give her cheek a light peck and pull her to his side. Several in the room snickered. Liza's already rosy cheeks seemed to flush even more. Something close to envy pricked Jon at his core, but he quickly shrank back from it. What business did he, the preacher, have envying one of his best friends? It wasn't as if he'd ever carried a torch for Liza Jane, or even that he resented the love and happiness Ben so deserved.

No, it was more like he longed for something similar, the satisfying love of a soft woman.

There's someone out there who can tenderize her spirit. Clyde's words echoed in his head until he gave himself a mental scolding and chased out the words.

"Someone's comin' up Sugar Creek Road," announced young Thomas Bergen, who stood peering out one of the windows. Sugar Creek Road was one of the main roads into town, so Jon figured it was just some farmer coming in for supplies. "He's drivin' a weird-lookin' wagon. There's colorful flags and ribbons blowin' from the sides of it."

This got his attention, along with that of everyone else in the room.

Chapter Thirteen

*S*tep right up here, young man."

Timid little Clancy Barton looked around as if to say, "Who, me?" His mother, Ophelia Barton, gave him a slight nudge in the middle of his back. Several had gathered around the yellow-and-blue wagon parked at the edge of town in the empty lot where the new church would stand and the former schoolhouse had once been. Brightly painted letters in many colors bore the name BILLY WONDER'S TRAVELING MAGIC AND MEDICINE SHOW across two sides of the gaudy, canvas-covered rig.

Midday sunlight filtered through low-lying clouds, and a gentle breeze rustled the leaves in the oak trees overhead.

"That's right. I'm talking to you. Come on up here, lad."

The man who called himself Billy Wonder appeared to be in his mid- to late thirties and wore a fancy, white, puffed-sleeve shirt with black trousers, shiny, black vest, and string bowtie. Perched on his head was a black top hat. Over one wrist, he'd draped a glossy wood cane; his other hand held a megaphone, which he used to project his voice to the town of Little Hickman. Up the street, a number of inquisitive folks made their way to the gathering crowd, children running ahead.

Jon watched with his own brand of curiosity, standing alongside the more dubious Doc Randolph. "He's one of those quacks," Doc muttered under his breath.

Jon shushed him with a grin and a nudge to the side. "Hear the poor man out, Doc."

Little Clancy was making his way to the platform Billy had set up at the rear of his wagon. Billy took his hand and shepherded him the rest of the way. Poor little Clancy looked as scared as a mouse in a snake hole.

Billy laid down his megaphone, apparently satisfied with the growing swarm of people, and rested a hand on the lad's shoulder. "How old are you, boy?"

"Six," came the nearly inaudible reply.

"Sick? You say you're sick, young man? Why, I wouldn't have bothered you if I'd known you were sick."

Clancy's eyes grew wide as he looked up at the man. "No, six. I'm six. *Six.*"

"You're sixty-six?" Billy's own eyes doubled in size. "My, my, you look awful good for sixty-six. Have you been taking my elixir?"

To this, the crowd guffawed, as if Billy Wonder had just told the funniest joke on earth. Doc groaned, and Jon laughed—more at Doc than anything.

"I'm just funnin' ya, young man. Step on back down to your maw." Clancy moved back down the steps, his mother beaming from one ear to the other.

Next, Billy took up a deck of cards and set to some fancy shuffling. Almost as good as Charley Connors, Jon mulled with narrow eyes, but not quite. He folded his arms and watched. Billy was a smooth-looking character with a smile that could charm the feathers off a duck. He was of medium height and lean, moving with finesse. Definitely a practiced spellbinder, Jon concluded, in both looks and personality. "Pick a card, any card," Billy said, stepping forward and bending down to poke the deck under the nose of Lydia Swanson, making a point not to watch.

Her husband, Amos, laughed. "Take a card, Lyd." She

pondered the cards with care, then finally took one from the center of the fanned-out selection.

"Show it to the crowd, but take care that you don't let me see it," warned Billy.

She lifted her hand with discreetness, and everyone could see it was a ten of spades.

"Now place it carefully back in my deck."

Lydia was vigilant about assigning it to an entirely different position in the deck. Billy shuffled the cards then fanned them, this time showing them to the crowd. Everyone leaned forward to give them close perusal, viewing them as a normal deck of cards. Once again, he set to shuffling faster than the naked eye could follow.

Then he laid the deck down on a small table in front of him, waved some sort of silver wand over the cards, and split the deck in half. With heedful eyes, he scanned the burgeoning crowd. When his gaze landed on Bill Whittaker, who'd apparently slipped out of the bank for a midday break, he pointed at him. "You back there in the suit; you look like an honest, intelligent man," he announced. Bill's chest seemed to balloon out past his buttoned vest.

"Well, I...."

"Come up here, if you please," Billy ordered.

Without so much as a moment's hesitation, Bill grinned with pleasure and moved forward, passing through the parting crowd until he reached the wagon's metal, collapsible steps. Taking hold of the rail, he climbed the stairs and came to stand beside Billy.

"Have we ever met?" Billy asked.

Mr. Whittaker studied the man's face. "No, sir, we haven't."

Billy looked him up and down, removed his top hat, bowed low, and then extended a hand. "Billy Wonder," he offered.

"Bill Whittaker," Bill said, chuckling. The two shook hands, as if they'd just closed on a large-size loan, Billy taking awhile to pump the banker's arm up and down. A twittering of hushed whispers fell over the crowd of curious bystanders.

"See these cards?"

Bill looked at the split deck lying on the table in front of him. "Yes."

For a bank president, Jon thought he looked a bit befuddled.

"I'm afraid we have a small problem."

"See there," Doc Randolph hissed, poking Jon in the arm. "He can't produce the card. He's stalling. I told you he's a quack."

"Hush before I put a muzzle on you," Jon warned him.

Bill Whittaker's frown deepened, and he shrugged his measly shoulders as if to ask what the Wonder fellow wanted him to do about it.

Billy shifted his weight and bit his lip, feigning uneasiness. "What's your job, Mr. Whittaker? You don't appear to be a farmer."

Bill stood as tall as his five and a half feet would allow. "I'm the bank president."

"Oh, my!" Wonder blustered, looking abashed. His gaze slid over the crowd, whose gaping mouths and wide eyes revealed their keen attentiveness. "Well, that does pose a problem, folks. It seems your president is a shyster."

"Now, see here," Bill started.

"Mr. Whittaker, would you mind opening your jacket?"

"What's that?"

"Your jacket, sir. Just reach inside, if you don't mind, and check that inside pocket."

"Well, I don't see...."

 144

"Just do it, Whittaker," someone from the crowd bellowed.

Bill Whittaker gaped at Wonder, but he did as told, stuck a hand inside his coat and reached into the chest pocket. When he drew out a card, the crowd gasped in amazement. But when he revealed it as the ten of spades, an even louder shriek skittered through the throng of disbelieving observers.

And it was right about then that Rose Marley fainted dead away.

*****

Emma stood back from the supper table to give it one last inspection. With Mr. Wonder joining them for the next few days—or weeks—it would mean setting an extra place at the table and preparing a dab more for each meal. But, of course, it would also mean a bit more pocket change. And who couldn't use that?

Ever since the arrival of this magic man—or whatever name he'd given himself—Luke had not stopped talking about him. And when Luke talked fast, his stutter only worsened. She smiled to herself. Perhaps one day she would pay a visit to one of Billy Wonder's shows. As skeptical as she was about such things, hand trickery was an interesting phenomenon, and she'd heard from everybody that there was no finer magician. The medicinal aids he sold by the flaskful might be questionable, but, after all, he forced no one to purchase. If folks wanted to throw away their money on a bottle of syrup that claimed to heal a body of everything from arthritis to poor eyesight to kidney pain, then that was their problem.

"Something smells awfully fine down here," said a familiar voice. Her heart lurched crazily when she realized Jon

Atkins had entered the dining room. She turned to give him a cordial greeting, but her breath caught at the sight of him. He was dressed quite smartly, as if he were about to go courting. Without thinking, she pushed several loose strands of hair back behind her ears. It'd been hours since she'd fashioned the thick bun at the top of her head and stuck a blue ribbon around it. And not only that; she had a gravy stain running down the front of her yellow blouse, one she'd tried to wash out but had only made worse by scrubbing. She pulled back her shoulders and studied him, though not too carefully lest he notice.

"We're...having gravy and meatballs with scalloped potatoes and corn," she replied, turning to straighten Charley Connors' cloth napkin. "And rhubarb pie for dessert. My rhubarb's straight from the garden."

"Hm. Sounds wonderful. Unfortunately, I've been invited elsewhere tonight. I only just realized that I forgot to tell you earlier. I hope I haven't inconvenienced you."

"What? No, that's fine." She hastened to walk around the table and remove his plate, fighting down deep-settled disappointment. She'd wanted him to help carry the conversation with their dinner guest.

"You sure?" he asked, sticking his hands behind his back. Out of the corner of her eye, she admired his fancy trousers and pale cotton shirt. His tanned, muscular arms made a fine contrast.

"Absolutely. Who's invited you for supper?" she asked, regretting her nosiness almost immediately.

"A new family that's just moved in down on Cream Ridge, just over the creek's bridge and not far from the Broughton's property line. I haven't even met them yet myself. Heard there are four kids and a father. Apparently, the oldest girl acts as mother to the kids since their own died in that diphtheria out-break last spring."

"I've heard of them. They come from Nicholasville. Fancy Jenkins met the oldest girl yesterday in Flanders' Foods. Said she's a pretty thing. The last name is—"

"Clayton," they both said simultaneously.

"That's it," Emma said, suddenly rattled. Was it because he looked so handsome and she didn't quite know how to act? Or was it that he'd been invited out for supper—and the cook was a pretty young lady? Fancy had said the girl looked to be in her early twenties with ink black hair and eyes the color of a summer sky. Of course, leave it to Fancy to keep everyone abreast of Little Hickman's happenings, big and small.

She couldn't help but wonder what had precipitated the invitation, particularly since Jon said he hadn't even met the family yet.

"It was Reverend Miller who set up the invitation," Jon added, as if he'd read her mind. "Seems he's known this family for some time, used to pastor their church when he was out riding the circuit. He wants them to feel at home here in Hick-man, so he figured my going out to their place for a meal and inviting them to Sunday services was a good start."

She nodded, remembering the upcoming community picnic day after tomorrow.

"How about you? Are you coming this Sunday?"

She'd been trying to decide that very thing when Lucy Fon-taine had knocked on her door two days ago and asked her to donate a casserole for the potluck. She gave a slow nod. "I've been asked to bring a dish to pass, so I might better go to church."

One brow quirked with humor. "You make it sound like a death sentence. It won't be that bad, Emma, I promise." His soft tone unnerved her.

"I'll keep that in mind." What would he think if he knew she'd been reading from Clara Abbott's Bible every night before turning down her lamp—had even pondered the meaning of the verse "**If ye shall ask anything in my name, I will do it**"?

Jon glanced down and saw the extra place setting. "You expecting someone else for dinner?"

She noted a badly folded napkin and decided to redo it. "That character, Billy Wonder, will be takin' his evenin' meals with us," she said. "Soon as he arrives in any town I guess he goes in search of a restaurant. Since I'm the closest thing to one, 'cept for the bakery, he asked if he could join us. I obliged." She replaced the refolded napkin.

He frowned. "You don't say. Well, I'd watch my step with that one."

She'd been about to ask him what he meant when the knocker on the front door sounded and Luke ushered their guest into the dining room.

"Madame," Billy greeted by way of a ceremoniously gallant bow, followed by his reaching for her hand and bringing it to his mouth for a tender kiss. The move so surprised Emma that it took a moment to register what he'd done. But when she felt his lingering hot breath leaving a damp spot on the upper part of her wrist, she quickly withdrew it, wiping it as discreetly as possible on the back of her skirt.

"Good evenin'—sir."

"Oh, please, Billy will do."

Jon chortled loudly. "She barely calls her closest friends by their first names, Mr. Wonder."

"Oh, but I insist," he said, winking at Emma as if they were old acquaintances. "I'll simply not answer to anything else." At that, he surveyed his surroundings. "What a lovely old house. Such intricate carvings on that old grandfather clock in the foyer. Where may I ask did you come across it? And the piano—my, what a fine piece. I'd ask to play it later—if I had a clue how to find middle C." He laughed at his own joke.

He continued scrutinizing the house. "Your paintings are quite grand, too. I'm assuming you must have inherited them—from a relative, perhaps—or maybe your own parents. At any rate, it's a lovely home. And the food." He put his hand to his flat belly and rubbed a circle. "Might I say your cooking must be quite superb if the fine aromas coming from the kitchen are any indication?"

"She's a good cook, all right," Elliott Newman said, entering the dining room. "Haven't heard the supper announcement yet, but I'm assuming it's pretty near ready."

"Yes, Mr. Elliott. If you'd like, you can call the others in."

"I'll do it," Luke volunteered, turning his head and bellowing at full voice, "Everyone c-c-come to the t-table. Now!"

An exasperated look crossed Elliott's face. "I don't think that's the sort of announcement Miss Emma was looking for, Luke."

Emma hid her smile with a lightly fisted hand as the boarders started trickling into the room.

Rather than apologize, Luke's eyes trailed over Billy with sheer adoration and fondness. "Can you sh-sh-show us some m-magic later?" he asked.

"Well, now, I bet I could find something up my sleeve, but what say we make the food disappear first?"

"Huh?" Luke asked, not getting the intended joke.

Billy laughed and turned his attention to Emma. "Where would you like me to sit, fair lady?"

Emma looked at the table. She could have had him take Jon's place, since he'd be absent this evening, but since the place setting was already directly to her right, she pointed.

"You'll be sitting right next to me, Billy," she replied, the first name unwittingly slipping out.

A great puff of air blew past Jon's nostrils, as if he'd just received the news that someone had stolen all his sermon notes. When she glanced at him, she found his expression pinched. Wasn't there something in the Good Book that warned against men of the cloth showing their wrath?

"Well, now, I consider that a place of honor," Billy cooed. "May I assist you?" At breakneck speed, he slid behind her and pulled out her chair.

Emma laughed. "I—thank you for that, but I'm not quite finished in the kitchen. Go ahead and take your seats—everyone."

Charley Connors was the first to sit, and the rest of them followed suit, no worries with any of them as to the proper protocol. Billy, however, remained behind her chair. "I'll wait for the lady to sit," he announced to the others.

Charley shrugged. "Suit yourself."

Flustered, Emma escaped to the kitchen, not surprised when Jon followed. "Doc was right; the guy's a shyster, a grease-coated snake," he spit in a whisper.

"Shh. I think he's charming."

"And I thought you weren't easily charmed."

He had her there. "And I thought you had a dinner date."

"It's not a dinner date—as such."

"Well, no matter. You don't want to be late," she scolded, taking up the mashed potatoes in one hand and the gravy in the other. "That pretty young lady is probably even now sitting on pins and needles." Without meaning to, she let her cynical tone slip out.

He leaned into her. "Are you jealous?"

She glared at him. "What? That's the silliest thing I've heard since—since—those horseless carriage contraptions!

The comparison earned her a frosty glimmer. He gave the kitchen clock a frenzied look and blocked her passage. "You called him Billy."

She rolled her eyes. "That's his name."

"And Jon is mine," he rasped.

The desire to laugh nearly overtook her. "Well, ain't that a mercy. You're sounding more like a spoiled child than a minister of the Word."

"I am not!" he hissed, his breath tickling the hairs around her temple.

She stared at him for a full ten seconds, forcing her lips to stop their trembling. Oh, if only she could smile, but with mere inches separating their stubborn faces, she dodged the impulse. What was this sudden battle of wills?

"I'm merely suggesting it wouldn't kill you to call me Jon once in a while."

Something melted at her core, and she felt herself caving. "Okay, *Jon*," she said. "Will you kindly step aside?"

Now his mouth curved upward, and the melting escalated. "Was that so hard?" he asked, moving out of her path.

She sighed. "I declare, for a preacher, you're not only a scamp, you're touchy, to boot."

When she returned to the kitchen for the remainder of the meal, she saw the back door slam shut.

Chapter Fourteen

y 9:55 a.m., five minutes before the start of the service, it was standing room only. Billy Wonder looked a trifle put out when he sauntered through the doors at 9:59 only to be ushered to a spot next to a back window along with several other latecomers.

Jon sat on the platform at the front of the schoolhouse while Bess Barrington played "Praise Him, Praise Him" on the school's donated upright as a prelude to worship, the buttons on his jacket nearly bursting with the joy of it all. Carl Hardy sat beside him looking equally gleeful, new hymnbook in hand. Some unidentified contributor had left several cartons of brand-new hymnals on the schoolhouse steps—and in the middle of the night, no less. Ah, the joys of humble, selfless giving, with no thought for recognition!

To add to his pleasure, there sat Emma, directly in the middle of the congregation, fifth row back, crammed in between young Lily Broughton and the rotund spinster, Esther Martin. It was a big step for her, coming to church, and he longed to tell her he was proud of her for doing it.

Thankfully, the schoolhouse fire had not touched the church benches, as they'd been stored in a shed at the back of the property. Every Saturday night like clockwork Harvey Coleson, Gerald Crunkle, Clyde Winthrop, and Tim Warner had shown up to push the school desks to the back of the room and haul in the benches. Of course, once the new church was in place, the new pews would remain stationary.

Jon had made a point to tell one of the ushers, Irwin Waggoner, to seat Clyde and Iris Winthrop in the front row. Iris would think of it as a position of honor, which was, of course, his purpose in putting them there. Not that he was into apple-polishing, but a little couldn't hurt where Mrs. Winthrop was concerned.

Irv and Flossie Martin, faithful attendees, had visited literally every congregant's home to take up an offering on Clyde and Iris's behalf. Quite surprisingly, folks had come through in their spirit of giving, their contribution amounting to enough to buy the couple a fine dinner at the recently built Hotel Nicholas in Nicholasville and to hire a driver to get them there in his new folding-top, four-seated surrey. Jon doubted Clyde would consider such a gift the height of enjoyment, but Iris would nearly swoon at the thought, and that was what counted. He planned to present it to them along with a well-written letter of thanks composed by Liza Broughton and signed by the church council. Besides that, he would hand over a bouquet of roses straight from Flora Jarvis's garden that even now wafted a fine aroma from its hiding place behind the piano. All this would occur at the conclusion of the service.

Jon perused the rest of Little Hickman Community Church's eager assemblage. The Crunkles and Martins sat in the third row, and next to them was the entire Clayton family. Hannah, the oldest of the Claytons, had prepared a generous meal of thick chicken noodle soup, cornbread, and orange marmalade cake on Thursday night. Fancy Jenkins had been right when she'd said Hannah was a pretty little thing, but in Jon's estimation, she didn't hold a candle to Emma Browning. He gave himself another mental scolding. It was a fine fix he was in, finding himself attracted to a woman who had no

153

interest in spiritual matters. But she was here, sitting in the fifth row, and shouldn't that count for something?

Behind the Claytons were the Haywards and the Jacobs, and then there were the Fontaines, Tom Averly, and Clarence and Mary Sterling. Even the Swains had shown up with their entire clan, including little Ermaline, who still sported a cast on an arm and a leg. Somehow, Fred had figured a way to carry her in and plop her into his lap in the front row beside the Winthrops, her broken leg sprouting forth like a young tree branch.

The service went well. The singing was heartfelt, Bess's piano playing masterful, the vocal solo by Anna Johnson not exactly polished, but at least above average, and his sermon, well, he supposed satisfactory, considering he'd taken less time than usual in his preparation for it. In the beginning, he'd intended to base his message on praise and thanksgiving, but mere days ago, the Spirit told him otherwise. And so his message centered on prayer.

"Unlike Billy Wonder, God's no magician," he'd stated during the course of his message, the remark gaining him a few snickers. Billy himself had looked tickled to have his name mentioned. "Does God still perform miracles? Of course. Does He always answer prayer? Yes! Are His answers consistent with our needs? Absolutely. But are the answers He provides always the ones we're looking for?" He'd paused for effect. "Not necessarily.

"God answers prayer according to His divine will and purpose for our lives. John 16:23 says, **'Whatsoever ye shall ask the Father in my name, he will give it to you.'**

"Did you get that, folks? Praying in Jesus' name is the key. However, it's not a magic formula; it is a plea that our petitions will align themselves with Jesus' perfect desires and that we will long to pray with this mind-set.

"Thus, the aim of prayer shouldn't be that we change God's mind about any given circumstance, but that we allow God to change ours.

"In short, His will becomes our will, and whatever the outcome, we find peace and assurance that He loves us and has our best interest in mind. That should be our prayer."

Among the congregation, he'd sensed a desire to know the mind of God, as if the Lord Himself had done the talking, a most humbling thought from Jon's perspective.

As for Emma Browning, he shouldn't have worried that she'd consider his sermon too heavy or too judgmental, or even too convicting. This wasn't about keeping Emma comfortable, he told himself; this was about simple obedience to the Father.

Besides, when he'd glanced at her midway through his sermon, she'd appeared intrigued.

*****

"Miss Browning, sit by us!" young Lili Broughton called, her squealing voice loud enough to shatter glass. Emma laughed with glee at the sight of her bouncing up from her place on the picnic bench and sliding over to provide space for her to sit.

"Yes, do," invited Liza Broughton, waving her over. The entire family had perched themselves at one of the many makeshift tables built from sawhorses and long pieces of plywood and covered with tablecloths of various colors and patterns. Hard benches had been fashioned to fit each table. At first glance, the schoolyard resembled a huge patchwork quilt, augmented by myriads of Queen Anne's lace, goldenrod, and pink curled thistle growing wild in the field. It was picture perfect. Emma approached the Broughton's table, plate of food in one hand, tin cup of red punch in the other.

"Thank you, Lili," she said. "I was just wonderin' where I might sit."

A light breeze picked up, creating a problem with her skirt, but she righted the situation when she set down her plate and cup and positioned herself next to Lili.

Two crows swooped down in hopes of finding a few scraps of food on which to feast, but Ben shooed them off with a wave of his hand. "How have you been, Emma?" he asked, little Molly on his knee stealing food from his plate, her fingers red and sticky. "Those boarders keeping you on your toes?"

She took a sip of punch, dabbed her mouth with her napkin, and nodded. "I thank ya for askin'. I'm busy, all right, but I like it that way."

Liza shook her head. "My goodness, I don't know how you do it, manage a houseful of men. I can barely keep one happy." She leaned into her husband and giggled.

He plopped a kiss on the top of her head. "I do my best to make life difficult."

"Do you like ar new school?" Lili asked, eager to change the topic to something of interest. "Ain't—um—isn't it just grand? I wonder who they'll get to teach us this fall. I hope it's Mrs. Barrington. She wants the job is what I heard. Course she won't be near as good as the teacher we had last year." Lili sent her stepmother an impish grin with twinkling eyes to match, causing the dimple in her lift cheek to spring forth.

"Oh, silly Lili," Liza jibed, laughing off the compliment with an exaggerated flip of her wrist.

"It's true," Lili argued. "You were a fun teacher. Then Papa went and married you, and you couldn't be our teacher anymore. Well, I mean, I'm glad he did and all, I wanted him to, but—oh, you know what I mean."

The adults laughed, seeing her predicament.

"Actually, it was the school fire that kept her from finishing out the year, Lil," Ben clarified. "And it's this upcoming baby that's preventing her from going back to the job."

All eyes except Molly's seemed to make a natural trail to Liza's rounded belly. As was typical with most pregnant women, Liza gently rubbed the mound while a tranquil smile appeared from nowhere.

"Anyway, Lili," Emma quickly inserted, "to get back to your earlier question about how I like the new school, I think it's positively wonderful. The menfolk did a fine job." She picked up her fork and started to dig into Iris Bergen's potato salad, actually strategizing which delectable item on her plate to try next—Martha Atwater's mouthwatering strawberry concoction or Gladys Hayward's cheesy macaroni. Then there was Frances Baxter's meatball recipe, Mary Sterling's apple and raisin salad, and—

"I helped!" Lili announced, interrupting Emma's absorption with her food choices.

"Really!" Emma responded between chews. "What was your responsibility?" She took another sip of punch.

"I held lots of boards for Papa so he could cut 'em straight. Well, and Reverend Atkins stood behind me and helped hold, right, Papa? Plus, I painted some of the wall. See that spot over there under the window?"

Emma turned and strained to see the area Lili indicated with pointed finger, but instead of finding it, her eyes fell on the reverend himself. He was facing her, squeezed in tight right between a little boy and a young woman with flowing black hair! Across from him sat a middle-aged man and two more children, and the entire lot of them were laughing hysterically over something Jon had said, their boisterous mirth carrying across the yard. The new family Fancy Jenkins had mentioned, Emma silently ruled. It had to be, for she'd never seen any of them before. And from what she could tell, Fancy hadn't exaggerated when she'd clued her in about the oldest girl's fair looks. Why, even from a distance, anyone could see she was a beauty.

"See it?" Lili was asking. "I painted that blue part around the window; well, just the bottom half."

But Emma barely heard the girl, so glued was she to the new family and its dinner companion. "Yes," she muttered. "I see it."

"Ain't it nice?" A second slipped past. "Miss Browning?"

Just then, Jon lifted his head and appeared to look straight at her, after which she quickly swung around on the bench and returned to her meal. Suddenly, for no distinct reason that she could determine, Martha's strawberry concoction didn't seem nearly so appetizing.

"Nice that new family could make it today," Ben said, nodding in the direction from which she'd turned. Had he caught her watching them?

"Oh, I agree," Liza said. "How sad about their mama's passing. It does appear they're all holding up well, though. They'll find acceptance here in Little Hickman, don't you think?"

"Hickman's a friendly place, I'll grant you that," Ben answered. "In fact, I believe Jon Atkins has been sitting close enough to that oldest girl to make her feel more than welcome."

Was it her imagination, or had he intended that statement for her benefit? Even now, his laughing eyes seemed to be studying her reaction to it. Emma dug into her meal with single-minded determination, eating as though she hadn't seen food in weeks.

"Oh, you!" Liza gave her husband a playful swat. "You mind your own business, Benjamin Broughton. Jon's the cordial sort. I declare, if a snake crawled under his feet about now, he'd find a way to welcome it."

Everyone laughed, and even Emma looked up and forced a flippant chuckle, feeble as it was.

As the afternoon waned, Emma prepared to head home. In the end, she'd truly enjoyed herself, despite the glitch in her emotions when she'd discovered the preacher in the company of the lovely Clayton girl. It was such a silly thing, she brooded, caring with whom he chose to associate, as if she had the right. Ridiculous. In fact, the town council could vote to hang her before she'd ever admit to caring one iota what Jonathan Atkins did with his life or how he chose to live it.

Still, she did catch herself spying on him from time to time, watching when he took his leave from the Claytons to mingle with the crowd, noting the way he showered everyone with affection and care, and witnessing his parishioners reciprocating his devotion. When the Claytons meandered back to their wagon, Jon ran to catch up with them, coming between Mr. Clayton and the pretty girl, resting his hand on Mr. Clayton's shoulder as they walked. Once at the wagon, they gathered in a little circle, and Jon bowed his head.

My, but it took a great deal of time and energy to be a preacher, she decided.

The Broughtons took their leave after little Molly fell asleep in her father's arms and Lili had fallen and skinned her knee while chasing some other children around the schoolhouse. The Callahans, with whom Emma had enjoyed chatting, left with their two sprouts shortly after Ben and Liza. Then, one by one, other families waved and shuffled off, dishes and youngsters in tow, horses and wagons waiting under shady trees. With a contented sigh, Emma made her way to the food table to collect her chicken casserole, the bowl scraped nearly clean.

"So you're the one responsible for that tasty chicken recipe. I'd wondered if it might be yours when I saw the familiar dish." Before turning, she recognized the voice of Billy Wonder. He lifted his tall-crowned bowler hat and bowed ever so slightly.

She smiled. "You guessed right."

He was another one who'd made his rounds with the crowds today, but for different reasons than the preacher, she suspected. He looked dapper in his gray striped trousers, white shirt, Windsor tie, and charcoal gray vest, a matching frock coat hanging over one arm. By most standards, one would even consider him quite a fine-looking man—square-set jaw, wavy, dark hair, snappy, coffee-colored eyes, a pencil thin moustache, curled just so at the ends.

Gathering up her large round container and wooden spoon, she politely remarked on the lovely day and the nice community picnic, while out of the corner of one eye, she glimpsed Jon heading in their direction.

"Might I give you a lift back to the boardinghouse?" Billy hastened to ask. "I brought my wagon, as you can see." He'd parked the colorful rig and horses in plain view, for advertising purposes, no doubt, but it being Sunday and all, had refrained from selling his commodities or performing any trickery. Now, wouldn't that have created a stir with the proper Mrs. Winthrop had he tried to push his wares on the Lord's Day?

"Well, I actually rode out with the Crunkles," she replied with some hesitation. "But I told them I preferred to walk back."

His thin, dark eyebrows drew into a frown. "But I insist. The road is much too dusty for walking, and with the afternoon sun beating down as it is, why, you'll be hotter than a chimney in December by the time you reach town. I won't take no for an answer."

She thought about telling him she was accustomed to walking everywhere, but he looped his arm for her to take and waited.

"Emma," Jon broke in, still a few yards away.

In an impetuous act, she curled her arm through Mr. Wonder's then lifted her gaze to the approaching preacher. "Yes?"

"I—just wanted to say hello," he said, quite out of breath, his eyes focused briefly on the hand looped through Billy's arm. "To both of you, of course," he added, giving Mr. Wonder a quick glance. Strange how he didn't appear as eager to lavish Hickman's newest stranger with the same sociability he'd afforded everyone else that day, in particular the Claytons and that lovely young woman.

"Nice you could join us for services, Mr. Wonder."

"Why, thank you, Reverend. I surely did enjoy myself," Billy replied, shifting his weight. "Even though my legs grew weary of standing."

Jon's expression seemed less than sympathetic. "Well, that was unfortunate." He twisted his wide-brimmed hat in his hands before turning his gaze on Emma. "Thank you for coming."

He looked as well turned-out as Billy, but in a different way. Whereas Billy dressed to impress, with his expensive shirt and tie, neatly pressed pants, gold watch chain draped from his vest pocket, hair parted and greased back to perfection, Jon dressed to match his jaunty, happy-hearted self, his sandy hair flying free in the breeze. Yes, he'd worn a frock coat, matching pants, and a nice white shirt with a bowtie to services, but sometime today, he'd shed the coat and tie and rolled up his sleeves to reveal tanned arms. She liked that about him, his unconventional manner, the way he fit so comfortably in his own skin. Somehow, she couldn't picture Billy Wonder ever learning the art of relaxation, so great was his need to uphold his enchanting personality.

"No thanks needed. I came of my own accord, and I enjoyed your sermon," Emma responded.

"You did?" He looked downright pleased.

Strange how his sermon had come at a time when she'd been questioning the aspect of praying in Jesus' name. Coincidental even. And what he said had struck a chord of truth in her deepest parts, made her want to sit down one day soon and write the mysterious Grace Giles.

His eyebrows arched in a questioning manner. "And what did you like about it?"

Not prepared to comment, she took a second to respond. "I just found it interestin' is all, your idea about prayin' with the mind of God. Askin' for things in His name, but makin' His will be our will and all. I liked how you said it."

He chuckled. "It all comes straight from the Word of God, Emma. I assure you it's not some notion I concocted. Christianity requires faith because parts of Scripture can be paradoxical."

Para-what? Dared she tell him he'd stumped her with the word? Oh, she hated that he was so book-smart and she was such a—a bumblehead!

Billy cleared his throat and clucked as if thoroughly bored. "Shall we go, Miss Emma? Sun's a beatin'."

She allowed Billy to give her a nudge. "It was nice the way you honored the Winthrops," she said with a quick turn of the head. "I thought Iris was going to faint dead away from all that extra attention. Did you see how she sped up that fan on her face?"

Jon gave a hearty laugh then rocked back on his heels. "She did appear delighted, didn't she? Can't say the same for poor Clyde. Course, he understands the importance of keeping Iris happy. If Iris ain't happy, ain't nobody happy." To this, he laughed harder, and she couldn't help the emergent giggle. Billy managed a weak smile, not knowing the infamous Iris Winthrop.

"You do have a way with her." *And with that pretty Clayton girl.*

He shrugged. "Just being myself."

"Well, we'll see you back at the house."

"Oh, don't plan on me for supper. I'm invited elsewhere."

"Oh." She tried to cover her ridiculous disappointment. No doubt it was that Clayton girl who'd extended the invitation. How silly of her to have rambled on like that—as if they were on friendlier-than-normal terms. "Well then...."

"We'll talk later," he assured her.

Humph. She didn't need his assurance. Bucking up, she pointed her gaze at Billy. "Shall we go, then?"

Billy sighed with pleasure and patted her hand, and together they walked to his gaudy, gussied-up rig.

Chapter Fifteen

*M*onday was Jon's day for making his rounds, visiting the sick and elderly, and calling on as many regulars as the day would allow. It was an overcast day, clammy and warm, and in the air there was a whisper of impending rain. Even the birds seemed less eager to move about, content to sit clustered on tree branches, chirping in a nervous sort of prattle, as if they were privy to something no one else could know.

Jupiter seemed skittish and touchy, throwing his head at the slightest sound, watching his footing with fastidious vigilance. No doubt about it, a storm brewed in the distance. That's why he'd decided to visit old Ezra first. If a storm was going to hold him up later, he'd sooner be stuck with someone other than Ezra Browning again. Even the elderly widows Marley and Jacobsen, sisters who'd been living together for the past ten years, sounded more appealing. At least they kept their cupboards well stocked with plenty of sweets.

Jon steered Jupiter down the trail toward the Browning farm. When he arrived, the goat greeted him, and the chickens came running. He climbed down from his horse and tossed the reins over the repaired hitching post, then sauntered up the narrow lane, shooing the chickens out of his way. So far, vandals had left the old man alone, and it even appeared by the look of the rose bushes Liza had planted on the north side of the house that he'd managed to get out and pull a few weeds. Would wonders never cease?

He gave a light rap on the door and peered through the window, hearing Ezra's cough before noting his plodding shuffle

 164

to the door. Jon stepped back to wait for the door to swing open. When it did, he witnessed something different in the man's eyes. A hint of pleasure, a flash of jubilation? Sadly, the expression quickly died.

"You again? What I got ta do to convince ya to leave me be?" he snapped, holding open the door and stepping back, neither inviting Jon in nor chasing him away. Jon took it as a definite invitation. He grinned and walked inside. *One day at a time*, he told himself. **Inasmuch as you have done it unto the least of these, my brethren, you have done it unto me.** *So You've said, Lord.*

He stayed for an hour, most of which passed with Ezra's coughing spells and bits of conversation. While they talked, Jon straightened the little shack as best he could, washed a few dishes, and scrubbed the table and tiny counter space. This time Ezra didn't question him as to why he'd come, just watched and wheezed, stubby fingers tapping away at the table.

"Haven't seen you in town for a while, Ezra," Jon said, finishing what he could around the place and deciding to sit for a spell before heading out. His next stop would be Clarence and Mary Sterling's neat little farm. Would she have any of her oatmeal raisin cookies on hand? "You still working at the saloon?" Ever since the drunken episode on the Fourth of July, there'd been little noise from him. Were his prayers working?

"Sure. Jus' not as often, that's all. I got—I ain't—uh...."

Jon waited before deciding to prod, edging forward on his chair. "You ain't what?" he ventured to ask.

Ezra shook his head and shot Jon a mocking smile. His filthy fingers tapped a little faster. It was clear he had something to say, but whether he would was another matter. "I go when I can," he finally conceded.

"Meaning some days you're not well enough?"

A simple nod was all he got in return.

"Have you gone to see the doc? He might be able to give you something for that cough. It's a nasty one. Seems to me you've been fighting it for some time now. Might not hurt to—"

"Yer a nosy cuss, ain't ya?" Ezra blurted. But even as he said it, Jon detected a faint teasing. "I never asked ya ta start comin' out here, preacher kid. And it still ain't clear ta me why ya do."

Jon sighed. "I'm sure you won't believe this, Ezra, but I enjoy our friendship."

Refusing to acknowledge his remark, Ezra sniffed and took out a thin piece of rice paper from his front shirt pocket along with a small, round container of tobacco, then set about to create a cigarette, his fingers so shaky he could barely make them operate.

"I've heard those things aren't good for your lungs," Jon remarked, somewhat fascinated as Ezra creased the paper then laid it flat on the table. With trembling movements, he poured a dense line of tobacco down the middle of the paper.

"Too late fer worryin' about that," he said with a snort, a sad, disparaging tone sneaking in to mix with the cynical. After a hearty attempt to roll the tiny paper, it slipped from his grasp, spilling on the table. Frustrated, he shoved the entire contents to the floor with a flip of his wrist and leaned back, breathless and weary eyed. "Can't even make my own cigarettes anymore."

Lord, help me reveal Your love to this man. Somehow, help him spot Your light in the midst of his dark, hopeless world.

"You see my girl much?"

The question set Jon back. "Emma? Sure, I see her every day. She's a fine cook and good housekeeper, takes her job very seriously." *Prettiest girl in town.*

"She come out here the other day."

Jon's spine went straight as a pin. "She did? Well, that's good news, right? Did you two have a nice visit?"

Lord, I've been praying for this, praying that You'd start to mend this broken relationship before it's too late.

A huffing sound spilled out. "Don't know as you'd call it that. It weren't a social call, but she did wind up stayin' awhile. Even cleaned up my place—like old times. Wanted ta know if I knew someone who's been sendin' 'er letters. Course, I couldn't help her any. I only know one person from Chicago and it ain't the name she give me."

"What name did she give you—if I may ask?"

"Don't 'member now."

Jon's body tensed. Was someone sending her intimidating notes? He thought about the letter George Garner had asked him to deliver and remembered how she'd quickly tucked it out of sight and pretended to act as if it meant nothing. But he'd sensed there was more involved than she let on.

"Who do you know from Chicago?" Jon asked. "Maybe there's some connection between the person you know and the one who's been writing to Emma."

He shrugged and turned his mouth under. "Doubt it. Don't matter anyhow." Ezra put his hands on the chair arms and with effort pushed himself upward then shuffled to a more comfortable chair, flopping down once he reached it, his breathing labored.

"What if it does matter, Ezra? Tell me who you know from Chicago."

When it appeared the old guy was about to fall asleep, Jon stood and strode across the room. "Ezra?" he asked, bending closer despite his stench. "Who do you know?" But a fresh coughing spell kept Ezra from answering. Helpless, Jon took a step back and waited for the coughing to subside, wincing at the sight of blood on Ezra's collar.

When it finally did clear up, Ezra took a labored breath and laid his head against the back of the chair again. "Edith," he muttered.

"Edith," Jon repeated. "Who's that?"

But it was like talking to a corpse the way the fellow had settled in for his nap.

On the ride to the Sterling farm, Jon pondered just who this Edith person might be. Could she be an old acquaintance from Ezra's past, a distant cousin, perhaps, someone who used to live in Little Hickman? Or was there somehow a link remaining with Lydia's family, someone vile enough to send Emma menacing notes? He recalled the time Ezra had divulged the story of his marriage to Lydia and her own parents' rejection afterward. It must have been a painful time for her.

He reined in Jupiter at the base of a hill where the little Sterling farm sat nestled amongst tall pines and rambling oaks. As usual, Clarence and Mary Sterling waited for him on the front porch, arm in arm. Some nameless emotion tugged at his heart at the sight. What would it be like to grow old with someone? He tried to envision Emma in her seventies and knew without a doubt she'd be just as lovely then as now.

Mary lifted a thin arm and waved at Jon. "Got some chicken sandwiches and a platter of fresh-baked oatmeal raisin cookies jus' waitin' to be et, Reverend," she called.

Jon dismounted and cast his gaze upward. The sky was still gray and overcast. Not much had changed in the weather

except for the eerily still air around him. In the trees overhead, not a leaf moved. Even the birds had hushed their
song. Jupiter pawed at the earth with a powerful front leg
and snorted.

"And the coffee's on, I presume," he returned, removing
his Bible from his saddlebag.

"Been percolatin' for awhile now," Clarence said.

Jon grinned and watched his steps as he headed up the
pebbled pathway.

*****

Emma hastened to remove clothespins from the line, toss
them into her apron pocket, and drop clothes, some still par-
tially damp, into the laundry basket at her feet. Black, looming
clouds promised rain, and as the wind picked up, she found
herself hurrying even faster to finish her task. Rather than
expose the clothes to driving rain, she would drape them over
her bedposts and the tub in her private bath to finish drying.

Luke stepped out on the porch. "N-n-need help, Miss
Emma?" he hollered.

"Could you carry in this basket?" she called back, thankful
for his offer. "I have just a few more things to get off the line
and then—I'll—be—finished—out—here." A heavy blast of
wind whistled around the house. Tree limbs bowed low, causing loose branches to break free and hurtle to the ground.
She ducked her head to dodge the worst of the gale. Not a half
hour ago, the air had been spookishly quiet, and now it howled
and shrieked like a rabid banshee on the loose. Miss Tabitha
meowed in protest and whizzed between Luke's legs, making
a beeline for the house, the mangy, no-name mutt Luke had
been feeding following in her wake.

169

Luke lumbered down the steps and picked up the laundry basket, darting back as fast as his awkward body would allow. Emma scampered up the stairs behind him, closing the door just as a sheet of lightning sliced across the angry, black skies, and an explosion of thunder reverberated off the walls. A second later, the skies opened up. Emma leaned against the door as if the weight of her body against it would keep them safe.

"Tarnation! What a storm." She breathed two full breaths before gathering her wits and pushing herself away from the door. "Those rascally varmints ran right past you, Luke. Where'd they go?"

They searched the kitchen and washroom for the skinny, orange feline and droopy eyed, brown mongrel, bent to look under the butcher-block table, then moved to the broom closet.

"They need to go back out," she insisted, looking around the doors, under the sink, and behind the stove, but with no luck.

"They can't hurt n-nothin'," Luke protested. "They j-just ascared."

"That may be, but we can't start lettin' them in every time we have a little storm." Little storm? This was hardly a typical summer squall, she mused, but she didn't show any mercy as the rain pummeled the windowsills. She could only imagine what it was doing to her precious flowerbeds and vegetables. "Those fleabags will start takin' us for granted." As if they didn't already. Every day, Luke saved a large portion of his meals for the critters, and now they'd come to expect it, standing on the back porch like two castaways, which, of course, they were.

Like flaming arrows, lightning bolts ripped the sky and instant thunder rattled the windows and foundation. "Land sakes!" she exclaimed, running to the window, the animals put out of her mind for the time being.

Luke came up beside her to gaze at the rain, which was practically falling horizontally now. "How will my p-p-papa get home?"

"Oh, goodness, you needn't worry about that." She put a reassuring hand on his shoulder. "This storm'll be over before you know it."

But even as she said it, she felt her confidence waning, watching her poor corn and tomato plants bend nearly to the ground, her rose bushes drowning in the waterfall coming off the roof, and more twigs ripping loose from their branches and soaring to the earth like wildly thrown darts.

"And what about M-Mr. Wonder and the p-preacher—and all the others?"

"They're all fine," she said, fighting down the tiny twinge of worry that erupted in the back of her brain, knowing that Luke had a sixth sense about such things, somehow managing to figure out before anyone else when things weren't exactly right with the world. "Come now, help me put down all the windows before this wind knocks the pictures off my walls."

Behind them, the ragtag brown dog whined and plopped himself in the doorway between the kitchen and dining room, his eyes darting nervously between Luke and Emma.

She suspected the dog and Luke shared that extra sense.

*****

Blast! He knew he should have stayed at the Sterling's a few more minutes. He could have waited out the storm with them and enjoyed another oatmeal raisin cookie and just one more cup of Mary's coffee. But Bill and Flora Jarvis were expecting

171

him and so he'd tried to stay ahead of the storm. Instead, here he was, stranded in a dark cave just west of the fork at Sugar Creek and Little Hickman Creek Roads. Jupiter was hitched to a tree situated in a cluster back on the creek bank near the bridge. It wasn't the best of situations, but at least it was better than standing in the wide-open elements taking the brunt of the driving rains. There was a single tree right next to the cave, a big oak, but he didn't feel good about hitching Jupe to one tall tree that might be a target for lightning. Hunkered down in the approximately six-by-six-foot cleft in the side of a sloped piece of earth, Jon sat against a lumpy rock wall, stretched his legs out, and thanked God that at least he was dry and shielded from the worst of the storm.

This part of Kentucky was home to dozens of caves much like the one in which Jon now found shelter. Wild animals called them home, children played in them, and the occasional outlaw had even been known to hole up in one until the coast was clear for moving on. Of course, many were much larger, big enough for walking through, and oftentimes long and winding enough to confuse even the smartest footsloggers.

Jon tried to pass the time by quoting Scripture, humming his favorite hymns, and planning the week ahead. It seemed such a waste to be sitting in a cave twiddling his thumbs, but he'd learned early on the dangers of lightning, having heard the story at least a hundred times about his Great Grandpa Martin's near-death experience with a deadly lightning bolt. Funny how the story changed with every telling, going from "It struck him smack in the middle of his back, paralyzing him for the rest of his born days," to "Got him square between the eyes, blinding him for life," to "Affected his brain somethin' fierce. That man never could get out a straight sentence after that." No matter how the story went, it had stuck with Jon as a lad, and to this day, he had a great deal of respect for electric storms.

As if Mother Nature herself had read his thoughts, she issued a bolt of lightning and a crack of thunder so loud that it shook him to the soles of his boots then echoed off the rock walls. He snapped to attention. Maybe this wasn't the time for humming, he decided, or maybe he should hum louder for distraction's sake. He thought about old Jupiter and hoped he was faring okay under that clump of trees.

The rain fell in torrents now, some blowing through the cave's mouth to form a narrow stream that ran down a slight incline and pooled around his boots. Leaning forward, he peered out the opening, glimpsed the tops of trees bending and twisting like angry giants, and tried to remember the last storm of this magnitude. A year ago, they'd had three solid days of rain that resulted in a swelling creek that rose to river proportions and knocked out the ancient bridge, even closing down the school for several days. But the winds hadn't compared to this storm's ferocious gusts.

Putting him in mind of the Independence Day's bountiful fireworks display, continuous streaks of lightning and powerful, pulsing thunder filled the skies, shaking the earth's foundation, making his heart pound and his chest constrict. "Lord Almighty," he whispered. Then he blew out little puffs of air from his clogged lungs when he realized he'd been holding his breath.

He folded his hands in his lap, an attempt to relax, but just as quickly unfolded them and got up on his knees to peer out the entrance of the cave, the cramped space not allowing him to stand. Moments ago, his watch had indicated it was mid-afternoon, but if one had only the blackish skies to go by, he'd think it was time to turn in for the night. Realizing he'd knelt in a puddle, he settled himself back against the hard wall and closed his eyes, releasing a brief shudder as chill bumps rose on his arms.

No point in trying to escape this dark hole until the rain slows, he told himself, which, by the look of things, could be awhile. He tried to think about next Sunday's sermon, his mind wandering to yesterday's instead, and then the well-attended picnic, and then to Emma. Despite his current circumstances, he felt a smile break through. She'd actually had some kind words to say about his message, a miracle in itself.

Just then, an ear-splitting peal of thunder resounded overhead, jerking him out of his thoughts, as lightning struck the tree closest to the cave, its immense trunk rupturing and plowing into the earth with such vehemence he thought he might be witnessing the end of time itself. The ground quaked as dirt and rock came loose from the cave's wall, pinging off his arms, legs, and face.

Death by suffocation didn't appeal to him, so with little forethought he jumped to his feet, thinking to get out before the place completely collapsed, but in suddenly standing, he smacked his head hard on a razor-sharp, jagged edge of rock hanging from the low ceiling. Searing pain surged from the fresh gash, first stunning him, then hurtling him backward until he stumbled in a heap against a cold, hard wall. Something warm and wet made a fast trail down his forehead. Rain? No, for when the wetness seeped into the corner of his mouth, he tasted blood, and lots of it. As quickly as possible, he searched his pockets for a handkerchief, but finding none, ripped off a big section of his shirt and pressed it against the wound, wincing with discomfort.

Disoriented, he put his shoulders to the wall and, breathing deeply, blinked once, twice, three times, as he sought to gather his wits and stop the bleeding, noting in that instant how dark his surroundings had grown.

Another burst of thunder erupted, but the flash of lightning that went with it seemed less luminous. In fact, only a glimpse shone through a tiny crack straight ahead of him. What in the world? In haste, he crawled across the space to investigate, and that's when he made his discovery.

The monstrous tree so brutally struck mere seconds ago had fallen like a dead giant and firmly planted its trunk directly in front of the cave's entrance, making it quite impossible to escape.

It was then he realized with chagrin that unless someone missed him and came looking for him, he was sitting in his own grave.

Chapter Sixteen

*E*mma tossed and turned in her bed, staring at the blank ceiling one minute and the wall the next, then gazing out the window where the rain still fell in sheets; the thunder, although now distant, still roared and rumbled like a fiercely disgruntled lion. It was deathly hot in her room, but opening the window much more than a crack would let in the rain, and she wasn't sure which was worse, lying in a pool of sweat or allowing the rain to pool on her floor.

Luke had asked at least a dozen times after supper what had happened to the preacher. "No idea, boy," his father had replied. "He's probably holed up somewheres, waitin' out the storm. Don't worry about it."

But a minute later, he'd turned his question on Emma. "Y-you think he's okay?"

"Of course," had been her pat reply, not wanting to think about it.

"W-where you think he is?" he'd asked Mr. Wonder.

The man had laid down his newspaper and shrugged his shoulders. "I haven't the faintest idea, son, but I'm sure he's fine. Probably someone from the parish has him tucked safe away. He's a friendly sort, that man." Clearing his throat, he'd added, "Surprised some woman hasn't snagged him up by now." With that, his eyes had traveled straight to Emma, as if to gauge her reaction. She'd promptly dropped her chin and returned to her mending, still irritated with herself for offering the little guest room off the parlor to

Billy for the night. Was he now going to assume it was his for the taking? Well, no point in worrying over that till the sun returned.

After Mr. Newman had ushered Luke to their room, the others had breathed a sigh. "That boy's worried plenty about the preacher," Charley said.

"You think he's okay?" Wes asked.

The room went silent. The no-name dog lifted his head from his napping spot and looked from one to the other. Sometime during the course of the evening everyone had come to accept the dog's presence, and so there he was, lying in the center of the room on the braided rug, acting as if he owned the place and everyone in it. As for Miss Tabitha, she hadn't shown her face to anyone.

"I'll be jig-swiggered if I know!" Gid answered. "Mr. Wonder's prob'ly right. Someone from the church talked 'im into stayin' in their guest quarters."

Wes pushed up from his chair and stretched. "You're probably right, but if he ain't back by mornin', we should probably investigate."

The lot of them nodded their heads then retreated to their rooms one by one, leaving Emma alone with her thoughts.

Now, hours later, she still couldn't sleep, the battering rain keeping her from it.

Jonathan Atkins, where in tarnation are you and what are you doin' to me?

"Lord, keep 'im safe wherever he is. Please."

It was the first time she'd prayed as an adult and, holy hog's tooth, if she didn't feel a sort of peace come over her, after which she fell into a semi-restful sleep.

*****

It was his own moaning that woke him hours later, utter blackness preventing him from seeing his hand in front of his face. In fact, for a second he feared his head wound had left him blind; then he remembered the huge tree that blocked his light source. Far-off thunder indicated the storm persisted, just not as close. Throat parched, he tried to swallow but found it hard to work up the saliva.

His entire body ached, his back from the fall he'd taken, his shoulders from lying on the hard floor, his hip, which had taken the brunt of his backward fall, and the gash on his head, from which he still felt blood oozing. Now he had dizziness to add to the mix, forcing him to lie still lest he lose what little remained in his gut.

"Lord God, I'm coming to You as Your child," he whispered into the dark, his voice blending with the pelting rains. "As You know, there is a hulking tree blocking this cave's passage, and it is beyond me how I'm ever going to escape. So I'm asking You, Father, to intervene, to send someone to get me out of here. Also, if Jupiter is suffering in any way, would you please help him with his circumstance or put him out of his misery?"

As if he needed reminding that he hadn't eaten a thing since Mary Sterling's oatmeal raisin cookies earlier that day, his stomach growled. He'd heard once that when a man starved to death, his hunger pangs eventually subsided. Therefore, the fact he was hungry was a good thing, he supposed.

He hoped to remain hungry until someone found him.

*****

Emma banged around in the kitchen, her mood less than chipper. Rain still drizzled from a murky sky, with only a hint of a sunrise in the east.

Jonathan had not come home last night. She knew it was silly to fret. After all, she'd never worried one jot about him before he'd moved under her roof, had barely let him cross her mind—and hadn't he fared just fine without her? Now here she was stewing over his safety!

She flipped an egg, intending to keep the yoke intact, but accidentally breaking it, broke the lot of them and quickly added milk and salt and pepper, scrambling the whole mess together. She mopped her sweaty brow with the corner of her apron and continued fuming. No wonder she'd dragged her feet in giving Jon Atkins room and board. Something had told her early on that giving him a room could jeopardize her heart, and she'd been right. Not that she'd ever let on to anyone, him least of all, but there it was just the same—out in the open—no matter how she looked at it. Oh, what a fix!

"Smells good," said Wes Clayton, passing by the kitchen door. He and Charley Connors were the only boarders living on the main floor, across the hall from the kitchen, a tiny washroom separating their small rooms. Quiet, sensitive, even considerate to those who knew him, Wes sometimes came across to those who didn't as cold, eccentric, and hard. For the most part, she related well to him, probably because she believed most viewed her in the same way they did Mr. Clayton, unapproachable if not impenetrable. In some ways, they shared a kinship. She suspected one reason Wes had never married was the barrier he put up keeping most everybody out except for those he sincerely trusted. She'd often wondered what it was that held him at arm's length, but then, everyone carried secrets, didn't they? She of all people understood secrets.

Was that how the preacher saw her, then? Cold, hard, distant? She gave her head a shake and went back to her eggs.

"Did he come home in the night?" Wes asked, still tucking in his work shirt. She scowled. Did he have no scruples, tucking in his shirt in her company?

"What? Who?" she asked, playing dumb.

Wes came up beside her, still adjusting himself. He smelled of sawdust, having worn the same pair of coveralls to the sawmill for at least two solid weeks now without washing them. "Don't think you're foolin' me, little lady. I know you were listenin' for the preacher's return." She felt her cheeks go red, and it wasn't from her cookstove. He chuckled to himself then ambled to the window. "I 'spect he's fine, but we'll go lookin' jus' the same. I'll run over to the sheriff's office, see if he's heard anythin'." There was a pause while he took a deep, audible breath. "Appears to be lettin' up out there. Maybe the sun'll pop out later."

She kept her eyes glued to the eggs. "What about the sawmill? Ain't you goin' to work today?" Try as she might to avoid it, her language sometimes slipped when conversing with her boarders, except for the cursing aspect. That she wouldn't stoop to—unless one counted the silent, in-the-head-only kind.

"Naw. I'll stop by and tell Grady 'bout the situation. 'Spect others'll want to help look—unless the feller gets back here before we form a search party."

A vexing notion kept pulling at the corners of her mind. What if something was terribly wrong? Jon didn't strike her as the type who would hole up at someone else's place for the night, regardless of the weather, hence creating undue worry in the town. He was kind and generous, always putting the concern of others ahead of his own.

It was the Christmas season. Someone had dropped a huge box of secondhand clothes off at the school, woolen caps, coats, freshly darned socks, knitted mittens, sweaters, scarves, and whatnot. The students gathered around the big wooden crate with eye-popping excitement, snatching up items from the box and holding them up for size, some greedier than others, pushing and shoving to paw through the collection.

"Now, now, let us be courteous to one another," Mr. Thurston instructed, trying to regain control of the riotous bunch. Big boys pushed the smaller ones aside in their haste to find something suitable.

Emma lagged back, not wanting to appear overanxious, even though she longed to get her hands on the velvety, soft-blue scarf lying at the top of the heap. Beside her, Jon Atkins also lagged. He was always like that, never pushy or audacious, unless it was to tease or pull at some girl's pigtail. He did so love to pester the girls, and they loved it right back. She watched him out of the corner of her eye.

"Get on up there, Emma," he whispered. "I see somethin' in that box that'd look mighty pretty around your neck. Bet it'd look nice next to your blue eyes."

She felt the blush of her cheeks and hoped he wouldn't notice, but still she didn't shove through the crowd. In one fell swoop, he sought an opening and reached his arm through it, snatching up the velvet scarf and handing it to her like it was some precious offering.

Amazed that he'd managed the maneuver, she barely eked out a thank-you. Holding the soft cloth to her cheek, she said, "You best get yourself somethin' 'fore it all gets took."

"Naw, I don't need anythin'," he replied, his smile lingering on her. "I get a bigger thrill from watchin' everybody else."

"Loosen up, Miss Emma," Wes said, snatching her out of her childhood remembrance. "Feller's probably on his way home as we speak."

But as Wes walked into the dining room to take his usual seat at the table, she sensed a worried tone in his voice.

By late-morning, Will Murdock and an assemblage of men, Wes Clayton and Elliott and Luke Newman among the dozen or so, headed out of town in search of the preacher, who was now considered officially missing. Will had ridden out to several homes earlier and managed to track down where he'd last been seen—Clarence and Mary Sterling's place. As far as they knew, he had been going to Bill and Flora Jarvis's next, but Will said he'd never made it to the Jarvis farm.

According to the Sterlings, Jon had paid a call on Ezra Browning before arriving at their place, so Will went to see Ezra on the chance that Jon had backtracked, but Ezra said he hadn't seen the preacher kid, as he referred to him, but once, and that was yesterday morning. Of course, Will said it was hard to follow the man's speech since his persistent cough interrupted every other word. Emma flinched at the remark. She'd noticed the cough herself and wondered what was caus-ing it. She made up her mind that while the men were gone today, she would go talk to Doc.

But Doc wasn't in his office when she arrived there shortly after 2 p.m., umbrella shielding her from the constant drizzle. What she did find was a note tacked to his door indicating he was out making calls and wouldn't return till early evening. She toyed with the idea of renting another horse and riding out to her father's place. But what excuse would she give for paying him another call? It wasn't as if she'd made a habit of checking on him. Heaven knew it made little difference to him if she showed up on his doorstep, and the only time he'd ever called on her was when he'd been too drunk to find his own way home. She tossed the notion aside and set off across the street to the post office.

George Garner greeted her with his usual friendly smile. At the door, she shook the rain off her umbrella as best she could before entering. "Afternoon," she said, returning the smile.

"You got another of them notes from Chicago," he announced right off. "It's in your mail slot."

Emma walked straight to her box and removed her mail. "Thanks."

"You're mighty popular with that Grace person. She an old friend from way back? I don't recall the Giles name bein' from around Hickman."

Not in the mood for his questions, she made up something on the spot while she perused her mail—a couple of advertisements, another postcard from Mr. Dreyfus, and the missive from Grace Giles. "She's been inquiring about my boarding-house," she answered, which was an out-and-out lie. "Wants to know how to start up one of her own in Chicago. I'm not sure how she come across my name. I've yet to write back to her, but I 'spect I will one of these days." At least that much was true. With every letter she received, her interest in Grace Giles mounted, not to mention new questions pertaining to the Scripture she'd been reading.

When she glanced up to observe his reaction, a suspicious line showed up at the corners of his mouth. "She's awful persistent, ain't she?"

The door opened and in walked Iris Bergen and her boy, Thomas. Emma breathed a sigh of relief to be let off the hook. "Afternoon, Mrs. Bergen," she greeted. "And Thomas, look at you. I believe you've grown at least half a foot in the last year." The way his pants came nearly to his calves, showing a good share of his boots, proved her point.

The boy grinned and stretched to his full height. "I'm almost taller than my maw," he announced.

Emma smiled. "I can see that."

Without further ado, the lad wandered over to the "wanted" posters, as most children were prone to do. She supposed it was fascinating reading to some, although she herself had never spent any time poring over the seedy looking characters who'd managed to dodge the law.

"Nice to see you, Miss Browning. Any word on the preacher yet?"

"Not that I know of," Emma replied, trying to put the matter out of her mind. The more she dwelt on the idea of Jon Atkins going missing, the deeper her heart sank.

"What about the preacher?" George asked.

"You ain't heard?" Mrs. Bergen asked, mouth agape. "He's missin'."

George frowned. "Missin' what?"

Iris looked perturbed. "*He's* missing, silly! Here I thought you kept abreast of all the news. How'd you miss out on that tidbit?"

"Nobody tol' me nothin'. He get waylaid in this storm?"

"No one seems to know," she answered. "There's a bunch of men out lookin' for 'im now."

George Garner scratched his head and looked genuinely concerned. "Well, I'll be. I hope he's all right. A feller can't go long without food and water."

Did he have to mention that? Emma's stomach turned over as she made her way to the door, mail tucked away in her pocket.

"Good day, Miss Emma," George called.

Without turning, she waved and walked out into the soggy air.

*****

Jon's craving for water grew with every minute. He'd managed to stick his hand through a tiny opening to get a bit of moisture, but had skinned his wrist badly in the process. Only glimpses of light shone through the cave's opening, the massive tree trunk completely covering the mouth, leafy branches protruding through the hole, making it impossible to see out. Hoping to find moisture on some leaves, he'd spent the morning breaking off branches, but his efforts had gotten him nowhere. Even the floor of the cave had dried up, and what hadn't, had turned to mud.

Throughout the course of the morning and early afternoon he'd taken to hollering, "Help!" thankful that the earlier dizziness had subsided, but then realized it was a waste of precious energy. Outside, the only sounds he heard were the persistent drizzle of rain and a light breeze. He'd called and whistled for Jupiter but had gotten nothing in response. The silence had him worried that his horse had been injured in the storm, might even be lying dead or suffering beneath the tree to which he'd been tied. For the umpteenth time he berated himself for his actions. The creature would have fared much better had he let him go free. Of course, he hadn't expected to spend the night in this bleak and barren hole in the side of a cliff.

Propped against a wall, Jon stretched stiff, unyielding muscles and heard an unexpected groan escape his mouth when he felt pain in muscles he didn't know he had. He'd always considered himself a strong man. Despite the fact that he wasn't a farmer, and wasn't accustomed to excessive labor, for the most part he kept himself busy and active. However, this predicament had him doubting his own strength.

"Lord," he prayed, "I've never confronted anything quite like this and, frankly, I'm baffled. Please give me wisdom as to what my next steps should be." Waiting for an instant answer from the heavens, he slumped back in frustration when it didn't come. What did he expect? That God would roll the trunk away from the opening just as He'd removed the stone from Jesus' tomb? Plainly put, he was at God's mercy.

He had spent a good share of his young life teaching others about learning to trust in a loving God despite their circumstances and obeying His call no matter where it led. Now here he was stuck in a cave, helpless to do a thing about it, and beginning to fear for his life. He felt his trust dwindling, his faith crumbling like a dried-up cookie. What if no one came? It would be easy for anyone to see that lightning had struck the tree, causing it to fall, but who could possibly know it blocked the entrance to a tiny cave? There were so many of these little holes in the side of a steep, rocky bluff. Few would suspect one was right behind a huge, fallen tree. Oh, he had no doubt folks would eventually locate him, but would it be his decaying body they came across or, worse, his skeleton?

In retrospect, it had been foolish to take refuge in the cleft of a rock. He should have pressed on to the Jarvis farm regardless of the lightning and holed up there till the storm let up. Bill would have fed and watered Jupiter and put him in his barn for the night. Flora would have offered him a warm supper and a spare bed. Though he wasn't accustomed to putting folks out, or accepting any kind of charity, for that matter, this might very well have been the exception. In short, he had no one to blame but his own cowardly self.

For reasons he couldn't explain, he thought about the time his father had caught him hiding out in the barn, avoiding certain punishment for failing to finish his chores before the supper hour.

"What you doin' hidin' behind that hay bale, boy, like you was some kind of gutless, yellow-bellied turkey? Come out here and face me like a man!"

Face him like a man? But he was only ten. Shoot, he still had trouble stretching tall enough to heave one bale onto the wagon, let alone a dozen or more. His muscles ached, his back and shoulders pained him, and his throat was parched. He'd only stopped for a minute's break. Was that so bad?

In his hand, Luther Atkins held a bottle of whiskey. He always had his ale close by. Jon shook like a leaf. He was a coward when it came to facing his father, and he hated that facet of his personality. Someday he would be big enough to stand up to him—and then he would tell him!

"Ain't I tol' you to get them bales loaded on that wagon?" Pa railed. "Why you draggin' yore feet? You been daydreamin'?"

"N-no, sir," he replied, feeling sheepish.

When Jon didn't move, his father reached down and yanked him up by the sleeve, ripping it free of its seam so that a gaping tear in the fabric exposed his arm to the chilly air. He flinched and shivered, gasping in pain when his father snagged hold of his arm as if trying to squeeze the blood from it.

"Don't hurt the boy," his mother said from the barn door. "He ain't done nothin' wrong." Despite her frail demeanor, his ma had always done her best to defend her only child, even though it did little good.

"No? What's he done right?" Luther laughed at his own words, thinking them funny, and spit on the dirt floor. His breath reeked of alcohol. Jon turned his head to avoid the worst of the stench, but he feared trying to wrench himself free of his pa's firm hold.

When his mother approached, Jon spoke up. "Ma, go back in the house. He'll hurt you."

"Better me than you, son," she said.

At this, his father spat and laughed again. "You askin' fer trouble, woman?" To him it was a game, a sick sport, this constant battle for control.

"Ma," Jon begged.

"Let 'im go," she pressed.

The closer she came, the louder Jon's heart pounded. He could handle this, he told himself. He didn't need his mother getting hurt on his behalf, and all because he'd grown lazy and decided to sit a spell.

Oh, if only he were stronger, taller, older—braver.

It felt good to have the pressure on his arm released when his father flung him aside, but seeing his mother hit the wall and slide to the floor from one solid blow turned his relief into instant rage. Oh, he wanted to jump on his pa's back and beat him with something hard and sharp and heavy, but instead, he watched the man saunter out of the barn, an evil smile of victory on his face, as if he'd just accomplished a major feat.

And it wasn't until his father disappeared from sight that Jon finally ran to his mother's side.

Jon closed his eyes against the senseless, irrelevant memory; he thought he even imagined a certain wetness building up behind his eyelids. Where had the childhood reminiscence come from—and why did it pop out at him now?

Shoot, Lord, I can't even think straight anymore.

Chapter Seventeen

After supper, Emma seated herself in a wicker chair on the front porch, waiting for her first glimpse of the search party. How long could it take a band of capable men to locate one man gone missing? Frustration made her jump to her feet to pace the length of the sprawling porch.

"Yer as fidgety as a pack o' cats in a gunny sack," said Gideon. "Yer makin' me nervous."

He, Harland, and Charley all sat smoking their cigarettes, Harland on the top step, Charley in the swing, and Gideon reclining in the ancient rocker. As soon as someone's cigarette smoked itself out, he rolled another. The porch was becoming a regular chimney, but since everyone's nerves were on edge, Emma bit back the itch to complain.

Billy Wonder pushed open the screen door, walked over to the chair Emma had vacated, and plopped himself into it. Apparently, he planned to use the guest room another night despite the orange sky in the west that promised a clear night. Emma decided to let the matter slide for now. "Any sign of them?"

"Nothin'," said Harland, blowing out a smoke ring then pulling a hand down his haggard face.

"Shouldn't be long now," Billy replied, his voice too chipper in Emma's opinion. "I still say he's visitin' someone, maybe not even acquaintances of the church. Could be hiding out in somebody's barn for all we know."

Gideon heaved an indignant sigh. "If that were the case,

he'd be home by now. Look at the sky, Wonder. Matter of fact, weather's clearin' real nice like."

Billy looked out at the still soggy treetops, gave his head a tiny shake, and remarked, "Anybody go out to that new family's house, the Claytons? Might be the minister decided to pay a call on that pretty young lady and wound up stayin' a spell."

For no reason she could think of, Emma's neck stiffened. "When the sheriff rode back with a report this afternoon, he said they'd checked with every parishioner, including the Claytons. No one's seen him," she replied, trying for all she was worth to keep the tartness out of her tone.

In the swing, Charley Connors pushed off with one foot and said, "Tom Averly discovered the reverend's horse out at his place. Went straight back to his old homestead, that horse did, a big ole branch draggin' behind him stuck to his bridle. Guess he was bearin' a few scratch marks, too. Makes one wonder if the preacher ain't throwed off somewheres in a ditch. I swear that thunder was loud enough to spook a stiff corpse in a bone yard. Plenty o' trees got struck by lightnin' out there is what I hear. I 'spect he could be lyin' under one of 'em."

The more the men speculated the sicker Emma felt. What was she doing listening to them when everything was gloom and doom? It was her porch. She had half a mind to send them all off to the saloon to drink their cares away. Instead, she turned to go inside. Her hand was on the doorknob when Harland stood and gazed down Main Street.

"Looks like they's finally comin' in," he announced. "Don't see no preacher, though."

Whirling on her heel, she ran down the steps to greet the search party then quickly halted at the bottom. There wasn't a one of them who looked jubilant. Her heart sank to her toes.

*****

So thirsty. Jon rubbed his tongue over the roof of his mouth and found it dry as cotton, his lips cracked and sore. He was burning up, but couldn't say if it was due to fever or the beastly hot temperature in the little cave. He swiped at his face with his sleeve and groaned. It seemed every muscle in his body ached as he drifted in and out of a restless stupor, his body quivering out of control.

He wasn't at death's door; of that, he was certain. No, in situations such as this, death tended to take its sweet time, but the question of how long a man could go without water did harass his half-witted mind. Was it three days or longer? The thought of waiting another day made his throat constrict, his heart jump erratically.

Confusing thoughts and images kept surfacing, his father's weather-beaten, hard-lined face evolving into that of Ezra Browning, then emerging into some kind of hairy varmint with black, stir-crazy eyes. He shuddered and fought down a queasy stomach.

Emma's face sprang up next, like a budding tulip just opening on a warm May morning, a refreshing sight in comparison. He reached up to cup her chin, but she shrank back.

Be Jesus to Ezra came the clear thought in the midst of all the fuzzy ones.

"Lord?" he asked.

The righteous cry, and the Lord heareth, and delivereth them out of all their troubles.

He recognized the words of the psalmist. "Lord," he managed in a hoarse voice. "If You bring me out of this black place, I promise to do all I can to bring Ezra to You."

191

My son, I am with you. I will never leave you or forsake you.

The last thing he remembered as he drifted off to sleep was the sweet, seductive song of a Kentucky bluebird.

*****

Dear Grace Giles,

I have no idea who you are or why you insist on writing to me, but I'll have to admit I'm curious, and yes yore letters have all reached me far as I know.

Emma sat and stared at the paper before her. Oh, what she wouldn't give for fine handwriting, the kind that swept across the paper with flare and elegance—the way that Grace Giles' penscript flowed so artfully. But, alas, hers was nothing more than chicken scratch, a mere scrawl of words, and probably misspelled ones, at that. *Far as I know?* Was that correct grammar? She debated drawing a line through it but decided that would only make matters worse.

It wasn't that she hadn't been a good student while in school; she'd done well with all three of her teachers. But English hadn't been her favorite subject or her easiest. To this day, she lacked confidence when it came to speaking and writing correctly, and why wouldn't she, surrounded as she was by a band of uncouth characters—save Jonathan Atkins, of course? It amazed her how he'd grown up in Little Hickman Creek, as everyone else had, but seemed made from different cloth. Had college and seminary done that to him, taught him the art of refinement and class? He was a finespun gentleman if ever there was one, but not the stuffy, stiff-necked type. No, Jonathan had a kind manner about him, the sort that fairly drew folks in, like a lure at the end of a fishhook.

Jonathan. Just as quickly as his face surfaced, she pushed it back. She mustn't think about him now, for whenever she did she thought the worst, imagined him lying under a log somewhere in deep suffering or, worse, dead.

Her eyes refocused on the task at hand, composing a letter to Grace Giles without sounding like a dolt. She turned the wick on her kerosene lamp up a notch, glanced at her clock, which revealed the midnight hour, and picked up her Lewis Waterman fountain pen, rolling it around between her fingers before putting it to the paper once again.

> *You'll be happy to know I been reading the Bible that Clara Abbott give to me. Was Clara a friend of yours? She was my closest friend, and when she died, I guess you'd say a part of me went with her.*
>
> *I read the entire contents of the book of John as you told me to do. And now I'll write down the questions that come to my head after reading it.*
>
> *1. Do you think Jesus really did all those miracles?*
>
> *2. Does He still do miracles today?*
>
> *3. Why did He have to die for our sins?*
>
> *4. How does a person forgive someone else for the wrong things he done to hurt her?*
>
> *5. How is it that you know about my father?*
>
> *6. Do you know where he came from, becus he wasn't ever clear on that?*
>
> *7.*

She quickly scratched out the number seven, figuring that she'd already given the woman plenty of things to ponder on. Then she reread what she'd written and felt a developing frown. Oh, how could she send out something so sloppily written, and with scratch marks, to boot? Shouldn't an adult like her be better able to compose a decent missive?

She looked at the one she'd received from Grace that day and compared the script.

My Dear Emma,

I worry that I have not yet heard from you. I trust that you are well and that you've had a chance to read the gospel of John. It is such a wonderful book about the life of Christ and His purpose in coming to earth—to bring us salvation. Can you imagine loving someone so much that you would freely sacrifice your life for him? Well, Jesus did that for the sin of the entire world.

Have you had a chance to visit your father? How are you finding him these days? How is his health faring? Has anything changed with regard to your relationship with him? Please remember I am praying daily for both of you.

Would you kindly write me and tell me if you have been receiving my letters? Also, do let me know if my letters bore you to high heaven.

I am your friend, Emma, and I long to talk to you about certain matters, but I do not wish to push too much. I anxiously await a letter from you.

Do feel free to ask me whatever you wish with regard to your Bible reading—and anything else.

I remain, yours truly,
Grace Giles

Emma reread the letter twice, then reread her own, finally deciding to scribble a hasty closing, fold it up, and send it regardless of its probable errors. After all, she wasn't out to impress Grace Giles...whoever she was.

After addressing the envelope, she prepared to seal it shut, then on a whim took it back out and hastily added a postscript.

> *P.S. The postmaster is most nosy about your letters, so I fear*
> *I lied and told him you were asking about starting up yore*
> *own boardinghouse in Chicago. If it wouldn't be too much*
> *trouble, could you ask me a question or two about my bis-*
> *ness? I think that would ease my conchense.*

While lying in bed later, she squeezed her eyes shut and tried her hand at another prayer.

"Dear Lord," she whispered into the night. "If You're out there, would You please help the men find Jon tomorrow? They're startin' out early after a good breakfast, Lord, and this time I've packed them plenty more food for nourishment, so they can ride until they find him. I s'pose I ask a lot, Lord, for one who's not accustomed to talking much to You, but one more thing...it would sure help a great deal if You'd show them just where to look this time. Seems to me, they haven't done all that well in using their own resources. Might You lend them Your eyes and Your wisdom?"

She stared at the ceiling, pulling her sheet up under her chin, thankful that the air wafting across her room tonight was cooler. "And one more thing, Lord." She licked her lips and thought on her words. "Is there any way I can ever forgive my pa? If there is, maybe You could show me how that would work."

Shadows from the distant streetlights Luke had lit that evening danced on her walls. She watched them flash and flicker until at last her eyes grew heavy.

"Amen." It was her second prayer in the last twenty-four hours.

*****

Jon lifted his arm, which felt about as heavy as a boulder, and tried to read his wristwatch, but no matter his efforts, the numbers and hands refused to focus. He knew his body was burning with fever, but there was little he could do to alleviate the problem. Even the muddy floor where he lay, knees propped up for lack of space, didn't appease his hot, dry skin.

The oven-like cave was stuffy, which he found interesting. Shouldn't it be damp and cool, stuck as it was in the cleft of a rock? Or was it the lack of fresh air in this rotten hole that made him so uncomfortable? Through a few tiny openings, he caught a glimpse of blue sky, caught the occasional ray of sunlight. What day was it? No longer could he form a clear thought, much less figure out something as complicated as the day of the week. Besides, what difference did it make?

"Abide with me...fast...falls the eventide. The darkness deepens—Lord, with...me...abide."

He barely eked out the words of the hymn, but what he managed brought comfort, so he continued.

"When other helpers...fail...and comforts flee, help of—the helpless, oh...abide...with...me."

Breathless, he fell into another erratic sleep.

*****

"Check this out. It's another of them fallen trees. This'n is huge. Anyone see anything suspicious, tracks maybe?"

 196

"I don't see anything, Will. Looks like it just come down in the storm like so many other trees around here. I tell you that was some powerful storm."

"There's a mound behind that downed tree, Ben. Think there could be another one of them hidden caves back in there?"

"As far as I know, we've checked every last one of 'em in these parts."

It was like pushing his way through dense fog to get to the other side, a heavy blanket of lead keeping Jon from moving, his eyes from opening to mere slits.

"H-here," he finally managed through a croaky voice. "In here."

"Nope, don't see a thing," someone said. Ben Broughton? "We best move on. Time's a wasting."

"Here," Jon screeched again, louder this time, determined to make his unused voice heard.

"You hear somethin'?" someone said. Rocky? A horse whinnied and stomped.

Oh, blessed Lord! I once was lost, but now am found, was blind, but now I see! "In—here," he repeated, the very notion that they were out there giving him strength.

"What in the...?" He heard the clatter of men dismounting, boots hitting the earth, and the approach of thumping feet. "Thanks be to God! You in there, Jon? You all right? Sound the gun, Will!" Rocky demanded.

Before Jon formed his next words, a round of gunfire blasted through the air, echoing off the hills and beyond.

"Reverend, how are you?" This from Will Murdock. "You hurt anywhere?"

"I'm—fine. One question though."

"What's that, Jon?" they all asked in unison. Jon pictured

197

them hunkered down on the other side of the tree, hanging on to his every word.

"What—took—you so long?"

*****

"They found him! Preacher's been found. He's alive!"

Emma heard the dish hit the floor and shatter into a thousand pieces before her brain transmitted the message that she'd dropped it. Picking up her skirts, she stepped over the broken mess and ran to look outside to see who was shouting. Next came the banging on her front door.

"Miss Browning, Miss Browning!" Peeking through the screen door was Gus Humphrey, the stock boy who worked at Eldred Johansson's Mercantile.

"Why, Gus, what can I do for you?"

"Doc sent me. He says he'll be needin' your guest room for the preacher. He don't want 'im goin' up and down them stairs to his room jus' yet. Doc says his office bed's bein' occupied by that old feller, Clarence Hazelton."

"Of course, of course, that's fine. Come in, Gus. Tell me what you know about the preacher." Like an anxious schoolchild eager to hear the news of whether she'd won first prize for the sack race, she bit her lip and held her breath.

She pushed open the door, but the boy remained firmly planted. "Cain't. I gots to ride back out to deliver some tools to the men. The preacher's been stuck in a cave about a half a mile off Sugar Creek Road. A humongous tree fell flat across the front of the cave. Men is sawing their way through it now to make way for 'im to escape."

"A cave? Is he—all right?"

"Doc says he's bad hurt on the head, gots a high fever too.

Called it de-de-dration 'er somethin'. That an' heatstroke and I don't know what all."

"Dehydration? Heatstroke?" she mumbled. "He'll be needing lots of fluids."

"After I drop off them tools Mr. Johansson rounded up, I gotta ride out to ol' Reverend Miller's place."

"Reverend Miller?"

"Mrs. Winthrop says someone's got to preach the sermon Sunday, and it won't be Reverend Atkins."

"Oh."

Strange, it wouldn't have occurred to her to worry about such formalities at a time like this, but leave it to the school board president and self-appointed general governing body of all of Little Hickman Creek to keep things running smoothly.

She watched the lad take off running across the street. Here and there, folks gathered in clusters, talking excitedly. Lucy Fontaine lifted a hand from one such cluster and waved at Emma, a baby on her hip.

"Oh, Miss Emma, ain't it grand news?" she hollered loud enough to shatter the new front windowpane at Borden's Bakery, the one on which they'd just painted the words

What a **BARGAIN!**
Fresh Donuts and a Cup of Coffee = Just 10¢ for BOTH
Hurry on over before the donuts dry out!

Every word held a different color of the rainbow, forcing passersby to stop by for a gander at the fancy letter work. And if one did that, why, the fine aroma of delectable baked goods wooed the "victim" the rest of way inside.

"Emma, you hear me? They found the preacher. Ain't it grand?" Lucy called again.

"I just heard the news," she returned, stepping out on her porch. "It is indeed a great relief."

"An answer to prayer is what it is," Lucy exclaimed. "There's some of us been prayin' 'round the clock. Praises be to Jesus!"

Well, then, there was her answer. "Yes, praises!" she exclaimed, unsure of the proper protocol for praising the Lord in public when one didn't profess to be a Christian.

Overhead, the jays and robins had some sort of jubilant chorus going between them. Emma walked back inside with a smile on her face.

"He's safe," she whispered, closing the door and leaning against it, aware that a tear drifted down her cheek. "Thank You, Lord."

This talking to the Lord business was becoming a regular habit.

*****

Jon practiced patience while the men worked, relishing in the canteen of water passed to him by Tom Averly through a small opening.

"Don't drink too much or too fast, Reverend," Doc Randolph instructed. "Unless you want it all comin' back up on ya. How's that head?"

"Shouldn't be long now, Jon," said Rocky, who seemed to be at one of the hacksaws now. One by one, they each took turns penetrating the mile-wide tree trunk, demanding every ounce of human strength. Grady Swanson had lent his best tools for grinding through the massive trunk, but even so, it took time and energy.

"When you got a weakling like Rocky Callahan at the saw, it slows down progress," said Ben. A band of laughter and lighthearted jeering followed the remark as the chiseling and sawing went on.

When there was a lull in the laughter and work, Tom Averly bent close to the opening. "Your horse is as good as new, Jon. Walked right up to his stall and helped hisself to some dried-up seed. Took me a day ta even realize he was in there. Sustained a couple of scratches, but for the most part he come through the ordeal jus' fine. Looked 'im over good, I did."

"Thanks, Tom."

"You best rest now, Jon. We'll have you out of here in no time," Doc was saying. "How's that head of yours?" It was the second time he'd asked, but so far, Jon hadn't gotten a word in edgewise.

"It's aching, but I'll be—fine—once I'm out of here."

"How's the vision? Have things been blurry?"

"Yeah, some. Right now all I want to do is—go home."

Home. He realized by home he meant Emma's Boarding-house—and Emma.

Doc used the word *concussion* in conversation before Jon drifted back to sleep.

Chapter Eighteen

*E*mma marched down the sidewalk, Billy's possessions in hand: a pillow and blanket, a change of clothing, a pair of socks, a vest, and a small, decorative box containing several items, such as cuff links, tiepins, and a gold chain. She passed by the bank, crossed the alley, and nearly collided with Mr. Wonder himself as he was leaving Bordon's Bakery, licking sticky fingers. Something custardy still lingered on his chin.

He removed his hat and bowed in his usual polite manner. "Afternoon, miss." Then, glancing at the items she carried, he raised his pencil-thin, dark brows. "You come bearing treasures?"

She extended her arms. "Actually, your treasures, I'm afraid. I'll be needin' the front room you've been using. I hope you don't mind that I went in and got your things. I'm sure you've heard by now they've found the preacher."

He nodded and took his belongings, though not with any degree of enthusiasm. "Yes, so I've heard. Wonderful news, simply wonderful."

"Doc doesn't want the reverend walking up and down the stairs just yet," she explained. "He suggested the front room would be appropriate."

One eyebrow quirked. "So you're kicking me out of my room?"

She wanted to ask when the room had become his but held her tongue.

"You're welcome to keep havin' your meals with us, of course, but I'm afraid you'll have to resume sleepin' in your wagon."

 202

He tossed a rueful gaze at his colorful rig, still parked in the lot where the new church would stand. The horses that went with it had taken up residence at Sam's Livery. "My dear Miss Emma, upon entering any fine town such as your own, I usually find folk quite magnanimous and munificent. Although I would prefer more comfortable accommodations, I suppose my wagon will have to suffice."

At the risk of sounding moronic, she did not ask him the meaning of the two M words, just clasped her hands behind her back and gave a weak smile, breathing in the fine scents of fresh bread coming from the bakery.

Seconds lapsed before he finally took up the slack. "Word has it the reverend was lost in some cave?"

"Not lost—just—hidin' out there is what I hear—until the storm passed. But then lightning—"

He flicked an impatient wrist at her. "Yes, yes, I've heard the story at least a dozen times and probably in as many versions. A fallen tree blocked his passage, leaving him at death's door." He looped a thumb through a buttonhole in his pricey, double-breasted jacket and sniffed the air. "Wouldn't have been a problem at all if he'd just ridden that storm out. Course, that's just my opinion."

"Anyone with an ounce of brain matter knows you don't fool with a lightning storm." An odd need to protect Jon Atkins' character, if not his person, came rushing to the surface.

As if he sensed it, he gave her arm a brief, gentle squeeze. "Now, now, Emma, I meant no offense, but, my dear, think about it." He leaned in to her, the dab of custard still sitting on his chin like a big pimple. "If he'd continued to the next house, the—hm, the Jarvis home, I believe, which, incidentally, was only one mile up the road, he could have stayed with them and come home the next day, thereby avoiding all this unnecessary hoopla. Instead, he stops to rest in a cave?" He shook his head to indicate his own disbelief. "Why, look at all the hours of pay the generous men of Little Hickman have sacrificed on his behalf, not to mention the worry it's caused all the women and children."

"The town loves Jonathan Atkins, and they weren't about to sit around on their backsides and concoct some notion that he'd brought this on himself. Have you forgotten the severity of that storm?"

"Don't get in a huff now. I was merely thinking aloud." He straightened, took a step back, and surveyed her face. "My, my! One would think you love him most of all. Is that the case, Miss Emma?"

So unprepared was she for his words that she stumbled. He reached out a steadying hand. Instantly, she withdrew and did the only thing she could think of to retrieve her composure; she lashed out at him. "I think what's really bothering you, Mr. Wonder, is that all this—hoopla—as you put it, has set your business back a bit. Folks aren't much interested in buying up your medicinal potion or watching your trickery when one of their dear citizens comes up missing."

Now, he was the one caught off guard. Good. "In the future, perhaps you'd be better off doing your thinking aloud in your wagon, not on Main Street."

His chuckle was dry and cynical sounding. "Well, I'll be, you *are* in love with him."

A bitter taste welled up in her throat so that she had the uncanny urge to spit—and make her target that yellow custard pimple on his chin. Instead, she threw back her shoulders and forced a smile. "Good day." She turned and started walking.

"Am I still invited for supper?" he had the gall to ask.

She paused. "Of course. But may I remind you the meals are a dollar a day, and I have yet to receive one dime from you. I'll expect payment by the end of the week."

"You'll have it, my dear Emma." His undiluted laughter mingled with the click of her heels as she made her way back to the boardinghouse.

In love with the preacher? The very idea!

*****

"Easy does it," Rocky said, helping Jon out of his prison. "He's burnin' up, all right. Dehydration does this?"

"Fever's just a sign that somethin's not right in the body. Could be coming from any number of things. More'n likely, he's caught a germ—or infection's set in from that head wound," Doc Randolph said, doing a quick perusal of Jon's vitals, sticking a stethoscope to his chest, pulling up his eyelids, feeling his forehead, and examining the wound, which made Jon flinch. Didn't he know the blasted thing still hurt?

"If you'll just get me back—to my own bed. Need a couple of days and—I'll be fine."

The men gathering around him, of which there looked to be a couple of dozen or more, chuckled under their breaths, and Jon could swear some were shaking their heads at him as if he were missing a few screws.

"You'll need more than a couple of days, son," said Doc, hunkered down next to him. "You've been through an ordeal."

Jon tried to focus on all the faces, but the only ones he could make out for sure were those of Doc, Rocky, and Ben. The others were a blur. He couldn't even muster up the strength to argue.

"W-w-we sure are glad we f-found you."

Okay, so he'd run out of steam for talking, but the familiar voice of Luke Newman did put a smile on his face.

He woke up sometime later, the quiet patter of footsteps in the other room persuading him to open his eyes and examine his surroundings. It was a small space they'd put him in, just big enough to accommodate the hard cot he was on, a small chest of drawers, and a wooden rocker with a colorful quilt thrown over it. Shoot, it wasn't much bigger than that miserable cave. On the wall to his left hung a framed painting, a print of a scenic countryside with a river running through it. It took him a moment to catch his bearings, but when he did, he recognized the room as the one just off the boardinghouse parlor. Why had they put him here? He preferred his own room with all his books, his desk and swivel chair. How was he supposed to prepare for Sunday's sermon if he couldn't get at his books? And his Bible. He needed his Bible. Disgruntled, he recalled having left it in his saddlebags. Had anyone thought to check them when they'd brought Jupiter back to the livery? It took a bit of effort, but he tossed off the cotton blanket and pushed himself up, fully intending to mount the stairs to his room, but quickly surmising he barely had the strength to sit, let alone stand. Instead, he sat there gathering his wits.

On the tiny table beside the bed was a tall glass of water, half of it gone. The vague remembrance that someone had been pouring water down his throat swam to the surface. And someone had bathed him, too, he recalled, glancing at the basin of soapy water on the floor. Doc and—Emma? Gingerly, he touched the bump on his head, noting the diminished size. Still, he felt weaker than a kitten.

"What do you think you're doing?"

Emma stood in the doorway, all business, hands propped on her narrow hips, a blond eyebrow quirked in question.

His skin felt dry and parched. "Going to my own room, the one I pay rent on," he answered, sorry for his curtness. Being a burden did not set well with him, and maybe Emma's shoulders having to take the brunt of it was what irked him the most.

"Not today you're not," she replied in just as curt a manner, stepping inside the room. Her hair, pulled back at the sides with two combs, hung down her back like a cascading fountain, and her yellow cotton dress, cinched at the waist, showed her curves in a pleasing way. He might be sick, but he sure wasn't blind.

"Doc says you're in no shape for climbing stairs. You got a high fever, brought on by a germ or infection from that bump you took on the head. Either way, Doc says what you need now is plenty of fluids and rest. Matter o' fact, he told me when you wake up you're to take some more water along with another dose of medicine."

He studied her face, wondering if she hid a smile behind that full mouth, but he was more likely to find gold in Little Hickman Creek than that.

She stepped up to him and pressed a cool hand to his forehead. "Fever's hangin' on," she announced.

Without forethought, he reached up and snagged hold of her wrist. She gave a quick intake of breath and paled. It was anybody's guess why he'd done it. He couldn't have her, not as long as she didn't profess to know the Lord. Yet having her near him brought a sense of comfort. He rested his gaze on her moist lips and wondered what it might be like to kiss them.

Lord, forgive me, but even in my sorry state, this woman tempts me.

207

Wait on the LORD: be of good courage, and he shall strengthen thine heart: wait, I say, on the LORD.

He'd run across the passage from Psalms a hundred times before, but this time it seemed to hit him square between the eyes. Did God have something up His sleeve, something to which he wasn't yet privy?

He relaxed his hold on her wrist and took up massaging the underside of it with the pad of his thumb, noting how she didn't pull away. Instead, she stood stiff as a starched pair of pants and started staring at something over the top of his head.

Seconds passed before he broke the silence between them. "If Doc's assigned you to be my nurse, I should warn you it might take me awhile to recover."

Suddenly, she pulled her hand from his grasp and blinked at him. Turning toward the little bedside stand, she picked up the glass of water and stuck it under his chin, her mouth pursed in a straight line. "Drink," she ordered. "Your medicine's in the kitchen. I best go get it."

He grinned and wrapped two shaky hands around the glass. "Hurry back."

Later, he woke to the sound of knocking at the front door. Still groggy from another bout of fitful sleep, he rolled himself over and watched Emma tiptoe past on her way to the door. The old grandfather clock's constant tick-tock seemed to parrot her footsteps. The rest of the house remained quiet. Had she shooed the bunch out or warned them against making too much noise? He hated the notion that he'd caused an inconvenience. He might be dog tired and feverish, but he wasn't an invalid and didn't need special treatment. He looked at the clock on the chest of drawers, straining his eyes before it came into focus. Near as he could tell it was 8:10, and by the dusky shadows outside the window, he figured it to be p.m.

He heard the screen door open and a gruff voice ask, "That preacher kid okay?"

"He's resting," came the terse reply.

The shock at hearing Ezra Browning's voice lent his body instant fortitude. "Who's there?" he asked, as if he didn't know, raising himself up on his elbows.

Emma appeared in the doorway. "My father's askin' about you."

He couldn't help the grin. "You don't say. Well, does he want to pay the preacher a visit?"

An inkling of a smile showed up at the corners of her mouth. Her azure eyes twinkled, then just as quickly turned steely. "You're not much up for visitors."

"How do you know? I haven't had any yet."

"That's 'cause you've slept through every one of them," she replied. "People been stoppin' in all day long."

He leaned back a smidgeon and grinned. "Well, I'll be. Why didn't you wake me?"

"I did. And you been friendly as can be—for a span of about three seconds per visit, long enough to drink a swig of water and smile a greetin'. Then, just like that, you're out," she said with a snap of her fingers.

"No kidding. How come I don't remember?"

She shrugged. "Doc did say that medicine he's givin' you might make you a trifle dopey, but you're meant to rest."

It made him wonder what exactly Doc was administering. He dropped back to his pillow, exhausted. "Well, that's a comfort. Send your pa in, will you? I'm feelin' like I might like a chat."

"A chat? With Ezra Browning?" she mumbled under her breath.

He squirmed on the bed. "A chat and maybe a little assistance."

A dazed look swept over her as she crossed her arms. "Assistance with what?"

He lifted one eyebrow a fraction. "You know all that water you been forcing down my throat? Well, it's created a need in me."

Her mouth formed a circle as instant understanding dawned. "Oh. Well, there's a—a—under the—I'll show you." She stepped inside and quickly hunkered next to his bed, pulling out a white bucket with a lid on it. "This."

Had he had the strength, he might have laughed, but as it was, he could barely offer up a pathetic smile. "How about you send Ezra in here?"

"I'm afraid he's not in the best shape for helping you. Surprisingly, he's not drunk, but he don't look good, either," she whispered. "I could go get Mr. Newman. He and Luke retired early, but I'm sure they're awake. Wes is ailin' tonight, so he went to bed already. The rest are out and about."

"I'll manage on my own then. I—"

"Hey, preacher kid."

Emma was right. Ezra looked spent, his face the color of gray paste. Suddenly he recalled the urgent message he'd received in the cave—*be Jesus to Ezra*—and his promise to do all he could if he came out of there alive.

"Hey, yourself. Come on in here. In fact, I need you for a leaning post."

"Huh?" The man took a shaky step forward. Emma's face went red as she turned on her heel and bolted out of the room.

A few minutes later, sweating bullets, Jon dropped back down on the hard mattress while Ezra plunked the lid on the white contraption and pushed it over to the door. "Emma, ya wanna empty this?" he called through the house.

To say Jon felt mortified was much too mild a word. He rolled his eyes and stared at the ceiling, wishing he could vanish.

"Ya liked ta knock me over," Ezra said, falling into the rocker in the corner. "Ya feel better now?"

Taking a second to think about it, he replied, "I'll grant you one part of me does, but my head, that's another story. Sort of feels like it's been trampled by an elephant."

Low and behold, Ezra cracked a smile, even let out a low, raspy chuckle. "Well now, that sounds familiar. I had me a few splittin' headaches in my day, all my own doin', o' course."

Jon allowed his head a minute to stop spinning. When it did, Emma showed up in the doorway, picked up the pot without a word, and disappeared again, her face still flushed, her purposeful footsteps taking her to the back of the house and out the door. He heard the screen bounce shut with a clunk and thwack, and figured she was heading for the little outhouse at the back of the property. It humiliated him to think of her performing this menial chore for him. And if it rattled him, what must it do to her? Or was she used to this sort of thing, having lived under the same roof with a houseful of untamed brutes for the better share of ten years?

Trying to put the matter out of his mind, he focused on Ezra again, who'd taken to rocking lightly, his head propped on the back of the rocker, arms folded across his wheezing chest. It struck him then how pleased he was to see the fellow. "Thanks for coming, Ezra. I'm glad to see you."

"Pfff. Don't go gettin' no big head about it now," he growled. "I was in town anyways."

Jon swallowed. "You're not working tonight, are you? Seems to me with that cough and all...." The poor man hardly looked able to leave his house, let alone work at that no-good saloon.

Ezra nodded.

"Why don't you quit that rotten job?"

His face crumpled. "Been thinkin' on it, but I need the money fer gettin' by."

"You mean for supporting your habit?"

"Naw, I been cuttin' back. Doc says I ain't doin' myself no favors if I don't."

That bit of enlightenment had Jon slowly propping himself up on his elbows. *Well, hallelujah!* "You talked to Doc, did you? What'd he say about that nasty cough?"

Ezra shrugged and turned his head toward the door. Was he looking for Emma? His mouth twisted downward, murky eyes stared into space. "I ain't wantin' that girl o' mine ta know nothing 'bout it," he muttered.

"Know nothing about what?" Jon pressed.

Seconds turned into a minute, during which Ezra closed his eyes. Using all the strength he could muster, despite his ringing ears and raging fever, Jon propped himself higher. "Ezra?"

Finally, the old man opened his cloudy gray eyes and focused on Jon. "Doc says I ain't long fer this world."

Exhausted, Jon dropped his head to the pillow and devoured a deep breath of air, thankful for the cool breeze wafting through the open window near his head.

"I got a bad thing goin' on in my lungs and liver," Ezra grumbled. "Doc says it's worse than bad, says my hard life done it to me." Again, he looked at the door. He waved his thumb in the direction that Emma had gone and shook his head. "I know she hates me, and I don't blame 'er none the way I treated 'er. She was good most times, she truly was. If I ha'n't been so blasted hammered my whole life I might o' been able ta raise her proper."

Ezra rocked forward in the chair. "She's a good girl."

A spot in Jon's chest clogged with emotion. "She is that."

Jon prayed while Ezra slowly rocked. He longed for the strength to rise up and go to him, wrap his arms around his frail shoulders. Instead, he lay in about as bad a shape as Ezra himself. "God can help you, Ezra," he managed. "You may not believe it, but even at this stage in your life, He wants nothing more than for you to surrender your heart to Him. He'll give you the strength and courage you need to fight this battle. It's no good trying to fight it on your own. Might be you'll even have time to settle things with Emma."

Having never resolved matters with his own father before he died still put an ache in Jon's heart. Exactly a year and a half after his mother's death, his father had drowned while fishing off a steep embankment. Hal Owen had found him in the river facedown, fishing line still tangled around his body, empty whiskey bottles at the river's edge. If it hadn't been for Reverend Miller's loving wisdom and the Callahans' remarkable, unconditional love in taking him into their household afterward, he may well have followed his father's destructive path. Instead, he'd learned about the love of his heavenly Father, and out of a great need for truth and meaning in life, had given his heart to Him at the age of sixteen-and-a-half years.

Ezra pushed himself up from the chair, the effort creating shortness of breath.

"Where're you going?" Jon asked.

"Back to work. Jus' stopped by for a second." Every breath carried a wheeze. "You don't go tellin' Emma 'bout my condition, you hear?"

"She deserves to know, Ezra."

"Maybe. But I don't want her feelin' beholden. It ain't right." He made a half-turn then stopped, not quite letting his eyes meet Jon's. "Sorry you got stuck in that cave," he mumbled.

"Thanks. When I get my strength back, I'll ride out to see you. Shouldn't be more than a few days. In the meantime, you take care of yourself."

"Yeah, yeah," Ezra said, waving off the comment with a flick of his wrist then sauntering out the door without so much as a fare-thee-well.

As soon as the front door opened and shut, he heard Emma enter through the back.

Chapter Nineteen

*E*mma glanced at the wall calendar. She'd just flipped the page to September. How was it possible? In a matter of weeks, the leaves would begin their transformation from green to orange, yellow, and red before turning a rusty brown and dropping to the cold earth. The air, once hot and steamy, would take on a shivery nip, calling for extra layers of clothing before venturing out. Families of squirrels and chipmunks would start the business of collecting food—not so different from the humans who had already started laying up jams, jellies, and sauces for the winter months. She'd been doing the same, filling up shelves in the cellar under the kitchen with canned peaches, pears, tomatoes, and applesauce, along with a large assortment of vegetables.

It was nearing the supper hour. Billy Wonder sauntered into the kitchen where she was stirring gravy over a hot stove. "I'll be leavin' town soon," he divulged. "Thought you'd like to know that." He plopped down a number of coins on the counter, which she quickly swept up and stuffed into her apron pocket. "Aren't you going to count those?" he asked.

Ever since their encounter on the street some weeks ago, she'd treated him courteously at her table but avoided any further confrontations for fear he'd bring up that silly notion about her having feelings for the preacher. Fool-headed, that's what it was.

"No need," she said. He'd been faithfully paying her the sum total of seven dollars every Friday, and she'd only had to remind him it was due twice. She had the distinct feeling he managed to finagle his way into most folks' lives on charm alone, then quickly wandered out before they caught on. Paying his way was a foreign concept to Billy Wonder. Yet in spite of his rather audacious manner, she had to admit he was a most likeable character, and the announcement that he was leaving not only took her by surprise, but also filled her with a twinge of regret. He'd become somewhat of a fixture around the boardinghouse.

"Where will you go next?" she asked.

"Further south, Tennessee, then Georgia. Might even go as far down as Florida. I'll want to get a head start on the weather. Cold winters spoil my temperament."

"Winters aren't so bad here," she remarked. "Hardly get any snow as a rule."

"No, but you get ice," he stated, as if he were the authority. "Might as well have snow for all the frigid temperatures. Nothing worse than freezing rain sluicing the cold earth. Makes navigating my rig nearly impossible." Billy found a spoon and dipped it into the gravy, then brought it to his lips, lightly blowing on it before closing his mouth around the spoon and sighing with pleasure. "That's delicious, madam. Have I told you what a wonderful cook you are?"

She smiled, staring into the saucepan of bubbling gravy. "Plenty of times."

"I'll surely miss your fine biscuits when I head for parts unknown."

There was a wistful tone in his words, and she wondered what it was that kept him moving. *Best not to pry,* she concluded. She'd always been adept at keeping her distance with regard to folks' innermost feelings, somehow knowing it could lay her open for questioning.

"Well, remind me, and I'll pack you some before you go."

He turned around, putting his back to the stove and folding his arms across his chest, his gaze zeroing in on her face. "I'm actually going to miss Little Hickman. Folks've been real nice to me."

"I'm glad to hear that. It's a pleasant place."

"It's the sort of place in which a man wouldn't mind settling down—if he was to find him a nice woman first."

Sticky heat inched across her cheeks, and she wondered if he sensed her discomfort. This was just where she didn't want the conversation heading. "You just finished sayin' you don't like the cold winters."

"Ah, but the warmth of a woman could easily persuade me to stick out a nippy Kentucky winter." She sorted through the silverware drawer in search of a wooden spoon and, finding one, set about shoveling mashed potatoes from a steaming kettle into a large serving bowl, her mouth clamped shut. "Course, it appears the only woman I'd be interested in pursuing has her eye out for the preacher."

She sighed loudly. Reaching into a drawer with one hand, she picked up two crocheted hot pads and pressed them into his palms. "Here, make yourself useful," she ordered.

"Doing what?" he asked.

She pointed at the heavy cast-iron kettle. "Hold that by the handles so I can scrape it out."

Looking about as blundering as an elephant balancing fine porcelain on its head, Billy Wonder situated the potholders on the handles and hefted the kettle up, tipping it to make the potatoes accessible. While she worked, she felt his eyes continuously boring holes through her damp cheeks.

"Just admit it," he quietly dared.

"There's nothin' to admit," she countered, drawing her brows together in a tight frown.

"Sure there is."

Her back went straighter than usual as irritation ran a line up her spine. "Tip it further this way," she urged, guiding the pan with her utensil. "More."

He complied. She scraped. "I've seen how you peer at him across the table," he pointed out. "Caught the fear in your eyes when he first came up missing, watched you care for him when he was down with that fever. Oh, and don't think the lot of us didn't notice that look of contempt on your face the night that pretty Clayton girl showed up to lend a hand." He laughed outright. "My, my, you looked ready to sweep her clean off your porch. And I believe you intended to use the wrong end of the broom to do it."

"Oh, pooh! You're being ridiculous," she snapped, a tight ball of apprehension rolling around in her gut. Had she really looked as riled that day as she'd felt? It had been another long twenty-four hours of caring for Jonathan, his fever refusing to break even after the third day, his sudden turn for the worse disarming everyone, including Doc. Day and night she'd cared for him, blotted his parched, fevered face with wet cloths, spoken in low, comforting tones to him when he got the tremors, and replaced his sweat-soaked sheets with dry ones. Sitting on the rocker beside his bed, she'd forced water down his throat, dozed when she got the chance, and prayed short prayers that gave little consolation.

Doc had just delivered another one of his lectures, insisting she needed rest. He'd been standing on the porch, preparing to leave, and talking to her through the screen door.

"I'll be fine," she'd muttered, watching a fly soar around Doc's balding head. Hannah Clayton had volunteered her services, he'd announced, and he wouldn't stand for any of her arguments. "What?" she'd fired back, aghast. "That's completely unnecessary. I'd have to show her where everything is."

Doc had blinked and shifted from one foot to the other, a loose board squeaking under his weight as he batted at the fly. "And your point?"

"Well, I...." What was her point? She'd been too exhausted to think clearly, but the one thing she had known was that she didn't like the thought of Hannah Clayton taking her place in the little rocker. For some reason, she'd wanted to be the one in Jon's line of vision when at last he opened his eyes, irrational as that was. She had glanced around only to discover her boarders, including Billy Wonder, had grown quiet as church mice, hanging on to every word spoken between Doc and her.

Bucking up, she'd dragged her gaze back to the town's doctor. He'd pulled back his shoulders. "She'll be here by seven and fully expects to stay the night," he stated, his eyes revealing he would have the last word. "You'll show her what you've been doing for the reverend, and then you'll take to your bed." Her back sagged on its own. A slow smile appeared on his face just before he turned to leave. "And don't worry, Emma. I'll see to it that he learns what you've done for him."

Mortification of the worst kind had jumped to the surface. "You'll do no such thing! Besides, it's nothin' different than I would've done for anyone else."

He'd grinned. "Then it shouldn't bother you one way or the other who I send over here to help, Hannah Clayton or my great uncle." He'd turned and headed down the steps, his throaty chuckle transporting itself over the air like a soft, wispy cloud.

"You love him, don't you?" Billy asked, breaking into her thoughts, his breath disturbing the tiny tendrils of hair at her temple.

The question left her so nonplussed that she dropped the spoon in the kettle with an impatient clunk, deciding the no-name dog could lick out the remains.

"Mr. Wonder, you are out of line in asking such a thing."

He tossed back his head and laughed. "You are a puzzle, Miss Emma. Pretty thing like you seeming content to run this boardinghouse of misfits." He set the cast-iron kettle down and tossed the hot pads to the counter. Then he stuffed his hands in his pockets. "Sorry if I've offended you, but you can't blame a guy for wondering why no one's snatched you up yet. How old are you anyway?" He tipped his face down close as if to judge her age by the tiny wrinkles in the corners of her eyes. In a regular huff, she gathered up several dirty utensils and carried them to the sink, pitching them down with a clang and a clatter.

"That is none of your business." So she was a spinster going on twenty-nine? These days, ladies were proud of their independence.

"I'm guessing twenty-three, twenty-four. You can't be a day over twenty-five," the galoot pestered, following in her steps. She turned the spigot and stuck a teakettle under the water's flow, studying its vigorous spray. "Anyway, doesn't matter," he finally relented after she'd filled the teakettle to the brim.

She turned off the faucet and flipped the lid on the shiny little pot before setting it on the counter, took a few steadying breaths, and raised up her head to gaze at him. It surprised her that his coffee-colored eyes weren't judging. Nor were they glinting with hilarity. Instead, a probing query came into them and something like genuine interest.

Her anger settled down. "I'm twenty-eight, if you must know."

"No!"

She dropped her eyes to the breadcrumbs littering the countertop and swept them into a neat little pile with the side of her hand, then set to poking the pile with her fingertip, arranging and rearranging. "I enjoy making my own way, not having to rely on another human being. Always have," she heard herself confess.

Hands still stuffed away, he gave a silent nod. "I can understand that. I've felt the same myself. I started making my own way as a boy of twelve after I lost both my parents in an ambush outside of St. Louis. I escaped with nothing but the shirt on my back, and that only because the desperados were too busy pilfering through the wagons to see me get away." A cynical snigger ripped past his throat followed by an angry curse. "They slaughtered eight adults and seven kids that day, my folks among them. We were traveling with a band of gypsies, you see." The smile on his face was cold and ghostly, his eyes icy with remembrance. "Took me weeks to come forward, maybe months. I was scared half out of my wits that if I did go to the law one of them would come after me. Hmph! They were long gone by the time I finally went to the sheriff. Far as I know they're still roamin' free unless the devil's taken 'em down."

The story horrified her. How did one come out of something like that and remain sane? So that explained his wanderlust. "How terrible for you," she managed on a hoarse whisper.

221

He shrugged and looked out the window overlooking the backyard. "Do you know that was exactly twenty-four years ago this month? I remember it like it was yesterday."

A cold, raw shiver flickered down her spine.

Lord, I don't understand You. Why would You allow such atrocities to happen? Where were You when Billy needed You—when I needed You? Where are You now?

In an impulsive act, she placed her hand on Billy Wonder's arm, allowing herself to care, wrapping her mind around the fact that she was even capable of it.

"I'm sorry, Billy," she said, meaning it.

He looked at her hand then slowly raised his face until their eyes met and held. "I'll tell you a secret if you promise to keep it between us."

Her chest tightened with anticipation. In her lifetime, she'd been privy to very few secrets, mostly because best friends often shared them, and she really didn't have a best friend. Her head bobbed up and down with nervous excitement. "I promise."

He swallowed hard then seemed to ponder where to begin. "My real name's not Billy Wonder."

"No." That was the secret? She'd suspected as much.

"It's Philip William Westerwunter. German I guess. Don't know what it means. Philip was my great-grandfather's name on my mother's side and William was an uncle to my Grandpa Westerwunter." He looked proud, if not relieved, that his secret was out.

"I don't think anyone would guess your real name," she stated, keeping a straight face.

"The first person who does is going on the road with me." At this, they shared a spontaneous laugh, after which Billy quickly sobered. "You never did get over to see one of

222

my shows, you know. Last one's tomorrow." His brown eyes sparked with a kind of impish innocence, and she decided he was really quite handsome—in an offhand sort of way.

"When does it start?" she heard herself ask.

"Two o'clock sharp."

She thought about tomorrow's list of chores: sweeping the floor and dusting the library shelves, baking a week's worth of bread, weeding the garden, picking the last of the ripe tomatoes, pole beans, peppers, and zucchinis, and writing a letter to Grace.

Grace.

As hard as she tried, she could not keep up with that woman's letter-writing skills. To every one of Emma's missives, Grace returned three.

A smile pulled at the corners of her mouth as Billy waited for her answer.

"I'll be there."

*****

No getting around it, Ezra Browning was a dying man. Jon steered Jupiter over rough terrain on his way back to town and rehashed his Saturday morning visit. Ezra's cough had worsened, choking the very breath from his diseased lungs, blood intermingling with spittle. Gray lines etched into his aging face, and bony, sagging shoulders only emphasized an obvious weight loss. He doubted the fellow had eaten a proper meal in weeks, perhaps months.

"You need to talk to Emma," Jon had said after spoon-feeding Ezra half a cup of chicken soup while he'd reclined in bed, his head propped up by two grubby feather pillows. "She deserves to know how sick you are."

"I ain't wantin' her ta know nothin'," Ezra grumped. "She don't much care anyway, so there'd be no point ta tellin' 'er." This he'd said between suffocating coughs.

"You're not fit to care for yourself, old man," Jon said. "Emma and I could help. You could move into the boardinghouse."

"Pfff. Been takin' care o' myself all my life. No reason ta stop now."

"You've never been this sick. Don't think I don't know how bad off you are. I talked to Doc myself."

"He had no right divulgin' my business."

"I forced it out of him." It was true. When he'd approached Doc Randolph about Ezra's health, the doctor had been hesitant to say anything, claiming he'd sworn to keep the matter quiet at Ezra's request. But Jon had convinced him he could help the old guy if Doc would just be straight with him. That's when he'd learned what he'd feared; Ezra had a large tumor in one of his lungs, and a rapidly decaying liver only added to the problem.

Deciding not to push him further where Emma was concerned, he'd asked, "Have you got any family—anyone you want me to contact for you?"

The old man shook his head and stared at the ceiling. "I done tol' the only person who'd care one whit. Wrote 'er a letter last spring—around April I guess."

"Would that be Edith?" Jon asked on a whim.

Ezra's eyes clouded with interest. "How'd ya know 'bout her?"

"You mentioned her awhile back. Don't s'pose you remember. Who is she?"

"Yer a nosy young cuss, preacher kid," Ezra grumbled.

Jon chuckled. "I've been called worse. Come on, who is Edith?"

 224

Ezra harrumphed and said, "She's my mother's sister and the only one from my family who ever gived a hoot 'bout me."

Jon's spine went straight. "You have an aunt?" He let the newfound information settle. "Does Emma know about her?"

"Never saw the need to tell 'er. I lost contact with ever'one after I left home. Heard from Aunt Edith ever' so often, but that was it. Ain't like she ever come to see me and Emma. She usually jus' wrote notes now and then, and sometimes I'd write back." Ezra shrugged. "Didn't hear back from 'er this last time though."

"Well, maybe she never got your note," Jon offered. "Or could be she's moved—or she's sick. Is your mother still living?"

His head moved from side to side on the filthy pillow. "Don't know nothin' 'bout my ma or pa, and there ain't no need tryin' to contact 'em," he groused. "They'd a writ me a long time ago if they gived a care."

Rivers of compassion washed over him. "God loves you, my friend. He wants to heal your heart from the inside out. Have you ever considered giving what's left of your life over to Him?"

Ezra's age-worn face creased even more. "Doubt God's much interested in what's left of me, a cranky, vile ol' coot. I ain't done much of anythin' good with my life. God knows my wakin' hours weren't worth a toot. Couldn't even take proper care o' my own kid. And that's the plain truth of it."

For the first time ever, Jon witnessed something different in Ezra, and it sounded like remorse, honest and genuine.

"God doesn't care about any of that. What He does care about is a penitent heart, a soul that's truly sorry for his sin and willing to accept the forgiveness that only Jesus can provide. How about I give you a Bible so you can read the very words that tell of His great love? Would you go for that?"

He didn't say yes, and he didn't say no. What he did do was turn his head away and close his eyes. Minutes later, he was snoring. Either that or feigning sleep to avoid further discussion.

After cleaning up the kitchen, Jon headed back to town.

Chapter Twenty

*J*on found Emma dusting shelves in the library upon his return from the Browning farm. She'd removed all the books and stacked them in several neat piles on the floor. He leaned in the doorway, hat in hand, and watched for several moments, his presence completely undetected. She wore a red gingham skirt, frayed at the hem, and a white cotton blouse with puffy short sleeves, dipped at the neck. Her pinned-back blond hair tumbled down like shimmering gold.

Lord, she's beautiful.

As if she'd heard his thoughts, she whirled about. Her face was pink with perspiration, and the notion struck him that she actually enjoyed laboring around her house, making it a comfortable dwelling place for all, even though its inhabitants failed to mutter their thanks.

"Smells fresh and clean in here," he stated, feeling obliged to convey his gratitude. It wasn't often he made note of the lemon-scented air in Emma's boardinghouse, even though it did appeal to him.

Emma bent to mop her brow with the corner of her soiled white apron then wiped her hands on it. She rewarded him with a rare smile, and his insides flipped. *Lord, have mercy.*

"I didn't know men noticed such things," she said, her tone facetious.

He continued using the doorframe as a leaning post. "Oh, they notice all right; they just don't let on because they're too blamed mule-headed."

A soft giggle erupted and his heart turned to mush. As usual, he needed to get a grip on himself before he revealed what she did to him.

"I suppose you've been out doing what preachers do," she said, turning back to her dusting duty. He watched her hand glide easily over the middle shelf. A stepladder shoved off to the side indicated she'd either already finished the two top shelves or she was working her way up to them.

He tossed his hat to a nearby table and stuffed his hands in his trouser pockets. "And what is it you think we do?"

Without turning, she replied, "Besides delivering a well-thought-out sermon every Sunday? Hm. I think you do a lot of gabbing with old farmers and charming their wives into feeding you whatever sweet they have in their cupboards. And when you're not doing that, you're buryin' your head in one of them books you got stashed in your room."

He laughed outright. "Thank you—I think—for your remark about the well-thought-out sermons. I notice you've been coming to services, so I'll take it as a compliment. As for the rest of your observation, you're not far off. How did you know?"

Leaning into her task with vigor, she said, "Intuition. I've watched you gobble my desserts as if you'd never eaten a dab of sugar in your life, and I've passed by your room a time or two to find you slumped over a book at that big ol' desk." Although he couldn't see her face, he could *hear* the smile in her words.

He grinned and bit into his lower lip. "I've always had a penchant for book learning. As for the sweet tooth, my mother wasn't much for baking. She cooked the essentials, but she left it up to old Ray Baker, who used to own the general store before Eldred Johansson took over the mercantile, to satisfy my longing for sweets. He always had jars full of jawbreakers, licorice and peppermint sticks, and every flavor lollipop you can imagine. And every so often, he'd slip me a big slice of warm peanut butter fudge hot off the slab. I hung around his store on fudge-making days."

"Oh, I remember Mr. Baker," Emma said with excitement, pausing to look at her work and let the memory sink in. "He was a nice old guy with a shiny bald head and a pencil-thin moustache. Whenever he smiled big, that thing curled up at both ends like a snake." She giggled at the recollection, the sound floating over the air like a sweet song. "I always thought he had a warm spot for Clara Abbott."

His ears perked. "The lady who willed you the boarding-house."

"Hm," she said with a slow nod. "He was forever stopping by for a visit. We'd be sittin' on the porch swing flappin' our jaws, Miss Abbott and me, and along he'd come. He'd ask me how my school day went and did I learn more than the boys did that day. And he always seemed to have a stash of gumdrops in his pocket." She turned and looked at him then, her sapphire eyes flashing with recollection. "He'd give me a handful, and I'd eat every one of them, the red ones first, pocket lint and all."

Jon tossed back his head and laughed, conscious of how refreshing it was to carry on a conversation with Emma Browning, discovering she preferred red gumdrops to all the other colors. On a whim, he shoved off the doorframe and went to the brocade sling-back chair, dropping into it with a sigh, hoping she didn't see the act as presumptuous. Would she now clam up because he meant to get comfortable?

"I've always wondered how you came to obtain this boardinghouse." He looked around the courtly room with its high ceilings and simple crown molding, a massive old landscape painting gracing the plaster wall opposite the one holding the bookshelves she'd been dusting. "I guess Mrs. Abbott thought the world of you, huh?"

"*Miss* Abbott," she corrected. "Far as I know, she never married. And yes, she cared for me, but no more than I for her. She was a dear old soul, always lookin' out for my best interest. One time she rode out to see my pa to have a word with him. She was angry because...."

Jon froze in place when her words halted mid-sentence. He swept his tongue over his upper lip, grazing his top teeth, gripped the ends of both chair arms, and waited while she struggled to compose herself, her back stiff, her hand moving mechanically over the smooth shelf. Finally, she shrugged her narrow shoulders and angled him with a desultory look. "That was a long time ago."

"Why don't you tell me about it?" he urged.

There was a quiet space of time followed by a slow nod. "I suppose it couldn't hurt." At that, she finished her chore, dropped her wet rag into the bucket of murky water, and bent to pick up a handful of books. He followed her with his eyes, reminding himself to exhale when his lungs filled with air. When she set to returning books to their proper place, he pushed himself out of the chair and resolved to lend her a hand.

Outside, horses' hooves pounded down Main Street, the sound echoing through town, interrupted by shouts of "Get up!" or the occasional squeal of an agitated child or a dog's shrill bark.

"I used to stop by to see Miss Abbott on my way home from school," Emma explained, picking up another book and perusing its title before deciding where to place it. He hunkered down beside the stack of books and without a word began handing her a few at a time. "She taught me woman things," she said, drawing out a long breath then placing the books on a lower shelf. When she turned around, he handed her four more leather-bound volumes, which she carefully studied then set on the middle shelf. If there was a method to her system of arrangement, he couldn't guess it. "Like how to cook and sew and weave a rug. She also loaned me lots of wonderful books, most of which Ezra disposed of when he got the chance." She gave a forced, cold smile. "He thought I was shirking my household duties if he caught me curled up with a book. He'd yank it out of my hand and toss it into the stove." A dull laugh sailed past her lips. "I always figured he was jealous 'cause he couldn't read near as good as me."

Jon nodded, the story tugging at a deep place in his heart. He pictured her as a young, defenseless girl trying to protect her precious property, envisioned her big blue eyes watering up with sorrow. A wave of disgust washed over him. *Lord, how can You expect me to care for a beast like Ezra Browning?*

"One day when I went to Miss Abbott's, she spotted bruises goin' up and down my arm. She got powerful mad—not at me, mind you, but at Ezra." The whispered assertion seemed to take the wind from her sails. All of a sudden, she dropped down beside him, folded her legs up under her full skirt, propped her elbow on her lap, and leaned forward to rest her chin in her hand. The books he'd intended to give her went back to the top of the pile as he positioned himself next to her, legs outstretched and crossed at the ankles, arms bolstering him from behind. They sat in unmoving silence for a full minute or more, her lemony scent wafting through the air.

"What'd she do?" he finally asked.

Her lips curved into an unconscious smile as she stared straight ahead. "Well, she put me in her rig and took me home, muttering stuff under her breath and saying she was going to make things right once and for all. I didn't know what she meant, still don't entirely. I kept begging her not to be mad at him 'cause I knew my papa would take it out on me after she left. She just patted my knee, told me not to worry, and said, 'You're comin' to live with me, child.'"

Her brows flickered as she straightened, dropped both hands to her lap, and toyed with the hem of her apron. "I should have known her scheme was too good to be true. When she offered to take me off Ezra's hands, he nearly exploded, saying he didn't need her help, and what did she know anyway about raisin' kids?

"I'll never forget that look he gave her. It was enough to freeze pig's snot. 'Sides,' he told her, 'who'd tend to the house chores and cook the meals?' When Miss Abbott argued that she'd go to the sheriff about the abuse he just laughed it off, sayin' something like, 'And who are you to judge me, Clara Abbott? It ain't like you know anythin' about raisin' kids.' He said it real hateful like, and I remember Miss Abbott went all white in the face, turned around without making a sound, and stumbled out of the house. She didn't even look at me on her way out, just walked away all quiet-like.

"When I went back to see her the next day it was like the episode with Ezra had never happened."

Emma lifted her face and met his gaze. "Strange story, huh? I can't believe I told you. I've never told that to anyone."

Jon's heart gave a painful pinch. "Then I feel privileged that you trusted me enough to repeat it. So how did you come to own this boardinghouse?"

Emma's eyes trailed to the window where the curtains floated in the breeze. "I continued visiting Clara every chance I got. When I was sixteen, I moved in with her. She was gettin' real sickly and needed the help. My movin' in took a load off her shoulders. By that time, Ezra had no say in my decision to move. He was drinkin' so heavy by then he could hardly walk a straight line, let alone order me around. It was so freeing to discover he no longer had a hold on me.

"On Miss Abbott's deathbed, she told me she wanted me to take over her place when she was gone. She told me she'd drawn up some papers to make it all legal. I tried to argue with her, but she swore there was no one else she'd rather see take ownership, muttered something about it being the least she could do."

Jon nodded, picturing the scene, a dying woman giving a young girl hope. "Why do you think Ezra was so hateful toward Miss Abbott?"

She looked thoughtful. "I don't know. Jealous, maybe? He knew how much I loved her—and how much she loved me."

His next words came after careful thought. "I believe Ezra loves you, Emma." He couldn't help it. He lifted a hand and fingered a wisp of golden hair falling around her temple. Surprisingly, she didn't shrink away from him, merely kept her eyes fastened on her lap. Her hair was feathery soft, as he'd imagined it would be, and the feel of it between his fingertips warmed the edges of his heart, made him want to test her lips to see if they were just as soft. "He's just got a pitiful way of showing it," he whispered.

Dear Lord, she's a beauty.

"Not for a second do I excuse the way he raised you, Emma, but something tells me your father never had a clue how to give or receive love. Your mother died and he was stuck with a newborn baby—and no outside support." He swallowed nervously, expecting her to bolt at any second or, at the very least, argue his claim. When she didn't, he asked, "Do you know anything about Ezra's background, ever met your grandparents?"

A cynical laugh blew past her lips. "I learned when I was about this high"—she laid her palm flat about two feet from the floor—"not to ask questions about my father's family. One slap across the face is enough to teach a kid when to keep her mouth shut."

Jon winced, marveling again that he cared for the old coot who'd abused his only child, his longing to lead him to the Savior still pressing in on him.

"Ever hear of a woman named Edith?" Jon asked on impulse.

She lifted inquiring blue eyes and shook her head. "No. Should I have?"

He swallowed a hard lump, let go of the wisps of hair he'd been fingering, and grazed the back of his hand over her pink cheek. "She's your father's aunt—*your* great aunt."

She pulled back and stared at him, which forced him to drop his hand away from her face. "She's from Chicago," he explained, spacing each word evenly.

"I have an aunt in Chicago? How would you know about any of this?" Big question marks seemed to pop into her vivid blue eyes.

"Ezra told me," he said. "He wouldn't say much of anything about her, except that she's the only member of his family who ever seemed to care about him. I got the feeling that she's kept in contact with him over the years."

Frown lines etched deeper into her lovely brow. "I don't know why he couldn't have told me about her. He's always been so hateful about anything relating to his past. The ornery old buzzard."

Jon wanted to comment that he worried Ezra's vinegary nature had rubbed off on her. Few had broken through the thick walls she'd built so craftily around herself. Walls that kept everyone at a safe distance. Was he managing—finally—to find a small crack in her exterior?

"I've been receiving notes from a lady in Chicago," she freely confessed. "But you probably already knew that, thanks to George Garner."

Jon chuckled low in his throat. "Can't slip much of anything past George's spectacles."

Ignoring the jest, she said, "No one named Edith, though. I wonder if…." Her fingers fluttered to the back of her neck to fumble with her hair. "If…there's some connection. This lady's name is Grace Giles, but aside from that, I know little about her. I asked Ezra, but he claims he's never heard of her. She knows about us, though—in particular, that Ezra and I don't get along. Every time she writes, she reminds me that time is too short to waste it on bitterness and hatred, and she defends her claim with a Bible verse. Then she tells me God loves me and that she's praying for me. She even talked me into reading my Bible—starting with the book of John."

"Hm, good choice of books. I think I like this woman," Jon said, dipping his chin and taking the liberty to lean in close enough to get a good whiff of her soap-scented hair. She seemed not to notice so he savored the moment. "Have you tried the direct approach, just asked her straight-out who she is and why the interest?"

"Yes, a couple of weeks ago," she answered. "But she hasn't responded. Oh, she's sent me others in the meantime, but none that answers that particular letter. I think it's because she just keeps writin' me, whether I write back or not, and now that I have, it's taken awhile for the post office ta deliver her reply. Truth be told, I'm not sure I want to know what she has to say—entirely. Maybe she will tell me stuff I won't like hearing—ugly things about Ezra's past that could make the situation even worse between us. I don't know." She grimaced and shook her head. He saw a battle of sorts going on behind her eyes and yearned to assuage her fears.

"Could things be worse? You don't talk to the old guy now. How will knowing what the connection is with this Grace person change that? Who knows? It could improve the condition of your relationship, give you a clearer viewpoint. Aren't you curious to know everything you can?"

"Psh! My father spent so much time squelching my childhood questions that I think he actually killed my adult curiosity. If anything, I want to forget he even exists in that little house a mile out of town. That being the case, why would I want to learn about his roots?"

"Because they're your roots, too, and they might explain some things." She merely shrugged and picked at a loose thread on her apron pocket.

He mulled over his next words then spit them out before he lost his courage. "Ezra is a sick old man, Emma. I'm thinking he should come here to finish out his years—if he has years." It was more like weeks probably, days even, but he kept that thought locked away.

She drew back from him, eyes round and glowing with befuddlement. "What?"

"He can't live on his own out there anymore. He's not drinking, as far as I can tell. I looked through his cupboards this morning and couldn't find his stash. I think he's run out."

"That's why he's sick then. He needs a drink. It's always been that way. He runs out; he gets more. He'll turn ugly if he goes very many days without his ale. Believe me, I know."

"I know you do, and I'm sorry. But he's not sick because of going without. He's sick because he's—sick," he said, remembering his promise to Ezra not to divulge the whole truth. "He needs our help. I'll do most of the work as far as his care goes. You wouldn't have to do much except supply the room, that little one I stayed in when I was ailing." He turned her chin with the tip of his finger. "And you did care for me very well, by the way. I don't know if I've thanked you sufficiently for that. I know you missed hours of sleep sitting by my bedside when the chills and fever hit. And on top of that, you still managed to take care of your boarders."

Their eyes locked temporarily before she flipped her wrist to signify it was nothing. "You thanked me with that big bouquet of flowers from the Hayward's garden, which was more than enough. I surely didn't nurse you back to health because I expected somethin' in return." She glanced away from him, unable to hide the flush in her cheeks. "And don't forget, that Clayton girl spent an entire night carin' for you. Matter of fact, you started recoverin' the very next day."

If he didn't know better, he'd say she was jealous the way her shoulders reared back and she frowned at the telling. He decided to test the waters.

"She is a mighty pretty thing."

She shot him a stony glare.

"What? You don't agree?" he asked.

Prickly as a new rope, she swiveled to retrieve a book from the nearby stack, a leather-bound copy of Mark Twain's *Life on the Mississippi*, and perused its cover.

She *was* jealous. Inside, he bubbled with pleasure. "Of course, she's not nearly as pretty as someone else I know." This he said while leaning in close to get another whiff of her lovely scent.

She drew back and angled him with a suspicious look. "I believe we were discussing my father. You mentioned bringing him here."

237

"Ah, yes, can we discuss that?"

"Have you talked to Doc?" she asked, standing and bringing some books with her.

He studied her demeanor, which had quickly reverted to the mode he'd grown accustomed to—distant. "I have, and he's not encouraging."

She straightened her shoulders and looked thoughtful. "You can ask my pa what he thinks about the idea, but I guarantee he'll hate it."

"I know. He's one cranky old man."

She blew a few hairs out of her face. He studied her nose, her eyebrows, the sweep of lashes that dropped lazily over her pretty blue eyes. Her lips were full and delicate, and he wanted more than anything to kiss them.

As if she'd read his mind and been scalded by the words, she turned in haste and set about replacing books to their proper places, according to color—size—title? He didn't know.

What he did know, however, as the walls of his chest felt ready to collapse, the beat of his heart drumming wildly out of control, was that somewhere between seventh grade and this very moment in time, he'd fallen completely, irrefutably, irrevocably in love with Emma Browning.

Chapter Twenty-One

This is it, folks; your final opportunity to see the amazing, the great, the wonderful Billy Wonder in action. I have enjoyed my time in Little Hickman, but I regret to say I am moving on."

Sighs of disappointment rustled through the crowd. "Do ya hafta go?" piped up Lili Broughton from her front-row position just two feet from Billy's makeshift stage at the back of his wagon. Along with Eloise Brackett, Sarah Jenkins, and Erlene Barrington, she had squeezed her way past the crowd to get a better view of Billy's closing act. Emma stood at the back of the throng, mildly interested, Liza Broughton at her side. The two had met on the sidewalk outside the boardinghouse and had walked together to see Billy's performance, Lili running on ahead.

About fifty yards behind the wagon, a couple of dozen volunteer workers had convened at the site of the new church, which, by the look of things, was coming along at a fast rate. The basic structure itself was up, shingled roof nailed in place, clapboard siding firmly fixed but still unpainted, windows fitted, and the big double-door entryway with ten-foot-wide cement steps inviting even the shyest stranger through its portals. Emma found herself watching the church construction with one eye and Billy's show with the other, torn between the two, especially once she spotted Jon Atkins amidst the group of church workers and recalled their conversation of less than an hour ago. She rebuked herself for her distraction and forced her focus back to Billy. After all, he was leaving Little Hickman; it was only right she give him her full attention.

Billy's firm mouth gave way to a smile as he eyed the young girls pressed in at the front of the crowd. With flare, he removed the black top hat he always wore, swept it wide, and bowed low. "Afraid so, my dear girl. The Southern states are calling me." He then straightened, looked out over the gathering citizens, and pulled back his shoulders. "But do not fear, my friends. I shall return—and when I do, I will bring with me the finest, most up-to-date products and remedies available." His voice had taken on a singsong quality, building with every syllable. "Why, I'm told that by the year 1900 we will have a cure for most everything that ails the human body." Enthusiastic smiles covered the faces of adults and children while murmurs of delight fluttered from one to the other.

"He's a curious sort of man, don't you think?" Liza Broughton whispered out of the side of her mouth. "He breezed into Little Hickman in that colorful rig of his, stirred up all kinds of skepticism about his medicinal herbs, potions, and magic, and now he's leaving behind a remarkable number of supporters. Frank Callahan claims his energy's improved since starting Mr. Wonder's Vegetable Compound, Gladys Hayward swears his Wondrous Nature's Balm has cured her arthritis, and Rhoda Marshall says her equilibrium's on the mend since starting his magnetic treatment. And there are multitudes more that will vouch for his tonics and cures. Of course, Doc's all tied in knots, thinks he's a quack, and says if Rhoda, for one, would lay off the nightcaps, her balance would return of its own accord." Liza giggled quietly and the lighthearted sound floated over the air like dust from a feather pillow. She rubbed her growing, rounded belly and added, "I'm not sure what to think of the man, a little strange, perhaps—and definitely a vagabond. Seems to me he'd grow tired of such a lifestyle."

Emma hesitated to comment, for she'd learned a side to Billy that few knew. Vagabond, yes, but with good reason. Who wouldn't want to escape a quiet life as a means of forgetting his past? Whether he'd found any kind of peace in doing so she couldn't say, but then who in this world could know true peace—especially after witnessing tragedy and loss? Her thoughts landed on Jon Atkins. Well, perhaps there were some exceptions. If anyone seemed at peace, it was him.

Then there were Ben and Liza, Rocky and Sarah, Carl and Frieda Hardy, the Crunkles, and the Jarvises, to name a few. All right, maybe peace was possible on certain levels—and the ability to forgive—as long as the infraction wasn't abuse or murder. She had a mental list that stretched a mile wide of reasons why it seemed impossible ever to forgive Ezra Browning.

"And now, before I unveil to you my most sought-after remedy," Billy was saying, "the one I've been withholding from you these past few weeks, I shall need a volunteer." Hands shot up all around, mostly from the teenage variety, with the exception of Lili Broughton, whose yellow-sleeved arm waved in the air, practically under Billy's nose.

Billy's eyes fell to her, as if they had a choice in the matter. "All right, young lady, get yourself on up here."

Without hesitation, or assistance, she mounted the steps leading up to the stage. Her braids flapped in the breeze, one of their red and yellow ribbons coming loose at the base to dangle down her front. "What do I have ta do?" was her on-the-spot question. "Can I help you do a magic trick? Can you make somethin' disappear before my eyes?"

"Oh, that Lili," Liza muttered.

Billy flung his head back and laughed. The crowd twittered with nervous excitement. Apparently he'd been delighting the crowds on a daily basis with his sleight of hand tricks, using his "magic wand" to make a playing card disappear from some unsuspecting hand then reappear in some unexpected place—like under his top hat, or in someone's pocket, or even inside Freddie Hogsworth's shoe, of all places! From what Emma had heard, that one gained the man an all new level of respect, especially when Freddie swore on a stack of Bibles that he hadn't so much as spoken a word to Billy Wonder before the trick transpired. Tongues wagged as folks speculated how he'd pulled it off.

From a hook on the wall, Billy removed a two-foot-long piece of rope. Giving it a couple of solid yanks on both ends to show off its sturdiness, he handed one end to Lili while he held to the other. "Pull as hard as you can, young lady. I want to make sure folks don't see this as flimsy." With gusto, Lili tugged at the rope, gritting her teeth in the process. "Harder," he pressed. Determined, she dug in deeper and pulled with all her might.

Billy laughed. "Well done, my dear." He took the rope from her possession and looped it over his shoulder, while from his pocket, he pulled a silky red swatch of cloth. "See this handkerchief?"

Lili nodded her head.

"Would you mind stuffing it inside this box here?"

Lili took the fabric and crammed it into a silver box sitting atop a narrow, wooden table at the front of the stage, then looked at him for further instruction.

"Very good." He handed her the box's matching lid. "Set this carefully in place if you don't mind."

Lili did as told.

 242

"Now, take the rope and tie it carefully around the box."

Billy retrieved the rope from his shoulder and handed it to her. She took it, but immediately the thing fell apart, one half of it falling to the floor. The crowd gasped and Billy feigned alarm.

"Well, would you look at that?" He bent to retrieve it, and when he put the two halves together, it seemed magically to reconnect before the eyes of every onlooker. Even Emma stood mesmerized.

"How'd you do that?" Lili's boulder-sized eyes fixed themselves on the now whole rope.

"It must have been your enchanting presence, my dear." The crowd cheered and clapped, and Lili blushed with excitement. Beside Emma, Liza clapped in delight.

Billy hushed everyone with a mere hand. "Now, if you wouldn't mind, tie the rope around this box."

Just as she was about to do it, someone from the crowd hollered, "First show us the scarf once more."

Billy looked slightly abashed. "Why, of course." Without hesitation, he lifted the lid and pulled out the scarf—then quickly jammed it back inside. That seemed to satisfy the heckler and Lili went back to her task, tying the rope around the silver box, fastening it with a double knot, and then stepping back when finished.

"Now I should like one more volunteer," Billy announced, looking out over the large group. Ignoring raised hands, he called on Emma.

Her hand went to her throat. She did not relish standing in front of folks, least of all on a stage where all eyes would be upon her. She felt her throat go instantly dry and shook her head, but the cluster of townsfolk wouldn't have it.

"Go up there, Emma. It'll be fun," Liza insisted. The people applauded and cajoled until, finally, she found herself pushed to the front and helped up the steps by Billy himself. Flustered, she looked out over the crowd and saw Jon Atkins and Ben Broughton standing on either side of Liza, Jon smiling with amusement, his hat resting low on his head so that she missed seeing that usual twinkle in his eyes. When had they wandered over? Already flushed from the excitement, she felt her cheeks go even redder. Lili jumped up and down, unable to conceal her enthusiasm.

Billy draped an arm around Emma's shoulder and turned her toward the audience. "This here is one fine cook," he announced, dragging her close to his side. "While in Little Hickman, I've had the privilege of taking my meals at her boardinghouse, and I must say I've never tasted finer food. And such a pretty thing, she is." He gave her shoulder a tighter than necessary squeeze. When she glanced at Jon, she found his smile missing.

Emma pursed her lips, feeling as if she were on display at the county fair. "Billy, get on with your trick before I introduce these delightful citizens to William Westerwunter," she hissed under her breath.

Good-natured laughter rumbled up from his chest. "Oh, you've cornered me, my fair lady," he murmured.

"You gonna show us some magic or what?" the heckler called.

Billy waved off the remark and proceeded, amazing his spectators with a disappearing scarf that, to the dismay of everyone, including Emma, somehow wound up in her apron pocket. And in the silver box? A bottle of Doctor Frunklemeyer's Essence of Life!

After wowing his audience with a string of tricks, Billy closed his act by explaining the benefits of the doctor's

"Essence," claiming it aided in preventing the common cold, cleared out the breathing passages, and even improved the condition of one's ailing lungs. "One dollar a bottle, folks," he sang. "I recommend a spoonful a day to prevent the germ from entering your body. One bottle will only last six months, though, so I'd suggest two bottles to last the entire year. And is it two dollars? Why, no. I'll sell you two bottles for just a dollar fifty. Now there's something you can't pass up."

Apparently, they agreed, for the majority of folks dug into their pockets and formed a line. In fact, Emma thought she'd never seen a longer one, unless she counted that line of youngsters who'd willingly waited more than an hour on Independence Day to ride Sam Livingston's prize mules.

*****

"You say that was your last show, Billy?" Jon asked over supper that night. He lifted a towel off the bread basket and helped himself to another roll.

Billy, seated catty-corner from Jon at the table, grinned and nodded. "Indeed it was, Preacher. I'll miss the good town of Little Hickman." As usual, Emma's boarders dug into their evening meal with gusto, injecting only sparse bits of conversation, barely taking the time to look up when someone spoke. And who could blame them? Tonight's meal was another winner—thick turkey noodle soup, fresh baked dinner rolls, a tangy cabbage slaw, and big, juicy slices of tomatoes and cucumbers straight from the garden. And if Jon's guess were right, by the aromas flowing from the kitchen, apple rhubarb pie for dessert.

"C-c-can you sh-show us some magic b-before you go?"

"Luke, you don't ask a man to work when he's off duty— much less without pay," his father scolded.

The unschooled boy's beady eyes brightened, unfazed by his father's words of reprimand. "He did some tricks in the p-parlor room. 'Member when he b-b-blowed on his hand and a nickel come up between his f-fingers? And then there was that trick with the b-ball. He'd s-start out with one in his h-hand and end up with three. He dint ask for no m-money then."

"Well, just the same...."

"Nonsense!" Billy interrupted. "I'll be happy to show the boy some tricks after he helps me pack up my wagon, how would that be?"

Luke brightened and pulled back his rounded shoulders. "Miss Emma says I'm a g-good h-helper."

Billy and Emma exchanged a friendly look. "That true, Miss Emma?"

"There's not much Luke won't do for a body when asked."

"Where you goin' from here?" Wes Clayton asked while chawing on a roll, a few stray crumbs nesting in his gray beard.

Jon's ears perked up, curious himself about the man's plans. Truth was, he didn't know what to think of Wonder. He was a crafty sort, and he did have a knack for entertainment, drawing crowds by the droves. There couldn't have been more than a handful of citizens who hadn't seen his show— and bought up his miracle cures by the carton-load after each performance.

And that was what troubled him.

In a day when money was already tight, had Billy Wonder taken advantage of the good people of Little Hickman by encouraging them to spend their earnings on worthless potions? According to Doc Randolph, these formulas consisted mostly of vegetable extracts and colored sugar water. Traveling medicine men such as Billy dotted the countryside, riding into unsuspecting towns to show off their masterful illusions. Then, while holding their audiences captive, they sold off their wares faster than the townsfolk could blink.

Newspapers and magazines were crammed with ads for medicines and miracle-cure devices. Most of these medicines were harmless, but many contained generous quantities of alcohol or opium, ensuring a quick feeling of well-being for first-time customers, followed by the possibility of habitual use—something for which these traveling salesmen dearly hoped. To them, the frequency with which patrons returned for more products determined the number of dollar signs flitting before their eyes.

He hoped that wasn't the case with Billy, but one couldn't be too sure about who to trust nowadays.

"I'm headin' south. Need to get settled in a warmer climate before winter sets in."

"Can't blame you for that," said Harland. "Wouldn't want ta be stuck in a blizzard with that wagon o' yours."

"You'd be surprised where that wagon's been. It's seen many a mountain range and crossed its share of rivers. Haven't passed through any blizzards yet, though, and don't expect to."

"Ain't you got a h-house somewheres?" Luke asked, showing his cabbage slaw when he spoke.

"He doesn't live anywhere to speak of," Elliott answered. "He moves from one town to another, never staying anywhere long enough to put down roots. Isn't that right, Mr. Wonder?"

Billy seemed unruffled by the remark. "It's true I never was one for putting down stakes, Mr. Newman." He speared several sliced carrot wedges with his fork. "That's not to say I'm opposed to the idea, though, given the right set of circumstances—and a pretty woman." He turned his smiling face on Emma, after which she dipped her head, a flush appearing in her cheeks. Was Billy sweet on Emma? The very notion set Jon's teeth on edge. He forced a demure smile behind the rim of his water glass and tried to ignore the sudden twinge in his neck.

"Course, I'd have to find me a whole new line o' work. Illusions and trickery's 'bout all I know."

"You seem ta be quite the salesman," Charley offered. *And a swindler, to boot,* Jon thought.

"I do enjoy the sales end of my business. It's brought me a hefty profit."

Jon thought he'd do well to keep his mouth shut with regard to his profits. Some might consider him a thief when they discovered his ointments, oils, and medicinal brews didn't accomplish their intended purpose.

"Perhaps I could find me a wife with wanderlust in her veins. Now, right there'd be the perfect situation." Humor sparked his countenance as he sought out Emma's eyes yet again. She scowled, plopped down her napkin, and pushed back her chair.

"I'm afraid you'd have to look far and wide for a woman like that," Jon said, disgruntled. "Most women want stability and comfort, someplace warm and inviting. And I'd vouch most want a place in which to raise a family."

Billy eyed Jon with particular interest, brow arched. "Is that so?" he quipped. His expression flickered with merriment. "I wouldn't think a man of the cloth would know about such things."

Jon had the distinct feeling he'd fallen smack into the middle of one of Billy's traps, and for the first time in a long while, he sorely lacked for a decent comeback. What had possessed him to make such a comment, as if he knew what women, Emma Browning in particular, really sought after?

Emma gathered up the serving dishes, starting with the ones in the middle of the table.

"You needin' some help there, Miss Emma?" Billy asked.

For a man of the cloth, Jon certainly felt hot under the collar.

"I can handle things just fine, Mr. Wonder."

"Humph. I wasn't even done with them rolls," Harland complained. Emma thrust the basket under his nose.

For reasons unbeknownst to Jon, Billy gave a full-hearted chortle—as if he were privy to some secret. He glanced around, put his palms square on the table, and nodded his head before pushing himself up. "Well then, folks, if you don't mind, I believe I'll call it an evening. You want to come help me load up my rig, Luke?"

"You bet!" the boy exclaimed. "C-can you show me how to make somethin' disappear?"

"Why, sure thing. How 'bout we start with you and me?"

"Huh? How you g-gonna make us disappear? You can't d-do that."

Billy winked at Emma and guided Luke into the parlor, giving everyone his back. "Course I can."

"Yeah, but h-how?"

"Like this. Now they see us..." he opened the door and stepped outside. "Now they don't."

With the closed door, the pair vanished.

Chapter Twenty-Two

*E*mma still couldn't believe Jon had talked her into bringing her father to the boardinghouse, but even as she
belabored the point, she knew there was no help for it. Why,
she'd be worse than heartless to ignore Ezra's helpless physical state, no matter that he'd treated her poorly most of her
born days. "It's just a matter of time, Emma," Doc had told
her yesterday. "About all we can do is keep him comfortable."
And the only way to ensure that was to bring him here, she
admitted—even though he had yet to agree to the plan. Merciful heavens! She could practically hear him wailing in protest now as she imagined Jon breaking the news to him, a job
he'd insisted on doing, even though she'd argued it wasn't his
responsibility.

Giving her head a little shake, she fastened the final
button at the front of her gingham dress, secured the tie belt
at the back of her waist, and hung her housecoat, which she'd
worn through breakfast, on the hook over her door. Next, she
moved to the mirror, trying not to think about Jon Atkins, or
her father, for that matter. Leaning forward, she surveyed her
reflection with grimness. When had she gotten those crinkle
lines at the corners of her eyes and mouth, and what was that
brown, freckly spot just over her right eyebrow?

She picked up a comb and ran it through her golden hair,
tipped her head to one side, and tried to decide how to wear
her locks, in the end, choosing the easiest method, a single
ponytail going down the middle of her back and pulled
together with a ribbon.

Most women want stability and comfort, someplace warm and inviting. Jon's words to Billy pulled at her memory. Had he been thinking about anyone in particular when he'd made the remark? Hannah Clayton, perhaps? Although he hadn't mentioned her for some time, Emma often wondered who he visited when he made his pastoral calls.

"Oh, pish-posh, why should it matter to me who Jon Atkins visits?" she muttered in the mirror. "I'm perfectly contented with my life. Don't need some minister of the Word fussin' with my head."

So why was it, she thought, as she pressed the front of her flared skirt with her palms, then surveyed herself one last time, pinching some pink into her cheeks, that she couldn't seem to shoo him out of her mind?

A sudden commotion coming from outside had her running to the side window to peer down at the street. Billy Wonder's garish wagon, pulled by his two horses, had halted outside the boardinghouse. He was coming to bid her good-bye. Grabbing up her sunbonnet from the bedpost, she plopped it on her head, then changed her mind last minute and tossed it on the bed. Finally, she snatched her reticule from its hook, stuffed it under her arm, and sailed down the stairs.

*****

"You're not staying here, old man, so you may as well stop arguing with me."

"I ain't goin' nowheres with you, preacher kid, least of all to the boardinghouse. My girl won't take kindly to my takin' up space there."

"Your girl's already cleaned out the guest room in preparation for your arrival. She wants you to come live with her."

251

It went against his grain to stretch the truth, but there was no help for it this time.

"Balderdash! If she'd wanted me ta come, she'd have told me herself."

Jon heaved a sigh. "I told her not to come out 'cause I knew what a fuss you'd raise."

His wheezing was especially bad today, and every word of argument that came from his mouth took great effort—so much that Jon feared he'd keel over right there if he didn't calm down.

"Cain't leave my animals."

"Sam Livingston's agreed to come get the horses, and Edgar Blake's taking the other critters to his place. They'll be well taken care of," Jon assured him.

Ezra dug in his heels, his face reddening as he gripped the arms of his tattered easy chair. The place stank to high heaven. The question of when Ezra had last taken a bath sat on the tip of his tongue, but he managed not to ask it, vowing that as soon as they got back to Emma's he'd start running the water. The old fool could fight him all he wanted, but like it or not he was going to soak for no less than thirty minutes.

"If I ever kick this cough I'm comin' back fer my animals," Ezra spat out, setting off a stint of hacking and spewing that lasted several seconds.

"And you'll get no argument from either Sam or Edgar." He reached out a hand. "Let me help you up."

"Don't need no help." But even as he said it, he took Jon's hand to pull himself up, shaking and teetering. Had Jon waited even one more day, he wasn't sure he'd have gotten the old guy out of his chair.

Outside, his friend Rocky Callahan waited in his wagon. They'd fashioned a bed of sorts in the back of the wagon in which to lay Ezra. It would be interesting to see how he took to the news that he'd be riding into town on a cot rather than atop his swayback mare.

"Catch your breath," Jon told him.

They must have stood outside the shack a full two minutes without moving, Ezra's eyes scanning the ramshackle place, thinking thoughts Jon would never know. A glint of remorse shone in his craggy countenance.

Wetness burned at the back of Jon's eyes.

"Come on, Ezra. It's time to go."

*****

"Here're your biscuits, Billy Wonder," Emma said, shoving the still warm batch into his hands. "There must be three dozen or more of 'em in there, so I hope you're hungry."

Billy lifted the towel from the basket and peered underneath, his eyes rolling heavenward at the fine aroma. "Hm. Give me an hour or so to let my breakfast settle and I'll be chompin' away on these delicacies before you can spit out the words 'Better 'n Boston's best batch o' buttered biscuits!'"

Emma laughed at his tongue twister. "Well, share them along the way if you can't eat 'em all. Otherwise they'll get too hard and go to waste."

"Share them, you say? Bite your tongue, madam. I will share them only if I run across a dying beggar lying along the road, and even then I'll make him give me the clothes off his back first."

She laughed again, harder this time. "Oh, Billy."

"You are beautiful when you laugh. You should consider doing it more often." She blushed at the compliment and clasped her hands behind her back. "And you are a smooth one, Mr. Wonder."

"So I've been told." He swept off his hat and clawed his fingers through his dark hair. Eyeing her with particular care, he bent forward and whispered, "I meant what I said, you know, about settling down someday—given the right woman and all. What if I'm looking at her now and just walking away?"

She looked him square in the face, which came as a surprise, considering she'd spent her entire life shunning the male species. Tipping her head just so, she gave him the beginnings of a smile. "You are a sweet man."

"But not the one to knock you off your feet."

There was nothing to say, so she stood mute. A gentle breeze cooled her cheeks, ruffled her long sleeves, and played with the hem of her skirt.

He looked up and down Main Street where folks were riding past, some calling out their good-byes from their high perches on dusty rigs, others smiling and waving as they rode their whinnying nags through town. Billy rewarded them all with polite nods.

"I saw it in his eyes, Emma," he muttered, kicking a stone off the sidewalk with the toe of his shiny, black boot. "Last night at the supper table when I was teasing about wantin' to find me a woman with wanderlust in her veins. The preacher thought I had eyes for you, and he looked plenty worried."

"Oh, phooey! What would the reverend see in me? He's a churchman. I'm a—a worldly...." She couldn't seem to finish her sentence. What exactly was she? She wasn't a heathen, for she'd never been one to use vile language, partake in bad habits, or engage in gossip. She'd rarely told a lie, never laughed at crude jokes, and tried not to covet her neighbor's things—although there were times she'd longed for Liza Broughton's sweet looks, refined manners, and intelligence or Sarah Callahan's delicate beauty. And she'd started attending

Sunday services, she reminded herself. That ought to count for something. Of course, her motives weren't especially pure. She had to admit that she'd fallen into the same category as Fancy Jenkins when it came to church attendance. The preacher was downright fine to look at.

So if she wasn't a heathen, what was she? Certainly not a *Christian*—for she'd never made a conscious decision to trust Christ. Too much bitterness, she decided, thanks to Ezra Browning. Despite Grace Giles' words that God loved her, she couldn't imagine God wanting someone with as dark a heart as she possessed.

So, no, Jonathan Atkins couldn't possibly be interested in her—unless it was her soul he sought to save and nothing more. She could see him caring about that. He was a compassionate man. Just look how he cared for her drunken father.

She put a hand to her brow to shield the sun from her eyes, wishing now she'd worn her bonnet, and looked up at Billy. "Are you a Christian, Mr. Wonder?"

The question must have thrown him, for he blew out a loud breath and twisted his mouth downward. "Well now, that's a blunt question, but since you ask it, I suppose I'd have to say no. Are you?"

Emptiness such as she'd never experienced crawled across her chest, its claws reaching out and pinching until it hurt, and she shook her head. "No."

"Well, then," he hemmed. "We're a pair."

His remark produced the tiniest of laughs, hollow and depthless. "Well," she said, swallowing hard. "You take care of yourself Philip William Westerwunter." She extended her hand. "Until we meet again."

"Until we meet again," he repeated, holding her hand in both of his.

Just then, Gus Humphrey stepped out of Johansson's Mercantile, three storefronts down, broom in hand. "Mr. Wonder!" he called. "We'll miss yer shows. Don't forget about us."

Billy turned. "No danger there," he called back, dropping Emma's hand in order to wave at the lad.

"Got any last-minute tricks?" asked Fred Swain, who, with his young wife on his arm and four trailing youngsters, was crossing the street, having just left the bank. Little Ermaline still had her arm in a sling, but her leg was free of its cast. With the use of a pair of crutches, she managed to limp along with her siblings, the smile on her face indicating the inconvenience didn't bother her in the least. Emma thought about the accident and marveled how well, and speedily, she'd recovered. Was that the hand of God, then? And if it was, why hadn't He simply prevented the accident from ever occurring?

Sometimes the Lord allows these things so His children will learn to trust Him more. Pure and clear, the words of Rita Flowers lingered at the edges of her mind. *Somethin' good will come of it*, she'd added. Had something good come of it? The family certainly didn't look any worse for the wear, and they still had their little girl, didn't they?

Suddenly, folks started gathering around the likable trickster to bid him good-bye. To be sure, he'd made his share of friends in Little Hickman. Of course, there was that faction of folks (Doc included) who claimed he was a shyster—bilking citizens of their hard-earned money for elixirs that weren't worth the cost of the bottles they came in.

Emma cared not what folks thought or said, for she'd formed her own opinions and planned to stick by them. As unconventional as he was, she liked the silly man, and truth be told, Little Hickman wouldn't be quite the same in his absence.

An hour later, Billy well on his way, Emma sat herself down under the big oak outside the post office, gathered her skirts about her, and carefully removed the seal from the envelope that contained her most recent missive from Grace Giles. A trace of some delicate perfume wafted through the air as she unfolded the onionskin paper and began to read.

My Dear Emma,

You will never know how pleased I was to receive your letter and to learn that you've been reading the Bible Clara gave you some years ago.

You asked me several questions that I will gladly try to answer, perhaps not quite to your satisfaction yet, but, rest assured, all in good time.

First, yes, I do believe that Jesus performed all the miracles spoken of in the book of John. Certain scholars have started rumors that perhaps we shouldn't take the Bible so literally, but I say that's blasphemy. If God could send His Son to earth by way of a virgin birth, why could He not heal the sick and even call back the dead? As to whether He performs miracles today—of course! The Bible tells us that Jesus is the same yesterday, today, and forever. That says to me that the same God who touched a hurting world nearly two thousand years ago longs to do for us today what He did then. You must believe it, Emma. We live in changing times, but our God's great love remains as strong and firm as ever.

You asked how one could learn to forgive another for the wrongs done against him. I presume you are asking how you could possibly forgive your father. Am I right? That is not an easy thing, I grant you, but it is far from impossible because of the power and strength that is ours through Christ

Jesus. If you believe that, you are already halfway there! Trust Jesus to heal the hurts of your past, Emma dear—then trust Him to lend you the forgiveness you need to show your father. Forgiveness is far more freeing than living with a heart of anger.

How do I know about Ezra Browning? Well, I know because my mother, God rest her precious soul, was your father's aunt. She passed away just over four months ago. Apparently, my mother and Ezra maintained minimal correspondence over the years, and before her passing, she had much to tell me about your father's own ill-fated childhood and the people who raised him. She also told me what she knew about you, which, unfortunately, wasn't a great deal. She heard stories of abuse, however, and because of that, her heart ached for you—as does mine. In your father's most recent missive to my mother, he indicated the two of you remain at odds.

I shall reserve the remainder of your questions for later (please be patient), my dear cousin—think of it; we are cousins—for the hour is quite late, and I must rise early to tend to my restaurant business. I am a childless widow, but very much at peace in my life. I have a fine little eatery in the heart of Chicago called Grace's Kitchen, and I reside in the upstairs apartment. Quite convenient, I must say, but not necessarily the place in which I wish to live out my remaining years. I shall post this letter tomorrow when one of my regulars comes in for his morning coffee. He will deliver my precious letter to the city post office.

Be well, and write back to me!

Your friend—and cousin.

Grace Giles

P.S. Let us say that I was perchance interested in starting up my own boardinghouse in Chicago—or someplace rural. Could you tell me what I might expect before undertaking such a project? (And you may tell your curious postmaster that I'm quite interested in knowing these things.)

Emma smiled at her cousin's postscript. At last, she had something legitimate to tell George Garner when he inquired about the mystery letters from Chicago.

"I have a cousin, a real live cousin," she whispered into the noonday breeze, fighting back the impulse to jump up and down, maybe even do a jig in the middle of the street. "Who would have thought?"

With her fingers, she retraced the finely penned words, rereading them at a snail's pace, taking them into her as if they were delicate morsels that required slow chewing and savoring.

Several questions still swirled in her head: Where was Ezra's homeplace, and who had raised him if not his own parents? How did Grace know Clara Abbott? How had Grace's mother learned of Ezra's poor parenting? However, she determined not to dwell on them another minute. Hadn't Grace told her to be patient? All in good time, she'd said, all in good time.

She folded up the letter, slipped it back into its envelope, and tucked it safely between the pages of the newest edition of *Ladies' Home Journal,* a splurge she'd made at the mercantile earlier when picking up a few household items.

"Hello, Miss Browning," called a male voice.

She glanced up to find a smiling Irwin Waggoner and Gertrude Riley, Hickman's latest "couple," entering the post office together, Gertrude's two youngsters, Charles and Jolene, trailing behind. His protective hand on the middle of her back as they'd traversed the sidewalk, and the manner in which Gertrude blushed with bliss, created a longing in the core of her being. What must it be like to have captured a man's heart? She returned the greeting and watched them disappear into the building.

Not ten feet away, a black squirrel scampered up a tree trunk, twittering for all his might at a blue jay who'd invaded his territory. Halfway up, the critter scuttled out on a limb then turned to finish his scolding. Sufficiently told, the jay took flight. Overhead, puffy, snowball clouds glided by, their shapes shifting with the air currents. It was so crowning a moment that in that instant everything in Emma's world seemed to glitter with tranquility.

That is, until she heard the sound of wagon wheels turning on the dusty, potholed street and witnessed two men sitting atop a wagon seat, carting something, or someone, in the back. "Ya ain't got no business," whined their passenger, loud enough to raise the curiosity of passersby.

And just like that, her peaceful moment vanished.

*****

As usual, he did his best to try her patience.

"You should drink some more water," she said, pointing to the glass on the bedside stand. "Doc says it'll help your cough."

"I could use a drink of the real stuff," he groused. "I'm plain sick o' water."

She counted to twenty in her head. "You're done with drinkin' ale, Pa. Water and milk's the only liquids you'll be gettin' under my roof. Now, stop bein' so cussed ornery."

"Phew! Yore the ornery one," he countered.

Not wanting to argue, she picked up the glass and shoved it under his nose, bending to lift his head with her other hand. His body trembled with weakness. "Drink," she ordered.

He drank to appease her. Two sips, three sips, four, then five. He was thirsty, the old coot.

When he finished, she set the glass back on the stand with a plunk, noting that at least half the water had disappeared down his gullet. "Was that so bad?"

He pointed his gaze at the ceiling, his stubborn chin jutting out. "I ain't needin' nobody ta wait on me," he muttered. "Been takin' care o' myself for nigh onto sixty years now." Emma wasn't sure how old her father was, for he'd never shared his birth date, but one thing was certain. He looked older than his years. And, yes, he did need a full-time nurse. As it was, he could barely walk from the bed to the necessary—a chair with a lidded hole and a chamber pot underneath that Doc had sent over.

Thankfully, Jon, true to his word, had been at the fellow's side most of the day, lending a hand and seeing to his personal needs, even giving him a bath in the portable tub in the main floor bathroom. Rocky had hung around long enough to help transport him down the hall, one man on each side. When the whole affair was over, she wasn't sure who was the more exhausted, Jon or Ezra, for both were sweating bullets by the time they got him situated in bed.

She ripped out a sigh, which probably amounted to about the fiftieth that day if she'd been counting. "Well, it's settled. You're stayin' here until you regain your strength," she said, wanting to sound optimistic, even though they both knew he'd never see his farm again.

For the first time, the notion that Ezra Browning's life was closing in on him cut straight to her core. As a youngster, she'd learned the art of compliance as a means of survival, counting down the days when she could strike out on her own, escape his disparaging, stony presence.

"Where you off to, girl? It's gettin' close ta dark time."

It was the evening of her sixteenth birthday. And her father hadn't once acknowledged it. He sat in his easy chair, feet propped on a wooden stool, one hand draped over his belly, the other holding to a bottle of whiskey. Dark spots shaded the underside of his eyes, the pupils glazed over.

She looked around the kitchen, brushing off his question. Strange. When she walked out that door it would be to say good-bye, but he'd so conditioned her to finish her chores that somehow she couldn't leave without first washing the dishes. She dropped the knapsack stuffed with her belongings in the middle of the room and went to the sink. She sensed his eyes following her every move.

"What you up to?" he asked again. His voice contained its usual gruff tone.

"I'm washin' the dishes," she answered. She kept her back to him so he wouldn't see the look of elation that surely gleamed in her eyes. There was a room waiting for her at Miss Abbott's Boardinghouse, the first one on her left at the top of the front staircase. A handmade quilt bedecked the Jenny Lind bed, which had a mattress made of real feathers and down. She couldn't imagine sleeping in such luxury.

Miss Abbott had extended the invitation to come live with her, and, by gum, she planned to take her up on it. Sixteen was plenty old enough to be out on her own, and she didn't care what Ezra had to say about it. She was done with the abuse. Done.

"What's in that ther' bag?" he asked.

She shivered despite June's hotter-than-normal temperatures. "Just some stuff," she muttered. After scrubbing clean the few dishes, she rinsed them and set them on a drying rack. As she'd done a thousand times before, she picked up the washbasin, dumped its contents down the drain, and then wrung out the rag and draped it over the edge of the sink.

Turning, she gave her father a long, assessing look. "I'm goin' to Miss Abbott's place," she announced, pulling back her shoulders.

 262

"She's invited me to come and work for her. I'll be takin' my room and board there."

When she would have expected him to blow up, he took a couple of steadying breaths and stared at her, seeming speechless. Minutes passed before he finally broke the silence. "What'm I s'posed ta do?"

She'd spent her life seeing to his every whim, even going out to the barn to take from his stash when he needed a drink and couldn't find a bottle in the cupboard. His very existence depended on her, and she was plain tired of it. "You can open a can, can't you?" she asked. "You'll have ta learn to get by. I ain't your slave, Pa." It was odd that her fear of him had vanished over the years, replaced by hostility and—what was it? Cold contempt?

She looked at her shoes and noted the holes coming through at the toes. Miss Abbott planned to pay her a small stipend on top of her room and board. She would save very carefully, and when she had enough, she would buy herself a nice new pair. Never again would she have to beg her father for money to buy the essentials.

Rather than rant, he sagged in his chair, looking spent. "Ya ain't old enough to go out on yer own."

She picked up her knapsack and tucked it under her arm. "I'm sixteen, Pa. Some girls get married at my age."

"Pff. Ya ain't sixteen yet. When did ya turn sixteen?"

She turned her mouth up and tilted her head, noting her lack of emotion. "Today, Pa."

At the sound of the tight little gasp escaping his chest, she walked across the room and out the door. And she didn't look back until she got to the top of the hill.

Oh, the sense of liberation, that day she'd walked out on Ezra Browning.

Which was why it made it so difficult to understand the overwhelming sadness she felt for him now.

Chapter Twenty-Three

*J*on hung back in the doorway and watched as she tended to her father's needs, fluffing his pillow, fixing his blanket, setting the glass of water in the center of the bedside stand.

"Jus' like old times, eh?" he murmured, his voice hoarse from hours of coughing.

She straightened to her full height. "Not quite. The difference is you're sober for a change. All you ever did when I was growin' up was drink." Her hair had long ago escaped its ribbon and was hanging loosely down her back.

"I know." It was nothing more than a whisper, but he'd heard it just as clear as if a bell had chimed in his ear. Regret. Deep, unwavering. He wondered if she'd heard it, too, or had she grown so accustomed to tuning him out that she'd missed it?

She pulled up a stool and sat, unaware that Jon lurked in the shadows. "Why did you drink so much?" she asked.

Jon held his breath. *Lord, be present in this room. Grant healing to these two hearts before it's too late. Turn Emma's animosity into love. May she find forgiveness in You and then in her heart. And grant hope and spiritual healing to Ezra.*

"Guess I dint see no way out. I lost my wife, and my world caved in. Life seemed prit'near hopeless."

"You had a kid to raise up. Did ya ever think of that? Couldn't you have sobered up for my sake?"

Jon winced, considered going into the room, but then thought better of it, reasoning that at least they were talking. He would act as referee only if necessary.

"'Course I did, but it wudn't easy. Once that stuff gets a hold on ya, ther' ain't no turnin' back. It eased my mind, took away the pain o' the past and the dread o' the future. I got me a powerful need right now, matter o' fact. Wouldn't hurt none ta give me just a li'l swig o' somethin' from yer cupboard. 'Bout anythin'll do."

Emma leaned forward in her chair. "What happened in your past?" she asked, deciding to skip over his need for a drink. "You've never talked about it. Who raised you?" Her voice dropped so low that Jon had to strain his ears. Immediate pangs of guilt for eavesdropping pinched his conscience, but he couldn't force himself to move away from the door.

"What kind o' birdbrained question is that? My ma an' pa did, who else?"

"How come you never talked about 'em then?"

He coughed, more out of a need to stall, though, Jon was sure. "They wasn't much worth talkin' 'bout. You wouldn't o' been interested. 'Sides, they was an uppity bunch, them and those two kids."

"What two kids?" Emma's back stiffened as if a bolt of lightning had just run the length of her.

"My older brother an' sister. Twins, they was. Spoilt ta high heaven, too. My ma and pa would o' give them the moon if they could've. Me? I was a knife in their sides my whole life. I guess you could say I wound up on their hate list, and the day I left home for good there weren't no weepin' over it."

"Kind of like the day I left, huh? The night of my sixteenth."

"Phooey, girl, that was different. There weren't no celebratin' 'bout that. If anythin' I hated myself, not you." His voice kept goin' in and out, as if a frog had suddenly leaped inside

265

his throat to croak out a few words of its own. "Don't you think I knew it was me what chased ya away? If I'd a just—" He mopped his brow with the corner of his sheet, clearly exhausted. It was all Jon could do to mind his own business.

Emma reached behind her back to gather up her thick golden hair and pull it off her neck. Then she dropped the mane, letting it fall where it would.

"You had twins in your family and you never told me? I always figured my grandparents died and you were an only kid."

The old man sniffed. "Don't know what give you that idea."

"Because you never talked about them!" she blurted. "What else was I s'pose to think? You warned me repeatedly to keep my questions to myself or you'd swat my behind—or make me stand in the corner next to that hot stove.

"Then there was that time I threatened to go find my grandmaw if you didn't tell me where she was, and you withdrew my suppers for a week of Sundays."

"Weren't that long. Two days, tops," Ezra murmured.

"Week."

"Two days."

"Week...."

"Two—" Another serious round of hacking drowned out the last of their sparring. Emma's questions were taking their toll on the old guy. Jon wondered if it was time to step forward. Ezra shifted on the bed, trying to get comfortable. Emma reached for the water glass, but he put up a shaky hand and flicked at it, refusing.

Seconds passed. Emma's shoulders remained taut and determined. "Are you sure you don't know Grace Giles?" This woman wasn't about to give up. She had him where she wanted him—flat on his back, sober, and immobile—probably a rare thing in her eyes.

"Who?"

"Grace Giles. The lady from Chicago I told you about. I found out today her mother is your aunt."

"I don't got no aunt with a girl named Grace. Least, none I know 'bout."

"Yes, you do. She tol' me so, and she also mentioned somethin' about the folks who raised you, as if they weren't your own."

"That's plain hogwash. Who's she think she is, this Grace person, and what's she tryin' ta pull by feedin' lies to ya, pokin' 'er nose in where it don't belong?"

"I don't think she's lying. And here's another somethin' strange. She talks like she knows all about Clara Abbott."

Silence. "I wouldn't know nothin' about that. I barely knew that Abbott lady." He made a big deal of turning over in his bed, situating himself so that he faced the wall. "I'm tired."

"I think Grace is your aunt Edith's daughter."

"Huh?"

"Don't play dumb with me. I know you've kept in contact with her. Why couldn't you have told me about her? Why the big secret?"

A shaky breath fell out of him. "It weren't no secret. Ther' jus' wudn't anythin' ta tell. I heard from Edith ever' so often, yeah. Fact is she was the only one o' the lot of 'em who ever cared if I lived or died. She never told me nothin' about any o' her own family, though, I swear. Never mentioned no Grace—jus' always asked me how I was and how—you—was doin'."

"I suppose you told her what a burden I was to you," Emma said, her words dripping with sarcasm.

He sighed again. "She knowed my life was rough."

267

"Grace's mother passed away four months ago, did you know that? If Edith is her mother, then that means your aunt has died."

Jon bit down so hard he thought he'd soon be tasting blood. Did she have to be so blunt in the telling? Or maybe she'd learned it was the only approach that worked with Ezra Browning.

Ezra stirred, turned his head halfway, and stared at the ceiling. Jon hung back further so as to stay out of sight. "She died, huh? Well then." And just like that, he went back to the wall. "I ain't answerin' no more questions."

"I have a right to know about my relatives, Pa." She sounded angry, but it was a contained sort of anger, desperate in tone, as if she worried that showing too much emotion would shut down the entire conversation and there might not be another opportunity like this one.

"Leave me be."

Emma heaved a sigh that reached across the room. Jon ducked behind the door, his conscience finally getting the best of him, and why wouldn't it? He felt like a bandit sneaking up on his prey, snagging every word that rose up between them.

He looked around the house. Should he go sit on the porch, park himself in the music room, walk down to the new church, or maybe walk out to the backyard and check on the garden? After supper, everyone had scattered, going either to their rooms or down to the saloon. He could always take advantage of the quiet house and have another look at Sunday's sermon notes, even though he felt quite studied up. He walked to the front door and looked out at the noiseless street. A sprinkling of townsfolk strolled along, stopping to peer inside shop windows or to have an evening chat with one of their neighbors.

"I don't see why you won't talk about it, Pa." Her muffled voice still carried to his ears.

He opened the door and moved out to the porch.

*****

It was the first time in a long, long while that Emma Browning felt near to tears. She'd always prided herself on her ability to stave off her emotions, but tonight was not one of those times. While it thrilled her to learn she had a cousin she never knew existed, her father's apparent lack of knowledge of the woman dropped a cloudy veil over her enthusiasm. Was he being truthful when he said he'd never heard of her? And what was the mystery behind his upbringing? Why had Grace alluded that his own parents hadn't raised him—or was that just her reading more into Grace's letter than she should have? One thing was certain; Ezra had never wanted to discuss his childhood roots, and tonight was no exception. What was the big mystery? And how was she supposed to forgive and forget the past if he never let her into his?

If ye continue in my word, then are ye my disciples indeed; and ye shall know the truth and the truth shall make you free.

She remembered the passage of Scripture from the book of John as if the Lord Himself had emblazoned it on her heart. What it meant, however, was another story. Was God trying to tell her something?

Outside Ezra's room, she dabbed at both eyes. His breathing had grown heavy, indicating he'd drifted to sleep. *Lord, how can You expect me to take care of him when he failed so miserably at watching over me?*

Bereft, she walked to the front door. She would gather her thoughts on the porch.

The porch swing swayed gently, as if the wind had set it in motion, except that there was no wind, not even a gentle breeze. She glanced up at the sky and noted a sprinkling of stars but no moon in sight. Hugging herself against the cool temperatures, she dropped into the swing and pushed off with both feet. A breathy sigh escaped as she leaned back and closed her eyes.

"I take a stroll through your garden and what do you do? Steal my place. Now you'll have to make room for me."

At the sight of Jonathan Atkins coming around the corner of the house, her breath caught. Why did he have this strange effect on her? She was no teenager, for mercy sakes, but a spinster for all practical purposes. But lately her mind had been dancing with all manner of fanciful thoughts. Shyness overtook her as she slid over.

"I thought you'd gone up to your room," she murmured.

"Too nice a night to be holed up in my room, even if it is on the cool side. Afraid fall is just around the corner." He settled in beside her and the swing moaned under the additional weight, but it was made of sturdy wood and hung by heavy chains. Truth be told, it would probably outlast the house.

"You chilly?" he asked.

"I'm fine," she whispered, even as her teeth chattered noiselessly, more from nerves than anything, she expected.

She felt his eyes bearing down on her. All at once, he stopped the swing and jumped up. "Be right back," he announced, scurrying into the house, the screen door shutting behind him with a thwop.

She gave her head a little shake. What was he up to? A second later, she had her answer when he reappeared with a quilt in hand. "Here you go," he said, positioning it across her lap, taking care to cover her completely. She regarded him with wide eyes. No man had ever treated her with such kindness, and the question of how to behave drove her a little crazy. In all her born days, she'd never required the attentions of a man, and now was no time to start.

"Th-thank you," she stammered.

"You're welcome," he said, dropping down beside her and setting the swing back in motion. "He's snoring in there," he said, angling his head in the direction of the front room window. "Guess he's finally tuckered out."

"Either that or puttin' on a good act."

His gentle chuckle rippled through the air. "He's a tough nut."

The swing gently swayed as ensuing silence seemed to stretch into tomorrow. Finally, they both spoke at once.

"It was nice of you to—" he said.

"Thank you for all you—" she started.

"Go ahead," she said.

"No, you go first," he insisted.

"Oh,…I was just going to thank you for all your help today."

"Didn't I tell you I'd do most of the work? He's a cranky old soul. No need for you to have to put up with that. Besides, you've a boardinghouse to run."

"And you've a congregation to tend to, sermons to preach, and a church to build," she argued. "Much as I hate to admit it, he is my father." She felt her chin jut forward. "And my responsibility."

Piano music, loud and twangy, carried from Madam Guttersnipe's establishment.

"I was going to say it was mighty generous of you to provide the room for him," he said in a soft voice. "I'm sorry if you felt pressured into it. That wasn't my intention."

Emma nodded, pulled the blanket up under her chin, and slanted her face in the direction from whence the music came. "I hate that place," she muttered. "Ezra Browning gave his life to that rotten slop house. Worked hours on end to support his wretched habit. It's ironic how he's wastin' away under my roof while up the road they're goin' strong as ever."

An owl hooted from three trees over, his spookish cry seeming to match her morose mood.

"My pa hung out there, too, you know," Jon acknowledged. "Heard it said when I was a kid that he and Ezra Browning used to have their drinking matches."

Emma's mouth fell open. This was news to her. She looked him full in the face. "What do you mean?"

A pathetic chortle cut loose. "Folks would gather around and bet on who they thought could guzzle down the most booze in one sitting, Luther Atkins or Ezra Browning. Guess it was a pretty even draw most nights."

In all the years she'd known him, she could count on one hand the number of times he'd mentioned his father. Oh, she'd heard stories that he was a no-good drunk like her own pa, but it'd never occurred to her that they'd been drinking buddies.

"What—was it like for you—growing up with your pa?"

The way his brow crinkled up, as if the question pained him, made her regret having asked it, but then he gave a loose shrug and grinned. "Truthfully? He was a mean cuss when he was drunk, which was most of the time; knocked my ma and me around if we so much as blinked wrong. I stayed clear of him as much as possible."

How could he appear so nonchalant? "And your mother?"

That sobered him some. "She took the brunt of it, always defending me, coming between us so that when his fists flew they'd hit her first. There came a day, though, when I was old enough and big enough to fend for myself, that she couldn't take it anymore. That's when she—well, you know."

She did know. News of any kind traveled through Little Hickman as swift as a grass fire, but folks particularly seemed to cherish sharing juicy gossip. Luther Atkins' wife had hung herself in the barn, and her teenage boy, Jon, was the one who'd discovered her body. Emma recalled how the news had sent a chill racing through her body. How did a boy go on living after making such a horrid discovery?

Where was his bitterness, the expected rage? If he had any, he'd hidden it well.

As if he'd read her thoughts, he tipped his face in her direction. "I hated him for what he'd done to my ma, Emma, but the Lord healed me of my anger a long time ago." He dipped lower until mere inches separated their faces.

In haste, she looked down at her shoes peeking out from the hem of the blanket.

"I was mad enough to kill him, don't think I wasn't. I knew where he kept his guns, and I was ready to go after him.

"I plotted how I'd march into Guttersnipe's, drag him away from whichever barroom girl he was cozied up to, and I'd haul him out to the middle of the street where we'd be in plain view. I wanted everyone to watch while I did the act."

His words chilled her blood, and she couldn't help but look at him again. His gaze had rested on something straight ahead.

"But God had His hand on me in the form of Reverend Miller," he continued. "As soon as he heard about the ordeal, he rode out to my place. He found me in the sorriest state I'd ever been in." He looked only a little sheepish. "By the time he arrived, I'd already torn the inside of our house to smithereens, ripped pictures off the walls, shredded my pa's clothing, broke dishes, ripped curtains off the windows, broke furniture with my bare hands. I mean, you want to see rage," he gave a slow nod, "that was a boy mad enough to kill.

"I remember Reverend Miller found a place to sit in a corner of the room to wait it out with me. Just sat there straight-faced and calm as a cat in the summer sun. He listened to me rant until finally I fell exhausted on the floor. That's when he got up, came over, knelt down beside me, and said, 'You're coming with me. The Callahans want you.'

"'The Callahans *want* me?' I asked. It was the first time I'd ever heard words like that. Someone wanted me. He said, 'Yeah, they sent me out here to tell you to pack all your things. You're goin' to live with them.' I couldn't believe it. Besides Ben Broughton, Rocky Callahan was the best friend I'd ever had. And I was going to live with his family.

"You might say they saved my life. They showed me God's love in action. I would expect Reverend Miller to show me God's love—but an entire family?

"It wasn't long afterward I gave my heart and soul to Jesus Christ, asked Him to reign over my life, give me a purpose. That family's unconditional love sent me straight to the cross, Emma, gave me hope for the future, made me realize I wasn't alone in this world.

"I can't say it was a happy-ever-after ending, though." He turned his gaze back to her, and in his eyes, she caught a glimpse of moistness. "I never made amends with my pa, although I tried. He wouldn't talk to me after I moved in with the Callahans. It was as if the hate in him increased a hundred-fold. I wanted to show him Christ's love the way the Callahans had me, but he wouldn't have it. His life took a steep, downward spiral after that.

"He died eighteen months later, a spiteful, embittered soul."

Jon shook his head, and Emma couldn't help it; she drew her hand out from under the blanket and placed it on his arm. A ripple of muscle moved beneath her hand, sending a nip straight to her bones. She'd never touched a man in this way, with tenderness and compassion, and the knowledge gave her pause. Jon Atkins did amazing things to her emotions. Compassion such as she'd never known welled up inside until a single tear rolled down her cheek, followed by another—and then another. She sniffed and raised the blanket to her face to swipe at the wetness.

Jon moved an arm around her shoulder and tugged her close. "Ah, Emma," he murmured in her ear. "What have I done? I didn't mean to make you cry."

It seemed that once the flow of tears commenced there was no stopping them. Hard and hot, they racked her from the inside out. She gulped, trying to stave them off, but the harder she tried, the faster they fell. Then came the choking sobs, worsened only by Jon's comforting arms that now both encircled her, drawing her close to his hard chest. "Let them out, sweet Emma."

His soft words didn't help, for she only cried harder. What was wrong with her? Why couldn't she get a grip on her conflicting feelings? And what had brought them on, Jon's sad story, so similar in nature to her own that it seemed to break her heart in two, or was it that this gripping, unforgiving spirit she'd buried deep inside her might never dig its way out? Jon seemed so at peace with his world, even though he had every right to be resentful. She was so angry, but no longer knew if she had the right. Sure, she'd been abused, but hadn't a million other kids like her suffered worse things? At least Miss Abbott had loved her—enough to set her up for the rest of her life. Of that, she should be eternally thankful. Wasn't it time she let go of the hateful spirit she carried for Ezra Browning?

Oh, it was all so confusing.

A light kiss on her cheek and then her temple turned her to mush. She wasn't accustomed to such tenderness, and the fact that the preacher himself was showing it to her melted her very core.

Oh, Lord, she whispered inwardly, *I want what Jon has. What do I have to do to get it?*

Yet while the question lingered in her heart, she kept it hidden from the one person who could give her the answer.

Chapter Twenty-Four

*E*mma," he whispered. There was no help for it; when she turned her face toward him, he trailed tiny kisses down the length of it, partaking of her delicate scent along the way, trembling with rapturous pleasure.

Her lips were full and waiting when he kissed them, salty tears mixing with their savory taste. His heart pounded through his chest until he thought it would burst the buttons on his chambray shirt. *Oh, Lord, Oh, Lord...I've wanted this for so long. I love her, Lord. I love her.*

My ways are perfect, My son. Do not rush My will. Give Me time to reveal Myself to her.

The hazy piece of reasoning sought to swim to the surface, but he kept pushing it back, not wanting to hear it, not wanting to break off this precious moment.

Rejecting the nudge, verse after verse of Scripture started plowing through his senses even as his mouth gently meshed with hers.

As for God, His way is perfect: the word of the Lord is tried...the secret of the Lord is with them that fear Him, and He will show them His covenant...commit thy way unto the Lord, and He shall bring it to pass...I delight to do thy will, oh my God: yea, thy law is within my heart.

With great reluctance, Jon stopped the kiss and cut loose a weary sigh. It couldn't be helped; there was no turning off the resounding voice of God.

Holding Emma at arm's length, he looked full into her face where fresh tears still rolled freely down her rosebud cheeks.

Cupping her face on either side, he wiped their wetness with the pads of both thumbs. She looked confused, to say the least, maybe even a little dumbfounded, and who could blame her? Blast if he wasn't speechless himself! How did he explain to her why he'd kissed her like that then suddenly pulled away? She would never understand the wrongness of it, even though he himself had sensed it with untold certainty.

Truth was, until she made her peace with God, broke free of her own spitefulness toward her father, he couldn't allow himself the luxury of her kisses. Nor could he trust himself to be alone with her. And the worst of it was that he'd done all he could to point her to the Father. The rest remained with her. Otherwise, he'd always question the earnestness of her decision.

When she came to Jesus, he wanted her to come of her own accord—not because he'd pushed her into making a decision to ask Him into her heart.

He dropped his hands to his lap and moved away from her. It wasn't hard to miss the tight little gasp that blew past her lips. He wanted to explain himself but couldn't find the words, couldn't even look her in the eye quite yet.

As if on cue, Luke's mangy brown dog sauntered up the porch steps, his droopy ears looking as if they needed scratching. Somewhere along the way—Jon wasn't sure just when— the mutt had managed to finagle his way into the household, as had the ginger-colored cat named Miss Tabitha.

"Hey, No-name," he mumbled for lack of anything better to say. The dog rubbed against his knee, a silent invitation for attention. Jon massaged his flea-bitten ear.

Emma stood to her feet, the impact of her sudden movement rocking the swing. "Well," she said with cool curtness, brushing down her skirt before swabbing her remaining tears with the end of her sleeve. "I feel foolish."

"What? No, you shouldn't. I—I can explain."

She raised a hand to put a halt to his next words, her throat sounding clogged and full with emotion. "No need. What just happened, well, don't worry 'bout it happenin' again. I saw your regret. Yo're probably kickin' yourself two ways ta Brooklyn 'bout now, you bein' the preacher an' all."

"No! Listen, I...."

"It was plain silly of me to cry like that. For gracious sakes, I don't know what got into me, but I'm over it. Yes, I am."

She swiveled on her heel and headed for the door.

"Emma, wait a minute. We should talk."

She paused, hand on the doorknob. "I don't need your sympathy, Jon Atkins. I can manage just fine without it."

So that was it, then. She was back to her stubborn, contrary self.

"Come and sit back down," he urged again. "We can talk this out."

But the door closed behind her, and none too gently, before he had time to manage another word.

No-name gave him a droopy eyed, if not scathing, look. "I've blown it, haven't I, buddy?"

*****

Dear Grace,

I thank you for the letter that came today. Since I can't sleep anyways, nows a good time to reply. Besides I'm feeling an awful need to talk to a woman, which don't happen that offen to me. I did something mighty foolish tonight concerning a man, and I don't need to tell you how imbarassed it's made me feel. And here's what it is—I let him kiss me. It don't make sense because I never have let a man do that before, and I don't think it came off too pleasant for him since he had the awfulest scowl on his face afterward. To make matters worse, he is the preacher. (Did I tell you the preacher lives at my boardinhouse?) He's a very nice man and I know he's sorry now for given me false hope. I ashurred him it won't happen again.

Well, you'll be glad to know my pa is livin' in my spare room. Jon—that's the preacher—talked me into bringin him here because he's so sick. I'm praying God will somhow give me strength. My pa's not an easy man. I did just come across that verse in the Bible that says with God, all things are possible, so that gave me some hope.

I was plain thrilled to learn I had a cousin. Maybe somday you and me can meet. Wouln't that be somthing? You could stay right in my room if you ever chose to visit. But Chicago is a long ways away so don't feel oblegated. (I wish I was a better speller. That wasn't my best class in school.)

Is your mother's name Edith becuse I know now that Ezra wrote letters to Edith and she wrote back? How do you know Clara Abbott? Could you tell me this ~~informashun~~ stuff the next time you write?

Who were the people who rased my father? Didn't he have his own parents?

I'm sorry for my pore writing. Yours is always so pretty and straight. My lines seem to go evry which way that it's a plane out shame you have to try decifer it.

But I'm glad I found you—or you found me. It's nice to know I have a cousin.

Love,
Emma

P.S. Write back!

P.S. again—I'm reading that book of John all over again and it seems to be makeing more sense to me the second time around. And I found another book called the Psalms that is just plain comfurting. I do think I want to learn more about God even though I never give it much thought before now.

*****

As the days rolled by, an amazing thing happened. Ezra Browning started to improve. Doc said it was due to the care he was getting, the square meals, the lack of booze in his system, and the much-needed rest. But he also said they shouldn't count on it lasting. He was a sick man and, unfortunately, still a dying one.

Emma scurried to wash the supper dishes, eager to go out to her garden before the sun made its final descent. Grapes ripe for picking hung from their vines, and she intended to make her father help her pull them off. If he was well enough to come to the dinner table, as he'd done the last few days, he was well enough to go out for some fresh air. If he tired, she would sit him on the cast-iron bench to watch.

Letters from Grace continued to pour in, with Emma answering every one of them. They had formed a fast friendship, knit together by the fact that Grace and Ezra were first cousins. Emma pored over Grace's missives, learning something new about her relative with every reading. She was forty-six years old, a widow to Wilburt Giles, having been married to him for twenty-one years before he suddenly fell ill. It was he who'd started the restaurant business, and Grace who'd carried it on. Her advice about Jon Atkins was that she must cease worrying over the kiss. If she had true feeling for him, and he did her, then the Lord would reveal His plan. "These things have a tendency to work out according to God's timetable," she'd said. At that revelation, Emma scowled and gave her head a tiny shake; not wanting to dwell on it, she quickly finished the note.

She learned, too, that Grace had never had the pleasure of children, although they'd wanted them. Over the years, they had come to accept the fact of her barrenness and invested time in other people's children.

Her father, John Fielding, passed away shortly after her wedding, having suffered from a chronic lung disease. She had two sisters, both older and living in Kansas and Colorado. To her great sadness, she seldom had the opportunity to visit either one due to distance and the inability to leave her restaurant for long periods. She employed a cook and two dining waiters, but since her thriving little restaurant had made a name for itself, she barely had time to read the evening newspaper, let alone leave town.

She implied that she had grown tired of the weariness of city life and had thought much about selling out and retiring to a quieter community, perhaps one of the cozy little towns that were popping up on the outskirts of Chicago.

As for the questions Emma had regarding her father's background, Grace's answers were slow in coming, noticeably absent, in fact, with the exception of her admission that, yes, her mother's name was Edith, and also that before she died she'd revealed some things about Ezra's family. Things that Grace preferred not to talk about via mail.

Well, if she wouldn't write them in a letter, Emma had asked in her last note, how was she ever to learn the mystery? "Furthermore," she'd added, "what about Clara Abbott? I still don't understand the connection."

Emma dried the last dinner plate and on tiptoe placed it on top of the other clean plates neatly stacked in the cupboard. She wrung out the dishrag and draped it over the edge of the counter, then hung the damp towel on a hook beneath the sink. Wiping her hands on her apron front, she turned and perused her neat-as-a-pin kitchen.

"Ya always was good at keepin' things all polished up nice-like." Emma whirled at the sound of Ezra's voice. He leaned the weight of his thinning body in the doorframe, too weak to support himself for long periods, his shoulders bent as usual, skin taut and ashen, but a spark in his eyes she couldn't recall ever having seen before. My, what a sober mind did for a body.

"Thank you—I think. Was that a compliment?"

The tiniest chuckle broke loose. "I s'pose it could be if ya want ta look at it thata way. Never was one for expressin' my gratitude toward ya, even though I should've."

Lately, Ezra Browning had been most hospitable, and she had no idea how to handle it. Even now, she felt a silly blush creep up her neck, as if this weren't her father standing three feet away from her but some stranger trying to butter her up. For that reason, she wanted to pick a fight with him, but she couldn't seem to conjure up a good enough motive for one.

"No need," she sputtered.

He started to cough but regained control of the episode much faster than normal. She walked the few steps it took to get to him and took his arm. His frailty did something to her innards, made her feel things she wasn't used to feeling. "Want to help me pick grapes?" she asked.

"Pick grapes, you say? Where's the preacher? That sounds like somethin' he'd want ta do." He was stalling, of course. No one she knew balked more at having to lift a finger. He was spoiled, and she had no one to blame for it but herself. Hadn't she catered to him her entire life just to keep the peace?

"I have no idea, and I wouldn't ask him to help me pick grapes anyway," she squawked. "Now, come on." She tried to hurry him, but it was like telling a baby tortoise to speed it up the way he gingerly put one foot in front of the other.

"You and that preacher kid fightin'? Don't seem like you two's lookin' at each other near as much as ya used to," he murmured when they finally reached the door.

"What? No." The muscles in her back tensed tighter than a drum as she reached for a big bucket sitting on the floor behind the door. It was plain mortifying to discover that her father had noticed something rising up between her and Jon, made her wonder what the others were thinking. Ever since those astounding kisses on the porch, the man had stepped cautiously around her, pointing his gaze to the floor in passing, conversing with everyone but her at the meal table, as if she carried some contagious germ and the only hope for not catching it was distance and complete avoidance. No, they weren't fighting—exactly— but then they weren't speaking, either.

Oh, it was all a big mess, and as far as she was concerned, they'd both do well to pretend the kiss had never happened. Clearly, he was swimming with regrets; why not let him off the hook and admit she felt the same? He was the pastor of Little Hickman Community Church, for gracious sake. If ever a mismatch existed between two people, it lay between them—her acting as "mother" to a beefy array of misfits, him a gentle shepherd leading his flock of Christ followers. Why, if Mrs. Winthrop ever got wind that he'd crossed the line from respectability into licentious revelry (for that is what she would call their innocent kisses), she'd see to it he lost his position, not to mention his preacher's license.

In fact, Emma had given serious thought to warning him of the dangers he posed for himself by even staying under her roof. Of course, in order to have that conversation, he would have to look her square in the eye again, and she couldn't guess when that might happen.

It had proven a chore getting Ezra down the back stoop, but once she did, they strolled slowly toward the arch where the grapevines grew thick and lush, their ambrosial scent wafting across the path. September's sun was fast setting, so rather than take him all the way, she stopped to lower him into the sturdy garden bench situated just feet from the vines. He huffed a puffing breath and grasped hold of the bench arms to steady himself. Once comfortable, he actually angled her with a crooked grin, which automatically drew suspicion.

"You seem especially chipper," she said, turning and walking to the grape arbor, bucket handle draped over one arm. Amethyst-colored grapes hung in chunky clusters, their mere sight sending her taste buds into a tizzy. On impulse, she popped a few into her mouth to satisfy her craving, savoring their luscious juices, swallowing them down, skins, seeds, and all.

"Ain't I got a right? I'm much improved, don't ya think?"

It *was* somewhat of a minor miracle, this newfound spurt. "Doc says your gettin' good rest and eatin' better has given you a new lease." She wouldn't mention that he'd also said it could be short-lived.

Moments passed, with the only sounds a few chirping birds, gentle breezes passing through the leaves, and a neighborhood dog barking up a storm. When the lull became uncomfortable, Emma glanced up from her picking and caught Ezra staring off toward the house.

"You thinkin' on somethin'?" she asked.

He cleared his throat. "Been talkin' to the preacher kid." His voice was hoarse from lack of use.

"About what?"

"Things."

She felt her brow pull down, but kept at her task. "Such as?"

"He got me ta thinkin', that's all."

Jonathan Atkins had a way of doing that. Did he hope to save Ezra Browning from his multitude of sins? Now, wouldn't that be a miracle? Her cynicism had her yanking grape clusters off their vines at record speed.

"Says I should try to make the end o' my life count fer somethin', maybe startin' with improvin' ar communicatin', yer and mine. I ain't been the best at it. Plus he got me ta thinkin' 'bout God an' all. Ain't that somethin'?"

Struck speechless, she picked faster. At the rate her bucket was filling, she would need to empty it soon.

"He tol' me the Bible's meant fer folks such as me—sinners, that is. Lord knows I'm the biggest one. Says it's a matter of askin' Jesus, God's Son, ta forgive me my past, and He'll do it. Seems a little far-fetched if ya ask me, but if it's that simple, I might give it a try. Course, I'd need to beg for pardon from you as well. That's what the preacher kid tol' me."

Was this one-way conversation really happening? And if it was, why couldn't it have taken place twenty years ago? For reasons she couldn't quite identify, the root of bitterness she'd nursed for most of her life sprouted tenfold. Did he really think it was as easy as that?

"I been a poor example, Emma. I done ya wrong."

Her basket full, she whirled to face her father. While plastered, he'd punched her more times as a child than she cared to count, screamed obscenities when she hadn't finished her chores, and belittled and embarrassed her in front of God and everybody. As if that weren't enough, he'd expected her to clean up after him when he lay in his own vomit. How old was she when he'd first handed down that chore, four, five? Looking at him now, hunched and old beyond his years, dying, to boot, she should have had some measure of compassion, but she simply couldn't muster it. What was wrong with her? The man was trying to make amends, for pity's sake, and her heart felt cold and stale, hard as a brick.

"The booze made me do crazy things," he muttered, head down, plucking lint balls off his pants. "I don't expect—" A bout of coughing forced him to halt mid-sentence. Emma pursed her lips tight and watched his struggle from afar, knowing there was nothing to do for it.

When he got a hold of the spasm, she slowly approached. "We should go in now. It's gettin' toward dusk." She set the bucket on the ground beside his feet and hauled him up. He rose slowly, his legs shaking when they took his weight. "I'll come back for my grapes after I get you settled."

She felt his eyes bore into her as they walked, her arm steadying him on the bumpy path. Not for the life of her could she say the words he wanted to hear—words like, "It's all right; I can put it all behind me; my rotten childhood never happened; let's start over."

Trust God to heal the hurts of your past, Emma dear.... The words from one of Grace's letters returned with punishing blows. *Forgiveness is far more freeing than living with a heart of anger.*

It was too much to think about right now. Perhaps tonight she would try whispering another prayer before going to sleep and see if that would help to piece together her frayed emotions.

Silly tears threatened at the corners of both eyes, and even as she pondered what she might say to God, she wondered if it would be worth the trouble.

287

Would He even hear her pathetic cries?

*****

Jon was waiting by the window when Emma brought Ezra into the kitchen. "I'll take over from here," he said, giving them both a start. "Sorry. Didn't mean to surprise you. I saw you coming up the path." When Emma shot him a hasty look, he noted her glistening eyes and wondered what Ezra had said now. She looked on the verge of tears—again. Had an argument ensued between father and daughter? He'd thought for sure old Ezra's heart was tenderizing, that for the first time ever he was seeing himself through different eyes, seeing what his life could have been like had he chosen God early on. But now he wondered. He'd certainly said something to make Emma miserable.

God, if he's hurt her, I'll be tempted to kick him into an early eternity, whether he's ready or not.

"Everything okay?" he asked, looking from one to the other. It was the first time in a long while he'd allowed himself to look deep into Emma's face, and what he saw there revealed a truth he'd been running from. He loved her deeply.

Her casual, polite nod did not convince him. Pulling back her chin, she handed Ezra off to him. "Since you offered, I'll leave you to his evening ablutions. I have to go get my bucket." With a turn, she left the kitchen, slamming the door harder than necessary behind her. Jon watched her out of the side of one eye as she strode down the path, and he saw her lift her apron to swipe her cheek. Blast!

"You say something to get her riled?"

Ezra's breathing seemed more labored than usual. "Jus' that I been doin' some thinkin'. Ya know how you been tellin'

me 'bout God and His love an' forgiveness? I thought it was all good stuff what I said, but it don't appear she liked it much."

Ah, so that was it. She didn't want to hear that Ezra's heart was going soft.

"Well, Ezra, forgiveness is a touchy thing. Might be you'll need to talk to God about that. I can't promise you she'll ever forgive you entirely, but you can't allow her lack of mercy over you to stand in the way of your own salvation. By asking her forgiveness, you've done your part. The melting down of her heart—now, that's God's business."

Ezra's legs trembled from weakness, so Jon set him down on a stool next to the butcher-block table. Once situated, he clasped his hands in his lap and fidgeted, his breaths coming out like a whole band of whistles. Jon stood next to him, worried he might topple. "I got to make her see."

"Maybe she's not quite ready yet, you know, to hear what you have to say."

A minute lapsed while Ezra seemed to collect his thoughts. "I left home at a ripe young age, you know. My ma and pop was glad ta see me go."

"I'm sorry to hear that."

"Phftt. Couldn'ta been much more 'n thirteen, fourteen." In his eyes was poignant sorrow, deep and cavernous. Of course, Ezra hadn't a clue how transparent they were, crystalline windows opening into his soul, as if they had a story all their own to tell.

Jon waited, then ventured a question. "What were they like, your parents?"

Tilting back his head to look at the ceiling, he gave a dismal snort. "Distant. They never had no use for me."

"Why do you think that was?"

"Never could figure it out, 'cept they liked Howard and Hester better."

"The twins." He remembered Ezra's revelation about his older sister and brother from when he'd eavesdropped from the doorway.

Ezra nodded. "Brats, they was. Always talking 'bout me behind my back, pokin' fun at me, kickin' me around, sayin' stuff like Ma and Pa liked them better, and I was nothin' but a crossbreed."

"Crossbreed. What would make them say that?"

Shriveled shoulders dropped even further. "Don't know, don't care. My folks was on trips a lot for business, left us kids with some neighbor lady. They never knowed half the time what was goin' on. When they'd get home from their long trips they'd haul out big presents for the brats and give me somethin' like a measly little writin' tablet."

Some nagging thought pestered Jon in his deepest part— like an itch he couldn't quite reach or an obliterated memory that refused to resurface. Something just didn't seem right here. He felt his brow crease, drawing his eyes into beady circles. "So where did you go when you left home?"

Ezra tipped his head at him and frowned. "Roamed the countryside. Picked up jobs here an' there, mostly in honky-tonk joints. I was big for my age. Weren't hard gettin' folks ta believe I was eighteen. Most places give me room an' board and all the booze I wanted. That's how my habit got off the ground.

"Once I met my Lydia, though, things started lookin' up." His eyes went wet at the corners and he shook his head. "Liked ta died when she stopped breathin' that hot day in June, leavin' me with that squallin' kid."

"And that's when the drinking started up again?" Jon took a long-held breath and swallowed.

Ezra's face lowered, making Jon wonder if he'd suddenly dropped off to sleep, but then he gave a slow, gloomy nod. "Got worse than ever after that. Ain't no excuse for my behavior, 'cept ta say I wasn't happy unless I was pub-crawlin'. Even that pretty li'l girl out there," he poked a finger toward the backyard, "couldn't turn my eyes away from the stuff. Now that I think 'bout it, I prob'bly resented her. Ain't that a rotten thin' to say?"

Jon patted the old man on the shoulder. With all his might, he wanted to dislike him, but it wasn't in him to do so. Almost from the time he'd taken the job as Little Hickman's pastor and committed to helping the helpless, he'd latched on to Ezra Browning. Now, no matter what, he couldn't let go.

"Best get you ready for bed," he said, having no idea what else to say. Out the back door, he noted Emma loitering in the garden, probably waiting for them to disappear.

He helped him off the stool. The fellow grunted and swayed, and if Jon hadn't been there to catch him, he'd have fallen flat on his face.

Lord, please live Your life through me. Make me a light that points the way to You. I never set things right with my own pa, and a part of me still mourns that fact. Maybe that's what draws me to Ezra. He reminds me of Luther Atkins. It may be too late for my pa, but it's not too late for Ezra.

He led Ezra to the washroom on the main floor, Ezra's feet shuffling along at a childlike pace, the floorboards squeaking under each labored step.

Chapter Twenty-Five

*F*renzied enthusiasm rippled through the congregation. It was a full house in Little Hickman Community Church, the new building drawing curious attendees from as far away as Nicholasville. Why, it was a celebration to rival the opening day of the new schoolhouse some two months earlier. Thankfully, the sun shone bright, even though the maple leaves in the churchyard had started dropping to the earth one by one, their flaxen hue a sure sign that cooler air would soon be blowing up the valleys and over the ridges, bending Kentucky's blue grasses and ushering in an all-new season.

Dressed in their Sunday best, which, for most men, simply meant a freshly laundered shirt tucked into a pair of trousers held up by suspenders, and for the womenfolk meant a simple cotton dress, folks sauntered down the center and side aisles seeking out spots in which to crowd together on shiny new pews.

With her usual flair, the church pianist and Hickman's newly appointed schoolteacher, Bess Barrington, treated the incoming church attendees to a rendition of "Onward Christian Soldiers" on the slightly off-key piano.

When the piano the Winthrops had generously commissioned to purchase for the new church had not yet arrived from the Michigan manufacturer, and Jon had decided the donated one at the school should remain intact, Emma had kindly offered the use of hers, saying it just sat in the music room like a big ol' hippo, anyway, collecting dust. "Makes nary a peep, 'cept for those times back when Mr. Wonder tried to play it," she wrinkled up her nose at the memory, "and Miss Tabitha decides at midnight to use it as a tactic to wake the dead."

Jon had laughed, glad that at least they were again treating each other with civility. He couldn't even count the times he'd wanted to share his heart with her, haul her into his arms again, and kiss her silly while savoring the scent of her hair against his cheek. Of course, he walked away from the temptation every time, knowing it could never work between them unless she dedicated her heart and life to Christ.

"Well, I appreciate that, Emma. I'll gather up some men to help me wheel it over there," he'd said just two days ago. "Maybe you'll come Sunday to hear the way it's supposed to be played?"

She'd awarded him with a half-grin, pausing midway in her mopping job. "I expect I will—just to hear how it's played, mind you."

"Of course. I wouldn't expect you'd come to hear my sermon."

With a hint of a twinkle in her eye, she'd turned back to her task. "And isn't that the truth."

And there she sat now, just four rows back, squeezed in tight between the Callahan family and Fancy Jenkins. Sarah Jenkins, Fancy's daughter, sat smack in front of them with Sully and Esther Thompson and their clan, holding their wiggling baby, Millie, on her lap. Jon suspected that before the service ended, Esther would be giving Sarah permission to take the toddler outside. When Jon failed to get Emma's attention—all he had in mind was a friendly smile—he turned his eyes elsewhere.

Amidst the commotion of incoming worshippers, he perused his surroundings from a chair on the two-step-up platform. It was a simple structure, simple but sturdy. High ceilings to afford that the sound would carry, a big potbellied stove situated at the rear, and floors made of four-by-four wood timbers, which even now carried their strong scent and probably would for years to come, graced the interior. Four big windows flanked either side of the room to allow for plenty of incoming light, and kerosene lamps hung six feet apart from the fresh painted white walls. It was that new-wood, new-paint smell mixed with the scent of fresh bathed children that made a body fairly keel over with delight.

The sort of pride a father must feel when his child takes his first steps pranced straight across his chest. So many men and women had pitched in at various stages of construction—he'd counted at least eighty—over the past weeks to accomplish the job of erecting Little Hickman Community Church, making its name all the more appropriate. Even folks who didn't normally attend Sunday services had rolled up their sleeves to see the building completed before the onset of bad weather. Sitting on the tiny platform now, with Carl Hardy seated on one side of him and church elder, Bill Jarvis, on the other, he felt as if he were walking through a dream. Wasn't it only yesterday he'd felt the nudge to sell his farm and donate his profits toward building a new church?

At the conclusion of Bess's hymn, the congregation hushed, settled into their spots, and pointed their gazes to the front of the sanctuary. With a smile on his face, Jon approached the rough-hewn pulpit, Bible in hand and bookmarked at Psalm 118.

Clearing his throat, he swallowed the unexpected nervous knot that had grown up in his throat, opened the book at the appropriate spot, and, with booming voice, read, **"This is the**

day which the Lord hath made; we will rejoice and be glad in it!"

*****

Emma's body shifted uncomfortably when she listened to the Reverend Atkins' pealing voice, his convicting words in his sermon titled "The God Who Hears" making her pulse tick at a faster-than-normal pace. When Fancy leaned into her shoulder mid-way through Jon's message and whispered, "My, ain't he a fine-looking man," Emma's jaw had dropped. Yes, he was that, but she wouldn't be admitting any such thing to Fancy Jenkins. Instead, she'd nudged her gently with an elbow and stifled a hysterical giggle.

For a change, though, it wasn't his superb looks that had her heart thrumming out of control. In fact, she couldn't quite pinpoint the root of the problem, unless it was the nudge in her own side that she suspected might be coming from the Lord Himself.

How much longer will you run from Me, My child? Don't you tire of carrying around all that bitterness? Won't you let Me help you take it off your shoulders? I can do that for you, you know. There is hope and healing.

"Are you seeking something, but can't quite figure out what it is? Are you looking for a purpose in your life, but finding little meaning?" Jon asked. "Do you have an empty heart that needs filling? Are you acquainted with the One who can fill it?"

All these questions, first from her head and then from that—that fine-looking man! Emma had the strongest urge to rise up out of this harder-than-a-brick pew—did they make church pews hard for a reason, so folks wouldn't get too comfortable?—and escape for a breath of fresh air. Suddenly she felt so hemmed in, so conscience stricken.

That morning Ezra had gotten himself out of bed and declared he was going to church, and she'd denied him that wish. "It's impossible!" she'd declared, easing him back to bed. Luckily, Jon had left the house at dawn or he'd have surely found a way to get him to services even if meant bringing him in on a stretcher. He'd looked as pale as the moon and as gaunt as a goat on its last legs. "I don't want to be responsible for yer fallin' or somethin'," she'd told him, hands on her hips. *Besides, what in the world would folks think?*—the words sat on her tongue as well. It would cause a stir, all right, his coming through the big, wide doors. Why, she could almost picture Iris Winthrop's pinched expression now as she craned her neck to watch the proceedings. As far as she knew, he'd never graced the inside of a church, and starting now, when he was so weak and frail, seemed a silly venture.

He'd looked at her from his spot on the edge of the bed, his deep-socketed eyes clouded with inquiry, his warbled breaths clamoring to get out. "Why you been goin'?"

He might have thrown her across the room the way the question hammered through her heart. Yes, why? She'd never gone to church in her life, either, but from the day Grace's letters started coming, an undetermined longing for something more had come to roost in her soul. She'd thought that going to church might alleviate that need, but so far, it had done nothing but make her vulnerable. In all her born days she'd never dealt with so much inner turmoil. Even as a child, she'd learned the art of coping under stress, strapping down her emotions so they couldn't bubble forth. Lately, though, tears threatened almost daily.

"I'm not exactly sure. I guess it feels like the thing to do." She dropped down beside him then and felt her shoulders sag, felt the ancient mattress tilt precariously with her added weight.

"It's that preacher," Ezra stated.

She slanted her head at him with a curious look. "What do you mean?"

He gave his gray head a half shake. "He talks to ya like ya was somebody important, like ya really matter ta him and ta God. I tol' ya I'm thinkin' deep about the stuff he's been sayin'. I ain't long for this earth, Emma. I'm squarin' things away with my Maker."

She should have viewed him with compassion, hauled him up and made an effort to get him to the church, but instead that old sense of anger circled around her heart again. She'd jumped to her feet quick, as if a bee had poked her in the backside, then pressed the wrinkles out of her skirt. Whether it was his admission that he was dying or his remark about setting things right with God that had her reeling with confusion, she couldn't say. All she knew was that she'd left him to his own defenses not ten minutes later, shutting the door behind her and heading up the street to Hickman's brand-new clapboard church, mingling in with the others who strolled up the sidewalk in their Sunday duds, and feeling like the worst kind of human being.

*****

Jon's sermon wound down with his final point: God hears the prayer of the righteous. In his deepest parts, he knew he held his audience captive, not because of anything he'd said, but because of the way the Lord's words had fairly flowed from his mouth. Not for a minute would he take the credit for the Spirit's moving.

Sunlight pierced through spotless windows, glancing off the faces of those sitting in its direct path. Emma's face, while lit with glowing rays, betrayed some dark emotion he couldn't

297

quite place. *Lord, help her find her way to You,* he prayed, even as he delivered the last of his message. *And help me to be patient while I wait for You to work.* ·

The big doors opened as he prepared to announce the benediction. Heads turned, eyes gaped wide, jaws dropped, and gasps of heaved-in air echoed off the plaster walls. Even Jon, hands extended to deliver the blessing, paused mid-sentence to stare down the center aisle with utter stupefaction.

"I got somethin' ta say—if ya don't mind, preacher kid." Uncommonly steady, considering his condition, Ezra Browning stood in the doorway flanked by Wes Clayton and Elliott Newman. Luke stood behind the threesome, his ear-to-ear grin nearly splitting his pudgy face in two. Not only that, he looked proud as a peacock, as if he alone were responsible for seeing Ezra to the church, and never mind their lack of punctuality.

Jon lowered his hands to his sides and cleared his throat, issuing a silent prayer for wisdom and guidance. In haste he sought out Emma but found her body turned full around like that of everyone else.

"May we be seated, folks? I believe this is important."

Hushed voices exchanged hurried phrases as, one by one, folks repositioned themselves, most looking bewildered, and who could blame them? How often did the town drunk come to Sunday service and ask for their ear? Of course, Iris Winthrop took the cake with her haughty, contorted smirk, her floral headpiece tilting to the point of almost falling off when she jerked her head around to watch Ezra Browning's grand entrance.

Whining children, obviously put out by the delay, precipitated the need for a few mothers to usher them out, but for the most part, everyone stayed, including the ashen-faced Emma, whom Jon worried might flee at any moment like a scared rabbit.

With assistance on either side of him, Ezra made his way to the front, shoulders straighter than usual, craggy face pulled taut by what could only have been sheer determination. His clothes hung rather off-kilter, but that was probably due to his weight loss. Had Emma dressed him before coming to church, or had one of the boarders? Jon had felt bad about leaving the chore to someone else when he'd been taking full responsibility for his care, but on this, his first Sunday in the new church, he'd wanted to spend some extra time in prayer, so he'd left the house well before Ezra's waking.

"He'p me up them steps," Ezra instructed in a hoarse tone when they finally reached the front, their progress so slow that Jon felt certain most watched with long-held breaths. "When I say my piece I want ta see their faces."

Wes and Elliott exchanged a look but helped him up the two steps, Luke standing at the ready, looking all-important. Jon would commend the pair later for their kindness. He doubted either one had seen the inside of a church in years, so to march before the congregation now, making spectacles of themselves, must surely have taken courage. What must Ezra have said to convince them to swallow their pride? Shoot, they'd even spiffed themselves up for the occasion, he noted, Wes's grayish hair plastered down with gel and parted down the middle, Elliott's white shirt appearing just pressed.

Jon stepped forward to relieve the men of their responsibility. When they turned, the front row quickly squeezed together to make room. Jon sent them all a grateful glance.

A quick assessment ruled Ezra capable of standing. *Lord, please lend him strength for whatever it is he wants to say, and plant a seed of compassion in the hearts of Your people*, he prayed.

His arm stationed around Ezra's curved shoulder, he asked, "What is it you've come to say, Ezra?"

The fellow breathed deep, and for a change didn't expel a loud wheeze. If anything, he stood taller than usual, chest out, chin held high. "I come to confess my sinfulness," he announced. The buzz that simple statement evoked nearly rocked the little church off its fresh foundation. Jon hushed them with a silent look.

"Go on," he urged, willing himself to remain calm despite the inner joy that sought to burst right through his shirt.

"I figure the whole town knows 'bout my past, what a scoundrel I been. I got no real excuse for my behavior 'cept to say that the devil hisself had a grip on me. But today I'm here ta tell ya the devil's got no more say. I give my heart to the Lord jus' the other night while I laid in my bed." An undertone of awe whistled through the place. Warmth, like wildfire, spread the length of Jon's tall frame. *Lord, is this really happening?* He wanted to gauge the look on Emma's face, but he dared not move his gaze from Ezra.

"I wanted ta get here earlier, but it weren't possible. Finally, I convinced these two fellers in the front row, well, Luke too, ta get me to the church. I felt like my seams would bust if I lost my chance."

Jon could feel the pounding of his heart clear to his temples. He squeezed Ezra's shoulder a little tighter. "Keep going, my friend."

"My wife died back in '68 right after Emma was born, an' my heart liked ta broke in two. I didn't know how ta be a pa, as most o' you know, so I did the worst thin' of all, I run from the responsibility, lost m'self in strong drink, treated my girl as if she wusn't even there, most days.

"It was a big mistake and one I been payin' fer ever since. Lost the respect of my friends, what few I had, but worst, I lost my girl."

At that, Ezra shot a fleeting glance out over the congregation until he found where Emma sat. He gave her a long, penetrating look. "Cain't blame 'er none for hatin' me as she does, but I'm here ta say ta her and ta you all that I'm plenty sorry for my acts."

Stunned was about the only word Jon could think of to describe her expression; that, and perhaps wariness and disbelief. If ever he'd prayed without ceasing, it was now.

"The preacher here's been tellin' me 'bout God's love. Seems unlikely the Almighty could love such scum as me, but accordin' to the Bible I been readin', it's true enough. Matter o' fact, He loves every one of you as well. **'Bless the Lord who forgiveth all our sins,'** is what I read three nights ago. **'His mercy endureth forever.'"**

Ezra paused and cleared his throat.

Had a pin dropped to the oak plank floor, the sound would have carried up the road. A baby's whimpering cries split through the hushed air.

"After I read that verse I closed my eyes right there on my bed and asked the Lord ta forgive me. A peace come over me like a flowin' river, ain't no other way ta describe it."

"Amen, brother!" came the resounding affirmation from someone in the back.

"Hallelujah!" someone else shouted, to which the congregation broke into spontaneous applause.

And that's when Jon's gaze snagged hold of Emma's and she leaped to her feet. It was perhaps, in her mind, her only recourse. Escape. She slipped past Fancy Jenkins and then the Warner family, and with head pointed downward, hurried up the center aisle and out the double doors.

*****

Emma clumped down the sidewalk toward home, her heart beating out of her chest, her eyes pointed to her feet lest anyone try to stop her along the way. Tears longed to explode from the back of her eyes, but she held them at bay. No doubt, it would have made more sense to sit there with the rest of the congregation while her father confessed, but she couldn't. His words had pulled too tightly at her heart, like a cinched cord that squeezed and squeezed. Mercy, if she hadn't left, she'd have passed out from lack of proper breathing. Even now, beads of sweat erupted on her forehead and drizzled down her face, a result of her burned-out emotions.

Imagine! Ezra Browning a born-again Christian. Why, he'd stood right there in front of God and everyone and confessed his sins. Yet, the most remarkable thing of all, she ruled, was that irrefutable look of radiance on his face. She couldn't get it out of her mind.

She passed the mercantile on her left, the CLOSED sign hanging crooked on the door latch, and then Winthrop's Dry Goods, the wrought-iron bench in front that usually held a body or two now sitting vacant. She stepped off the sidewalk and crossed the dusty alley. When she shot a glance sideways, she saw Edgar Blake and Amos Jordan sitting on the steps of Zeke's Barbershop. Both lifted their hands and waved. She responded in kind, taking care not to slow her pace.

A giant step up and she found herself on the sidewalk again, tramping past a closed Flanders' Food Store. Orville

Bordon crossed the street in front of her, giving her a tip of his hat and a casual nod. "Mornin' to you, Miss Emma," he called. "Or perhaps good afternoon is more like it. I see you been goin' to church lately. How you like that brand new building?"

"It's fine, very nice." She hoped she didn't sound too curt.

"Service must be over then?" he asked, pausing in the middle of the quiet street to ask the question.

"Just about," she said. Oh dear, what kind of answer was that? Now he'd know she'd left before the final benediction.

But if he thought it odd, he didn't say; he merely nodded and smiled. "Well, you have a good day now."

She resumed her hurried steps, anxious to reach the confines of her private quarters. Since Sunday's meal always consisted of leftovers, there would be plenty of time for her to gather up her frayed nerves and put them to rights again before facing her boarders—and her father. What would she say to him—to Jon? What did they expect her to say? She batted at damp eyes, glad that Mr. Bordon hadn't lingered.

Anxiety seized her chest as she thought about Jon, so tall and handsome standing there before his little congregation, so full of goodness and compassion. What a contrasting pair they made; he so faith-driven, she so faithless; he contented and at peace, she still gorging on the pain of the past.

Let it go, Emma, Grace had said in one of her letters. *It isn't worth the battle.*

She sighed as she lengthened her gait, staring down at her dusty high-top shoes.

Up the street, a horse-drawn rig, driven by Mort Brackett and carrying a female passenger, pulled into a spot in front of the post office. Since the stagecoach rarely stopped in Little Hickman, the fellow often delivered folks to and from Lexington for a fee. Rather curious about the woman he'd transported, Emma stopped at the base of her porch steps to have a look. Mr. Brackett jumped down, had a word with his passenger, and walked around to the back of the wagon.

Something stately and proper about her manner kept Emma gawking. My, she was a fair-looking type with her green—what was it? Brocade?—traveling gown and matching jacket, a feathery, flowery hat sitting at just the right angle on her head, a shiny black bag resting on her lap, a parasol hanging over one arm. She spoke to Mr. Brackett in a soft voice then pointed at her trunk. He heaved it off the back of the wagon, carried it around to the front, and then returned to fetch her off her high perch. Even from where she stood, Emma heard the very cordial "Thank you, sir."

She had to be well bred, Emma thought. No one she knew ever gave the scruffy Mr. Brackett the title of *sir*.

After giving a little shake of the head, she was about to turn when Mr. Brackett caught her eye. "There she is," he said, pointing. "Afternoon, Miss Emma!" he hollered.

She made a shield from the noonday sun with her hand. "Good day to you, Mr. Brackett."

Not wanting to appear overly nosy about the female traveler, she took to her steps again.

"Wait! Emma?" the woman called to her.

She paused and turned. "Yes?"

The woman approached, parasol in hand, bag hauled over her slender shoulder. The smile on her face, warm and vaguely familiar, caused a catch in Emma's throat, which kept her from swallowing. No, it couldn't be.

"I-I'm sorry to say I don't have any extra rooms," she sputtered.

The fair lady looked to be in her late thirties or early forties. And, yes, it was a fine brocade she wore, definitely store-bought, and looking mighty expensive.

The smile on her face never let up. If anything, it broadened as she looked Emma up and down.

"You're even prettier than I imagined."

"What?"

Miss Tabitha meowed from the screen door, letting it be known she wanted out. From under the porch, No-name emerged, stretched his long, scrawny frame, and yawned. As if he'd just noticed the stranger, he hobbled over to her and greeted her by way of a sniff.

"You told me your hair was blond, but I didn't picture it quite so long and flowing, and your lovely face, well, how often does a person describe herself to a tee?" She giggled and revealed bright teeth, the middle front one turned slightly in.

"Pardon?" Emma took one step down, bringing her that much closer to the regally clad woman. "You aren't...." She squinted, swallowed, tamped down a wave of excitement.

She nodded, fast, several times. "Yes! I'm Grace. Grace Giles."

"No. Grace? My cousin, Grace?"

The rapid nods continued.

Emma's hand pressed flat across her open mouth.

"I hope I'm not coming at a bad time. Your last letter, well, it sounded somewhat desperate. And you said if I ever wanted to visit, I could share a room with you. My cook and wait staff urged me to come. Matter of fact, I told you in one of my letters I was thinking of selling. My cook is very interested in buying my business—he and his wife, of course. She also works for me. They're giving it a trial run this next week."

Her babbling persisted while Emma's mind tried to sort it all out. Grace, her only known relative, had come all the way from Chicago just to see her? It seemed too good to be true.

It took two steps down to get to ground level, and when she did, she threw her arms around her cousin's neck and wept.

Chapter Twenty-Six

I still can't believe you're here," Emma said. She plopped down on her bed, exhausted. "That trunk was heavy. What on earth did you put in it?" She slid over and patted the place beside her, a silent invitation to her cousin to sit.

"I can hardly believe it myself." Rather than sit, though, Grace ran to the window to look out. "Oh, my, what a lovely garden. Your sunflowers reach nearly to the clouds."

"Aren't they somethin', though? I didn't expect such a crop of 'em. I guess I threw out more seeds than I realized."

"I do so miss flowers in my little Chicago apartment. There's just so much room out here. I can't get over the lush trees, the green, rolling hills, the lovely, wide-open skies— and the birds. My! Everywhere I look, nature abounds. Why, you must awake each morning and thank God for the beauty of His creation. Me, I wake up to the sights and sounds and smells of the city. Oh, it's not that I'm ungrateful, mind you. I'm thankful for my very lucrative business. It's just that as I age, I find the city less and less appealing."

Emma dawdled on Grace's assumption that she thanked the Lord each day, and realizing she fell short, swallowed a lump of guilt.

Grace whirled away from the window, making her skirt flare out with the twisting motion. Her sun-pinkened cheeks glowed bright. "Oh, Emma, I'm so happy to finally meet you." In one fluid move, she strode across the room, tore the pins from her hat, laid them on the dresser, and tossed the flowery bonnet like a soaring kite across the room, letting it land

307

where it would. The move made her golden brown hair stand up in places, and Emma nearly laughed aloud. Grace smoothed the stray locks down with her hand and closed the distance between them by throwing herself on the bed next to Emma. For a woman of forty-six, she certainly had a springy manner about her, springy yet graceful, living up to her name.

"You came at the perfect time," Emma told her.

Grace looked only a little hesitant. "You're not just saying that?"

The bed jiggled while Grace made herself comfortable. Two pairs of feet dangled over the edge of the high bed, the simple sight of which produced a wave of giddiness in the pit of Emma's stomach.

"From the moment I learned you were my cousin, I've been dyin' to meet you."

Grace smiled, showing that slightly crooked front tooth, which only lent to her charm. "Me too."

"Are you hungry?" she asked.

"Famished."

"Then we should go downstairs and produce a sandwich and a bowl of soup for you."

When she would have leaped off the bed, Grace grabbed her arm and pulled her back. "All in good time, cousin, but first, tell me how your father is faring."

Over the next several minutes, Emma told her cousin about Ezra's dire condition, how he'd come in weak as a motherless duckling but rallied under their care. How he seemed to have good days and bad days with nary a hint the night before of what to expect in the morning.

Unsure whether to tell her about her father's conversion, she decided there was no reason not to, except for the fact that Emma herself was still trying to digest it.

Cinnamon eyes sparkled like winter stars when Emma divulged the story. "But that's wonderful, Emma. It's exactly what I've been asking God to do for Ezra." She tipped her head and leaned in close. "Why so downcast?"

"What? Oh, I'm not. I just—it seems unreal to me, that's all. I don't understand how God could take the reckless ruins of my father's life and make him into a new person. I'll grant you he does seem different—there's a glow about him—but I can't help but wonder if he's riding on some kind of emotion. It all happened so fast."

Grace gave Emma's arm a gentle squeeze and curved her mouth into a thoughtful smile. "That's what God does for us, honey; He takes us just as we are, no matter how sinful or vile. Nothing we do will ever make us worthy of Him, but that's the good news. We don't *have* to be worthy. Christ paid the ultimate sacrifice for our sins when He died on the cross, so the worst is over. All that remains is for us to ask Him to forgive us and believe that He does. There's nothing more to it than that."

She made it sound so simple. Had Jon presented it to Ezra in just as simple a manner? If so, she could almost understand why Ezra had prayed the prayer. It would be nice to live a peace-filled life, free of anger and inner resentment.

A tiny seed of interest sprouted from within, making her hungry, not in the physical sense, but in the spiritual. In fact, her soul burned with need. To ward off the feeling, she pulled herself up. Grace followed suit.

"Want to see what I brought you?"

Relief filtered through her veins when Grace didn't push the subject. That and a ripple of excitement. "You brought me something?"

"You don't think I would come all this way without bearing gifts, do you?"

Grace tugged her to the floor next to the big black trunk, and in the next several minutes, she emptied the thing of a myriad of items. Besides those things she'd packed for herself, clothing, nightwear, cosmetics, and such, she presented Emma with an array of gifts: expensive perfume, a large supply of two different colorful fabrics, a selection of threads and sewing accessories, a lovely quilt, and a box of delectable chocolates. Emma couldn't help but notice that most of the items bore the name of *Marshall Fields*, either on tags or, in the case of the perfume and chocolates, on the bottom of the boxes.

"Oh my!" Emma rasped. "This is just too extravagant."

"Nonsense."

"But I've never owned anything from Marshall Fields."

"Well, now you do," Grace said with a shrug and a smile, as if the items were nothing more than a few grains of sand. "And I loved every single minute I spent shopping for them. I had your sweet face, although I'd not seen it yet, pictured in my head the whole time. You would love Marshall Fields, honey. Why, you can nearly get lost in there if you don't pay attention."

"Oh, mercy. That seems far-fetched, but I'm sure it's true. I saw a picture of it once and read an article when I was skimming through a magazine in Johansson's Mercantile. It looked to be quite somethin'."

Emma stared at the outlandish assortment spread out before her, the lovely quilt, the perfume, the fabrics. Wetness spilled out the corners of her eyes. "I don't—know what to say, 'cept—thank you."

Without hesitation, Grace drew her close. A soft chuckle breezed past her lips. "That'll do."

The two rocked back and forth for what must have been a full two minutes. Emma relished in the warmth of her cousin's embrace, still hardly believing she was here.

They both pushed apart at the same time. "And now I have one more thing to give you."

"Oh no, I couldn't accept another thing. Really, this is too much already."

Grace laughed and poked her hand into the trunk, feeling around until she produced the item she sought, a tiny, red velvet box.

"But, what is this?"

"Open it and find out," she answered, shoving the box precisely under her nose.

Emma looked from Grace to the precious little box, shaking with hesitancy. Without even looking, she knew something priceless lay within the velvet confines. But what?

"Go ahead," Grace urged. "I'll explain after you open it."

With trembling fingers, she took the tiny case. She used her other hand to lift the lid, and when she did, she nearly swooned at the sight. A gold pendant with three glistening diamonds and hanging from a gold chain winked back at her. She'd seen this piece before, had admired it countless times over, remembered commenting to its owner on how very pretty it was, the way the diamonds swirled in that half-moon effect.

Eyes swimming, she felt her jaw drop nearly to her waist. "I don't understand. This is...but how did you...? This once belonged to Clara Abbott."

Grace smiled. "I know, honey. She wanted you to have it, and so she mailed it to my mother before she died and asked that she give it to you in due time. Before Mother passed, she and I had a long talk—about a lot of things. She gave me this necklace and made me promise I would bring it to you."

"But—how would your mother know Miss Abbott?" Confusion wove its spindly fingers through Emma's mind.

"They were sisters."

"Oh." That information took a moment to settle.

Grace leaned forward and took a long breath. "This necklace"—she put her hand on Emma's arm and gently squeezed, her eyes welling up with inexpressible emotion— "belonged to your grandmother—Ezra's birth mother."

*****

Jon held to one of Ezra's arms and Luke the other as they mounted the porch steps. "I'm plain tuckered," Ezra mumbled, breaths coming in wheezy intervals.

"I imagine you are. Going to church was quite a feat for you," Jon said.

Wes and Elliott had stayed behind, finding folks to visit with in the churchyard. Jon had thanked them profusely for bringing Ezra to the service and, while neither had attended church prior to today, the way folks had welcomed them, he wouldn't be surprised to see them again.

Jon pulled open the screen door and ushered Ezra inside. A woman he'd never seen before looked up from the settee in the parlor and gave a bright smile, her eyes crinkling in the corners. He peered at her for just a moment before returning a smile. Emma, who sat in a chair across the room, gave a tentative nod and made eye contact with Jon. The faint ticking of the grandfather clock mingled with a whistling teakettle. She leaped to her feet at the teakettle's tune and disappeared into the kitchen, leaving him to guess as to the newcomer's identity.

"You must be the Reverend Atkins," the woman said, rising to her feet, her movements nimble as a practiced dancer, her back as straight as the stem of a fresh picked daisy. *Lovely* was about the only word that came to mind, that and *regal*.

"Yes. And you are...?"

She laughed, a winsome sound, and extended her hand. "Grace. Grace Giles." Something he couldn't begin to discern rippled through his chest. Grace Giles. *The* Grace Giles?

She had a wealth of golden brown hair tied back in a bun, a good share of which escaped to fall haphazardly around her oval face. A sprinkling of silver grew in at the temples, revealing a bit about her age. Her handshake was firm yet feminine, her gaze penetrating yet warm.

"So nice to meet you, Reverend. I've heard about you."

"Really. All good, I hope. Call me Jon, by the way. And I've heard about you."

She nodded and swept him with a twinkling gaze; for an instant, he felt her scrutiny, but just as quickly, she withdrew her hand and looked at Luke. "And you are Luke."

Pulling back his rounded shoulders, Luke put on his best smile. "Y-yes, ma'am."

She laughed again, the sound fairly floating on the air, warm and rich. She took his outstretched hand. "Nice to meet you, Luke."

Luke looked tickled that the stranger knew his name. "Y-yore p-p-pretty," he said.

She brushed a hand over her throat. "Oh my, well, aren't you a dapper gentleman, and a mighty handsome one at that."

The lad's mouth twisted downward. "D-dapper?"

"It means you're terribly smart looking," she said.

Luke tossed back his head and snorted as if she'd just said the funniest thing. The hearty peal made Jon chortle to himself. What a charming woman. He liked her on sight.

Her eyes made their way to Ezra. Jon swiped him with a sideways glance, waiting for a reaction, noting the tiny flicker above his brows.

"Grace Giles?" he asked. When he faltered slightly, Jon steadied him with a firm hand. "Yo're that one's been writin' to my girl. You hail from Chicago, do you?"

If the woman was uncomfortable with the question, she didn't let on.

"I do. My mother was your aunt Edith. Edith Fielding. Therefore, you and I are cousins."

Ezra gave a slow nod before tilting his face in a suspicious gaze. "Emma tol' me."

"And she told you of my mother's passing, I presume."

He shifted on tired feet. Jon grew impatient to seat him before he keeled over, but when he tried to guide him to a chair, the fellow kept his feet planted firm. "She did. I'm—sorry to hear 'bout it. She was—a fine woman."

"Thank you." Teeth pinching down on her lower lip, Grace leaned forward. "I want you to know she cared about you. She saved every missive you ever sent her."

"It weren't that many."

She laid a hand on his arm. "She tried keeping track of you through the years. She would be thrilled to hear the news that you've committed your heart to the Lord. I know she prayed long hours for it."

"It done took me awhile," Ezra said with a sniff.

No-name sauntered into the room to check things out, the mangy critter resembling an old shoe with its tongue hanging out. "Luke, why don't you take your dog to the backyard?" Jon said. "He looks like he could use a long drink."

"'Kay," Luke said. "C'mon, you ol' m-mutt."

Grace watched the unlikely pair exit the room. "What a lovely young man."

A light breeze lifted the curtains and stole across the room. Outside, passersby, on their routine Sunday strolls, conversed, competing with the chatter of overhead birds. "Yes, he's quite something," Jon conceded. "A favorite in the town."

Emma entered at that precise moment, rubbing her hands together in a nervous gesture. Something very important had transpired between the women; Jon sensed it in his gut. He tried to discern the look on her face but found it unreadable.

Lord, be at the center of this situation. Bring it to a peaceful conclusion, whatever it may entail.

*****

A knot of balled-up nerves rolled around in Emma's chest. This was just too much to take in, she thought, the news that Grace brought with her. Oh, she was plain thrilled that Grace had come—no question there—and not all the news was bad, but it'd caught her so off guard that her stomach felt queasy, her nerves trampled upon.

Grace believed that Ezra deserved to know the truth about his roots.

"What good could come from learning the truth at this stage in his life?" Emma had asked.

"In his final days, it might do him a world of good, lend some closure to the whole question of why the people he thought were his parents treated him so badly," Grace had said.

"But that's the part I don't understand. He was the innocent party, and yet they treated him as if he were at fault."

A wave of compassion such as she'd never experienced turned over in her heart, and the notion that she might finally be able to eke out some forgiveness for her father parked itself in the bottom of her soul.

She stole a glimpse at Jon and found him studying her, as if trying to size up her turmoil. Another wave of nausea poked at her gut. Did he have to make her feel so vulnerable, staring

315

at her like that through cobalt eyes, peering into her soul as if it were transparent?

"I think my father should sit," she said, averting her gaze to Ezra and thinking he looked especially pale.

"Yes," Jon said, steering him to the divan. The women sought a place to sit while Jon situated Ezra then dropped into the cushion next to him.

"Tell us about you, Mrs. Giles, or is it Miss?" Jon asked.

"Neither. It's simply Grace. Mind you, I'm a widow, but I prefer not to be reminded of that, so hearing my first name used keeps me feeling young."

He laughed. "All right then, Grace, what do you do with yourself back in Chicago?"

Her lips curled up, and she clasped her hands together in her lap. "My late husband started a restaurant several years ago, which I've been maintaining ever since his passing. It's proved quite profitable, but I'm nearing the point of selling out. As I was telling Emma, the city life is wearing on me."

"Why not come to Little Hickman and open a dining establishment here? A fine eatery is sorely missing in this town."

"The saloon serves food, but it ain't no good," Ezra put in. "The stuff she serves over there is enough ta choke a rat. Probably has, in fact. Ever hear o' beef liver soup?"

Grace wrinkled her nose. "Never."

"Wull, she serves it 'cause it's cheap, and I swear one bowl of it turns a body green."

"Pa."

"It's true."

"I think it's a wonderful idea, Grace, you moving here," Emma said. "You could stay upstairs with me. I've plenty of room."

"Well, I wouldn't impose on you for long. I'd find my own place in short order. Are there any vacant buildings in the town, or any empty lots for erecting a two-story structure? I could do what I've done in Chicago, live above my establishment. Oh, I can actually envision myself living out my remaining years in this wonderful community."

It was clear she'd given thought to the idea long before Jon's mention of it. Imagine her cousin living right here in Hickman. A flutter of pleasure pushed past Emma's bundle of nerves.

"It'd be a mighty big change for you," Jon said.

"We ain't no fancy city," Ezra said.

"But we're friendly," Emma inserted. "And like you said earlier, nature abounds."

Grace laughed, giving Emma an endearing smile. "You don't need to convince me, honey. I've been thinking about this for quite awhile."

Just as she'd thought.

Jon hauled one leg up by the ankle and propped it across the other knee. "Hm," he said. "There aren't any vacant buildings that I know of, but there is that empty space at the end of Main Street right across from the new church. Seems to me that'd be an ideal location. You could talk to Clyde Winthrop, who owns the property. Matter of fact, he might know of some other spots around town if that one's not available. He owns a good share of real estate in these parts. I'd be glad to talk to him if you want."

"Oh, would you? It'd be nice to have you broach the subject with him first. Then I can follow up."

Jon's enthusiasm seemed to match that of Emma. "You'd need to contract with a builder outside of Little Hickman, though, probably go into Nicholasville or Lexington."

"I could do that," Grace said, eyes twinkling with delight.

The three of them conversed for the next several minutes while Ezra dozed.

At 1:15, Wes and Elliott rambled up the steps, all loud talk, and walked through the door. Their jaws dropped, however, at their first glimpse of the attractive female visitor.

*****

Over supper, Jon watched Emma's boarders eat with particular care. Gideon had tucked in his shirt, Charley had greased his hair down, and Elliott looked to have shaved for the second time that day. Wes sat straighter than normal and cleared his throat often, and Harland, who wore dirt beneath his fingernails like he would an article of clothing, had scrubbed them spotless. Even Luke sported a new shirt. It appeared every male there, with the exception of Ezra, had come to the table with the intent of impressing Grace Giles.

Jon had to admit she was an appealing woman, full of zing and zip, a regular fireball. Even Ezra had warmed to her stories. Every time Jon had tried nudging him to his room to rest, Ezra declined the offer, seeming more interested in hearing what his cousin had to say.

And she'd said plenty, from her accounts of her childhood and the wonderful parents who had raised her and her two sisters to her recollection of her several aunts and uncles—and grandparents—all of which would have been Ezra's family as well.

"We had plenty of reunions," she'd said.

"I never went," Ezra said. "Least, not that I can recall. Most times my folks kep' me home or just didn't go ta family gatherin's."

Emma had shifted in her seat and shot Jon a worried glance. What? he'd asked with his eyes, but she merely shook her head at him.

Grace leaned forward in her chair. "Grandfather was an old sourpuss. Do you remember anything about him?"

Ezra looked thoughtful. "Naw. I don't recall much about 'im or my grandmaw. Seemed like my family was all distant from me. Even my own ma and pa was absent most o' my growin' up years. Them varmints, Howard and Hester, was meaner'n goats on a leash, too. Pushed me around ev'ry chance they got. Called me names crude enough to turn snakeskin inside out. Once I left home I didn't care if I ever laid eyes on 'em again, and I don't know ta this day what become of 'em."

A shadow had darkened Grace's face. "I can't say I know myself. In my opinion, they were ignorant people, not worth worrying over. I was just a wee thing when they were teenagers, but I recall Mama saying they were troublemakers, spoiled rotten, she said. And by the time I was old enough to remember anything about you, you'd already gone out on your own. Mama said she used to bring you to the farm from time to time. Before any of us girls were born. Do you remember that?"

Sparks lit in the old guy's eyes, and he tried to pull himself upright. "Course I do. I couldn't have been more'n five, though." His lungs rattled noisily. "Your ma used to make fine oatmeal cookies; I remember that. I'd sit high as I could in a chair at her big table and dip a cookie into a tall glass o' milk. Your pa'd take me fishin'. But there come a day I quit goin' there. Couldn't tell ya why. That's when she took ta sendin' me little notes."

"Mama says Aunt Phoebe stopped allowing the visits."

"My ma, ya mean." Ezra had angled her with a curious look.

319

Grace crinkled her finely sculpted brows. "Uh, yes."

Jon turned his attention back to the polite conversation taking place at the supper table. Ezra nodded off a couple of times while trying to spoon applesauce into his mouth. Jon nudged him awake.

Emma shook her head in dismay.

Something was seriously amiss, but Jon couldn't put his finger on it. He determined to corner Emma later that evening.

Chapter Twenty-Seven

*E*xhausted from her exceedingly long day, Grace excused herself to go upstairs shortly after dinner. Emma, standing in the entryway to the music room, book in hand, promised to join her soon.

"No need to hurry, honey. I'm plum tuckered out and won't be good company. You take your time and don't waste a second worrying over me. I'll be sleeping before the first stars come out." She looked around the room at the gawking boarders, all of whom had lingered in the main rooms after supper. "Good night, gentlemen."

Everyone leaped to his feet when she started up the stairs and wished her a pleasant evening. Jon nearly laughed aloud at the way they stumbled over each other to make the best possible impression. He might have told them none of them would ever measure up to the genteel Grace Giles, but he kept his thoughts to himself.

"Emma and I are going for a walk," he announced from Ezra's doorway, having seen the fellow to his bed. He stared her down, as if daring her to challenge him.

Her lips parted in surprise. The book went to her chest, where she clutched it with both hands. "I am—we are?"

Grace halted midway up the stairs and pivoted. "That's a lovely idea. I'd take a wrap, though, Emma dear; there's a chill in the air."

Jon pushed down the urge to tell her a wrap wasn't necessary. He'd be glad to keep her warm.

As if she read his thoughts, Emma sent him a warning

glance. "Well, I suppose a short walk couldn't hurt. I'll get my cape," she said, disappearing into the kitchen.

"Nice night for a stroll," Wes said, reseating himself on the sofa. "Appears someone's finally caught that girl's eye."

"Ain't no man ever succeeded in courtin' 'er, far as I know," said Harland.

Gideon sniffed, pulled a hand down over his sallow face, snagged a cigar from his front pocket, and meandered toward the door. "Ain't no man ever come along *good* enough for courtin' 'er." Gid angled Jon with a flicker of amusement. "Till now, anyways."

Jon worried that his heart had jumped to his sleeve several weeks ago. Had everyone been watching his reactions to Emma's every move? He laughed, albeit a weak-sounding chortle. "Don't go jumping the gun, fellas. We're just going for a walk."

Charlie stood at the base of the stairs just feet away from Jon. He finger combed his reddish-brown hair and gave a churlish grin. "Uh-huh."

"Ain't got no intentions of lookin' at that full moon, do ya?" Harland asked. That got a rise out of everyone.

Grace cleared her throat, stilling the laughter. "You men are too much. Why, you'd think you had nothing better to do with yourselves."

As if duly reprimanded, Gideon opened the door and disappeared to the front porch, Harland walked to the parlor table and removed a deck of cards from the drawer, Wes snatched up the detective novel he'd been reading, and Charley headed for the library.

Grace winked at Jon and turned on her heel.

*****

They passed Luke lighting the lamps on Main Street. His grin took up his whole face when he spotted them, the long pole he held in his hands to light the gas lamps weaving precariously. "H-hey, if it ain't M-miss Emma and the p-p-preacher."

Jon laughed. "You're doing a fine job there, Luke. Don't know what Hickman would do without you." The lad's smile grew wider yet, his pudgy cheeks fairly glowing with pride.

They strolled by. Emma tried to count the stars that peeked out one by one, marking their spot in the dusky sky. A squirrel bounded down a tree, darted past the post office, and headed for the alley. No-name, who'd come out from under the porch to follow Jon and Emma up the street, perked up at the sight of the critter, but quickly lost interest when it looked like chasing it would require more energy than he was willing to sacrifice. A few townsfolk mingled about, most on a mission to head home, either on foot or on horseback. Jon lifted a hand to wave at everyone who passed.

"Is there anyone in this town you don't know?" Emma asked. She'd clasped her hands behind her as they walked, taking care not to brush against him. A case of the jitters made her legs feel weak and quivery.

Jon gave a quiet laugh. "I suppose I do make it my business to know folks. Goes with the job."

His deep voice resonated off the walls of Sam's Livery when they walked past it, setting off a string of whinnying noises from several horses locked away in their stalls.

"You're a friendly man. You talk to everyone who crosses your path."

"You meant that in a good way, I hope."

"Of course."

Jon kicked a pebble, which sailed several feet. Emma couldn't help but glance down at the size of his feet. *Long* best described them. Like the rest of his frame. Why, her head just reached his shoulders.

"It's nice your cousin traveled all this way to see you."

Keeping pace with him, she lifted her face to look at him and smile. "You wouldn't believe how shocked I was when she climbed down off Mr. Brackett's rig at noon today and said, 'Emma?' Oh, my stars, I almost fainted when she introduced herself." They shared a moment of easy laughter. "She's so—so vibrant and interesting, and pretty, don't you think?"

He gazed down at her and winked. "No prettier than you."

The lump that formed in her throat went down hard. "Oh."

He gave a deep chuckle. "You're a beautiful woman, Emma Browning, and the strangest part is you don't even know it."

Now it was her turn to kick a stone. "I look in the mirror every mornin', Reverend Atkins. I must be lookin' at someone different than the lady you're describin'."

When the sidewalk ended, he took her by the elbow and helped her down. They'd reached the end of Main Street. Stopping on the dusty path, he turned her to face him, gently cupped her chin, and leaned in close. "You need to start seeing yourself as God sees you, Emma, and stop putting yourself down. He has a purpose and plan for you that far exceed your imagination. If you could learn to trust Him, that plan would begin to unfold before your eyes."

His touch set off a warmth that tingled down her spine. "I think I'm beginnin' to see that. At least, somewhat."

"Really?" Surprise mixed with pleasure washed over his face. He pulled back his sturdy shoulders and straightened to his full height. "Tell me about it."

She bit her lower lip until the pressure stung. "Grace told me some things today, things about my father's past. It's helped to put things in perspective for me, but it's also filled me with concern."

His expression stilled. "I knew something had you troubled. I saw it in your eyes all day." The hand that cupped her chin now moved to her shoulder. In the distance, a twig snapped and an owl sent out a lonely sounding, "Whoo—whoo." No-name took a moment to poke his nose in a nearby bush then sat on his haunches and sniffed the air.

"What kinds of things did she tell you?"

She sucked in a heavy breath. "Well, for starters, the people who raised my pa weren't his real parents."

He looked only mildly surprised. "Who were they?"

"His aunt and uncle." A tiny tear pushed out the corner of one eye, and she felt a stinging sensation in her throat. "His birth mother's stepfather raped and—and impregnated her when she was only thirteen."

A look of disbelief crossed his face as he heaved a choked sigh. "Oh, dear God, what is this world coming to?"

"When she gave birth to her baby, she didn't know what to do with him, so she gave him to her older sister, Phoebe.

"Phoebe and Oscar Browning already had a set of five-year-old twins, but they agreed to take Ezra off her hands in an attempt to cover up the horrid circumstances of his birth. Truth be told, they didn't really want him though. My father grew up in a loveless home. And the worst part—he never knew why. Apparently, the twins found out about the adoption, but their mother made them swear to keep the hideous family secret to themselves. They managed to do that but found ways to torment him, make it clear they resented him."

325

Jon's eyes narrowed as he shook his head. He shot a glance up Main Street then back at her. "Any idea who this birth mother is?"

"I'll get to that. Accordin' to Edith, Grace's mother, her youngest sister never could convince her mother of the rape. In fact, after confessin' it, her own mother—my great-grand-mother—refused to believe her and went so far as to accuse her of seducin' her husband. Can you imagine?

"My great-grandmother took to her bed and fell into some kind of deep depression, and the only solution was to send Ezra's birth mother away, young as she was. She went to live with her older sister, the one who took Ezra. But it was a bad situation. The girl wasn't much more than fifteen when Phoebe told her to leave, saying it'd be better for all concerned if she simply found a way to disappear. They gave her plenty of money to set out on her own, so she moved to Chicago, far from family—and her son—even changed her last name, so the association with family would cease to exist. In time, Edith and her husband, John, also moved to Chicago. They started having children and decided to settle there.

"Edith kept informed of Ezra's whereabouts, especially after he left the Browning household, and she relayed the information to Ezra's mother, who by now was filled with deep regret for having abandoned him. When Ezra and his new wife, my mother, moved to Little Hickman, his birth mother started devisin' a plan for movin' here."

A light seemed to dawn in Jon's eyes. "You're talking about Clara Abbott, aren't you?"

Emma paused and swallowed down another hard knot. She gave a slow nod. "Clara was my father's mother, and he never knew it. That's why she took such an interest in my life, left me the boardinghouse, tried her best to look after me, and was so concerned when Ezra failed miserably in bringin' me up."

A look of wistfulness stole into his face. "If only she'd told him who she was. It might have helped."

Emma nodded. "According to Edith, she was too ashamed. She was afraid what his reaction would be after so many years. She did desert him, after all. She thought he might punish her by refusin' to let her see me, and you and I both know he was just ornery enough to do that. I was the one light in her life that kept her going, gave her hope."

Jon's other hand came up to brace her other shoulder. He looked down into her eyes, searching, probing. "This explains a lot. The old fellow never had a clue how to give or receive love, and the death of his young bride only taught him how quickly it can vanish. He didn't have any idea what to do with you, Emma. He had no clue how to raise you, how to love you.

"With no role models, he stumbled through the whole process, and then the alcohol only made matters worse. But you have the power to stop that pattern of abuse, give yourself to another, namely our Lord Jesus, and allow *Him* to father you. He can heal your hurts and give you a brand-new beginning. He can help you forgive the years of abuse you had to suffer.

"If Ezra Browning can seek and find forgiveness for his past, surely you can do the same."

New tears rolled down her cheeks, making a hot path. Without help for it, she dropped her head into his chest and felt his arms go round her. While in his embrace, he took her to the alley behind the livery. There he held her and listened to her sobs, wracking sobs that nearly swallowed her whole.

"I—I want to do that, Jon. I want to ask Him to come into my heart."

She felt a tiny quiver pass through the preacher's body and heard a gentle sigh. His chin came to rest on the top of her head and his embrace tightened.

"Oh, honey, there is no better time than the present to make that happen. No better time than now."

*****

"Are you going to tell him?" Jon asked later on their walk back to the boardinghouse. No-name sauntered along behind, the old mutt's loyal presence contributing to the friendly atmosphere between them. As much as he wanted to hold Emma's hand, declare his love for her, give a hallelujah whoop that all of Little Hickman was sure to hear, he kept his emotions carefully contained, wanting to give her time to ponder on the decision she'd just made. He hadn't even kissed her, although he'd wanted to, longed with all his might to hold her soft body close to his for hours on end. But the Holy Spirit's nudging won out. Too much too soon could scare her off. No, he didn't want to throw his tender love for her into the mix just yet, not when she had so many other things to chew on.

She looked at him. Her eyes still shimmered with wetness, but in their depths shone peace and resolve, despite the little frown that crinkled her brow. "Grace thinks we should, and I suppose he deserves to know that his mother did love him, even though she never came forward. What do you think?"

Jon wasn't sure what to tell her. The man's health was precarious. Could such an announcement make matters worse? *God, please lend Your wisdom to this situation. Give Grace and Emma peace and direction.*

"I'm afraid I can't tell you what to do. What we can do, though, is pray about it. God will make it clear when the time is right."

And so they sat on the little bench in front of the post office and bowed their heads while Jon said a brief prayer.

*****

When the grandfather clock downstairs bonged three times to mark the early morning hour, Emma punched her pillow and turned over. Sleep refused to come even though exhaustion overtook her body. Beside her, Grace slept like a kitten, every measured breath emitting a tiny snuffling sound. Despite her predicament, she smiled. Who would have thought just twenty-four hours ago that she'd be lying next to her cousin, that her lush of a father would have gone to church to declare his new-found faith and ask forgiveness from his daughter and the entire church community, or that she would have made the same life-changing decision to follow Christ later that day? And what of the fact that the woman who'd bequeathed her the boarding-house was her actual grandmother? Her mind reeled.

If that wasn't enough, there was the matter of Jon Atkins.

She'd fallen in love with him—head over heels, to be exact. And it blew her away. Two months ago, she hadn't thought her-self capable, or even interested, and now here she was fairly swooning over him behind his back. What were the chances of him reciprocating that love? Anybody with a brain knew she wasn't preacher's wife material—no matter that she'd asked Christ to forgive her sins. She had so far to go in this Christian walk, so much to learn. An ordinary Christian man wouldn't fool with her, let alone the preacher, for mercy sakes! Yes, he'd kissed her that one time, but surely he'd done it in a moment of weakness, perhaps pity—and with obvious regrets—for he'd never attempted it again, not even after she'd prayed the prayer of forgiveness.

Was he looking for a woman like Hannah Clayton, someone well established in her faith? The Clayton family had attended services Sunday morning, but a handsome young man sat next to Hannah. "That's her old beau from Lexington," Fancy whispered loud enough for anyone within two pews, in front or behind, to hear. "Mrs. Winthrop claims they's gettin' married after Christmas."

Well, Iris would know if anyone would, Emma thought to herself. For once, she was glad the woman made it her business to learn the affairs of others, for it meant she could rest easy where Hannah Clayton was concerned.

Her mind spun crazily as she wrestled with her thoughts. Suddenly, they drifted to Ezra. One part of her wallowed in peace such as she'd never known before—she was a Christian now, an actual child of God—while another grappled with what that entailed; how, if at all, it would change her relationship with her father. Could she forgive him? Yes, she'd decided she could. But would God give them time to reshape the snarled mess they'd made of each other's lives? And if He didn't, would it really matter? So much had transpired through the years. Was it even worth the bother of rehashing it? Wasn't it enough simply to let it all go? Moreover, should she tell him about his tangled past?

She had a sudden need to peek in on him. She got up, donned her housecoat, and tiptoed barefoot down the stairs, frowning at the fifth step when it gave its usual creaky announcement that someone was out of bed.

As if sensing her presence in the doorway, he jerked awake. "What…?" he murmured, eyes gone big. That set off an unwelcome string of coughs.

She crossed the room and offered him water, trying to prop him up as he gasped for air. Guilt for having startled him coiled around her like a snake.

When the raspy hacking finally settled, he took a sip then fell back on the pillow, obviously bone weary. "What you doin' up?" he asked.

"Couldn't sleep," she said, pulling up a chair and situating it next to him. "How are you feelin'?"

His lungs wheezed and whistled. Doc had said there were no pat answers as to how long he would hang on. Could be days, could be weeks.

"I been better," he said. "Ever since I give my heart ta God I been hankerin' fer a drink. Tonight's been the worst. Ain't that strange? Preacher kid says the devil'll do that to a new child o' God 'cause he's plain mad you decided to go the other way."

She pondered that thought. "I don't have any brew in my house, and my boarders know I'll have their throats if they slip you anything. Hopefully, the cravin' will pass in a day or so."

"This trustin' the Lord business is new ta me, but the Scripture I been readin' says God gives strength ta the weak. I'm believin' He'll see me through this powerful want."

Emma leaned back in her chair and gave her father an assessing look, awed by the fact he'd changed so drastically. She longed to tell him about her own profession, but the subject of faith had never come up between them, and the notion of vocalizing it touched a weak spot that needed coddling. Despite his own forthrightness in unloading his confession before the whole church—and surely by now all of Little Hickman had heard the news that Ezra Browning, the town drunk, had found religion—her own decision felt too private to share just yet. Oh, she'd told Grace, but only because she'd nearly dragged it out of her, wanting to know the details of her evening stroll. But it hadn't felt natural. She longed for the confidence to let it come easy.

He pointed his gaze at the ceiling. "I been a worthless fool, Emma. Never treated you like ya deserved."

"Don't think on it now, Pa. It's not worth worryin' over." If that was her way of accepting his apology, it was lame at best.

Moments of silence lay between them. Finally, he cleared his clogged throat and aimed a questioning look at her. "I s'pect ar cousin knows ya got the bad treatment from me. Seems like she knows quite a lot 'bout my growin' up years, too, her bein' Edith's daughter an' all. What all'd she tell you?"

A stone of worry nestled in her throat. When she'd come downstairs it was to check on him, not to talk into the wee hours, least of all to divulge ugly family secrets.

Besides, Grace wasn't here to lend support.

God will make it clear when the time is right. Jon's words bore a hole in her memory.

"She told me you sent her mother a letter back in April telling her how sick you were."

He nodded. "Never heard back from 'er."

"She was too ill to reply. She gave the letter to Grace to read." Emma swallowed hard. "She also told her about your upbringin'."

Ezra adjusted himself on the narrow cot and grunted. "She tell you why she don't think it was my own parents what raised me? Or how she happened to know Clara Abbott?"

"I—she—had a few things to say on the subject." She stood and stretched. "I'm tuckered. Can we talk in the mornin'?"

"It shouldn't take ya long to tell me what she said," he pressed.

The old house creaked and groaned as if in dire pain. Even when no one was about, the thing had a way of talking to its residents, and if she weren't so used to its varied sounds, she might have thought it ominous. Outside, some cats yowled, probably tussling over a mouse. A dog barked into the mix, disturbing the otherwise tranquil early hour.

Emma sat back down as the grandfather clock chimed the half hour. When was she going to get some sleep? Plain weariness pushed a yawn through her clenched teeth.

"Did you ever question whether the people who raised you were your actual parents?" she asked, bracing herself.

"Sure." That set her back. "We never was close, so I can truthfully say it wouldn't have mattered one way or the other ta me, and it'd be a pure blessin' to discover them twins weren't my real blood."

"Oh, you shared the same blood, all right. They just weren't your siblings," she dared to add, keeping her shoulders erect.

"Eh? How do ya mean?"

She sucked in a cavernous breath and blew it out slowly. Whispering a hasty prayer, she proceeded with caution.

"The twins were actually your cousins."

Clouded eyes gave her a blank stare as he let that piece of information set awhile. Then, as if a light had dawned, he quirked one gray brow. "That'd mean that my ma and pa was actually...."

He didn't finish.

"Oscar and Phoebe Browning were your aunt and uncle."

"Then who...where...?"

Oh, Lord, how to tell him. Another sigh blew through her chest. "You had a mother, but she—was too young to care for you, a mere fourteen years old."

"Not married?"

She shook her head.

"Who was my pa?"

333

The old rattle came back to announce the coming of another hacking spell. She pursed her lips, willing it to halt their discussion, then feeling guilty for wishing it. Determination seeped out his eyes as he fought back the want to cough.

"Who?" he repeated on a rasp.

"He—was—he was your grandmother's second husband. Your birth mother—your birth mother was Phoebe's youngest sister, Clara. Clara Abernathy—Abbott."

*****

Jon listened from his room as Emma tiptoed up the front staircase. He'd been tempted to leave his bed when he awoke to Ezra's terrible hawking, but then heard Emma's voice and figured she had things under control. Long after the coughing spell had ended, their voices carried up the register, but not enough to ascertain their topic. Now and then, he'd catch a word or a small piece of a sentence—cousin—aunt—Chicago—was a long time ago—right here in Little Hickman. He wondered if Emma had decided to tell her father about his past, and if she had, why in the middle of the night?

He could tell when she rounded the hallway at the top of the stairs because the board that he usually stepped over to avoid its creak sounded loud and clear. He leaped from his bed, threw on his trousers and shirt, and raced to the door.

She turned around when the door opened and gave a jolt of surprise. "What are you doing up?" she whispered.

He hooked a finger at her to encourage her return. Slowly she tiptoed toward his room. Her eyes, red-rimmed and weary looking, held another indefinable emotion. Caution? Insecurity?

"I couldn't sleep."

She shrugged. "Join the crowd."

"I heard you talking to Ezra. Couldn't make out your words, but I got some of the drift of it. Did you tell him—about his past, about Clara Abbott being his mother?"

She nodded slowly.

"How'd he take it?"

"Better than I expected. I think God was right there in the room, Jon. The words seemed to come out pretty good—from both of us."

"You get things talked out between you then?"

"Not as much as you'd think, but it was a start. Mostly we talked about the people who raised him, what memories remained, what, if anything, he could recall about his grandmother's second husband, which really amounted to nothing. I 'magine the man wanted nothing to do with him. In fact, I'm sure every time folks laid eyes on Ezra, they thought about the awful disgrace, even though it was all Orville Lindsay's fault."

He quirked his eyebrows.

"That was the name of the man who married my great-grandmother less than one year after her husband passed," she explained. "Accordin' to Grace's mother's account, he was a mean cuss, abused in some way or another every one of the six children, including Edith, until one by one they left home, leaving Clara, the youngest, with nowhere to go. When she was just thirteen, he...well, you know."

"Yes."

Her chin dropped and she seemed to study her toes, which peeked out from the hem of her sleeping coat. He did the same and found them slender and well formed. In fact, if one could look at feet and call them pretty, he'd never seen prettier ones. He leaned a shoulder against the doorframe and gave her a sweeping gaze, which she never detected. Exhilaration soared through his veins despite the hour. She was a Christian now.

Didn't that free him up for courting her? The idea of courting Emma Browning set off a tingling in the pit of his stomach.

He tipped her chin up. The shift caused several tendrils of her golden hair to tumble in an elegant manner around one small shoulder. Without forethought, he twined a strand of it around his finger. Her eyes widened with surprise then focused on something over his shoulder. He smiled. "It was good that you told him, Emma."

She glanced at him for one second. "You think? I hope the timin' was right. I did pray about it."

Warmth curled through his veins. "Then all you can do is trust that the Lord was in it."

"I s'pose you're right."

"It's been a long day for you. You best get a couple of hours of sleep."

She nodded, her hair still entwined in his finger. When she turned to go, he tugged at the lock, forcing her to stop and look at him. He leaned forward, one hand on her shoulder pulling her close, intending to kiss her, intending to make it one she wouldn't soon forget, but the door across the hall opened before he had the chance.

Emma lurched backward. Jon's hands dropped to his sides.

"W-what you t-t-two doin'?" asked Luke in a voice loud enough to wake the whole town.

Chapter Twenty-Eight

*G*race's presence in the house added life and luster, if not a sense of style and civility. It was a downright shame she was leaving in less than a week, Wednesday morning to be exact. Everyone from innocent Luke to rough-and-tumble Gideon seemed bent on minding his manners. They came to the table with pressed shirts and clean hands and faces, and cleaned up speech, to boot. More than once Jon had to close his gaping mouth when the men raced to be the first to pull out Grace's chair. Often, glances of amusement passed between Emma and him, and when her smile reached her eyes, it was all he could do not to proclaim his love for her right there on the spot.

The last four days had found Ezra bedridden and with a worsening cough. Emma tended to him more than Jon did, insisting he take in water, fluffing up his pillow, straightening his bedcovers, and administering medicine prescribed by Doc. She fed him spoonfuls of soup, read to him from the Bible Jon had given him, and sat in the chair beside his bed while he dozed. Jon watched in amazement as the flat-out miracle took place before his eyes, the mending of two wounded souls. Ezra complained one night that she still hadn't told him she forgave him, but Jon had said, "Actions often speak louder than words, my friend. She's doing the best she can right now."

Doc Randolph had shown up on Tuesday morning just before Jon headed out to make a few calls on parishioners. He'd hung back to watch while Doc put the instrument to Ezra's heart and lungs then caught the solemn look Doc shot him. On the porch a few minutes later, the old doctor shook his head and said, "It shouldn't be long now."

"But he's been pretty good of late," Jon argued.

Doc shrugged. "Sometimes it works that way. He'll be good for a few days at a time then take a big turn the other way. I'm not saying he won't swing back again, but you should tell Emma to prepare herself."

He wanted Doc to tell her, but she and Grace had been out running errands at the time. *Just a little more time, Lord,* he'd prayed. *Please, don't take him yet.*

It was Friday afternoon. The Sterlings were expecting him for supper, but he had to track down Clyde Winthrop first. Jon directed Jupiter up Main Street, tipping his hat at folks as he journeyed past the post office, Doc's place, the bank, and Flanders' Foods. At Winthrop's Dry Goods, he reined in his horse, tied him to a post, and walked inside.

Busy with a customer when the bell above the door sounded, Iris glanced up and gave him an instant smile. "Well, Reverend," she fawned. "How lovely to see you."

Fancy Jenkins emerged from behind a bolt of linen and fairly gushed. "Reverend Atkins! You comin' in ta buy some thread, are ya?"

He tossed back his head and laughed, fumbling with his hat. Millie Jacobs, the woman who assisted Iris at the counter, turned and gave him a pleasant smile. In her arms, her one-year-old daughter, Rose, stuck a couple of fingers in her mouth and stared at him.

"Afternoon, ladies. No thread needed today. I'm looking for Clyde. Didn't find him over at the house."

"You won't find him there, Reverend. A wagonload of inventory came in three days ago, and he's been busy in the back room sorting shelves," Iris replied. "I'll get him for you."

Clyde appeared from behind the curtain just as Iris turned. "Well, howdy, Reverend. Thought I recognized that boomin' voice. How you been? Life seem different for you living over at that boardinghouse? Fine sermon, Sunday."

"I've adjusted quite well, and thank you."

"It was a downright surprise to have Ezra Browning show up in church," Clyde added. "My!"

"Surprise. It was a shock," Iris chimed.

"It's been the talk o' the town," Fancy put in. "Folks is just plain blew away by it. Who would've thought Hickman's biggest elbow bender would find the Almighty?"

"Of course, he *would* wait until he landed on his deathbed," Iris chortled, her face a marble effigy of contempt.

"Iris," Clyde said.

"Well, it's true. How convenient for him after having lived a completely reckless life to suddenly get saved."

A cool breeze stirred through the open windows at the front of the store, which was a good thing because Iris's comment made Jon's blood boil. "The Lord is not fussy about who He accepts into His kingdom, or when they come, Iris, as long as they come with repentant hearts. Look at the thief on the cross. In his final hour he asked the Lord for mercy, and Jesus promised him a place in Paradise."

"Well, that may be true, but was he a worthless drunk on top of being a thief?"

"Iris, for goodness' sake, what difference should that make?" Clyde scolded. "I don't know why it should ruffle you that the old guy's found peace with God. It took a lot of courage for him to come forward the way he did last Sunday, sick as he was. I can think of a few folks who'd benefit from goin' up front and askin' forgiveness from those they've offended." Clyde aimed his statement straight at his wife so that she dropped her gaze to her register and started punching keys, shoulders squared, her breaths coming out in short puffs.

Jon cast an eye at Fancy and found her mouth agape, but her eyes dancing with amusement.

Millie kept her eyes trained on Rose, but it was clear her pursed lips were fighting off a grin. "I'll take this spool of thread, too," she muttered to Iris, pushing it across the counter with her other items. Without so much as an upward glance, Iris completed Millie's dry goods order.

"Now then, Jonathan, was there something you needed from me?" Clyde brushed his hands together and stuck them in his pockets.

"Actually, I was wondering about that vacant piece of property across from the church. I'm told you own it."

"Well, I do, yes. Were you thinking the church might have need of it?"

"No, not the church. Emma's cousin, Grace, is interested in purchasing it. I told her I'd speak to you about it."

"Why, what would she want with it?" Iris asked, her head shooting up.

Clyde leveled Iris with a warning look. She shrugged. "I'm merely asking," she crowed. Huffing, she handed Millie her change then set to wrapping her purchases in brown paper, tying it shut with a piece of twine.

"She owns and operates a successful restaurant business in Chicago, but she's ready to sell it and move to Little Hickman," Jon explained. "If she can find the right piece of property, she'd like to build an eating establishment right here in the middle of town, maybe put her living quarters above it. I think it'd do well, don't you? Aside from the three stools in Bordon's Bakery where Orville and Winnie serve up a hot cup of coffee with a slice of fresh bread or a donut, there's no place besides their homes for the citizens of Hickman to take their meals."

"There's the saloon," Fancy said, as if she were being helpful. Clyde and Jon both raised their brows at her. "Not that it's suitable, mind you. Certainly, *I* wouldn't darken its doors. I only *hear* there's food in there."

Clyde whistled through his teeth and looked at Jon. "Well, I'll be. I been wondering when someone with the culinary skills might come along and build us an eatery."

"I know Herb and I would love the chance to eat the occasional meal out. Sounds like a downright luxury, if you ask me." Millie hoisted Rose more securely on one hip and tucked her parcel under her arm. "Good day, folks." At the door she turned. "Oh, and do tell Emma's cousin that I hope things work out for her."

Jon waved at Millie as she opened the door. "I'll do it, Millie. You have a good day now."

"I ain't ever et in a restaurant before," remarked Fancy after the front door shut with a thump. She laid her purchase of one twelve-inch black zipper on the counter. Iris snagged it up and rang up the total.

"There's a first time for everything, ma'am," Jon told her. The wide smile she returned was missing a few front teeth.

After a satisfying talk with Clyde, Iris tending to a sudden swarm of new customers, Jon left the store. Grace had to work out a number of issues before purchasing the property, but as far as Clyde was concerned, the lot was hers.

Reins in hand, he clicked Jupiter into motion and headed up Main Street again. He passed the mercantile on his right and the saloon on his left. Looking through the swinging doors, he glimpsed someone swaying on his feet. Even in the afternoon hour, it echoed with boisterous sounds, an off-key piano, raucous laughter, and some woman's crude remark.

Thank You for saving Ezra from that pit, Lord, even if it was in his eleventh hour. Give me a heart for more souls like him, ones who look for peace at the bottom of an empty bottle but fail to find it. Help me reveal Your redeeming love to them and, more importantly, show me how to do it.

An empty field separated the bawdy establishment from the new church. His mood changed at the sight of the freshly built structure. He perused it with pride. There was still a pile of debris at the back of the property, leftover building materials, Tim Warner's tractor, and a stack of unused lumber, but with the help of several men who continued to work on cleaning up the yard, the mess grew smaller every day. Already the new church had brought a fresh sense of community, drawing in folks who hadn't attended services in years. Perhaps this Tuesday's church supper would lure even more unchurched citizens.

He veered Jupiter up Hickman Creek Road. The horse snorted and sniffed the air, eager to speed things up. Jon gave in to the critter's urge and clicked him into a faster pace. He must have sensed the sweet oats awaiting him at Clarence Sterling's farm, and Jon couldn't blame him. His own mouth watered at what fresh-baked delicacy Mary would have sitting on her kitchen table.

As usual, Clarence and Mary Sterling sat on their front porch awaiting Jon's arrival. Clarence lifted a thin arm to wave then pushed himself to his feet and hedged down the steps, not as surefooted as he once was, but not frail either.

Mary rose and looped an arm around a post, putting the other hand to her brow to ward off the sun. Even from a distance, Jon caught the glint in her eyes when their gazes met.

"You bake me any cookies?" he called.

"That and a chocolate pie," she returned on the breeze. "We got roast beef and taters for supper. Baked your favorite rolls, too!"

Clarence arrived to take Jupiter to the watering barrel. "Got some oats waitin' for ya, feller." Jupiter's friendly snort indicated his gratitude as the two sauntered off to the barn.

These Friday evening suppers at the Sterlings made for a fine routine.

There was only one problem with them. He missed Emma.

*****

Besides the thrill of having Grace at her side when she walked through the doors of Little Hickman Community Church on Sunday morning, Emma had an uncommon peace. No longer did she enter weak-kneed and with a sense of dread. *You don't belong here, you're not good enough, you carry shame on your sleeve, your pa is nothin' but a drunk*—those nagging thoughts had all but vanished, and perhaps it was because Grace had told her those were the devil's lies to keep her locked away from Christ all those many years. Now that she'd discovered Him as her Savior, the devil had lost a great deal of ground with her.

Oh, but it gave her joy to discover the devil had not only lost ground, he'd lost his battle for her life.

Her relationship with Ezra steadily improved, although it had its bumps. Jesus may have saved his soul, but He'd pretty much kept his stubbornness intact. If he wasn't complaining about the horse pills Doc insisted he needed, he was grousing over the soup and water Emma kept shoving down his throat. She mostly ignored his rants, though, figuring they were due

343

to the battle he was losing against his illness. Every day he looked a little thinner, grew a little weaker, and coughed a little longer, his coughing spells often producing blood, which landed on his shirtfront.

Folks were plainly curious about the fashionable newcomer whose presence carried rumors about a possible restaurant coming to Little Hickman. "Oh, wouldn't it be grand?" someone had whispered from two pews back before the opening song that morning. "Imagine not havin' to cook a meal." "Wonder what will be on the menu," another remarked. "I hope it's meatloaf," chimed a child's voice.

Grace hadn't heard the talk, for she'd been conversing with Gladys Hayward, who sat on the other side of her, but the remarks brought a smile to Emma's face. The restaurant would be nice, yes, but restaurant aside, she'd have her cousin close by, and that's what led to her excitement.

After the service, folks gathered in the churchyard in clusters to visit. Glorious sunshine fell on shoulders wrapped in jackets and capes. Orange-tinted oak leaves fell one by one as early autumn kicked up its breezes. Across the yard, Emma caught sight of Irwin Waggoner and Gertrude Riley, a known couple these days. In fact, Emma wouldn't be surprised if they married soon. Hickman was due for a wedding, after all. Last winter it'd been Liza Jane Merriwether and Benjamin Broughton, and not long after that, Sarah Woodward and Rocky Callahan. Who would it be this winter if not Irwin and Gertrude?

Grace's arm tucked in Emma's, the two of them walked along, stopping every so often to chat with whoever vied for their attention.

"You're comin' to the church supper Tuesday night, I hope," Flora Jarvis had said, hugging Emma's shoulders. "It couldn't be a prettier day if it was the middle of July," remarked Tom Averly, coming up from behind. "That sure is a perty hat you're wearin', Miss Emma. You, too, Miss Grace," said the middle-aged Eileen Crunkle in passing. "I do hope you won't wait a full year to build that restaurant, ma'am. I could use a mite of good cookin'," called the elderly Elmer Hayward from five feet off, taking a punch in the arm from his wife, Gladys. Everyone who'd seen and heard laughed with glee.

And so it went.

"This sure is a friendly town, honey," Grace whispered in her ear as they moved along. "I can hardly wait to call it home. And look at Jon over there." They both paused. "Why, you'd think he was royalty the way folks swarm him like bees to a comb. That laugh of his, my, it's plain contagious."

Emma had been watching him ever since the benediction. Fact is, if the man left her sight for long, he slipped right into her mind, a true predicament if there ever was one. Yes, he'd been more than kind to her and had even attempted to sneak a kiss the other night before Luke interrupted them. It'd been another one of those moments of weakness, that's all. Simply put, she'd looked weary, and he'd taken pity.

If ever she needed to stay on her guard, it was now. Somewhere along the line, the Reverend Atkins had overtaken her heart—and now he had the power to break it in two.

*****

On Tuesday morning, Jon readied Ezra for his day as best he could. Lately, the fellow hadn't wanted to rise for his morning ablutions, much less get dressed, but Jon believed in keeping him moving.

"Up and at 'em, my friend," he insisted. "We're going to

sit on the porch this morning. It's a fine day." With assistance the fellow stood.

"What's the date?" he wanted to know.

"The date. Let me think."

"October 6," said Emma, breezing into the room looking prettier than a spring flower in her yellow flowered skirt and pale green blouse, dust cloth in hand, a wisp of hair falling square between her eyes.

Jon smiled but got nothing in return. The woman was nothing this morning if she wasn't business. He wondered if she'd spent any time thinking about their near kiss, which Luke had so rudely interrupted a few nights ago.

"That right?" Ezra took a step and paused, took another and rested again. "Time's a wastin', ain't it?" he said.

"Don't know why you'd say that," Emma mumbled. "You got no cause to be worryin' over the date." She started dusting the dresser despite its spotless sheen.

"Course I do. My days is numbered."

"Don't be silly," she said.

"I ain't bein' silly, girl," he argued. "I got a feelin' the Lord and Gabriel's been discussin' my homecomin'."

Emma's skirt flared when she whirled about. She set both hands on her narrow hips and fixed him with perturbed blue eyes. "Don't be talkin' like that."

Jon watched the two shoot daggers at each other with their pinned gazes and nearly laughed aloud. He'd come to believe they enjoyed sparring.

"We're going outside to sit a spell, Emma. Care to join us?" he asked, already knowing she'd turn him down. Lately, she'd taken pains to give him the cold shoulder.

She stuck out her pert little chin and shook her head. "Enjoy the fresh air."

"I'll join you," said Grace, coming out from the kitchen and wiping her hands on her full skirts, having just finished the breakfast dishes. "Lord knows I won't have another opportunity what with my getting back on that train tomorrow. Emma, sweetie, I plan to make pies for the church supper tonight. Can we walk to the food store later for some fresh apples?"

"Of course. I need a few supplies of my own."

Jon held the door for Grace so she could slip out ahead of Ezra and him. "How about filling our heads with more stories of Chicago?" he asked.

"Oh, pooh, I've talked enough. I want to hear about you for a change."

"Ask me anything you like," Jon said, noting with a side glance that Emma was watching. He took the opportunity to wink at her and chuckled to himself when she blushed.

*****

As quick as the menfolk set up makeshift picnic tables in the churchyard, the women tossed tablecloths over them. Families arrived by foot, wagon, and horseback, each with some sort of covered dish to contribute to the supper.

Grace tossed a red-and-white checkered cloth over the table, long boards placed across two sawhorses, which Benjamin Broughton and Truman Atwater had just set up. The men tipped their hats at Emma and Grace and moved on to the next location.

"This should do nicely," Grace said, a look of pride set across her face as she placed plates, silver service, napkins, and tall glasses on the table. "Do you think anyone will join us?"

"You are a magnet, dear cousin," Emma said.

"Oh, pooh!" Grace said, flicking her wrist. She looked around the churchyard where folks big and small, old and young, were arriving in droves. "It's you they want to sit near. Jon, for one, asked me to save him a spot, and I doubt it's because he wants to hear any more of my senseless blather. That boy has his eye on you, Emma Browning, and don't try to deny it."

Jon was going to sit with them? "But there are so many others whose table he should share. Won't folks be put out with him?"

"Now, darlin', you need to stop worrying what folks think. Jon Atkins has an interest in you, and it's high time the citizens of Little Hickman realized it, yourself included."

"But that's plain silliness." The chill in the air had her pulling her cape closer.

"Is it? Why, a person would have to be blind not to notice the way he watches you."

That's what Billy had said, and for just a fleeting moment, she wondered how the eccentric character was doing. She thought he would've at least sent a postcard by now.

"You two saving that table for anyone in particular?" asked Rocky Callahan, Sarah at his side, their two youngsters, Rachel and Seth, in tow. Rocky carried a covered casserole and Sarah had her hands full with table service.

"You come right over here and join us," said Grace. "We've only to save this spot right here for Jon." She leaned across and pointed to the space beside Emma. Emma felt her cheeks go pink.

If Sarah noticed, she didn't let on. Instead, she gifted them with a radiant smile, revealing glistening teeth. "Oh, I'm glad you've made room for us. I've so wanted to talk to both of you."

While the ladies set the table, Rocky went off in search of folding chairs and Seth prattled about the puppies the Warners had carted with them and the "Free Pups" sign Tim Warner had leaned against their crate.

"How is your father doing, Emma? I've heard there's been good and bad days."

"You heard right," Emma said, thankful at least that Jon's name had dropped from the conversation. "Today proved to be a better one. In fact, Grace tried to talk him into joining us tonight, but he begged off. We left him sitting on the porch where he's been most of the day. He'll be fine for a couple of hours."

"That's good to hear. I'm sure your excellent care has made a big difference."

"That and the reverend's," Grace put in. "He's a wonder, that man, the way he finds time to tend to the needs of his flock, reads volumes of books while studying for his sermons, works at the church, and still spends hours caring for a dying man."

Emma flinched at the words *dying man* then chided herself for it. She knew as well as anyone that Ezra wasn't long for this world, but did folks have to keep reminding her of it, her father included? Why, just this morning he'd made mention that time was wasting. Was he privy to something, some keen perception of things to come?

Seeming to sense Emma's sudden discomfort, Sarah stood silent before taking in a deep breath. "Well," she pointed her gaze at Grace, "have you enjoyed your stay in Little Hickman?" She tossed a lock of red hair over her shoulder as she positioned a silver fork just so.

Across the way, the Broughton family gathered at a table with the Swains. In the midst of arranging her table service, Liza shot a glance around the churchyard. When she saw Emma, she gave a hearty wave. Her pregnant belly so protruded that Emma wondered how she'd ever scoot close enough to the table to reach her plate. She returned the friendly gesture.

"Very much," Grace was saying. "I can hardly wait to

return. I've only to make final arrangements for the sale of my restaurant in Chicago and pack up my belongings. I'm aiming for late November, early December. I hope I'm not being unrealistic."

"Oh, I shouldn't think so," Sarah said. "As long as you have good attorneys who can draw your papers up in short order. These things can happen relatively quickly if you've already procured a buyer."

"Oh, I have. I sent a wire to the interested party just yesterday, in fact, and his return message was one of utter delight. He and his wife have been a great help to me over the years, particularly after my husband's passing, and I shall miss them greatly. They would be the only basis for my regretting leaving the big city."

Sarah looked thoughtful. "I can surely understand that. You'll purchase the property across from the church, then?"

Vivid eyes lit with excitement. "I met with Clyde Winthrop yesterday morning. As soon as I return home, I'll wire the money from my bank to his. It was a very simple transaction. Jon promises to make the arrangements for finding a builder from Lexington."

"I'm sure Rocky would be happy to assist him. He knows a great many people in the contracting field."

Rocky returned with several folding chairs under both arms. "I believe I heard my name mentioned. I hope it wasn't in vain." The ladies laughed and continued their chatter, Seth started begging to go see the puppies, and Rachel spotted her friend, Lili Broughton, and announced her departure. Rocky whisked the two of them off with a warning not to go far and started setting up chairs.

Chapter Twenty-Nine

*T*he church supper accomplished everything Jon had hoped, bringing folks together for a time of laughter and pleasant conversation. He'd moved from one table to the next, not wanting to leave anyone out, making certain to approach newcomers first, of which there'd been several. To his delight, established church members took these visitors under their wings, inviting them to their tables. It seemed the folks of Little Hickman Community Church were learning the art of compassion, and he guessed Ezra Browning's confession had had a hand it that, inspiring folks to take greater risks, care more, love more deeply.

Emma's gentle laughter carried over the breezes, something Seth had said having sparked her mirth. Then, when Rachel jumped in, it made Emma laugh harder. He'd missed the joke entirely, of course, his mind wandering to church matters.

"What do you think of that?" Rocky asked, zooming in on Jon, a twinkle in his eye.

Time to confess his inattention. Grace reached across Emma and put a hand on his arm. "Oh, he's in favor, I'm sure."

"I am?" he asked.

"Of course. It could draw a big crowd."

"It could?"

"You don't think the preacher kissing a pig's snout would attract attention?"

Ah, so that was it. "Depends on which preacher does the deed. Now if we're talking Reverend Miller, I could see—"

351

"We're talking you, my friend," Rocky inserted. "The Sunday we reach two hundred in attendance, you kiss a drooling pig the next week."

"Oh." Growing the church by artificial means didn't appeal to him, but on the other hand, if it meant increasing his audience for receiving the gospel message, what preacher wouldn't go for it?

"That's something I would like to see," said Emma, giggling.

He leaned into her, daring her to pull back. "What? You don't think I'd kiss a pig?" he asked. "I've kissed worse." As soon as he said it, he noticed his error. Her eyes lost all their humor; her face paled like a summer moon. Surely, she didn't think he meant *her*. That time he'd kissed her had been nothing short of spectacular. "Not you! I mean, your...." Well, wasn't this a pickle! Emma slapped a hand over her mouth. He felt his face go beet red.

"What I meant was—Georgia Whitehead!" He threw Rocky a pleading glance, but his friend just crossed his arms over his chest and gave his head a slow shake.

"You remember her, Rock." Desperation crawled up his spine. "What was it? Third grade? You guys dared me to kiss her out behind the school, said you'd each give me a penny if...."

Grace and Sarah sat wide-eyed and gape-mouthed, and he didn't even dare look at Emma. He could be mistaken, but hadn't he just given away the fact that he'd kissed his landlady?

"Reverend! Reverend Atkins!"

Just when he thought up a believable explanation, he heard someone call his name. To his surprise, rounding the church, and in a great hurry, were Harland Collins and Gideon Barnard.

Instinct told him something wasn't right, so he pushed back and stood, hands steepled on the tabletop. "What is it?"

"You better come," Harland said on a shaky breath. He eyeballed Emma. "You too, Miss Emma."

Emma wiped the corner of her mouth with her napkin and stood beside Jon. "Where? What's going on?"

Gideon swallowed hard. "It's Ezra. He's—over at the saloon."

"The saloon!" Emma shrieked. "Oh, no! What in the world...?" She tossed down her napkin and started marching across the yard.

"Emma, wait!" Jon called.

When she didn't slow down, just picked up her long skirts and walked faster, Grace leaped from her chair and took off after her. Jon let them go.

"What's he doing at the saloon?" he asked both men, practicing his preacherly, calm demeanor, but feeling anything but relaxed. Before he ran off half-cocked, he needed details.

Harland shook his head. "Craziest thing you ever did see. Gid and me was just sittin' there at the madam's place enjoyin' ar ale when in comes Ezra. At first I didn't think nothin' of it 'cause he used ta be a fixture there. Then it hit me he ain't s'posed ta be there.

"Me and Gid both thought it at the same time. We was goin' ta take 'im back to the house, but then he walks up on the stage and gets everyone's attention. Even Gus stopped playin' the pianer."

Jon motioned for them to start moving toward the saloon. "Keep talking," he said, giving Rocky a silent invitation to follow. Without a second's hesitation, he leaped from his chair. Several other men who'd noticed the commotion, perhaps expecting trouble, tagged along. Jon was thankful for their presence.

"Well, once he got the place all quiet like, he started up preachin'," continued Harland. "It was just like God Hisself was doin' the talkin'. Folks was lendin' 'im their ears, and even the madam had a tear in 'er eye. He was talkin' about how he got—what you call it—salvation, and sayin' that any of us could experience the same thing. Weren't no special formula, he said, 'cept to take Jesus as your Savior.

"Well, he had one coughin' spell toward the end of his preachin' episode where blood was comin' out, but then he got control. He said a few more things about havin' regrets and whatnot, and asked folks to think over what he said. That's when it happened."

Jon felt his brow crinkle and a knot start to form in his gut. "What do you mean?" he asked.

"He toppled over right there on that stage."

Alarm curled through his veins. "Toppled?" He stepped up his gait, eyes zeroing in on the saloon, where a crowd had gathered outside the swinging doors.

"Several of us men carried him to that bench there," Gideon offered, pointing straight ahead. "We sent Henry Watson after the doc, but I ain't sure...."

That was all he needed to hear before he set off on a run.

*****

"Pa, say somethin'. Please. Talk to me." Emma cradled her father's head in her arm, body bent over him. Beside her Grace prayed in low murmurs, her hand on Ezra's arm.

"Didn't I tell you—they was discussin' my homecomin' up there?" he muttered, his voice shaky and scarcely audible.

A well of sadness dug so deep in her soul she had to fight to keep her own self breathing. "Papa, please don't talk like that," she begged on a hoarse whisper. "We're not done yet, you and me."

He closed his eyes and swallowed. Blood oozed out the side of his mouth and made a straight path down his chin. The sight unnerved her.

"It's nearin' my time, girl. I won't be a burden to ya any longer."

It seemed to take him longer than usual to suck in his next breath. When he did, it came out raspy and hollow sounding. His eyes opened to slits and fixed on her face for the briefest time. "You was always a good—girl. I'm sorry I...."

"Shh. I know, Pa. I'm sorry too."

A strange groan broke loose from his chest, and his eyes fluttered shut.

"Pa?" When he made no further attempt to open them, she leaned close to whisper in his ear. "I still got things to say to you, Pa. You hear me?"

"Emma." Doc had been prodding her to move aside, but she wouldn't listen.

Another shallow breath slipped past his sagging mouth. Desperate to say her piece, she put her mouth close to his ear. "Jesus saved me—just like He did you, Papa. I meant to tell you sooner, but I was too piggish to do it. I meant to tell you it was brave of you to walk in front of the church like that, too, and I was, well, proud of you for doin' it.

"I love you, Pa, I really do, and I wanted so bad to tell you, but—well, it just wouldn't come out o' me. But you knew it, didn't you, Papa?" Only inches from his face, she saw a slight movement behind his eyelids. He battled to open them further, and when he did, it was to give her a glazed-over look, as if his spirit had

355

flown away. Panicked, she started to shake him, barely aware of the growing crowd of curious bystanders.

"Don't go yet, Pa," she begged.

"Excuse me, folks," came a male voice—deep, lulling, soothing—familiar. *Jon.* "Let me through, please. Emma," he whispered in her ear. "Come on, Emma; let's get out of Doc's way now, shall we?" His warm hand came to rest on her shoulder, big and long-fingered. She leaned into it.

A stream of tears coursed down her cheeks. "I love you, Pa," she repeated, willing him to open his eyes.

"Come on, honey."

She tipped back on her heels and fell against the preacher's firm chest, unable to see through the hot blur of tears. "Tell him to wake up, Jon. He'll listen to you."

She felt his chest heave. "I'm afraid he wouldn't hear me," he whispered.

She refused to accept that. "Wake up, Ezra Browning, you ol' coot," she ordered.

But Ezra Browning did not move again.

*****

The funeral had been a quiet affair, attended mostly by Emma's close friends and very few of Ezra's, which was to be expected. Over the years the man had made little time for friendship building.

Naturally, Jon performed the ceremony, although his words were few due to his clogged-up throat. It was his first funeral as a minister of the gospel, and he decided it would forever be his least favorite obligation.

Emma had sat in a chair in the parlor, shoulders straight, face serenely peaceful, though not naturally so. It was as if she'd determined to turn off her emotional faucet. She shook the hands of friends and thanked them for their concern, pasted smile in place. Grace stood behind her acting as host and doing a fine job of it, protective of her younger cousin, her hand set squarely upon her shoulder. Jon would have liked to assume the role of protector, but, alas, Emma didn't know his full intentions, and now didn't seem an appropriate time for telling her, considering her grief.

Afterward, in the following weeks, Emma's boarders walked around the house with sullen faces, keeping the noise down, and going to their rooms at decent hours. Even Luke seemed to recognize the need to hold back his blather, although Jon thought his senseless chatter might do everyone some good. Around town, talk was that Madam Guttersnipe had considered closing down the saloon for lack of business. It would seem Ezra Browning's "sermon" had touched a tender chord in many a heart, Gus Masterson, the saloon's pianist, for one. Ever since Ezra's passing, he'd been attending Little Hickman Community Church, and Sunday before last, had walked to the front to express his need for the Savior. Jon suspected it wouldn't be long before Bess would start trading off with him at the piano, and wouldn't that be a flat-out miracle!

From saloon honky-tonk to church hymnal. Would wonders never cease?

Of the boarders, Wes Clayton and Elliott Newman seemed most affected by Ezra's passing. Three Sundays in a row now, they'd faithfully sat in the third row from the back, all ears at Jon's messages. Luke came, too, of course, his perpetual smile a joy to watch, a regular boost to Jon's confidence.

Folks stopped by almost daily to deliver big casseroles, pies, cakes, platters of cookies, and pans full of fried chicken and scalloped potatoes, freeing Emma of the need to spend

357

long hours in the kitchen. Even Iris Winthrop dropped off a meatloaf hefty enough for serving an army. Seeming genuinely concerned, she stood on the porch and chatted with Grace for at least ten minutes, Jon standing at his window just above and catching bits and pieces of the conversation.

"Well, it was a shock to that poor girl, I'm sure," Iris had said. "Of course, she suffered years under that man's abuse, so one part of her ought to be relieved."

"Ezra found forgiveness in his latter days," Grace put in. "He and Emma had just started to make amends."

"Well, yes, and I'm sure that must give Miss Browning some sense of peace. Still, it does amaze me."

"What's that, Mrs. Winthrop?"

"Why, this whole business of God's grace and forgiveness—no matter how great the sin, no matter how late in life... there is always forgiveness for those who seek it."

Grace's low-throated chuckle rose to Jon's second-story window. "I see you've been paying close attention to our pastor's sermons, Mrs. Winthrop."

Grace stayed on a full ten days after Ezra's passing, tending to the house chores and the meals; weeding the garden, even though most of it had withered, save the pumpkins and squash; and running errands, affording Emma the opportunity to hide out in her private quarters like a hermit, as if she had need of a refuge. Jon grilled Grace more than once about Emma's reclusive behavior.

"She needs time to process all that's happened to her, Jon. In some odd way, she feels guilty—about Ezra."

"Guilty? Why should she feel guilty? It was Ezra who wronged her."

"And she who carries the responsibility for not freeing him of his guilt."

"That wasn't her job to do."

"You and I know that, but try convincing her. I've told her till I'm blue, but it doesn't seem to matter.

"She spent the better share of her life hating and resenting her father, and then in the end, it occurred to her that she truly loved him. Now she faces the harsh reality of what might have been if they'd have communicated their hearts to one another long ago."

Jon shook his head. "But the timing would have been all wrong before. It took Ezra's illness to bring him to his knees before Almighty God and your timely letters to alert her to her need for Christ. Can't she see that?"

Grace placed a hand on his forearm. "I've no doubt you'll find a way to make her see it, Jon."

His shoulders slumped. "She won't talk to me. Every time we meet in the hallway, she makes an about-face. My presence has always disarmed her, reminded her that her heart wasn't right with her Creator, but now that she's a Christian, it puzzles me how she's more determined than ever to avoid me. It doesn't make sense." He looked to Grace for some kind of encouragement, but she remained quiet. "Unless she just plain dislikes me and I'm too thickheaded to see it." His insides panicked with raw realization. "Well, blast if that hasn't been it all along! She does hate me."

Grace cackled. "Oh, listen to you. If you believe that, then you have slow-of-wit to add to thickheaded, my dear Reverend."

"Really?" He studied her now-smiling countenance. "Believe it or not, you've just made me feel better, Grace Giles."

She laughed outright. "You'll be fine," she'd said, patting him on the arm. "What you need to do is help her overcome her feelings of inadequacy. It is quite beyond her that you, a minister of God's Word, could possibly be interested in her—in any way but friendly, that is."

"No kidding? Did she tell you that?"

She gave a casual shrug. Her eyes glinted with humor. "Perhaps a bit of courting would do the trick?"

*****

"You take care now, Miss Emma," George Garner called as Emma made her exit from the post office, another missive from Grace tucked safely away in her coat pocket. She'd torn into it immediately and had thrilled to read that things were progressing at a fast rate concerning the move to Little Hickman. All that remained was to settle up with the new owners, pack her belongings, and set off on her journey. She'd hired a friend to drive her this time, someone familiar with the roads to and from Lexington. It should make for a more pleasant ride, especially when considering the fellow's wife planned to join them on the journey.

"And you, Mr. Garner," she replied.

For the first time in days, a tiny seed of expectation sprouted in her heart and made her step a little lighter, made a smile inch its way past her chattering teeth. Was it because a golden sun shone through thinning trees, making a valiant effort to warm the late-October air, or was it that Grace's letter had boosted her spirits?

She pulled her collar close and paused to sniff the scent of autumn, much like No-name did when he crawled out from under the porch, senses sharp and vigilant. One block off Main Street, at the corner of Washington and Mayfield, Gerald and Eileen Crunkle sat bundled up together on their porch swing.

A fire of leaves burned itself out where their front yard met the road. She'd noticed Gerald earlier raking dry leaves into a giant pile and toyed with the notion of running up the street to ask if she might dive into the middle of it, but figured he'd think she was missing a screw or two if she did.

Jon Atkins spotted her as he was leaving the livery, no doubt having turned Jupiter over to Sam. He lifted a hand and waved, causing her heart to scuttle off track. Lately, he'd been all smiles and attention, leaping to his feet to pull out her chair at the table, helping her haul out the trash barrel, rising before her most mornings to start the coffee, and even standing next to her at the sink to dry the dishes while she washed. Ever since Grace's departure, he'd stepped into her cousin's shoes, making it his job to look after her. She'd been careful to guard her heart, not wanting to read more into his actions than necessary, telling herself his kindness came from sympathy and a need to fulfill his pastoral duties rather than from genuine tenderness. Still, she couldn't help but wonder.

And now that she had set off for home, she knew he followed her.

"Emma, wait," he called.

She turned to find him jogging across the dusty street, darting out of the path of Fred Swain and his team of horses.

"I just came from Ben and Liza's place," he announced. "They've invited us for supper next Wednesday night." *Us?* "She's expecting that baby any minute now, but she still insists. Says she's better off staying busy. I guess they've asked the Callahans as well." When she didn't immediately answer, he added with a smile, "It'll be a regular party. Are you game?"

"Me?"

She still couldn't get past the "us" part of his earlier statement. "They've invited *us*" was what he said. There wasn't an "us," was there?

"Yes, you." In broad daylight, he took a section of her hair between his fingers and gently tugged. "It will do you good to get out of that house, Emma. You've done nothing but hide out for the past five weeks. Folks are starting to worry about you."

That was it, then. As her pastor, he saw the need to draw her out of her self-made cocoon, and what better way than to surround her with friends? But would her pastor also finger her hair and make chill bumps race up and down her arms?

Carl and Frieda Hardy walked by. "Afternoon, Preacher. Miss Emma," Carl said.

When Emma would have stepped back for propriety's sake, Jon leaned closer, nodding as the couple passed, but keeping his eyes trained on her.

"My! Did you see that, Carl? Emma Browning and Jonathan Atkins...." Frieda's voice drifted off.

Jon smiled. "We're the talk of the town, Miss Browning."

She snapped out of her trance, felt a soaking blush. "I don't know what there'd be to talk about."

He chortled, and she noted he hadn't dropped her wisp of hair; rather, he studied it with care as he rolled it around in his fingertips. "You don't think they're curious about us?"

"There is no 'us.'" *Is there?*

"They probably think something's going on right this minute."

She drew back and followed his gaze, which landed on Doc Randolph. Taking a rare break on his front stoop, the old gentleman, tin mug in one hand, newspaper in the other, looked up and nodded. Even through the cloud of dust hovering over Main Street, Emma swore she saw him wink.

Then there were Truman and Martha Atwater, Ila Jacobsen, and Rose Marley all engaged in conversation in front of the bank. The names Bryan and McKinley drifted past her ears, indicating their discussion centered on the upcoming presidential election. She sighed with relief—until they all turned to gawk at her and Jon, at which point Rose made an indiscernible remark and Ila covered her mouth to stifle a giggle.

In haste, Emma resumed her steps toward home. She refused to be the topic of folks' conversations. If her sudden move surprised Jon he didn't let on; he merely fell into step with her, their heels clicking out a similar rhythm as they traipsed up the sidewalk.

"Your reputation will be tarnished."

He looped his arm through hers. "My reputation is what it is."

"Jonathan." She could almost hear his smile. "I'm not— you shouldn't...."

When she would have mounted the steps to her porch, he snagged her by the arm and halted her progress. "I shouldn't what?" he prodded, turning her. "Love you? Is that what you're trying to say?"

"What?" A gasp of air whistled through her lungs. "Jonathan."

His hands settled on her shoulders as he bent close. With the pad of his thumb, he drew little circles around her shoulder blades. Tenderness that went beyond a pastor's call to duty swirled in his eyes.

"Jonathan," she repeated.

He chuckled. "You're going to wear my name right out, woman. Was there something you wanted to add to it?"

She blushed with wonderment. "I don't know what to say... exactly."

"How about telling me you'll be my bride?"

Another gasp put her lungs in danger of draining completely. "Your—bride?"

No-name sauntered out from under the porch and stretched, sniffed the air, and stood in sober contemplation. Soon, he ambled to his favorite bush and lifted a leg. Overhead, two squirrels scampered across a branch and vaulted to the roof just over Jon's dormer window.

"But I—I couldn't."

His whole face spread into a smile. "Of course you could."

She managed a small one in return. Could it be? After all these years of running from Jon Atkins, starting with the playground when he'd chased her around the rope swing, then into adulthood when he'd hounded her very soul with his overt testimony, had she finally run out of reasons for escaping him?

"I'm not exactly preacher's wife material." She dropped her chin, and he promptly lifted it.

"Why would you think that? People love you. You're warm, generous, funny, kind-hearted…passionate." He looked to the heavens. "Help me make her understand, Lord."

She laughed from sheer joy. "I don't think I'm any of those things."

He touched the tip of her nose. "Then it's time you started thinking more highly of yourself, young lady. God sees you as His precious child, someone worthy to be loved and cherished. I want you to start seeing yourself in that light."

She regarded him with somber curiosity. "Are you talking to me as my pastor now? I can't tell."

His brows flickered a little. He leaned forward and planted a soft kiss on her cheek, letting his lips linger at the spot, warming her with his moist breath. "Indeed I am," he whispered. "In fact, your pastor is about to kiss you more heartily, so if you don't want all of Little Hickman to watch, perhaps we should go inside?"

A ball of tension knotted in her throat and refused to move. "Oh."

With nary an ounce of strength left in her to argue the matter, she allowed him to lead her up the steps.

Chapter Thirty

To Jon's great relief, the house was as quiet as a bare tree in the dead of winter, but it wouldn't be that way for long. In less than an hour, Emma's boarders would amble through the door expecting supper. Good thing he smelled a simmering kettle of stew in the kitchen. A glance into the dining room indicated a set table.

He shut the door behind them. Giving him her back, she unbuttoned her coat and slipped out of it, hanging it on the coat tree next to the door. The linen scarf went with it. It was impossible not to admire her belted waist, the flare of her narrow hips, and the rest of her shapely form beneath the blue cotton of her dress. To add to his torture, her blond hair fell in graceful curves around her feminine shoulders.

Lord, give me strength.

He'd asked her to be his bride, but now he questioned the manner in which he'd done it. Too hasty? Too forward? Too presumptuous? "Perhaps a bit of courting?" Grace had said. Blast! He knew nothing of courting. How did one ease into a marriage proposal? Was there any way to go about it other than straightforward? He loved her; he wanted to marry her. That should be sufficient. And yet Grace's assertion that Emma felt inadequate beat dully away in his head. Ezra had done it to her, of course, had drilled into her the notion of her insignificance. Though not intentional, his hurtful words and actions had followed her into adulthood, making her believe she neither needed nor deserved the love of a man.

Well, tonight that ended. From this day forward, if he accomplished nothing else, he would make her understand this single truth: she had worth. The question was, should he prove it to her with an immediate kiss? He had warned her that he intended to kiss her thoroughly, but now that he'd tucked her away from Hickman's watchful gazes, he suddenly felt the need to wait for the perfect moment—if there was such a thing.

Emma glanced at the vacant room where only weeks ago her father lay ailing. Something drew her to the doorway. Jon followed close behind, resolving not to speak without first weighing his words. She leaned in the doorframe and sighed. He placed a hand on her shoulder and breathed deep of her scent.

Seconds flew by as they stared at the empty room, the single cot with its fresh washed bedding, the unlit lantern on the tiny bedside table, the motionless rocker sitting in the corner. A single rose stood straight as a pin in a crystal vase atop the chest of drawers, the Bible Jon had given Ezra lying next to it. The poignant moment gave Jon pause. With a little imagination, he could almost hear the old fellow's hacking cough, see him hunched over the edge of the bed, his rounded shoulders trembling with weakness. As he'd done a number of times before, he reminded himself that Ezra Browning had passed into his eternal home.

"There were things I didn't get to say," she muttered.

"You said everything that needed saying."

She gave a half-turn and looked into his eyes. Her own shimmered with moistness. It took every ounce of willpower he could muster not to put on his preacher hat and tell her God wanted all her leftover pain.

"I should have spent more time with him."

"The time you spent with him in the end was quality. Ezra Browning was a hard man, and considering everything he put you through, I commend you for taking such good care of him. It was a selfless act, you taking him into your house."

Her eyes trailed back to the empty bed. "You didn't give me much choice, if you'll recall." Her tone was just shy of facetious, and he smiled.

Giving her shoulder a gentle squeeze, he asked, "Can you look back now and see the bigger picture—see that God had a hand in all of it? Starting way back when you were just a little thing?"

There was a long pause.

"Think about it, Emma. If Edith hadn't kept track of Ezra's whereabouts and relayed the information back to Clara, there never would have been a Clara's Boardinghouse back in the seventies and eighties. There never would have been a woman looking out for you while you were growing up, a place for you to kick off your shoes after school, enjoy an afternoon snack, learn womanly things. Maybe you didn't recognize God's love back then, but Clara paved the way for you to know Him by giving you that Bible.

"If Ezra hadn't written to Edith last spring to tell her he was sick, she might have taken the family secret to her grave, but she recognized the need to share it with Grace. If she hadn't, you and Grace might never have met."

"And I would still be without a Savior," Emma added. "Grace shared Christ with me woman-to-woman in those letters she sent." Suddenly, she looked away from the empty cot and tilted her gaze at him. "I see what you're sayin'—about the bigger picture."

His heart swelled with triumph. "Romans 8:28 says, **'And we know that all things work together for good to them that**

love God, to them who are the called according to His purpose.' He knew all along what it would take to bring both you and Ezra into the fold, but all the pieces had to fit together first."

"Yes."

"God has been looking out for you all your life, Emma, protecting you even when Ezra was at his worst. You lived through it, right? And now you can be a beacon of hope for others who have suffered. You never know how God may choose to use you. Think of the possibilities."

Her eyes lit with fresh excitement. "It's too much to think about right now."

He turned her body full around and swung her into the circle of his arms. Wonder of wonders, she didn't even fight him. "Emma, Emma, think about this, then," he whispered, grazing her earlobe with his lips. "I love you and wish for you to be my wife."

She buried her face against his chest and wrapped her arms around his back. "You really do?"

"I really do."

He bent and kissed the hollow part of her throat then drew back to look into her summer-sky eyes. "What do you say?"

For one heart-stopping second he thought she might turn tail on him. Instead, she stood on tiptoe and kissed his chin. "I suppose I could confess my love for you as well."

He exhaled a long sigh. "I would like nothing more."

She picked at something on his lapel. "I have loved you, Jonathan Atkins, for a long time, but it didn't seem possible you could love me back."

His confidence spiraled upward. "Silly girl. I loved you first. In fact," between each word, he planted kisses around her lips and along her jaw, "I've loved you since you were a girl in yellow pigtails."

She pulled back and squinted up at him. "I was a scrawny kid. How could you have...?"

But he blocked her words with a sound kiss, one that sent them both reeling, her trembling limbs clinging tightly, him barely able to keep his knees from buckling under.

The rapid thudding of his pulse was what finally stopped the kiss.

"Do I have to court you before you'll agree to marry me?" he asked, breathless.

"Of course. It wouldn't be proper otherwise."

He brushed his lips across her forehead. "What would this courting business entail and how long should I persist?"

An infectious giggle floated upward. "To the first question, flowers, bushels of them; and to the second, years. Years and years."

He set her back from him. "Years?"

"Look at the Crunkles. Wouldn't you say they're still courting?"

If anyone presented the perfect picture of a sound marriage, it was Gerald and Eileen Crunkle. He bent to kiss the tip of her nose. "I see what you're saying. Get married now and continue the courting for decades to come."

She pushed back and sent him a raking gaze. "Did I say that?"

"Maybe not in so many words." He angled a mischievous grin at her. "But it sounds like the perfect plan to me."

*****

Jon and Emma married the Saturday after William McKinley won the 1896 presidential election. It was also the Saturday after Liza Jane Broughton gave birth to little Amos Benjamin.

No one had expected to see her at the wedding, but just five days after delivering the seven-pound bundle, she entered the church on her husband's arm, albeit slowly, baby swaddled in a white blanket, Lili and Molly in tow. They seated themselves in a pew toward the back on the chance that Amos would object to his first-ever wedding ceremony.

Almost the whole town showed up for the celebration, fully supportive of the preacher marrying Emma Browning, and Rocky joked later that because the number had surely exceeded two hundred it warranted the preacher having to kiss a pig the next Sunday. Jon's defense, and it was a good one, was that his wedding hardly counted as morning worship, and besides, he was taking his bride to some undisclosed location of which only Grace was privy. If there were to be any pig kissing, he'd announced, Reverend Miller, who was not only marrying him but also standing in for him at the pulpit, would have to do the honors.

Grace managed to return just three days before the wedding, carting a wagonload of possessions for setting up housekeeping in Little Hickman. She would stay in Emma's quarters until the couple returned from their honeymoon, for which she had made all the arrangements—seven nights in a first-class hotel in downtown Lexington. Both Jon and Emma balked at the extravagance of it all, but Grace insisted. While Grace was humble and unpretentious on the outside, she made it clear to the pair the gift would in no way break her financially. Her late husband, rest his soul, had invested wisely, leaving her with a hefty bank account. The least she could do was lavish her precious cousin and her preacher husband with a lovely honeymoon. Put that way, Jon and Emma could hardly refuse.

Upon their return, the couple planned to settle in Emma's spacious quarters, converting Jon's former room into his private library/office, transporting the bed to Ezra's house for Grace's use. Grace intended to stay at the old homestead until the newly hired Lexington Construction Company completed her two-story building in Little Hickman, tentatively fall of 1897. It could prove to be a long, cold winter for the Chicago native, but she claimed to look forward to the peace and serenity, and, besides, she'd said, if the quiet got to her, she could always look in on the newlyweds and the bunch of hooligans who made up the boardinghouse.

Grace and Rocky served as witnesses to the bride and groom's nuptials. Sarah, rumored to be three months pregnant, fairly glowed as she watched the proceedings from her front-row pew, Seth and Rachel sitting on either side of her.

Besides the gold, princess-length necklace with the three-diamond pendant, the bride wore a white cotton gown with Battenberg lace around the scooped neck and a wide silk belt at her tiny waist. The bodice had large tucking and the sleeves were puffy with pleats in the center and cuffs, and straight down the middle of the back were about a hundred or so tiny mother-of-pearl buttons, the kind that required assistance to hook.

It was a lovely thing, the dress, sewn in record time and with much skill and loving care by Fancy Jenkins. When Grace asked her why she didn't sew for a living, the woman gave a sheepish look and said she hadn't the business sense or the money for setting up such a venture. Grace had pooh-poohed that idea and said when things settled down for her, they would talk.

It would seem Grace Giles had more than a new restaurant on her mind for Little Hickman.

One week before the wedding, a postcard came from Billy Wonder addressed to the entire town. In it he stated he'd found a ladyfriend in Georgia to whom he'd grown quite attached. He never had made it down to Florida, he'd said, and after having met Millie Grunder, a dancer who'd once traveled with the circus but now taught ballet at a downtown studio, chances were good he'd remain near Atlanta for the winter months. Folks always gave a chuckle when they stopped to read the postcard George Garner had pinned to the corkboard right next to the wanted posters. Billy Wonder and Millie Grunder? How strangely comical.

Would *wonders* never cease, Eileen Crunkle commented after reading about the unlikely pair.

After a long afternoon of celebrating in the schoolhouse, student desks pushed back against the walls to accommodate tables of food, cakes, and pies, a large crowd assembled around the newlyweds, who'd changed into their traveling clothes and had seated themselves in a rented carriage parked in front of the boardinghouse. The hired driver from Lexington, donning black suit and top hat, sat tall in his seat, all business, awaiting orders to proceed up the road toward the big city.

"I've never ridden in anythin' so luxurious!" Emma gushed. In the glow of the lowering sun, folks could see the blush of pink stealing across her cheeks.

"Miss Emma looks like royalty sittin' up there," Wes Clayton remarked.

"Ain't Miss no more," corrected Harland, pulling at his long white moustache and looking particularly pleased.

Emma's boarders closed around the conveyance in a protective air. "Guess we don't need ta tell the preacher ta look after ar landlady," Gideon said, a waggish look washing over his features. A rare smile eked past his thin mouth. "Seein's as he's been givin' 'er the eye fer some time now."

Chortles rose up all around.

The reverend pulled his bride tight to his side and grinned. "Didn't know I was that obvious." His eyes had fastened to his one and only as he spoke.

"You best get a move on 'fore ya embarrass us all by kissin' 'er in plain sight," Charley issued, taking a step back, his move prompting everyone else to do the same.

"I s-seen 'em kiss a'ready," Luke announced.

Emma whirled on her seat and looked at the lad, eyes round as saucers. "You did not."

"D-did too. I was hidin' 'round the c-corner, and you was b-by the w-w-wash machine."

"Luke Newman, that's spying," Emma scolded.

When the crowd of onlookers started laughing, Jon motioned to the driver, and just like that, he set the team of horses in motion. Last-minute felicitations sailed through the air as the carriage jostled up the road, leaving everyone in a swirl of dust.

Grace Giles and Fancy Jenkins swiped at tears, the Callahans and Broughtons exchanged knowing smiles, and Iris Winthrop leaned into Clyde and gave an audible sigh, as the whole of Little Hickman celebrated with the happy couple.

A mile up the road, the driver passed a little cemetery where a fresh marked grave bore a simple, engraved message.

EZRA BROWNING

MARCH 1, 1840–OCTOBER 6, 1896

"WHOSOEVER BELIEVETH IN CHRIST SHALL NOT PERISH, BUT HAVE ETERNAL LIFE."

—JOHN 3:15

Excerpts from Sharlene MacLaren's next novel,

Hannah Grace

First in The Daughters of Jacob Kane Series

~ Chapter One ~

Sandy Shores, Michigan
August 1903

...HANNAH sat on the cushioned bench in front of the mirrored vanity, happy to be upstairs preparing for her evening out rather than downstairs with all the commotion. She leaned forward to study herself in the mirror. Her lower lip went out in a pout as she viewed her plain looks—grayish eyes, neither true blue nor clear green, a thin, longish neck and narrow shoulders, pointy chin, square jaws, and a plumpish mouth. To top matters, she had a skinny frame with very little up front to prove her womanhood. Matter of fact, she'd thought more than once if she'd wanted to pass as a boy she could pile all her hair under a cap, if ever there was one big enough, don a pair of men's coveralls, work boots, and a jacket, and no one would be the wiser.

She thought about Maggie's fair-haired beauty and Abbie's dark eyes, sallow skin, and flowing, charcoal hair. Assuredly, they both outshone her pasty features by a country mile, Abbie's assets originating from their mother's Italian heritage, and Maggie's coming from their Grandmother Kane. To be sure, Helena Kane was an aging woman in her sixties, but anyone with an eye for beauty could see she'd one day had all the makings of elegance and charm, high cheekbones, perfectly inset blue eyes, well-chiseled nose and chin, and clear, nearly wrinkle-free skin.

But where did she, Hannah Grace Kane, fit into the picture? Certainly, she'd inherited her grandmother's curly hair, but where Helena's lay in perfect, gentle waves, a tidy silver bun at the back, Hannah's crimped and coiled atop her head like a thousand rusty-colored bedsprings. And nothing she did to tame it seemed to work. She'd even lain her head on an ironing board some years ago, like a sacrificial goat, and allowed her sisters to straighten it with a hot iron—until they came too close to the skin and burned her scalp. About that time, Grandma Kane, having heard Hannah's yelp of pain, came into the room and put an end to the hair-straightening stratagem, spouting something about Hannah's hair being just as God intended it to be, but wasn't it a shame He hadn't granted all of them a bit more common sense.

The silly recollection made her brow crinkle into four straight lines. "What could you possibly see in me, Dr. VanHuff?" she murmured, squinting in the mirror. Then pulling back her shoulders, she dipped her chin and tried to look dignified in her ivory silk afternoon gown with the button-down front and leg-o'-mutton sleeves.

"Hannah Grace VanHuff." She tested the name aloud wondering how it would feel to say it for the rest of her born days.

Tonight they would dine at the Culver House in downtown Sandy Shores and afterward perhaps walk down to the harbor to watch the boats come and go. Along the way, they would pass the closed shops on Water Street and possibly do some window gazing. Ralston would speak about his practice, tell her about the patients he'd seen that day, the broken bone he'd set, or the wound he'd wrapped. He would speak about his dreams for erecting a new building, one that would allow him to reside apart from his practice. Not for the first time, he would mention his hopes for a partner with which to launch this undertaking, someone who shared his passion for medicine, of course, and had the financial wherewithal to pitch in his fair share. There would be a placard above the door and maybe larger signage in the front yard. They would hire a nurse, of course, and down the road, a bookkeeper to keep the mounting records straight.

He would ask her about her day at Kane's Whatnot, her father's general store, and inquire as to how sales had gone. She would be vague in her answer, knowing it would bore him to tears to hear the details. Nevertheless, he'd smile and nod, and appear deeply interested, but then quickly commence to speaking about his medical practice again.

Perhaps Abbie was right in saying Ralston was a tad stuffy and one-sided, but she liked the dear man. Besides, at present, there was no one better suited for her, and at twenty-one, one couldn't be too choosy. Grandma Kane had warned her that once a woman reached her twenties, her chances of landing a genteel man narrowed considerably. Thus, she'd already decided that when the time came, and Dr. Ralston VanHuff offered her his hand in marriage, in all probability she would accept—providing it was God's will, of course.

And why wouldn't it be? He was a churchgoing, decent, educated man, greatly respected in the community, and well on his way to becoming highly successful in his field. Certainly, God would not look poorly on such a union. True, Ralston rarely spoke about his personal faith in God, but surely that would come in due time.

As the racket continued downstairs, Hannah proceeded to pile her mass of reddish curls on the top of her head, using every available pin to hold them in place.

"Thank heaven for hats," she muttered to herself.

～ *Chapter Two* ～

...HANNAH lifted her skirts and climbed each step leading to the county courthouse's double-door entrance with quiet determination, planning her words with care, going over the events of the morning in her mind, wanting to be sure to give an accurate account. When questioned, she would say the man was tall, dangerous—but, no, in fairness she couldn't use that word. The sheriff would call it, what, supposition? Stick to the facts, he'd say. I want details.

Details. In her head, she began again. He was tall and broad-shouldered. He had freshly cut blond hair, a nice style, you might say, the sort that…facts. He had a square jaw, sort of a square *face*, actually, now that she thought about it, and his eyes, oh, those eyes.

The sheriff would be leaning forward now, pencil in hand, perhaps even tapping one end of it on his fresh polished desk, impatient for the particulars.

They were blue, she would state, almost iridescent. Iridescent? She would have to clarify its meaning. Blue like the sky, and, well, shimmery.

His lack of understanding would put her over the edge.

Oh, never mind, she'd concede. Don't you have one of those books with all the criminals' faces? I'm sure I can identify him at first glance.

The solid door opened when she used all her strength.

"Kitty?" she called. "Are you about?" On the marred counter at the front of the office stood piles of papers, thick volumes of information, a Mason jar containing pens and pencils, a flower gone dry in a vase, and a couple of ashtrays. At present, Kitty's little desk in the middle of the room, also piled nearly to the ceiling with paperwork, appeared unoccupied. Several plaques framed in dark cherry wood hung from the walls, as did a large painting of President George Washington. A United States Flag graced one corner, its six-foot pole jutting out from the wall so that the flag lay at a nice angle.

She knew the sheriff's office was down the hall, first door on her right, but to get there, she needed assistance from someone on the other side of the counter who could unlock and lift the gate. She couldn't imagine why the sheriff's office, or the other rooms down the hall, for that matter, had to be so inaccessible to the public.

From one of the back rooms off the main one emerged Nathanial

Brayton, Sandy Shores' community treasurer. In his fifties and of medium height, he wore a perpetual smile. Round faced and bulbous nosed, he also sported a gray, bushy moustache. Hannah remembered as a child standing beside her father in the churchyard after services, feigning interest in their conversation, but more intent on watching Mr. Brayton's bobbing moustache.

"Wull, hello there, Miss Hannah. Kitty's out t' lunch, I'm sorry to say. What can I do for you?" With hooked thumbs, he held to his brown suspenders, suspenders that didn't seem to serve their purpose if one considered where the waist was supposed to fall, and where it actually wound up coming on a protruding belly.

"Oh." She stretched to her full five-foot-seven-inch height and stepped forward. Why suddenly did she feel like shrinking? She'd hoped to find Kitty at the counter. Kitty to bolster her reasons in coming.

Beads of sweat pooled and trickled down her back. She removed her hat, a fool thing to wear anyway on a day pushing ninety degrees, and laid it on the counter. As a result, though, her russet-colored curls fell in complete disarray. "I've come to pay the new sheriff a visit."

Something happened to Mr. Brayton's perpetual smile. "Um, now might not be the best time, ma'am."

"But I insist on seeing him."

"He's had a bad morning."

"Already? It's his first day on the job."

"That it is—but, well, let's say better first days have gone down in history."

Though she wasn't normally one to stand her ground, she felt her heels dig in. "That may be, but I've an important crime to report."

This got his interest. His eyebrows twitched and flickered. "A crime, ma'am? What sort of crime are we talking? Was the Whatnot robbed?"

She shook her head. "I think it would be best if I dispensed with matters of the crime in the sheriff's private quarters, Mr. Brayton."

Mouth opened and prepared to argue, he clamped it shut at the first sounds of a door coming uncracked.

Both heads turned in the direction from where the sound came. One mouth remained closed, the other gaped in disbelief.

~ Chapter Three ~

…"You!" Her breathing seemed to come in short spurts, her otherwise pretty face having taken on a sour expression. "What are you—what exactly is the meaning of this?"

Gabe smiled, enjoying this other-side-of-the-fence feeling. "Was there a problem?" he asked.

She made a grumpy, disdainful noise, not at all of the ladylike variety, as it wound up coming out both her mouth and nose. Pellet-like eyes shot him a piercing, no, murderous, look. "Problem? Of course, there's a problem." With every word, her voice rose in minute decibels. "And you know exactly what I'm talking about, Mr.—Mr. Deluder, Mr. Deceiver, Mr. De—"

"—lightful?" he supplied.

"Argh!" Another unbecoming growl came from somewhere deep in her skinny frame. He stepped forward to lift the gate and proceed into the lobby area where he hoped to be able to calm the waters of misunderstanding.

"No need to scream."

"I am not screaming," she *screamed*. Mr. Brayton, appearing completely bewildered, had not yet made one move to speak.

"First of all, my name is not any of those D words you mentioned; it's Gabriel Devlin, Gabe to my friends." He extended a hand and she conveniently ignored it. His eyes made a quick pass over her mop of rust-hewed hair then moved on down to her dusty shoes peeking out underneath the hem of her full-skirted yellow calico. Clearly, she didn't intend to shake his hand, so he dropped it. "And whom do I have the pleasure of addressing?" he asked, knowing full well, thanks to Kitty, her name was Hannah Grace Kane.

"You are a beast. An abusive beast."

A good deal of throat clearing came from Mr. Brayton. "Miss Hannah, you are speaking to our new sheriff."

"Hannah. I like that name. I'm Gabe," he repeated.

Her face looked near the popping stage, red and silky with perspiration. "If you are who I think, you have no business holding the sheriff's title."

He smiled. "More than likely I'm not who you think then."

She nearly sucked the air out of the room then slowly gave it back. "Where is that child?"

"He's sleepin' in the cell," offered Mr. Brayton, suddenly all eager about jumping into the conversation. "Little whippersnapper, he is. Don't mind saying I'll take my leave when he wakes up. No telling what'll happen."

"In a cell, did you say? You're holding that poor, innocent child in a jail cell?"

If looks could kill, he'd be lying flat out on a board. "Innocent, you say? If he's innocent, I'll eat my socks for dinner. That boy's been—" But she whirled around, skirts flying, before he could finish and made a beeline for the gate he'd failed to lock.

He chased her through the office and down the hall. "Just a minute there."

"Where is he?" she asked. "And where's his mother."

"Just hold on," he said, watching while she opened one door after another.

"Where did you put the jail?" she asked.

The question struck him as humorous, so he laughed. She turned and stomped her foot. He quickly sobered and put out a hand in much the way he would to calm a wild filly. "I did not put the jail anywhere, my dear lady. It is in the basement, where it's always been."

Stepping forward, he seized her by the arm.

"Unhand me," she ordered, viewing his hand as she might a snake.

Frustrated, he murmured into her ear, knowing Nathanial Brayton stood at the end of the hall watching the fiasco. "I've a mind to slap some sense into you. You're about as obstinate and willful as Zeke."

She blinked twice, and suddenly their eyes connected. "My mule," he explained, drawing close enough to pick up her lovely citrus scent.

"Everything okay?" asked Nathanial.

Snapping to attention, she threw up her arm and stepped back, glaring at him with the eyes of a woman who means business.

"If you'll settle down, I'll take you to the boy, how's that?" And to Nathanial, "Everything's fine. Go on about your job."

That curbed her little conniption. They walked to the next door and Gabe pulled it open. Wooden steps led to a dimly lit basement. When she meant to proceed ahead of him, he grasped her arm midway up, noting how his thumb and middle finger met at the back. Bean pole woman.

"Be forewarned," he whispered. "The boy does not speak, and need I remind you that the last time you talked to him, you scared the living caca right out of him."

"Mr. Devlin!" she exclaimed.

He grinned and let her go. "Just warning you is all."

She hesitated when he nudged her forward. "I asked you where his mother is," she reminded.

Besides underfed, he could add persistent to her wonderful list of attributes. He sighed in spite of himself. "Well, that's the rub. I haven't got a clue."

. . .

About the Author
Sharlene MacLaren

*B*orn and raised in western Michigan, Sharlene MacLaren attended Spring Arbor University. Upon graduating with an education degree, she traveled internationally for a year with a small singing ensemble, then came home and married one of her childhood friends. Together they raised two lovely daughters. Now happily retired after teaching elementary school for thirty-one years, "Shar" enjoys reading, writing, singing in the church choir and worship teams, traveling, and spending time with her husband, children, and precious grandchildren.

A Christian for over forty years and a lover of the English language, Shar has always enjoyed dabbling in writing—poetry, fiction, various essays—and freelancing for periodicals and newspapers. Her favorite genre, however, has always been romance. She remembers well the short stories she wrote in high school and watching them circulate from girl to girl during government and civics classes. "Psst," someone would whisper from two rows over, and always with the teacher's back to the class, "pass me the next page."

Shar is an occasional speaker for her local MOPS (Mothers of Preschoolers) organization, is involved in KIDS' HOPE USA, a mentoring program for at-risk children, counsels young women in the Apples of Gold program, and is active in two weekly Bible studies. She and her husband, Cecil, live in Spring Lake, Michigan, with Dakota, their lovable collie, and Mocha, their lazy fat cat.

The acclaimed *Through Every Storm* was Shar's first novel to be published by Whitaker House. *Courting Emma* completes the trilogy of the Little Hickman Creek Series, which also includes *Loving Liza Jane* and *Sarah, My Beloved*. Look for Shar's latest contemorary romance, *Long Journey Home*, in July 2008. Her newest historical trilogy, The Daughters of Jacob Kane, is scheduled to be published in 2009.

You may e-mail Shar at smac@chartermi.net or visit her website at www.sharlenemaclaren.com.

Long Journey Home

A Contemporary Novel

Sharlene MacLaren

After divorcing her abusive husband, single mother Callie May is still nursing emotional scars when a handsome but brooding stranger moves into the apartment across the hall. Former church pastor Dan Mattson may be attractive, but his circumstances certainly aren't. He abandoned his flock and turned his back on God following the tragic death of his beloved wife and baby daughter. When Callie's ex-husband shows up to wreak even more havoc in her life, Dan finds himself coming to her defense—and being forced to face his own demons in the process. Will Dan and Callie allow God to change their hearts and mend their hurts so they can take another chance on love?

ISBN: 978-1-60374-056-2 • Trade • 400 pages

WHITAKER HOUSE

www.whitakerhouse.com